Saving Grace

Saving Grace

Fiona McCallum

HARLEQUIN® MIRA®

First Published 2013
Second Australian Paperback Edition 2014
ISBN 978 174356772 2

SAVING GRACE © 2013 by Fiona McCallum
Philippine Copyright 2013
Australian Copyright 2013
New Zealand Copyright 2013

Published by
Harlequin® Mira®
An imprint of Harlequin Enterprises (Aust) Pty Ltd.
Level 4, 132 Arthur Street
NORTH SYDNEY NSW 2060
AUSTRALIA

Printed and bound in Australia by Griffin Press

MIX
Paper from
responsible sources
FSC
www.fsc.org   **FSC® C009448**

In memory of Panda.

Acknowledgements

Thank you to my wonderful editor, Lachlan Jobbins, for making sure my stories are the best they can be, and to Haylee Nash, Cristina Lee and everyone at Harlequin Australia for turning my plain pages into beautiful books, and for continuing to make my dreams come true.

Huge thanks to Deb McInnes, Kate Taperell and the team at DMCPR Media for spreading the word, and to the media outlets, booksellers and libraries for your interest and support.

It means so much to me to hear of people enjoying my books and connecting with my characters and stories. Thank you to all my wonderful readers. I may not have met you, but please know you are special to me and I am very grateful for your support. Without you my manuscripts might remain doorstops!

I am truly blessed to have a handful of wonderful friends who provide a lot of love and support and help me weather the ups and downs. Some are new, but most have been a part of my life for many, many years and were always steadfast in their belief of me and my dream to be a novelist. I owe you so much. Special thanks to dear friends Carole and Ken, Mel, Arlene, Sonia, and Tamara. You guys mean the world to me.

About Fiona

Fiona McCallum spent her childhood years on the family cereal and wool farm outside a small town on South Australia's Eyre Peninsula. An avid reader and writer, she decided at the age of nine that she wanted to be the next Enid Blyton! She completed her final years of schooling at a private boarding school in Adelaide.

Having returned to her home town to work in the local council office, Fiona maintained her literary interests by writing poetry and short stories, and studying at TAFE via correspondence. Her ability to put into words her observations of country life saw a number of her feature articles published in the now defunct newspaper *SA Statewide*.

When her marriage ended, Fiona moved to Adelaide, eventually found romance and followed it to Melbourne. She returned to full-time study at the age of twenty-six and in 2000 graduated with a Bachelor of Arts (Professional Writing) from Deakin University. While studying, she found herself drawn to writing fiction where her keen observation of the human condition and everyday situations could be combined with her love of storytelling.

After brief stints in administration, marketing and recruitment, Fiona started Content Solutions, a consultancy providing professional writing and editing services to the corporate sector. Living with a sales and marketing executive and working on high level business proposals and tenders in Australia and overseas gave Fiona great insight into vastly different ways of life.

Fiona continued to develop her creative writing skills by reading widely and voraciously, and attending short courses. In 2001 she realised her true passion lay in writing full-length fiction, and in 2002 she completed her first manuscript.

In early 2004 Fiona made the difficult decision to return to Adelaide alone in order to achieve a balanced lifestyle and develop a career as a novelist. She successfully re-established her consultancy, and now enjoys the sharp contrast between her corporate work and creative writing.

Fiona describes her books as 'heart-warming journeys of self-discovery stories'. Her first novel, *Paycheque*, was released in April 2011 and became an 'instant bestseller'. Her second novel, *Nowhere Else* (released in December 2011), was an even bigger hit. Fiona's third novel, *Wattle Creek*, was released in April 2012. Fiona was thrilled and deeply honoured when *Wattle Creek*'s success saw it chosen as one of the 2012 Get Reading! campaign's '50 Books You Can't Put Down'. *Saving Grace* is Fiona's fourth novel, and is the first in *The Button Jar* series.

More information about Fiona and her books can be found on her website: www.fionamccallum.com and on her Facebook page: Fiona McCallum – author

Prologue

When John encouraged Emily to resign from her secretarial position with the insurance firm, telling her he'd rather his wife was at home, she thought it rather nice; antiquated, but nice. It meant they would stand shoulder to shoulder and run the farm together. She was really looking forward to that: mucking in and getting her hands dirty, and learning how to be a farmer.

Finishing work two weeks before the wedding meant she could attend to the final preparations in comfort, without the flurry of last-minute hiccups and the stress other brides faced. The only problem was all the extra time she was expected to spend with her mother. Still, it was easier than the confrontation and inevitable sulking that would follow if she avoided her.

At twenty-eight, Emily was an old bride by Wattle Creek standards – the average age being around twenty-three – and for a few years now her mother had been voicing her concerns about having a daughter 'left on the shelf'. With the day finally approaching, Enid Oliphant was desperate that nothing prevent her daughter being married. She was determined to present a wedding that would be the talk of the town for months, for all the right reasons.

Frankly, Emily would have been just as happy barefoot on the beach, but she didn't have the courage to tell her mother that. Instead, she quietly went along with all Enid's plans, which in her opinion involved far too many bows and way too much white satin. Experience had taught her that there was no point putting up an argument; when dealing with her mother, it was best to just grin and bear it.

The day went off without a hitch and the couple spent their first night as husband and wife in the local pub's honeymoon suite – a room that differed from the others in the row only in the length of stained white tulle draped across the ceiling and windows.

Emily barely noticed the décor; she was too caught up in reliving her perfect wedding to the most eligible farmer in the district. They had indeed made a handsome couple. The photos would be great.

She still sometimes found it hard to believe he'd chosen her. But he had! And now she was free from all Enid's pointed comments and could get on with her own life out of her mother's shadow. She, Emily Oliphant, would live happily ever after.

'Come on, how 'bout it,' John Stratten said as he dragged his new wife towards him. Emily closed her eyes on the first kiss and cringed at the beer on his breath.

Afterwards, she retreated into the bathroom and sat down on the plastic toilet seat. As she pulled a wad of paper from the roll to dry her eyes, she wondered if she'd made a terrible mistake. Maybe John liked sex a little rougher than other blokes, not that she had much previous experience on which to go by. It felt like he'd been drumming into her – that she was now his to do with as he pleased.

Perhaps she was imagining things, the exhaustion of the day making her overly sensitive. But the more she tried to mop away the tears, the more they fell. Meanwhile, her husband of nine hours and twelve minutes was snoring loudly in the saggy bed in the next room having – apparently – made love to her.

If they hadn't been setting off early in the morning for their honeymoon interstate, Emily would have consulted her gran about it. She felt the cold raking its way up her body from the tiles beneath her bare feet, adding to the emptiness in the pit of her stomach. She pulled a towel from the nearby rail and wrapped it around her shoulders. *What would Gran say?* First, probably, 'It's never as bad as it seems,' and then, without a doubt, 'You'll just have to make the best of it.'

Then she brightened a little. Eleven days on Great Keppel Island; a source of great envy for those past and future brides who had to be content with their family's fibro shack amid the dunes of Pigeon Bay. That was something to look forward to.

Her only other choice was to slink back home and become the talk of the tiny town and district for having the shortest marriage in its history. Ordinarily the bridesmaids' dresses, quality of the food, who had and had not been invited, and who had made a drunken fool of themselves would be enough to occupy the gossips.

No, Emily decided, she was not about to disrupt the natural order of things by running out on her new husband. Enid would probably drag her straight back to John anyway. She dried her eyes, hung the towel back over the rail, and returned to bed.

On the plane back home Emily thought about the irony of what a waste the resort had been – they may as well have been in Pigeon Bay. Each of her suggestions of things to do – snorkelling, kayaking, horseriding, romantic walks along the shore – had been rejected. Emily had tried to excuse her husband; holidays were *meant* to be all about sitting around drinking, weren't they? But by day seven she was bored.

After snapping at him to get up and get his own bloody beer, she had left him at the poolside bar and stormed off for her own long stroll along the beach.

Upon their return, Emily spent a week unpacking her few possessions and giving the bachelor pad farmhouse a sense of homeliness. After stepping around her husband watching daytime television for five days in a row, Emily came to the conclusion that the man she'd married was indeed pathologically lazy. Damn love being blind. Hopefully, with her buzzing about, he would pick up some of her energy.

Having run out of domestic chores, Emily began tidying up the office, only to be yelled at not to touch his paperwork – it was private. But the warning came too late; she had already perused a couple of bank statements lying on the desk. With a shock that hit her like a four-by-two across the temple, she realised that John Stratten, best catch of the district and legendary big spender, was almost totally broke.

He was wild when Emily innocently enquired if there was another working account she should use for buying groceries. After he'd got through screaming that she had no right to go through his things, he simmered down enough to explain that he had plenty of money thanks to his parents. Rather than feeling buoyed, Emily felt like enquiring if there was such a thing as a money tree. But she was already learning to keep her thoughts to herself – life was easier if he was kept calm and happy. He clearly had no intention of them working together in a partnership. No, she was expected to spend her days chained to the sink, vacuum cleaner and washing machine.

While preparing dinner, Emily tried to get rid of the biting nag deep inside her by telling herself she didn't care if he didn't have a cent – what mattered was they had each other. Oh, and not admitting to her mother that she'd made a huge mistake. She shuddered at the thought.

Over golden syrup dumplings, her offer to go back to work was met with such forceful opposition she actually feared for her physical safety. No wife of his was going to work in town and show the world he couldn't support his own family, John bellowed.

But any tension he took to bed that night evaporated as Emily let him have his way, 'Just lie back and think of England' running through her head. They'd been married eighteen and a half days.

With the house immaculate and both lunch and dinner organised by ten most mornings, Emily began taking daily walks to the crumbling old stone cottage across the creek. She'd first fallen in love with it while being shown around the farm. At the time, in answer to her remarking it should be preserved, John had said it was earmarked for demolition to make way for a hayshed – when he got around to it. Emily had almost cried at the sacrilege, but was now somewhat soothed by the thought that he was unlikely to 'get around to it' for years, if at all.

Sitting amongst the rubble and pigeon poo, Emily whiled away the hours daydreaming of structural renovations, colour schemes and décor for the bed and breakfast she pictured it becoming. Back at the main house she indulged her reverie further by putting together a scrapbook of ideas and samples. One evening, desperate to tell someone her thoughts, Emily shared her aspirations with her husband.

'I told you before, it's a knockdown job. Anyway, who'd want to stay out here? I've never heard of anything so ridiculous!'

'You're probably right,' Emily said, and closed the scrapbook with a heavy sigh.

John went off to the pub that night while Emily was taking a long, hot shower to hide her tears. Afterwards, she put all remnants of her musings into a box and stuffed it into the bottom of the linen press. He was right: it was a ridiculous idea. No one would want to stay so far out in the bush.

Emily didn't waste her time wandering the semi-ruins again. Instead she began to take walks in the other direction, towards an old concrete water tank. It took a few weeks before she stopped looking up and offering a regretful grimace to the old cottage as she turned the corner into the driveway by the house.

Chapter One

Around three years later...

Emily checked her watch and gathered up her handbag and car keys. John had stopped deriding her for her visits to her gran a while ago. In his mind, Rose Mayfair wasn't worth wasting the time on. It was a view shared by Emily's mother Enid and her aunt Peggy, especially since Rose had begun to show signs of dementia. But to Emily, her gran was still one of the wisest, kindest women in the world.

Above all, she loved and respected Granny Rose for the strength of her inner conviction – the ability to make her own choices, no matter what others thought. As a young woman, Rose had upset her parents by choosing to marry a farmer rather than a wealthy lawyer or doctor. Emily thought that maybe if she shared this trait, she'd have the guts to leave her husband. Or was it strength that made her stay and try to make it work?

Before her marriage, during the four and a half years she worked at the insurance company in Wattle Creek, Emily had made the short stroll up the street to have lunch with her gran every day. Although she no longer worked, she still managed a visit most days when she drove in to get the mail and groceries.

Gran was now in the old folks' home on the hill. For Emily's mother, the last straw had been when she caught Rose defrosting a loaf of bread in the oven – inside its plastic wrapper. To Enid Oliphant, her mother's condition had been an inconvenience, and she had been waiting for the opportunity to hand her over to someone else. After the incident with the bread, she bolted off to see the people at the home, leaving Emily scraping the melted plastic bag from the oven racks. Emily and Gran shared a laugh about it, with Gran calling herself a silly old fool. But things had already been set in motion.

Two years on, Emily still hated seeing Granny Mayfair confined to the nursing home, though she consoled herself with the thought that the dementia was a mixed blessing. On the one hand, if Gran didn't have it she wouldn't have been there; on the other, she didn't remember she had lost her independence and should probably be miserable.

Enid Oliphant regularly grumbled that the 'old bat' was otherwise healthy as an ox and would probably live forever. Emily hoped so, and not just to spite her mother. Granny Mayfair was her best friend.

Emily knocked gently on door 221 and called, 'Hello, Gran? It's me, Emily.' She held her breath while waiting for an answer. Would it be one of Gran's good days or bad days?

On a good day she would be welcomed, offered the lone armchair or end of the bed to sit on, and would spend an hour or so listening to Rose talk about days gone by. Most stories she'd heard dozens of times, but she never tired of hearing them.

On Gran's bad days Emily would be told, usually without the door being opened, that all donations were handled by her husband and that he would be home around six that night. On these occasions, Emily would let herself in and spend ten minutes explaining who she was, where she fitted into Gran's life, and convincing the old lady that she was just there to visit. This Gran invariably accepted with a sceptical but resigned frown and waved a hand to indicate she find somewhere to sit.

Today the door opened suddenly, startling Emily slightly.

'Come in.'

Emily couldn't tell from the greeting whether it was a good or bad day, and she frowned as she entered the room. She settled herself in her favourite position: cross-legged on the multi-coloured rug Gran had crocheted back before her memory and eyes had let her down. Gran went over to the only available chair but remained standing, wringing her hands. There was something different about her, but Emily couldn't put her finger on what it was. And she was still none the wiser as to her mental state.

'Emily, I need you to listen to me.'

Phew, it was a good day. 'I always listen to you, Granny Rose.'

'I know, but this is important.' Granny Rose seemed agitated.

'Okay. But Gran, please sit down, you're making me nervous.'

Instead, Rose Mayfair knelt and retrieved a large rattling jar of buttons from under the bed. Emily recognised it at once. She had loved the colourful collection since first being allowed to touch the outside as a four year old. For as long as she could remember she'd been fascinated by the fact that Gran had often added buttons but had never taken any out. She'd once asked why and had been told they were too precious; it was easier just to buy some more. Emily had always accepted the explanation without further question.

When the old lady struggled to get back to her feet, Emily rushed to her aid.

'Don't ever get as old as me, dear. It's horrible.'

'I could have got it for you, silly,' Emily scolded.

Granny was slightly out of breath when she finally settled in the chair.

'Thank you, dear. Now, it won't be long before I'll be pushing up daisies and...'

'Don't talk like that, Gran.'

'Oh fiddlesticks. It's the truth and the inevitable...' she waved a dismissive arm. 'But now, I need you to have this and take good care of it.' Gran pushed the jar towards Emily.

'Of course I will,' Emily said, clutching it to her chest. 'Thank you.'

'Best not to let anyone else poke about with it,' Gran said solemnly.

'Right, okay,' Emily said, thinking it an odd thing to say.

Later, as Emily was preparing to leave, Gran prodded at the large jar clutched to Emily's chest and told her in a hissed whisper that she was now in charge of something very precious and to take very good care of it.

Emily nodded sagely while stifling a smirk, patted the jar, and said she would guard it with her life.

After kissing Gran on the cheek, she left, driving home with the jar rattling beside her on the passenger's seat. *Precious!* She silently scoffed, shaking her head. Gran had become so serious about the smallest things.

That night, as Emily tucked the jar under some clothes at the back of her wardrobe, Rose Mayfair died while propped up watching the cricket on television, aged eighty-nine and three quarters.

Chapter Two

Emily stood next to her cousin, Elizabeth, who was a head taller, a few years older, much more sophisticated and – Emily had always felt – much better looking. She'd always envied her cousin's extra height, larger breasts, and lean, long legs. Emily was slightly stockier and curvier by comparison, except in the bust region, where she thought it counted.

Liz had been born and raised in Adelaide, but moved to Melbourne years ago, where she lived in a swanky inner-city apartment, drove a flash BMW convertible, and spent all her spare time eating out and shopping. She was a business analyst. No one in the family could explain exactly what that meant, except to say she earned stacks of money.

Mention of her by the older generations was usually accompanied by rolled eyes and exaggerated gestures. Thirty-four, childless and single, Liz was regularly referred to as 'Poor Elizabeth'.

Part of Emily wondered if Liz was the one who'd got it right; maybe the rest of them were the ones who'd got it all horribly wrong.

Together they nodded and murmured greetings to the mourners filing past them out of the cold dark church and into the brisk spring day. Small groups hovered nearby in the bright sunshine, away from the shade of the large, sprawling pine tree. Emily had been relieved to wake that morning to a clear sky for Rose Mayfair's send-off. She and Elizabeth remained standing like statues a full minute after the last person had passed: a wheelchair-bound woman of their late gran's vintage.

'I don't think I'll ever stop missing her,' Emily said with a wistful sigh. She'd spent the whole week in tears, with John telling her the old dear was almost ninety, what did she expect?

'You're lucky. I feel like I hardly knew her.'

'She was my best friend. I could talk to her about anything,' Emily sniffed. *Well, almost* she silently conceded. She'd never confided in her about how unhappy she was with John. She'd come close a few times, but now she'd never be able to. And she'd never know if Gran would have supported her leaving him, or if she'd shared Enid's view that marriage was for life, no ifs or buts about it.

'I'd sit on a stool next to her while she knitted, did the mending or her tapestry – until her eyesight went, that is,' Emily said.

'I just remember her at family functions – never making a fuss, just there. She and Grandpa always arrived with a boot full of biscuits and cakes. I don't remember her ever really having much to say.'

'That's probably because she chose her words so carefully.'

'I don't think she even knew who I was last time I saw her.'

'I'm sorry, that must have been hard.'

'Was she as bad as Mum says at the end – that she'd completely lost her marbles?'

'Not to me she hadn't. The recent past was a bit of a mystery, but we used to talk about her early life and school days like it was only yesterday. I think our mothers just chose not to see it for what it was.'

'Must have made for interesting listening.'

'It did. But what amazed me the most was how she never lost her wisdom.'

'What do you mean?'

'Well, I used to talk to her about stuff. You know, problems, mainly just to get them off my chest. But sometimes, even if she wasn't making much sense otherwise, she'd suddenly focus her eyes on me and say the most profound thing. It was quite spooky.'

'Problems? You?' Elizabeth laughed. 'Isn't this meant to be the simple life?' she said, sweeping an arm around.

Emily swallowed hard. Tears filled her eyes.

'What's wrong, other than being at a funeral, of course?'

'I don't know – everything.' Emily cast a glance at John, who stood in a group with their male cousins, already clutching a beer bottle.

'What is it with these country guys and always having to drink? Come on, let's go for a walk,' Elizabeth urged.

'We're meant to help set up for the afternoon tea.'

'Do you always do as you're expected?'

'Pretty much; it makes life easier.'

'Oh well, tell them I kidnapped you or something – come on.'

After waiting for a couple of utes with barking sheepdogs aboard to pass, they crossed the road to the empty golf course and sat down on the slatted wooden bench at the fifth tee.

They stared down the rustic fairway of naked brown earth dotted with tufts of barley and nut grasses. Tall weeds swayed in the breeze beyond the mowed area. Birds chirped. Crows crowed. Large limbs creaked overhead.

'God I wish you didn't live so far away,' Emily sighed. She bent down, picked up a stick and started scratching randomly in the dirt between her black patent leather court shoes.

'I *could* say *you're* the one who lives so far away. And you could call or email once in a while.'

So could you, Emily thought. 'So how long are you staying?'

'A couple more days. Tomorrow we're going through everything, remember? That should be fun.'

'John's convinced we're going to benefit – you know, financially.'

'What rock's he been living under – doesn't he know there's nothing left? Uncle Richard had the farm and everything of value signed over to him years ago so they could get Granny and Grandpa on the pension – crafty bastard.'

'I know, but he's got this idea there's a fortune hidden in the sock drawer or something.'

'And they say farmers aren't creative.'

'Gran always said you and I were to get her diamond rings – since we're the only two granddaughters,' Emily said.

'Well, try getting them back from my mum – they're probably on their way to the jeweller for redesigning as we speak.'

'You know, I must have sat for hours watching her fiddle with them over the years. As a kid I was mesmerised, but as I got older I realised it was a thing she did when she was thinking, or holding her tongue. I learnt a lot about her from watching those rings twirl.'

'Wish I'd known her better. Do you want me to say something to Mum about the rings?'

'There's no point. No offence, but your mum was always going to make sure she ended up with them.'

'I know, and she doesn't have a sentimental bone in her body. I'm probably a bit too like her in that regard,' Elizabeth said.

'So what of Gran's would you take if you had a choice? Or Grandpa's, for that matter?'

'The painting of the sad girl with the puppy. It was always the first thing I saw when I walked into the house. And I know it's awful to say, but that girl was me – I always cried when Mum left me with them, I hated it. But Mum'll take that too because it's probably worth heaps. What about you?'

'Her old recipes and a couple of the tapestry cushions – they kind of sum up who she was to me.' Emily wasn't sure why she didn't mention the button jar.

'I think that's nice, and much more likely to happen,' Elizabeth said, arching her eyebrows.

'Well, don't tell anyone, especially my mum,' Emily warned her.

'Why not?'

'She'll want them if she thinks I do.'

'I don't think she'd be so...'

'No one does. Everyone thinks she's just oh so lovely.'

'Ah, the old mother-daughter chestnut – none of us is immune. But it's not just that and losing Gran, is it?'

'What isn't?'

'Em, I might only see you every couple of years, but I can tell when things aren't right. What's wrong? Are you and John okay?'

'Oh Liz, I made a big mistake marrying him.' Emily expected another flood of tears, but they didn't come. She examined her fidgeting fingers. 'I knew it was wrong from the first night, but I hoped it would get better,' she said quietly.

'Maybe it will.'

Emily shook her head slowly. 'It's been three years. It's not any better. If anything, it's worse.'

'Well, leave.'

'I can't.'

'Of course you can. You pack up your things, tell him it's over, and drive into the sunset. You're welcome to come to Melbourne and stay with me.'

'Thanks, but it's really not that simple.'

'Why not?'

'Mum would say that now I've made my bed I have to lie in it.'

'Great advice if you're living in the nineteen-fifties – which you are not, in case you haven't noticed.'

'I knew you wouldn't understand,' Emily said, getting up.

Elizabeth grabbed her cousin's arm. 'I'm sorry, that was insensitive. Don't go. Come on, tell me what's wrong – everything.'

Emily sat back down and took a deep breath before pouring her heart out for almost twenty minutes while Elizabeth sat in stunned silence.

'So let me get this right. You're not allowed to have a job, he won't let you be involved with the farm in any shape or form, and he thinks all your ideas are stupid. Well, all I can say is he'd have to be a damn good shag for me to hang around – though I'm guessing things are pretty crap in that department too.'

Emily blushed. 'Well, I…'

'Oh God, you're not about to say it's your fault – that it's a woman's job to keep her man satisfied?'

Emily turned away from her cousin's incredulous look.

'You cannot be serious! Em, what's happened to you? You used to be so sure of yourself.'

'I guess I grew up,' Emily said with a shrug.

'Growing up doesn't mean losing your identity.'

Emily continued staring at the random patterns she'd made in the dirt. Tears flowed steadily down her face and she dabbed at them with a ball of soggy tissues.

'What you need is a puppy, or a kitten,' Liz said after a long silence.

'Come on, you hate pets. "Smelly, slobbery, bloody things", I think you once said,' Emily said, looking up and offering her cousin a slight smile.

'Well it isn't for *me*, is it? You always had cats and dogs. Anyway, aren't they an important part of a farm?'

'John's allergic to cats. And we did have a kelpie – he shot it a few months ago because it wouldn't come when it was called.'

'What?!'

'Apparently it's the way they do things on farms.'

Emily shuddered at the memory. First John had held the dog by the collar and laid into it with his steel-capped work boots. She had seen it all unfold from the kitchen window, and decided then and there that she could not – *would* not – have children with a man so cruel. If he could do that to a dog that had continued to show unconditional love despite rough treatment, what would he do to a baby who wouldn't stop crying, or a child who dared talk back to him? She'd felt sad at the realisation that she might never be a mother.

'Well it's bloody barbaric from where I'm sitting.'

'I love border collies – I think David Burton was trying to get rid of a couple the other week...' Emily mused, more to herself than to Liz.

'Do you have his number?' Elizabeth asked, pulling her mobile phone from her pocket.

'But I think John only likes kelpies.'

'So? The puppy is for you.'

'I don't know...'

'Jesus, Em, if you won't leave the bastard, the least you can do is make your life bearable. You've just got through telling me how lonely and miserable you are.'

'He'd be furious if I...'

'Em, there's no way to say this nicely, so I'm just going to get it out. He hasn't ever hit you, has he?'

'No.' *Not yet.* Emily stared at her shoes.

'Not that the emotional and mental abuse you're already suffering isn't bad enough.'

'We'd better get back,' Emily said, checking her watch and getting up.

'You're probably right,' Elizabeth said. She looked at Emily intently before pushing herself up from the bench with her hands. 'Seriously, though, think about the puppy. And remember, Em, it's one thing to make the best of what you have, but quite another to make it better. If you're going to lie in the bed you've made, at least make it comfortable.'

Emily smiled to herself. It sounded like something Gran might have said.

Chapter Three

Emily stood in the oversize double garage that once housed her grandfather's treasured Jaguar and farm ute. Stacked against the back wall were the items of furniture, garbage bags of linen and clothes, and boxes of household items and books that hadn't fitted in Granny Mayfair's single room at the nursing home. She wondered if Gran had remembered to miss all the treasures she had to leave behind.

To the left, just inside the roller door, was an untidy pile of items from the nursing home – they'd had only twenty-four hours to empty the room, such was the demand for aged accommodation in the small town.

Emily was relieved to be the first to arrive; it gave her time to silently remember her gran, grieve for the imminent loss of her worldly possessions, and breathe in her fading scent for the last time in peace.

Standing there looking at the empty armchair, Emily pictured Rose's crooked smile and felt her throat tighten.

The thought of her mother and aunt going through Gran's things like scavengers caused a few tears to spring forth and trickle down her cheeks. But it had to be done. It was either that or haul it off to the local tip for all and sundry to rummage through.

Emily smiled, imagining those her mother and aunt referred to as 'ferals' sipping tea from Granny's Wedgwood cups, having tossed the saucers back for being a 'pain in the arse'. Gran, with her benevolent yet cheeky soul, would have got a kick out of that.

Emily's thoughts were cut short by a voice behind her. 'Thought you would have been halfway through by now.'

She turned to find her mother, aunt and cousin standing in the light of the open roller door.

And let you miss out on the pick of things – I wouldn't dare, she almost said, but instead, with a smile plastered on her face, replied, 'I was merely awaiting your instruction.'

'Well, we're keeping the furniture, jewellery and anything of value. The rest can go to the op shop – unless you have any objections, Enid,' Aunt Peggy said to her younger sister.

Elizabeth and Emily shared knowing grins and rolled their eyes.

'Sounds about right to me – just toss everything else in the middle and we'll bag it up later.'

Before long they were all scurrying about like vermin, clouds of dust rising into the air after being released from the folds of plastic bags, drop sheets and the flaps of cardboard boxes.

The piles of clothes and accessories, books and assorted household items grew in the middle of the dusty concrete floor.

'It's a pain we have to go through *everything*, but I suppose we must,' Peggy said half an hour later as she stood up and put her rubber-gloved hands to her hips.

'This dust is *killing* me,' Enid announced, pausing to blow her nose.

'Sooner we get on, sooner we get finished,' Peggy said, and returned to her pile.

Emily would have preferred to do the task alone. She'd have given Gran's things the respect they deserved. Every now and then something discarded caught her eye and she'd rush to retrieve it for her own growing pile just outside the roller doors. She noticed Elizabeth was amassing a pile of her own as well. It was considerably smaller, but Emily was pleased to see her rich city cousin wasn't totally devoid of sentimentality. Liz was collecting mainly fiction books and kitchenalia: scales with cast iron weights, rusty hand beaters with wooden handles, chipped enamel mixing bowls, and an old Mixmaster – things that held no particular interest for Emily as she'd been given all new stuff for her wedding. Maybe Liz was keen to add some rustic touches to her apartment.

Occasionally, a commotion from the far side of the garage caused the cousins to glance over at their mothers squabbling over something or other. The arguments between the sisters never lasted long as, invariably, Peggy would strike the winning blow by trotting out the line that she was the elder and therefore should have first right of refusal.

While the older two women were otherwise occupied by one of their tussles, Elizabeth and Emily took the opportunity to escape into the sunshine and fresh air for a short respite from the dust.

'Reckon I'm not far away from the recipes if you still want them,' Elizabeth said quietly.

'Thanks. Thought of anything you want?'

'Other than the painting, you mean? Actually, I wouldn't mind some of her costume jewellery – it's so *in* in Melbourne at the moment.'

'I'm going through a heap of bedroom bags right now – they're probably in there.'

'Better get back to it before we're told off for slacking,' Elizabeth said, making her way back inside.

★

Enid slipped out to get lunch about two o'clock, and arrived back from the shops with brown paper bags glistening with oil from the pies, pasties and sausage rolls within.

'Sorry, it's all the roadhouse had left, and the bakery was shut,' she offered as she slapped the bags onto the dining room table.

Peggy, obsessively healthy, grumbled that she would have fixed a salad had she known it would take this long and be this greasy. Nonetheless, Emily and Elizabeth noticed – they shared a look, but said nothing – that she polished off her lunch quicker than anyone, before voraciously retrieving the last crumbs of pastry from the bottom of the bag and licking them off her fingers.

They finished their sorting just as the last rays of late spring sunshine shone through the dust-speckled windows at the front of the garage, packing what they could fit in their respective vehicles. Emily – knowing she'd cop it for bringing 'more crap' into the house – hoped John was at the pub so that she could stow the boxes in the bottom of the large wardrobe in the spare room without him knowing.

After a sleepless night and a day spent amongst Granny Mayfair's things, feeling the wise old woman's spirit all around her – not that she'd tell anyone – Emily knew Elizabeth had been right the day before, and that Gran would have agreed: she had to start standing up for herself.

Emily parked the car and carried the largest box to the house, pausing at the door to take a fortifying breath before entering. She stopped in the hallway when she heard the television. *Damn.* She thought about taking the box back to the car and dealing with them when he was out tomorrow. But somehow she found the strength to walk forward and, with the box hoisted on her hip, opened the door to the lounge room.

'Hello,' she said, her voice coming out a little squeaky because of her nervousness.

'Oh, so you're finally home. I was thinking I'd have to go to the pub for tea.'

'There are plenty of leftovers in the fridge,' Emily answered, surprising herself.

'How many bloody boxes of crap have you brought home?'

'Just three.'

'All useless stuff, I suppose.'

'Pretty much,' Emily said, feigning joviality. 'How was your day?'

'Boring, absolutely nothing on the TV today. Hey, now you're here, can you get us some tea?'

'Sure. How hungry are you?'

'Starving!'

Emily gave a deep sigh as she shut the lounge-room door behind her and offered silent thanks to the hallway ceiling. There had been no confrontation. *Slowly but surely*, she told herself, quoting one of Gran's favourite sayings, as she divided up the leftovers.

While she watched the first plate revolving slowly inside the microwave, Emily felt a wave of comfort envelop her like a nice warm blanket around her shoulders. Part of her said it was Granny Mayfair protecting her. Another part told her not to be so bloody ridiculous; she was just tired from a long day.

The microwave's shrill cry, signalling the end of its program, startled Emily, and she put her thoughts aside to attend to the demanding appliance before it screamed again and brought John into the kitchen.

The next morning Emily cooked bacon and eggs – their traditional Sunday breakfast – but today she chose to mix things up a little. John's broad boyish smile and hearty answer of 'Yes please' to her offer of sausages with his bacon gave her a glimmer of the man she'd met and thought she'd fallen in love with. Her heart ached for a split second before she was reminded of everything else that had gone on between them.

It took her almost to the end of their meal to summon the courage to mention what had been on her mind since she'd awoken in the early hours of the morning.

'What do you think about getting one of David Burton's puppies?' she asked, after running the line through her head a dozen times.

'I'm not having a border collie – they're too bloody timid,' he said through a mouthful.

'I was more thinking house dog – for me. I could do with the company,' Emily said.

'Oh,' he said, before picking up his last piece of bacon with his fingers and shoving it into his mouth.

Emily was left to endure an excruciating silence while wondering what was going to happen next. It hadn't exactly been a flat out no, had it?

'Fine, as long as it stays outside and away from my sheep,' John said, pushing his plate away and getting up from the table.

Emily sat in stunned silence, her mouth gaping slightly. *Had he really said it was okay?*

'May as well see if Bill Angas has got any kelpies left while you're at it. I'd prefer a male but a bitch'll do,' John said from the doorway with his greasy, battered Akubra in hand.

She *had* heard right! Emily practically ran to the telephone to ring David Burton. After agreeing to take the last puppy, a female he described, apologetically, as a bit of a runt and therefore a giveaway, she rang Bill Angas and kept her fingers crossed that he had a male left. He did: three. Her day was getting even better.

Emily hung up and hurried off to find John – she wasn't going to tempt fate by choosing a useless dog herself. He was in the shed changing the oil in the ute and said he'd head off soon.

Back in the house, Emily hummed her way through the dishes and the rest of her Sunday. For once she actually had plans for the following day. *Yay!* At nine o'clock she would catch up with Liz for a coffee at the bakery before she left town, and then she was, quite literally, off to see a man about a dog. She chuckled to herself.

★

Emily didn't tell Elizabeth that John had agreed to her getting a puppy. She wasn't sure exactly why, except that she didn't want her cousin telling her she'd blown everything out of proportion and that John was clearly nowhere near as bad as she made him out to be.

At ten to ten, her cousin announced she had to go – her mum wanted to leave at exactly ten o'clock.

Emily was distracted when she hugged her goodbye, her head swimming with possible names and the things she had to get for the puppy.

'You okay?' Liz asked when they pulled away.

'Yes, fine. Why?'

Elizabeth looked at her with a quizzical expression and said, 'Nothing. Call me, any time, if you want to talk – I mean it.'

'You can call me too, remember,' Emily shot back quickly.

'Take care,' Elizabeth called from the open window of Aunt Peggy's late model red Commodore.

'You too,' Emily replied, waving as the car pulled away. She waited until it was out of sight before making her way across the street to the rural supplies shop to buy everything she would need for the new puppy.

Chapter Four

The Burtons' stone farmhouse stood grandly on the top of a small rise. Emily approached it, feeling excited and a little unsure. Was she really doing the right thing? Definitely. She couldn't believe she hadn't thought of it earlier.

The plain four-panelled door opened before Emily had the chance to lift the ornate brass knocker. Before her stood a lean but robust woman of similar age and height wearing sandals, beige tailored pants and a neatly pressed but untucked, pale pink, short-sleeved linen shirt. Emily blushed slightly and wished she had dressed better than her usual attire of well-worn denim jeans, plain navy t-shirt and Rossi work boots. But she was here to collect a puppy, not indulge in high tea, she reminded herself.

'Hello Mrs Burton, I'm Emily Stratten – I'm here to…'

'It's Barbara – none of this *Mrs* rubbish,' she said, accepting Emily's hand. Emily felt an instant connection.

Barbara Burton was what locals referred to as a 'ring-in'; she was from elsewhere.

'Would you like a cuppa?'

'Only if it's no trouble.'

'I'd be glad of the company, actually,' she said, stepping aside to let Emily in. 'I was just about to have one myself.'

'In that case, I'd love one,' Emily said, returning Barbara's warm smile. 'I'll just leave my boots at the door,' she offered, looking down the expanse of what appeared to be a horribly expensive, handmade Persian runner.

'There's really no need.' As Emily looked dubiously down the hall, Barbara added, 'It may look posh, but they really are the easiest things to keep clean – hardly shows the dirt with that pattern. Once a year you just drag it outside, hang it on the fence, give it a good beating with the back of the broom, and then hose it off.'

Emily couldn't hide her look of disbelief. She still hesitated.

'Come on, I'm serious,' Barbara laughed. 'They're not as delicate as you'd think.'

Emily stepped onto the rug, and then followed Barbara past a narrow antique hall table on which stood a tall vase overflowing with long-stemmed roses directing the eye towards a pair of large floral oil paintings in ornate gold frames.

'Are you sure I'm not intruding?'

'I've got nothing on that can't wait. I'm here all day on my own most of the time – you have no idea how nice the prospect of another woman to chat to is. But don't let me keep *you* if you're in a hurry.'

Emily was surprised to hear herself saying to this complete stranger, 'I'm in much the same boat myself, actually.'

They entered a large tidy country kitchen. It was bathed in bright light from two skylights above a massive antique pine table. It reminded Emily of what she'd chosen for her B&B project before it was banished to a cardboard box.

'Wow, what a gorgeous kitchen,' she said.

'Thanks, it's only just finished. It kept me out of trouble for three months. Next is the office. I have to have a project else

I'll surely go mad – God knows what I'll do when the house is finished; garden, I expect. Please, sit.'

Emily carefully pulled one of the plain pale timber chairs out from the table. The upholstered seat matched the cranberry checked curtains that hung above the sink. She noticed that the classic black and white tiles laid in a diagonal pattern on the floor were not ceramic at all, but lino.

'I can't get John to spend a cent on the house,' Emily said wistfully, now staring up at the expanse of timber cabinetry running around almost the entire perimeter of the room.

'John Stratten, big spender,' Barbara said, stopping herself abruptly and blushing slightly. 'Sorry, I should learn to keep my big mouth shut.'

'That's okay. You know what farmers are like – they'll only spend money on something that has a chance of making them some more.'

'Oh yes, only too well. That's why I made the renovation a condition of the marriage.'

'Sorry?'

'I told David I wasn't moving here unless I had somewhere nice to live – not necessarily overnight, but eventually. Mean, I know, but I figure if they love you enough, well…'

Emily stared in awe at the woman who had her back to her as she pulled cups from a glass-fronted cupboard.

'So, tea or coffee?' Barbara asked, half turning from the sink as she filled the kettle.

'Coffee would be great, thanks – white with one.'

Barbara joined Emily at the table as the kettle slowly began hissing into action.

'How long have you lived here?' Barbara asked. 'Sorry to be nosy, but David didn't tell me anything about you.'

'All my life.'

'Raised on a farm?'

'No, a townie – over at Hope Springs. My parents still live there. And you?'

'I grew up on a farm near Millicent, in the south-east.'

They were distracted by the roar and then click of the kettle signalling it had finished boiling. Barbara got up to tend to their drinks. After placing two plain white tapered mugs on pewter coasters, she disappeared into the pantry and returned clutching a large square glass jar full of homemade melting moment biscuits.

'My other hobby to keep me out of mischief,' Barbara said, sounding a little apologetic, as she took off the lid then pointed the open jar towards Emily.

'I love them, but I've never tried making them,' Emily said, taking one out.

'They're actually a lot easier than they look – remind me to copy the recipe for you before you leave.'

They became engrossed in discussing their favourite recipes and it seemed only minutes later when Emily looked at her watch to find it was almost one o'clock – John would be furious.

'I really had better get going,' she said with a groan. She was disappointed her morning was ending.

'Have some egg sandwiches before you go – I made them first thing, before I found out David wouldn't be home.' Barbara got up and went to the fridge.

'Only if you're sure...' *Let John be furious*, Emily thought, feeling a rare surge of boldness.

'Of course – it's so nice to have a visitor.'

'Just don't let me leave without a puppy,' Emily laughed.

'Yes, quite,' Barbara giggled, as she placed a small white oval platter of plump sandwiches, garnished with sprigs of parsley, on the table, and went back for a large jug of homemade lemonade.

How very postcard, Emily thought, feeling somewhat insecure about her own domestic skills, which she'd thought quite adequate until now.

At three o'clock Emily announced that she really did have to get going if she was to have the puppy settled before nightfall.

'Come on then,' Barbara said, getting up and leading the way back down the hall.

As they crossed an expanse of rubble to the shearing shed, Barbara said, 'I hope you like her. I'm not sure what will happen if you don't take her, dear little thing. She's a bit too timid for a sheepdog, but she really does have the sweetest nature.'

Emily had already made up her mind she was not leaving without a puppy; they'd learn to like each other. 'She's for me – a housedog – so she can be as timid as she likes.'

'Oh, that's a relief. Even though I'm a farmer's daughter I've never got used to the matter-of-fact way they deal with these things...'

'No, me neither.'

'Sasha, come on, girl,' Barbara called as she pushed a huge corrugated iron sliding door aside. A large long-haired border collie waddled out of the shadows.

'Sorry, I didn't even bring you anything,' Barbara said, ruffling the dog's ears. Before long, a small puppy emerged tentatively from the darkness. It hid behind its mother and peered out from under her belly at Emily and Barbara.

Emily's heart melted. 'Ooh, aren't you just the cutest thing,' she cooed, bending down to examine the fluffy little bundle. Sasha stepped aside to expose the puppy, and Emily, seizing the opportunity, scooped the creature up into her chest. It whined and wriggled a bit before snuggling into her armpit. Sasha looked up, wagging her tail.

'Look, she's happy her last one is going to a good home,' Barbara said.

Emily looked down at the large eager eyes of the mother dog and felt her throat tighten. She bent down, still clutching the puppy tightly, and patted Sasha's head.

'I'll take good care of her, don't you worry. You need a name, little one,' she said, holding the puppy out from her and examining her markings. She was the quintessential black-and-white border collie, with one exception: she didn't have the broad white collar.

'I've been calling her Grace,' Barbara said.

'That's perfect. What do you think, little Gracie?'

Emily put Grace gently on the towel in the bottom of the box she'd brought, placed it on the front passenger seat, and pulled the seatbelt around it. All set, she offered Barbara a broad smile and an extended hand to complete the transaction, thinking as she did so that their lovely day together warranted more. Barbara, clearly thinking along the same lines, acted, drawing her into a tight hug.

'I've had the best time – promise you'll come back soon and bring Grace for a visit with her mum,' Barbara said.

'I'd love that, but it's my turn next. What about next week?'

'Okay, but call me tomorrow and let me know how she settles in. We'll organise something then.'

'Thanks for a truly lovely day, Barbara, and for Grace, of course.'

'Pleasure. Drive carefully.'

Emily's bright mood was tinged with a touch of sadness as she drove back down the Burtons' driveway. Her heart ached for taking the tiny dog away from her mother, but she vowed to be the best, most loving replacement mum she could possibly be.

Chapter Five

Grace didn't make a sound the whole way in the car, and when Emily pulled into the shed and the box beside her was still silent she was suddenly concerned – maybe she hadn't put enough air holes in it after all. With her breath held and a slow thudding heart she carefully prised the flaps open and peered inside. Two eager eyes greeted her. The puppy was in almost the exact position she'd placed it in forty minutes earlier.

'Thank God you're all right – I thought you'd died or something!' she cried, scooping the black-and-white bundle up and pressing her cheek to the puppy's fur. Grace gave a little whine in response and tried to lick her face. Emily got out and closed the car door.

'Come on, little one. This is your new home.' Emily carried the pup around the yard and sheds in the immediate vicinity. She thought it strange the dog didn't wriggle or insist on being put down. She looked at her new friend with concern. What if being the runt meant it wasn't right in the head or something?

Back at the car she put Grace down, saying, 'You'll have to walk now while I carry all your things. Come on.'

On the verandah, just outside one of the four doors that led into the house, Emily placed the pet bed, a bowl of dampened biscuits with the contents of a small tin of puppy food on top, and a bowl of water far enough away to avoid being knocked over during any ensuing feeding frenzy. As Emily explained everything, Grace looked on with great, yet solemn, interest, though with no apparent inclination to eat. Emily then placed the puppy in the centre of the plush foam pet bed and told her that this was where she had to stay.

'I'll be back soon to check on you,' she reassured, one hand on the door handle ready to step inside the house. But the puppy was so tiny, and looked even more so perched on the large bed, chin on her outstretched legs and sad eyes peering up at her. For the second time that day, Emily's heart melted almost to the point of tears.

'Oh, come here,' she said, scooping the puppy up and taking it inside. She'd worry about training her to stay outside later. After all, she was only a baby and it was her first night away from her mum – she'd be terrified.

'This is the house,' she told the puppy, as she walked through, opening and closing doors. 'You're not allowed in here, though, because you live outside,' she explained to the solemn ball in the crook of her arm.

Emily got a fright when she opened the lounge-room door to find John watching TV. She'd been so caught up organising Grace she hadn't even thought to check if his vehicle was in the shed. She went to quickly shut the door again, hoping he hadn't noticed her or the puppy. But she wasn't quick enough.

'What the hell is that thing doing inside?' he bellowed. 'Get it out!'

'I was just showing her around. John, this is Grace; Gracie, this is John.'

'Emily, for God's sake, it's not a child – it doesn't understand what you're saying!'

'Shush, you're scaring her,' Emily said, stroking the bundle that was trying to push its way under her arm.

'Just put it outside,' he groaned.

Emily did as she was told, but every time she tried to leave it, Grace would scratch and whine at the door. And every time, Emily would give in and sit with the puppy until it was settled again.

She was still sitting with the pup later when the door suddenly opened, startling her. John stood in the doorway looking down at them. She rubbed her eyes, realising she must have nodded off in the lovely late afternoon sunshine.

'Are you going to cook dinner or sit out here with that damn dog all night?'

Her response was to uncross her jeans-clad legs and get up.

'I knew I'd live to regret this,' he said, shaking his head and turning on his heel.

'Now, Gracie, I need you to be a good girl and stay here – quietly. I'll be back a little later to check on you.' She gave the puppy's kinked ears a ruffle.

Emily busied herself with fixing a dinner of grilled T-bone steak and steamed vegetables. She hoped Grace had had enough excitement to have finally dropped off to sleep. So far so good, she thought as she put the meals on the table and called John in from the lounge room.

They ate in silence, except for John's brief statement that none of Bill Angas's kelpies had been suitable. He didn't elaborate and Emily didn't enquire further.

She collected the plates and was turning to put them on the sink when something caught her eye. Grace had somehow got into the kitchen and was curled up under the meat safe cupboard against the end wall.

'I'll bring your dessert into the lounge,' she told John, trying to sound nonchalant. He shot her a quizzical frown before pushing back from the table.

He had to pass right by where the puppy was hidden, and Emily held her breath as he did. But just as he passed, the tip of the puppy's tiny tail flopped out onto the dark stained floorboards.

'And what do you think you're doing?' he asked, bending down and giving the white tip a gentle tug.

Grace emerged from under the cupboard with a shy expression that seemed to convey both guilt and pride.

Emily rushed over. 'She must have come through the old cat door.'

Grace was now looking gleefully up at them and wagging her little tail furiously. Emily leapt to the pup's rescue, but John beat her to it, bending and scooping her up himself.

'Well, aren't you a clever little thing?' he said, rubbing her taut belly. Grace let out a little burp and Emily and John chuckled.

Emily was so relieved she could have cried. In their time together she had never seen her husband so doting. *Maybe he would make an okay father after all*, she thought wistfully as she watched him play with Grace.

'Now, you, little monster, live outside – got it?' he said, giving the pup's belly a poke before handing her over awkwardly to Emily.

'You'd better block up that damn cat door,' he said as he left the kitchen.

Emily sighed. What was she expecting: that he'd crumble and agree to the puppy sleeping at the end of their bed? Well, yes. That was exactly what she'd been hoping for.

'Sorry, little one. You heard him, outside for you,' she said, and reluctantly took Grace back outside.

★

Grace's first night was a disaster. Having apparently searched the verandah that wrapped around the house and found the door nearest the master bedroom, she whined and scratched for hours before Emily, fearful that John would completely lose his temper, took a thick coat and rug and joined her outside. Thankfully it wasn't one of the unseasonably chilly nights they'd been having lately.

'We can't have a repeat of that performance tonight,' John announced the next morning upon finding Emily curled up on the pet bed with Grace.

'She has to get used to being alone. Poor little thing has always had her mum.'

'Well, how's she going to do that if you keep giving in to her?'

'I don't know,' a tired Emily confessed with a sigh. She was beginning to wonder if she'd done the wrong thing taking on a puppy.

When John headed out to check the sheep, Emily took Grace into the lounge and plonked her on one of the chairs while she lay down for a catnap on the three-seater couch.

'Please, just stay put,' she said. 'And don't you dare wee or poo anywhere – John will kill us both.'

A little later the phone began to ring. Emily tried to ignore it, but it got the better of her, and she eased herself to her feet. She smiled at seeing Grace curled up and sleeping soundly on the chair.

'Hello,' she said quietly, after picking up the portable phone from the small table. She went back into the lounge.

'Hi, Emily? It's Barbara Burton.'

Shit, Emily thought, frantically checking her watch – it was almost lunchtime.

'Barbara, hi, sorry I haven't got around to calling you yet...'

'It's fine. Listen, sorry if I'm being pushy, but I wanted to know how little Gracie's first night went.'

'Not very well, I'm afraid,' Emily replied. 'Actually, we were just having a nap. She's meant to be outside – John would kill both of us if he knew she was in the lounge – but it's the only peace I've had. She scratched and howled all night until I joined her. I'm a bit of a pushover, I'm afraid,' she said with a laugh.

'Poor little thing must be missing her mum.'

'Any suggestions, Barbara?'

'David's the dog man, but I'm a softie like you – I'd have her inside.'

'Not an option – John won't have it.'

'Well, there's an electric blanket we sometimes use. It's got a pulse that's meant to simulate a heartbeat. I can bring it over if you like – I have to go into town anyway.'

'I don't want to put you to any trouble.'

'It's no trouble.'

'Well, I could do with the help – I'm afraid if we have another sleepless night John will insist I get rid of her.' *Or worse.*

'We can't have that. Shall we say two o'clock, then?'

'As long as you're happy to drive out here – I could always meet you in town.'

'No, this way I can help you set the blanket up and see if I can offer any other suggestions.'

'Okay, great, I look forward to seeing you then.'

'See you then.'

'Come on, you, we've got things to do,' Emily called to the slumbering puppy, who responded by opening her eyes and giving a big yawn. Reluctantly Grace stood up, stretched, hopped off the chair and followed Emily into the kitchen.

'You sit down there under the cupboard you seem to like so much,' she said, pointing to the meat safe. Grace obliged her by making her way under and getting comfortable. Emily couldn't believe the dog had done as it was told.

She busied herself with making a date loaf for afternoon tea, and then preparing sandwiches for lunch while it was in the oven.

She'd fully intended on sending Grace outside well before John came in for lunch, but the puppy was so quiet, tucked almost out of sight, it completely slipped her mind.

'Emily, the condition of you getting a puppy was that it would live outside,' he said, entering the kitchen and again spying the tip of Grace's tail poking out from under the cupboard.

'I know. Barbara Burton rang. She's bringing a blanket with a heartbeat. Hopefully Grace will think it's her mother and be happy to stay outside on her own from now on. I think she just wants the company.'

'Of course it does – you're being pathetic. Just stop giving in to it!'

Chapter Six

'What a gorgeous setting!' Barbara exclaimed upon her arrival. 'You are so lucky to have lovely big gum trees all around you – the mallee scrub at our place really doesn't have the same grand effect. What's the story with the cottage across the way? It would be just gorgeous done up.'

'Yes, well, that's what I keep telling John. But apparently it's a knockdown job.'

'Oh no, you can't let that happen. There's so much potential. It could be an art gallery, or an artist's or writer's studio – not that I'm either; I'm just being a silly romantic.'

'I thought it would actually make a great B&B. Far enough away from the house for privacy, but close enough to service.'

'You're absolutely right – it would be brilliant! Come on, I *must* have a closer look,' Barbara said, already halfway back out the door.

They walked across to the steel mesh gate into the paddock, which Emily opened. Grace was panting heavily, having struggled to keep up, and she flopped down in the paddock while Emily shut the gate after Barbara.

Thankfully this was one of the easy ones, not the wire 'cocky' gates that could be tricky to operate. Even though she hadn't been raised on a farm, Emily knew to leave a gate exactly as she found it. Not to do so was practically a hanging offence in the country.

They reached the ruined cottage, and Barbara's excitement increased. 'Oh, wow, what gorgeous tiles,' she said, squatting down to look more closely at the tessellated verandah. 'It's in amazing condition, considering.'

'There are a heap missing up the far end,' Emily said.

'They're making them again, so you could easily replace them. I had to get some new ones for our verandah, and apart from looking a little newer and shinier, you can hardly notice.'

They wandered through the derelict building and the area around it, where fallen limestone and bricks lay about in piles here and there, each offering comments and suggestions.

'These floorboards are still pretty good too, considering the state of the roof. And I can't believe the fireplace mantle is still here,' Barbara said, running a hand over the grey, weathered timber surface.

'Hmm,' Emily said wistfully. The more enthusiasm Barbara showed, the more despondent she felt.

'It's such a pity John doesn't share your passion. What if you *showed* him your ideas, like took cuttings from magazines or photos of other old cottages done up?'

'I did – it didn't work. He reckons the hayshed is going here when he gets around to it.'

'Aren't there, like, thousands of other acres he could choose from?' Barbara asked, looking around her.

'Apparently not.'

'Well, we'll just have to hope it takes him ages to get around to it.'

'Hmm.'

Back at the house they enjoyed a few moments of silence sipping their coffees and savouring the rich nutty cake liberally spread with butter.

'This is divine – is it the date loaf from the CWA book?'

'Yes, with a bit of tweaking.'

'I've never made it. I've had it heaps of times, but never as good as this. What is it you've tweaked – or will you then have to kill me?'

'No,' Emily laughed. 'I just double the dates, walnuts and golden syrup. I find the CWA recipes are often a bit stingy. Maybe because the old dears who wrote them went through the Depression – or wrote them during it. I quadruple the cocoa for the Two Minute Chocolate Cake, otherwise it's quite anaemic looking and bland.'

Just then they heard the sliding back door, and turned as John strode into the kitchen.

'Hello, you must be David's wife. John Stratten,' he said, offering his hand, which Barbara accepted. 'Come to sort out the wretched puppy, I hope.'

'I hope so. Emily told me you had a pretty disturbed night.'

'Emily, how many times do I have to tell you? The dog is to be kept outside,' he said, poking at the tail protruding from under the meat safe with his foot. 'You're just making it harder for it – and yourself, for that matter.'

'I'd better get going,' Barbara said, getting up. 'Come on, I'll give you a hand setting up the blanket before I go. Nice to meet you, John.'

'Yes, goodbye.'

Out on the verandah, Barbara cast her eyes around where Emily had set up Grace's things. 'I think a basket with sides she could snuggle against might be better. And couldn't she be just inside the door here?'

'You heard him – dogs are for outside.'

'But if the blanket got wet she'd be electrocuted.'

'Don't give him any ideas.'

'She's just so exposed out here. That's pretty terrifying for a pup who's just left her mum.'

'I know, but I think the shed would be worse – too far away.'

'Yes, you're her mum now; she needs to know you're close at hand and she's safe. I hate the thought of her being miserable.'

'Me too.' Emily bit her lip for a moment, then made a decision. Speaking almost in a whisper, she said to Barbara, 'Look, I'm going to take the risk. Let's set her up inside here – just by that power point – and hope John comes around. When she's a little bigger I'll try to retrain her to live outside.'

'Blame me,' Barbara offered. 'Tell him I said she's too little to be outside on her own just yet.'

'Thanks. I'd have her at the end of the bed if I had any choice about it.'

'You and me both,' Barbara agreed. 'I'd better get cracking. Thanks for a lovely few hours – let's do it again soon.'

'Yes. And thanks again for the blanket. I'll return it as soon as I can.'

'Hopefully it will do the trick.'

Emily saw Barbara out to her car, where they hugged like old friends. Emily almost skipped on her way back into the house.

She fed Grace and stood for a few moments watching the dog tuck in to her dinner. She already seemed much more content for being inside.

When Emily returned to the kitchen, John looked up from the newspaper. 'Hope you've got the damn dog sorted out. I want to get some sleep tonight.'

'We've put her just inside the door at the end of the verandah. Barbara thinks she's a bit little yet to be outside on her own.'

'Well, she would, wouldn't she?'

'What's that supposed to mean?'

'All you bloody women are the same – weak as piss.'

Chapter Seven

When Emily awoke the next morning, the sun was beginning to peep through the small gap in the bedroom curtains. She was a little surprised to have, apparently, enjoyed an uninterrupted night's sleep.

The electric blanket must have done the trick; that or Grace being inside rather than out. Either way, it didn't matter. What did matter was that her husband was still sleeping soundly beside her, snores vibrating from his loose lips.

Unable to quite believe Grace could still be asleep, Emily stretched slightly and eased herself up. But something caused her to look down before putting her feet onto the floor: two tiny black eyes blinked back at her from where the puppy lay curled up beside the bed.

Realising she finally had conscious company, Grace slapped her tail lightly on the carpeted floor and then sat up at attention. Emily held a silencing finger to her lips, to which the puppy responded with a tilt of her little head. She got out of bed, pulled her robe from the end, scooped Grace into its folds, and practically bolted from the room. As she closed the door she heard John stir and mutter something unintelligible.

'I should be telling you off, you naughty little thing,' she said sternly to the puppy, which was now fidgeting playfully with the terry towelling fabric wrapped around it. 'But you're just far too cute.'

As she pulled the tin of puppy food from the fridge and grabbed a spoon, she wondered how long Grace had been in the bedroom. *Thank God she hadn't jumped on the bed*, she thought with relief.

'What am I going to do with you?' she said as she sat cross-legged on the floor watching Grace devour her breakfast. *Let's just hope there aren't any nasty surprises lurking on the carpet*, she thought, and got up to check while the puppy was busy eating.

Emily was in the dining room when John appeared in the doorway yawning and rubbing his head. 'What are you up to?'

'Just looking for, um, my book – I'm not sure where I left it.'

'Well, it would hardly be in the dining room, now would it?'

'I vaguely remember putting it down somewhere.'

'You'll find it eventually. Come back to bed,' he urged, pulling at the tie on her robe.

'I, er, just have to check on Grace.'

'She's fine – was just finishing eating. I turfed her outside and shut the door. Thank God she let us get some sleep last night. Now come on, I've got something for you,' he said, suggestively.

Emily cringed as she allowed herself to be steered back to bed.

A few minutes later a series of barks and whines came from outside the bedroom window.

'Damn dog. It managed to sleep all night alone...'

'Just ignore her,' Emily urged in a whisper from underneath John, hoping he wouldn't put two and two together.

Emily waited until she saw John driving away from the house before phoning Barbara.

'Hi Barbara, it's me, Emily.'

'Hi Emily. Did our little Gracie enjoy her blanket?'

'I'm not exactly sure.'

'Oh no, she didn't keep you awake again?'

'No, but I have a sneaking suspicion she may have slept on the floor next to my side of the bed – I found her there when I woke up.'

'What did John say?'

'Didn't notice, as far as I know.'

'Naughty little monster.'

'*Clever* little monster,' Emily corrected. 'She didn't make a sound; I almost stepped on her when I got up.'

'Maybe you can teach her to sleep there and go back to her bed early in the morning before John gets up.'

'Surely she's too young to be *that* clever. Anyway, John would have a fit if he found out – it's not worth the risk. I'll just have to shut the kitchen door and hope she doesn't scratch it to shreds.'

'You'll work something out. So, what about lunch next Tuesday at the bakery in town – say, one o'clock? I'll be in doing my groceries.'

'Sounds like a plan. I'll see you then.'

'Okay, good luck with Grace.'

'Something tells me I'm going to need it,' Emily said with a laugh.

'Come on,' Emily called to Grace from the back door. 'We're going for a little walk.' Emily walked out the short driveway and onto the road, Grace trotting quickly behind her. When she got level with the old cottage, fifty or so metres back from the road, she stopped to let the panting puppy catch up.

It would have been so lovely in its day, she thought, looking over at the stone building flanked by majestic gums. There really was no good reason why it couldn't be beautiful again with a bit of hard work. And she wasn't the only one who thought it: Barbara had also seen the potential and seemed genuinely sad to hear of its future demise.

Emily sighed deeply. There was nothing she could do about it; it was earmarked for demolition, and in a matter of time all trace of it would cease to exist.

Standing there on the threshold of the bare paddock, Emily felt a wave of comfort wash over her, similar to what she'd experienced in the kitchen a couple of days earlier. She was relieved; she'd been afraid she'd imagined it. Or worse, that it had somehow served its purpose and left her.

'Hi Gran,' she said, smiling, looking up at the thick white clouds crawling across the brilliant blue rural sky.

'Had enough walk, Gracie?' she said absently, looking back down. But there was no sign of the pup in the immediate vicinity.

Glancing towards the cottage she noticed something white flickering above the short grass. She steadied her gaze and spotted the border collie's small black body bobbing up and down.

'Gracie, we're heading back now.'

But the waving white tail tip continued to move away from her. Emily followed it and arrived at the cottage to find Gracie stretched out panting on the cracked, uneven front verandah.

'See, silly thing? It's too far for a little puppy to walk,' she said, plonking herself down beside the dog. She lay back onto the tessellated tiles, closed her eyes and listened to the sounds around her. Timber joists creaked and groaned, and iron squealed and squawked in the brisk breeze that whispered through the large surrounding trees. A couple of cockatoos shrieked at each other nearby.

Another waft of fresh cool breeze tickled Emily's bare hands, face and neck; the verandah catching the gully breezes coming up from the ocean some twenty miles away would have been a godsend on hot summer days.

She could picture the original owners in their wicker armchairs, a yard apart, right where she lay, taking in the cool, relaxing after a hard day's pioneering in the harsh South Australian sun.

Perhaps the parents discussed their day while children were sent out to collect eggs, gather firewood, or throw a ball about, or just leave the weary parents to themselves. Perhaps there were no children – they hadn't been so blessed – and they had only their hopes for the success of their land on which to focus. Emily's heart felt heavy, but she took a deep breath and banished the feeling.

She imagined them to be people not to make a fuss or dwell on this misfortune life dealt them; they had each other.

She could picture the man and his wife. He was wiry, muscled, but not overly bulky. She was shorter than him, with a lean frame that hid the fact she could give any man a run for his money stooking hay. They were as strong of mind and resolve as of body. Tomorrow they would again work together, doing their darnedest to tame their patch of this wide brown land.

Maybe they lived in a tent or a small hut cobbled together from whatever they could scrounge. Maybe this was their dream house – the reality many years in the making.

She sat up with the overwhelming desire to keep their dream alive. Grace, sensing the changed mood, leapt up to kiss her mistress's face, only to collide with her chest and fall into her lap. Emily gave the puppy a cuddle and a kiss on the forehead before putting her down again and standing up.

'Come on, Grace. This is a special place. Let me show you around.' Emily wandered through and around the building, pointing out this and that feature to the pup and explaining her plans for each room, down to the detailed colour schemes and curtains. She half expected the puppy to bolt off on her own adventure, but instead she trotted along next to Emily, stopping when she did and standing still, her head tilted and ears kinked in the intelligent, concerned expression that is almost a trademark of the border collie.

When they finished their tour, Emily picked the puppy up and made her way quickly back to the main house, the phrase 'If at first you don't succeed, try, try again' coming to her as she stepped back onto the road.

Emily had retrieved her scrapbooks from their bottom-of-the-cupboard exile and was furiously committing her new ideas to paper, making notes and rough sketches, when John arrived home for lunch.

'God, not that *bloody* cottage again,' he cursed, taking his seat at the table. 'I suppose you've been too busy with that to get me some lunch.'

Without a word, Emily went to the fridge to retrieve the plate of ham and salad sandwiches she'd prepared that morning and, as she did, offered Granny Mayfair thanks for passing on the gene for being impeccably organised. She tried to focus on eating her share of the sandwiches, but the encouragement to 'try, try again' kept running through her head.

The phone rang, relieving Emily from the pretence of being interested in how many sheep had made their way into the wrong paddock. As John got up to answer it, she returned to the scrapbook.

It's all well and good to have ideas, she thought, but what she really needed was some action. *But how?* She didn't have much money to speak of – probably five thousand at best. But it was a start.

And what should she do first? Re-roof the intact portions of the building or rebuild the fallen stonework? She didn't have a clue.

Barbara might know, she suddenly thought; she'd ask her at lunch next Tuesday. It was a pity it was almost a whole week away.

Until then she had a small mountain of washing to do, the house to clean and vacuum, and the boxes of Gran's things to sort through. *Bless her*, she thought, tears beginning to well; she was missing their chats terribly.

She left the kitchen under the guise of taking the tea towels out to the washhouse. Her mood was instantly buoyed when Grace greeted her like she'd never expected to see her again, running in circles, jumping about and trying to lick her all over. Emily scooped the puppy up and hugged her tightly to her chest, smiling. There really was nothing like the unconditional love of a pet.

Chapter Eight

Later, standing in the doorway of the spare room, John announced that he was going out and probably would not be back for tea. Only when she heard the ute leave did Emily fully relax and engross herself in the contents of the first box of Granny Mayfair's things she had retrieved a few days before.

Emily took three tapestry cushions from the top. She frowned as she ran a finger over the intricate floral design that Gran had worked many years before, wondering where they should be kept. The logical place would be on the chairs in the lounge, or on their bed, but John hated cushions anywhere, especially floral ones.

Early in their marriage, Emily had brought some home from a shopping trip to Port Lincoln, only to have John throw them back across the room, telling her she was stupid to waste money on such crap. The fact that these were sentimental would make little difference.

Emily sighed and put them aside to be reconsidered later. Next in the box was a stack of large black-and-white and sepia photos of Granny and Grandpa and an assortment of relatives and ancestors Emily had never met.

The contrived backgrounds and grim smiles were reminiscent of old studio portraits, as were the discoloured cardboard mats surrounding them.

She would see to it they were finally framed, Emily decided. Surely John could not object to them taking up space on the wall. And if he did, she would just have to stand her ground. But he *would* object to her spending the money on frames, she realised with a deep sigh, and put the pictures aside in a neat pile next to the cushions.

Next, she brought out Granny Mayfair's treasured writing companion, an eight-by-twelve-inch box, four inches deep. It had a padded lid covered in pale vinyl with an all-over pastel floral design. Engraved on the tarnished gold clasp were Granny Rose Mayfair's pre-marriage initials – R.D. – in elaborate flowing script.

Emily remembered Granny Mayfair sitting at the dining table with it beside her when she wrote letters to her friends. *What to di with it*, she wondered as she lifted the lid and breathed in the unmistakable, sweet, slightly sickly scent of stale vinyl.

Underneath the lid were stiff compartments, empty except for a tiny manila envelope with the word 'KEY' stamped on it in blue ink. *It was so typical of Granny to never lock anything*, Emily thought, smiling, after checking the envelope, wrapping the key up again and placing it back in the pocket.

She checked the other pockets thoroughly – for what, she wasn't sure. All were empty. The box itself was brimming with folded yellowing papers. Among them were a number of old share certificates and bank statements. Thumbing through them, Emily indulged in the brief fantasy that she'd uncovered a forgotten fortune, before reminding herself that even if she had it would belong to her uncle Richard – he'd got the farm and everything else of value. She thumbed on, only finding a few piles of brightly coloured chocolate wrappers smoothed out and bound with string.

Emily sighed deeply, closed the lid, snapped the metal clasp shut, and put the box aside. Next she turned her attention to the bundle of Granny Mayfair's recipes – tied tightly with Gran's trademark grey string. With the bundle on the floor in front of her, Emily bent forward and carefully prised apart the knotted bow. Released, the collection of magazine and newspaper cuttings, scraps of paper, recycled envelopes, and well-thumbed Country Women's Association cookbooks slid away from each other and across the floor.

Picking up an envelope on which was written a grocery list in Gran's abrupt angular hand, Emily smiled as the saying 'Waste not, want not' – another of Gran's favourites – came to mind.

Below the list was a series of mathematical calculations – another of Gran's talents. Even with the onset of dementia, Granny Mayfair could calculate the most complex problems as long as she had a pen or pencil and something to write on.

Emily put the envelope aside and picked up another – this one with her grandpa's mix of small and large rough script making up what looked like a record of sheep and cattle numbers.

She smiled, imagining Grandpa cursing the whereabouts of his precious note and Granny shrugging and saying she 'didn't have the foggiest idea' what he was on about. This happened all the time, thanks to Grandpa's habit of littering the dining table with chequebooks, bank statements and assorted paperwork, and Granny's of regularly 'tidying up' by scooping everything into a pile and depositing it in the pantry, or anywhere else that had available space out of sight. This had gone on forever, well before there'd been even a hint of dementia.

Until the onset of her condition, Gran remembered exactly where everything was, and when asked, would go off, fossick about for a few moments in a cupboard or drawer, and return with the requested item.

Emily wondered if Grandpa's heart attack had anything to do

with his exasperation at items being lost, with denials from Rose of having touched his paperwork, and with the same questions being asked over and over.

Putting the envelope aside, she continued to sort through the mass of papers spread out before her, separating the recipes from the shopping lists and jottings.

About halfway through her task, a piece of folded notepaper caught her attention. Its quality made it stand out like a neon sign from the scraps of butchers' paper, thin-lined notepaper, and used envelopes with corners missing where Gran had cut out the stamps for forwarding to charities.

The thick, textured paper of the note had once been white but was now more a dirty pale grey, greasy with smudged finger-prints across the neat cursive script and large sloping signature at the bottom. There was a jagged, torn edge in the top right-hand corner where the full name and address of the writer would have been.

The delicate state of the crease suggested it could have been a recipe for one of the family favourites – shepherd's pie, pavlova or Gran's famous chocolate raspberry shortcake – but what Emily read bore no reference to cooking.

October 18ᵗʰ, 1947

Dear Miss Rose,

It really was the greatest pleasure to again make your acquaintance in London this last year.

Your uncle tells me you are betrothed to a grazier and soon to be married and then make your new life in the interior of the wide brown land that is Australia. He tells me the place is a small village called Woop Woop, but the twinkle in his eye, not unlike your own, and the fact I could not find the name on any map, suggests he may have been doing what you taught me Australians are very apt to do: that is, 'pulling my leg'. You are indeed an intriguing people with a peculiar language. But I digress.

Please accept my gift for your nuptials of seven (a sacred number in my land and faith, and I believe your own) of Golconda's finest – left rough for you to have cut and set as you desire. They are, I think, almost the exact shade of your unusual and enchanting eyes.

You and your husband would be extended the most gracious welcome should you ever find yourselves in my, what would you say, 'neck of the woods'? (See, I have managed to retain some of what you taught me in our short time together!)

I wish you all the very best of health and happiness for the future.
With the kindest regards,
Prince Ali

Emily reread the letter and continued staring at the paper twitching in her slightly shaking hand. Granny Mayfair knew a prince!

It made sense; one of Emily's great-uncles had been a diplomat and travelled widely, mixing with high society across the world during the nineteen-forties, fifties and sixties. It was a far cry from Emily's upbringing.

I could have had a prince for a grandfather, she thought. Except the note gave no indication of romantic involvement. But what if…?

Family lore had it that Rose had essentially been excommunicated from her family after her marriage. Emily wondered if her grandpa had known the true extent of what Rose had given up. Other than a few bits and pieces from an aunt – who was considered a little wayward, anyway – Granny never benefited from the family fortune that supposedly existed upon her parents' deaths. Good on Granny for sticking to her guns and marrying for love and not wealth or power.

What had the prince sent her for a wedding present, anyway? All the letter said was 'Golconda's finest'. *Finest what?* What could be left rough? Emily leapt up and bolted into John's office and turned on the computer. She tapped her fingers while she waited for it to boot up.

Finally she had the Google search box in front of her. She put in 'What was Golconda famous for in the 1940s?' and waited. Seconds later she was staring at a list of links, including a number of pages about the famously cursed Hope Diamond – apparently the inspiration for the jewel in the movie *Titanic*.

Fuck! Had Gran had been given seven of Golconda's finest *diamonds*? What else could the letter be referring to?

And if so, what happened to them? Had she sold them along the way? Granny and Grandpa seemed to have done all right financially. Despite a number of crushing droughts and devastating floods, they'd always driven a good car – a Jaguar, second-hand but a Jaguar nonetheless – taken a major overseas trip every few years, and built a large home with all the mod-cons for retirement.

Emily found herself wondering if all this had been provided by her grandfather – or by Gran's friend, the prince. But if the diamonds had been sold and the proceeds used to make up shortfalls on the farm, wouldn't she have heard? Wouldn't someone in the family have mentioned it?

Perhaps Gran had had them cut and set in jewellery like the letter suggested. She frowned as she tried to remember the few pieces of quality jewellery Granny had worn or kept in a box on her dressing table.

Green, being her favourite colour, had featured prominently amongst her costume jewellery, but always in a bright emerald shade. There was nothing that could be described as the same colour as Gran's eyes, which were an odd smoky blue grey; exactly the same as Emily's.

Surely such a gift from such a person would have been mentioned somewhere along the line. And if it had been, she'd definitely have remembered. Her overactive, romantic imagination would have woven a fabulous tale of intrigue around it.

Perhaps Grandpa had insisted Rose return the gift. Or maybe they had accepted it and sold the stones straight away, long before Emily's birth, or even her mother's.

Google then revealed that there was a Prince Ali in Golconda at that time. Emily clicked on the link and, as she waited for the page to load, found herself fantasising about rushing off on a romantic adventure to find him and introduce herself.

Moments later she was quite devastated to learn that the prince in question had died a mere five years ago. And that was the end of that.

Ordinarily Emily loved a good mystery, but now she found herself frustrated; there was no way of solving this one. If there had been diamonds, they would have been sold or fought over and distributed long before now. And asking her mother or aunt would be like opening a huge can of worms.

For some reason, the secret had been kept. And she would continue to keep it, she decided, refolding the letter and putting it aside. Though she couldn't help feeling a little disappointed.

Emily got up and went to the bathroom. While washing her hands she stared into the mirror. She'd been told so many times, mainly by Gran's friends, that she had eyes the exact hue of her grandmother's. She'd always hated her dead straight, mouse brown hair that she kept just below her shoulders, but she liked having eyes that were a little different. People always had difficulty putting a name to the colour – they were not really blue and not really grey – and Emily liked that.

So what *had* happened to those diamonds that were supposedly the same colour as Gran's eyes, and therefore her own? Damn not knowing. Damn Gran for dying and not telling her.

Emily splashed cold water on her face to ward off the threatening tears, just as the phone began to chirp. She dragged the handtowel from the rail and hurried to the kitchen to answer the call.

'Hello, Emily speaking.'

'Emily, it's your mother.'

Emily swallowed hard, trying to push the lump forming back down her throat.

'Are you there?'

'Yes, sorry, I'm here,' she said, her voice coming out as more of a croak.

'You sound terrible – you haven't got a cold, have you?'

'No, I've been sorting through the things of Gran's I brought home.'

'Load of old rubbish – don't know why you bothered.'

Emily sniffed.

'No point crying over spilt milk, she always used to say.'

'I don't think her death could be considered *spilt milk*, Mum.'

'She lived a full life. Now she's gone – no point dwelling on it.'

Emily wondered if it was all an act or if Enid really was this cold; she was talking about her own mother, for goodness sake.

'Well, I miss her.'

'Emily, you do realise she probably didn't even know who you were from one day to the next, don't you?'

'She remembered lots from her early life. I loved listening to her stories.'

'You can't possibly have believed a word she said for the last ten years – the woman was gaga.'

'She seemed pretty sure about some things to me.'

'One of them being some Indian prince sending her diamonds as a wedding gift, I suppose?' The sneer in her mother's tone was obvious.

Emily's heart skipped a beat. 'You know about…'

'Oh Emily, don't you think if it were true someone would have actually *seen* them?'

'I suppose so. But why didn't anyone ever say anything?'

'Because it isn't true, that's why.'

'Maybe Grandpa was jealous and didn't want it mentioned or something.'

'Oh Emily, you really do have far too vivid an imagination,' Enid Oliphant said with a brittle laugh. 'Face it, darling, you were duped like the rest of us. Look, I really must be off – Janet will be here in a tick to drive me to lunch. Bye for now.'

'Bye.'

Emily hung up, but stood staring at the phone in her hand. Her mother hadn't said why she'd phoned. She shrugged. *Probably just checking I haven't done anything to embarrass her, like leave my husband,* she thought with another shrug, and let her mind go back to the diamonds.

Gran *hadn't* told her about the gift – the diamonds – from the prince. She only knew about it from reading the letter, which her mother didn't seem to know anything about.

She'd said, 'duped like the rest of us', which suggested the rest of the family had heard the story. That still didn't explain why *she* hadn't. Perhaps it had been consigned to the gaga bin along with Gran when no evidence was found to corroborate it.

But why wouldn't Gran have told her? They'd spent hours candidly discussing her life, especially the early days. How could she have left this out?

Emily's heart sank. Her mother was right: she'd been duped. But in a different way. A lump lodged tight in her throat and tears burned her eyes. Part of her wanted to sit and have a good sob, but another part of her was too angry to give in.

Grace was demanding attention at the glass door. Emily, welcoming the distraction, headed outside to join her.

Chapter Nine

Emily and Barbara, neatly and casually dressed in jeans and recently ironed shirts, sat across from each other at a picnic bench in the mottled shade of a large tree on the median strip dividing the main street.

Grace lay on the ground between them, having exhausted all options for escaping the lead attached to the leg of the bench. Every now and then the dog scratched at its ears and shook its head to shoo away a fly or insect out enjoying the warm late spring day. Her tail flapped in a slow gentle beat against the dirt, which was worn into a bare shallow trench from the feet of locals and visitors over many years.

The two women chatted easily between mouthfuls of their egg, lettuce and mayonnaise wholemeal rolls from the bakery and sandwich place across the road.

Emily closed her eyes and sighed. She was so lucky to have met Barbara. She wondered for a moment if somehow Gran had had something to do with it, but dismissed the notion. She didn't believe in God – in her opinion too many bad things happened in the world for there to be one – but she did believe that there was a force out there more powerful than the human race. And she believed in karma – people getting what they deserved, both good and bad.

Perhaps she was being rewarded with a new friend because she'd been good to Gran when everyone else in the family was just interested in securing her money and keeping her out of the way.

A shrill female voice pulled her abruptly from her thoughts. 'Ooh, fancy seeing you here!'

Emily closed her eyes briefly, took a deep breath, and then turned towards the voice while fixing a pleasant expression on her face.

'Hi Mum.' A slight groan escaped Emily's lips after her greeting. She got up to accept Enid's vague air kiss before sitting back down again.

'You didn't tell me you were lunching! You're Barbara Burton, aren't you? Finally we meet.' Enid Oliphant extended a hand across the table.

'Um, yes, I am,' Barbara said, accepting the hand.

'Sorry, Barbara, this is my mother, Enid Oliphant. Mum, Barbara Burton.'

'Yes, thank you Emily, I think we have established that,' Enid said, sitting down beside her daughter. 'Terribly uncomfortable on these benches; I don't know why you wouldn't eat in the hotel's dining room,' she continued, shuffling and twisting about in an exaggerated gesture of trying to get comfortable. 'And sandwiches really are so *ordinary*,' she added, looking down her nose at Emily's half-eaten roll lying nearby on its brown paper bag.

Emily was about to respond when a yelp rang out from under the table. They all peered down.

'Ooh, a dog! Sorry, I must have kicked it. Barbara, how sweet of you to bring it to lunch,' Enid said, failing to completely erase the disapproval on her face. 'Now, as President of the combined Wattle Creek and Hope Springs Lions Club, let me extend a personal invitation to you to attend our next meeting: Tuesday evening fortnight – the twenty-second. We thought we would have had the pleasure of your company well before now. Your reputation for being such an active member of your old branch preceded you, I'm afraid.'

'I am rather busy with CWA at the moment,' Barbara stated.

'I'm sure you can find time to contribute to a number of worthy causes. And Emily, it's high time you started putting a bit back in to your community as well. I've been meaning to say something. Perhaps you'll both come, though Barbara, I'm sorry, the little doggy will have to stay at home.'

'She's my dog, Mum,' Emily chimed in.

'Oh, Emily, whatever would you want a dog for?' She shot Grace a look of pure distaste before continuing. 'Well, better be off, cards at three. Perhaps you'll consider learning to play bridge, Barbara – if you don't already know how?'

'Maybe when I have more time,' Barbara said through gritted teeth.

'Lovely to meet you. Goodbye Emily. See you both on the twenty-second, if not before.'

'Bye,' Emily and Barbara said in unison.

'God, sorry about that,' Emily said.

'Don't be, but gosh, she's a bit full-on. I feel like a small tornado just passed through.' Barbara grimaced. 'Sorry, I shouldn't say that about your mother.'

'They don't say "You can choose your friends" for nothing,' Emily said, picking up her half-eaten roll.

'Is she always so, um…?'

'Caustic? Bossy? Aggressive? Yes, all of the above,' Emily said.

'Sorry, but I don't think I could spend a lot of time with her.'

'Let alone a lifetime?'

'Well, yes.'

'Now you see why I was so desperate to get married.' Emily couldn't believe she was being so candid.

'What about your dad?'

'Henpecked. We get on pretty well, but I wish he'd stand up to her occasionally.' Emily didn't like to think disrespectfully of her father, but she couldn't help it: Enid bullied him and he just seemed to take it. *Why didn't he stand up for himself, or leave?*

'Perhaps it's easier for him to just keep the status quo,' Barbara offered.

'Hmm. There's probably a bit of that in me too. So are you close to your parents?'

'My dad died years ago...'

'Oh, I'm sorry.'

'Don't be, it was a long time ago.'

'What about your mother?'

'Usual story: drives me mad too – why do you think I live over here? We get on quite well now we never see each other,' Barbara said with a laugh. 'Did you hear they did a study around the complexity of the mother-daughter relationship and found that the problem comes from being either too alike or too different? What a ridiculous conclusion.'

'Hope they didn't spend a lot to find that out.'

'Anyway, let's change the subject. How is John?'

Emily groaned audibly.

'You're really not happy with him, are you?'

'No, big mistake – I think the phrase is "From the frying pan into the fire",' Emily said quietly. She still couldn't believe she was saying all this. Her mother would have a fit if she knew.

'How long have you been married?'

'A bit over three years.'

'You know they're saying three and a half years is the new seven-year itch – apparently because of the fast pace of life these days. Maybe you'll be through it and blissfully happy again soon.'

'Actually, I'm struggling to remember what it was I fell in love with,' Emily said.

'Probably the idea of him – of being married, setting up house, getting away from home, you know. I did the same thing, but was just lucky David turned out to really be the one.'

A wave of envy and longing washed over Emily.

'That's not to say it's always perfect. We've had some ripper fights, don't get me wrong. But I wouldn't stay if he didn't make me happy most of the time. Well, anyway, it's only just over a year for us,' she added, noting Emily's downcast expression.

'I'm sure if I left John, Mum would physically drag me back, tell him I made a mistake and beg him to give me another chance.'

'So you've thought about leaving?'

'All the time, lately.' *Shit!* She hadn't meant to say it.

'Not waiting until he hits you so you can justify it to your mother – and yourself – are you?'

Emily stared down at the table, her face beginning to flame with embarrassment.

'It doesn't have to be physical to be abuse, you know.'

'I know.' Emily thought back to her conversation with Liz at the funeral. It was like hearing an echo. 'But where would I go, what would I do for money?'

'You'd come and stay with me, for one.'

'Thanks, you're too kind. But I mean long-term.'

'I don't know, but remember, whatever money he has is half yours.'

'There isn't any. We're practically broke. Don't tell anyone; he probably *would* hit me if he knew I'd said anything.'

Emily felt tears fill her eyes and was glad she'd kept her sunglasses on despite the heavy shade under the tree. *God, what is with me?* She seemed to burst into tears at the drop of a hat these days.

'I'd be happy to loan you some money if it would help.'

'Thanks, but I couldn't. I've got a couple of grand of my own tucked away.'

'You don't have to wait for something major to happen, though I suppose it would help justify things if you have a reason,' Barbara said thoughtfully.

'No reason would be good enough for my mother.'

'So there's no point waiting then, is there?' Barbara said brightly.

'I'm sure it's not as bad as I'm making it out to be – my marriage, that is. I'm just being a drama queen. Everyone goes through their ups and downs.'

'Only you know how bad the downs are. But remember, I'm only a phone call away if you ever need me,' Barbara said, patting Emily's hand.

Emily swallowed hard. 'Thanks, but I'm sure everything will be fine.' Just how long had she been saying that to herself? 'Gosh, it's almost three,' she said, checking her watch. 'I'd better get cracking.'

'Yes, I've still got to get the groceries done and catch the butcher,' Barbara said, leaping up.

Barbara scrunched their lunch wrappers up and tossed them in the nearby bin. She then gave Grace's head a ruffle and said to Emily, 'It really was lovely to catch up – let's do it again soon.' She strode off after giving Emily a tight, lingering hug.

Emily waited for a few cars to pass. As she watched Barbara wave and drive off, she felt a heavy sadness engulf her.

When her throat tightened and a couple of tears escaped, she told herself sternly to get a grip; she was being ridiculous, there was nothing to be upset about. She'd had a lovely lunch out with a friend. And now she was going home.

'Come on, Gracie, let's get you home,' she said, untying the dog and trying to feel as enthusiastic as she'd made her voice sound.

Emily felt a familiar sense of dread biting at the pit of her stomach. It wasn't normal, was it, to feel like this, returning to your home and husband? She pictured Barbara beaming as she threw her arms around David, who'd be standing on the verandah awaiting her arrival.

'Beware the green-eyed monster,' Gran might have said. 'You've made your bed, now you must lie in it,' her mother would have added.

Chapter Ten

The closer Emily got to home, the heavier the feeling in her stomach became. She was beginning to find it difficult to breathe. It had never been this bad before.

Talking had made everything she'd been trying so hard to suppress bubble up to the surface. It was now just waiting to spill over.

Suddenly Emily found it hard to see. Everything before her through the windscreen was a blur. She pulled over to the side of the road and wiped her hands across her face, startled at how shaky they were.

Now she was stopped and didn't have the vibrations from the corrugated dirt road pounding through her, she noticed how hard and fast her heart was beating. What was happening to her? Grace looked up from where she'd been sleeping on the passenger's side floor, her head tilted in question. Emily reached down to offer reassurance. The dog licked her shaking hand and gave a couple of whines before settling back down onto her front paws.

Okay, breathe in, slow, out, slow, Emily silently instructed herself. It took a few full minutes for the panicky feeling to recede.

She'd driven home from town hundreds of times before. What was she so afraid of today? That he would actually hit her? Then she'd have the bruises to prove he was a bully and would be able to leave. Wouldn't she?

Emily's heart sank further as the reality set in like a cold fog rolling across a paddock in winter. She couldn't leave him.

Having her mother tell her she was a failure, or worse, not tell her – just give *the look* – was too much to contemplate. That would be worse than the whole town talking behind her back, taking the side of their wealthiest family.

Why not leave the area altogether, then? But where would she go? Hope Springs and Wattle Creek were all she'd ever known.

Melbourne, she could go to Melbourne – Elizabeth had offered. But there was no way she'd be able to keep up with Elizabeth's legendary spending habits, and she couldn't bear being paraded around as the poor hick cousin whose marriage had just ended and who didn't have a clue what to do next.

And of course there was Grace to think about. As if sensing her gaze, the pup looked up and wagged her tail. She hopped onto the seat and put her head in Emily's lap. No, there was no way she would do anything that didn't include Grace.

When her breathing returned to normal and she could see clearly again – though she now had a cracking headache – Emily put the car into gear. Had she just had some sort of mental breakdown?

No, it was probably just an anxiety attack, she told herself. People have them all the time. *I'll be fine; it'll all be fine.* Though the nagging feeling remained, telling her that if it was to be fine, something had to change – things just could not go on the way they had been.

As Emily rounded the first of the sharp bends two kilometres from home she realised what she needed to do. She had to get a job. She'd just have to present the idea to John the right way. If nothing else, surely he'd appreciate the extra money.

Feeling significantly buoyed, Emily tried to remember where she'd put her résumé and when she had last updated it.

Rounding the final corner, she saw a large plume of dust rising a little way off. Her foot automatically came off the accelerator and the car slowed. She frowned slightly, taking it in. *That's odd*, she thought. Definitely not smoke; too reddish brown.

She stopped the vehicle and stared. Her heart lurched before skipping a couple of beats. Half of the old cottage was a pile of stone, concrete, timber and iron. All that remained was the chimney and part of the northern and eastern walls. But not for long. Emily held both hands over her gaping mouth and watched as a large green front-end loader lined up and drove forward, the bucket hitting the brick chimney structure mid-section. After a few moments it wavered and began to topple.

Unable to bear seeing the final walls come down, Emily moved the car slowly forward before picking up speed and driving around the corner, past the house, and into the shed.

So he'd actually done it. She shook her head, surprised at how calm she felt; she wasn't even that angry. What was the point – it wouldn't rebuild the cottage, would it? And it was his farm; he had every right to tear down a dilapidated building to make way for a hayshed.

Emily felt a tug of sadness for the people who had spent possibly years building what had been rendered a pile of rubble in a matter of minutes. Would their angry spirits now haunt them?

Part of her hoped there would be some sort of karmic payback for John, but another part told her he was already difficult enough to live with. She sighed deeply.

'Come on, Gracie, let's get these groceries unloaded.' Walking to the house felt to Emily like wading through mud. She could smell the dust that coloured the sky the full length of the house and beyond.

She sighed again. There was no way John would have thought to shut the windows. The place would be a mess thanks to the stiff north-easterly breeze.

As Emily walked up the path, she tried to block out the hum and intermittent roar of the tractor. She sternly told Grace to stay outside, instantly feeling guilty at the dog's downcast look. But she had to start staying outside, else risk a boot from John.

Entering the kitchen and seeing the leg of lamb defrosting on the sink, Emily regretted her decision to cook John's favourite meal.

She sniffed at the air. There was no mistaking the faint scent of red loam. After dumping the bags of groceries on the floor, she wiped her fingers across the dark surface of the antique timber table. As expected, a film of red-brown dirt clung to them.

Emily made her way through the house, shutting the windows and cursing John for his lack of forethought – she'd just done the vacuuming the day before. She thought about leaving it so John would see the mess he'd caused, but what would be the point? He'd just say something like, 'How was I to know you'd leave the windows open all day?' And she'd still have to clean it up. Vacuuming, just like cooking and washing, was 'women's work' that he had no intention of participating in.

Emily had just finished vacuuming the house when the roar of the tractor became considerably louder. She looked up as the big green machine made its way past the bedroom window toward the shed, and hoped John had other things to do before coming in.

Minutes later, Emily was at the kitchen sink peeling vegetables when she heard a loud bang. She jumped slightly with fright.

A gun shot? Definitely sounded like it; she'd heard plenty before. But this one seemed awfully close, and it wasn't dark enough yet for spotlighting. John must have seen a feral cat or something, she decided, and went back to what she was doing.

But she couldn't concentrate. God, she hoped Grace was on her bed by the house. She brought a hand to her heart as it began to race, and was just about to look for the dog when John entered the kitchen.

'Keep that mutt out of the paddocks and away from the sheep,' he said, before Emily had a chance to say anything. She felt the colour drain from her face.

'You shot Grace?' she said in a quiet, shaky, but slightly incredulous tone.

'No, but next time it won't be so lucky,' he said, tossing his filthy Akubra onto the bench in the far corner of the room. Emily had to grip the kitchen sink for support. Her hands shook as she put the tray of vegetables into the oven.

John got a beer from the fridge, sat down at the end of the table, and turned on the small television set with the remote beside him.

Emily cringed at the little clouds of dust that rose from his clothes with every sudden movement, but held her tongue.

'Well that was the best fun I've had in ages,' he announced. 'What's for dinner? I'm starving. Ah roast, good,' he said, rubbing his hands together. When Emily didn't reply, he looked at her. 'What's wrong with you?'

'You shot at my dog, and you say it's the best fun you've had in ages!' she said, willing herself not to cry.

'It needed a fright,' he said, waving a dismissive arm. 'If I'd meant to kill it, I would have. And, for your information, I was talking about having fun with the loader and the old cottage. They certainly don't build 'em like they used to.'

'John, shutting the windows on the house would have been helpful; I've just spent the last hour vacuuming.'

'Didn't know they were open,' he said, twisting the cap off his beer and taking a long sip. John Stratten gave his customary shoulder shrug and turned-down mouth expression. 'Took ages to bring the old girl down,' he mused, before taking another large slug of beer.

'I thought we didn't have the money for the hayshed this year,' Emily said, setting his place around him.

'We don't,' he said, looking up at her with a lopsided grin.

'So why pull the cottage down now?'

He shrugged. 'Something to do while the weather's too cool to reap. Dad wants to borrow the loader for a few months straight after harvest.'

'What are you going to do with the pile of rubble?' Emily cursed the words as they escaped her lips.

John shrugged yet again, and for the first time Emily realised how much she hated it. Had it once been one of his endearing mannerisms?

'It's fine as it is; maybe push it into the creek later if I can be bothered.'

If it was going to be left where it was, why did it need to come down?

'But I thought you needed the space,' she said.

'Nup – there's five thousand or so other acres to choose from.'

And then Emily saw the truth, the realisation hitting her like a sharp slap to the face. She stared at him, unable to stop her mouth from dropping open. But she couldn't speak.

'Maybe now you'll stop with all this bed and breakfast nonsense,' he said with a smirk.

Emily felt her face begin to flame. Had he really done it just to kill her dream? And had he smiled while telling her so? Surely even John wouldn't be that cruel?

'You demolished the cottage so I would stop thinking about the B&B?' Emily said, incredulous.

'Well, it'll stop you going on about it.'

Emily clenched and unclenched her hands. She wanted to scream at him that a dream, a scrapbook and the odd mention were hardly 'going on about it'. But there was no point. No matter what she said, John Stratten would have the last word. And anyway, there were more important things to consider, like the fact he'd just shot at her dog – a harmless, defenceless puppy.

Emily finished preparing dinner, served it, and ate in a trance, barely tasting each morsel. Chewing was a struggle that seemed to take forever. But she pushed on, refusing to give John the satisfaction of knowing just how much he had hurt and upset her. How could she have ever fallen in love with this man?

Emily thought about what Liz said at Gran's funeral. Her cousin was right: she hadn't grown up – she'd lost her identity. At some point she'd stopped standing up for herself and her dreams. But it wasn't just her she had to stand up for now, was it? It was up to her to protect Grace. And she would.

With a shock Emily realised that she was actually going to leave her husband. She had to; for herself, and also for Grace.

She felt oddly calm. There would be no hysterics, no 'hissy fits', as John called them. No, whatever it took, she would deny him that satisfaction.

That night, as John snored loudly beside her, Emily lay awake, seething and resisting the urge to smother him with a pillow. *It would be so easy*, she thought, and eventually had to leave the room lest she try to find out.

Chapter Eleven

The following morning was just like any other.

Emily brought John Stratten his breakfast of toast and jam, and packed his lunch for the Agricultural Bureau 'sticky beak' day. Then she waved him off from the glass door – more to make sure he left the property without harming Grace than from any affection.

After doing the dishes, putting them away and leaving the kitchen tidy, she made the bed and tidied the bedroom. Her order of morning tasks rarely changed, and ensured that the house was perfectly presentable by nine o'clock should unexpected guests arrive. The routine was another inheritance from Granny Mayfair, and today she was especially grateful for a well-honed system that she could work through with little thought; she hadn't had much sleep.

Emily packed her clothes into her large and medium sized suit-cases and then added her toiletries. The only other things she would take were Grace's bits and pieces, the three boxes of Gran's belongings, and the button jar. She'd have liked to arrange a truck to empty the house, but she wasn't prepared to take so much time and risk John coming home early. And where would she send it anyway? Her mother's? Enid would have a fit. No, she'd worry about furniture and household effects later, or not. She could live without it all if necessary. She didn't like the idea – there were some really nice things she treasured. But at the end of the day it was only *stuff*, and stuff could be replaced.

After putting everything by the sliding door leading outside, Emily checked the rest of the house to make sure there wasn't anything else she needed. She kept seeing things she'd like to take, but resisted. Her main concerns were to get out of there and to leave the house in good order. Her mother-in-law would most likely be the first to arrive when the news hit.

Mrs Stratten – Thora – was one of those women about whom you got the feeling you'd never get approval or praise from, even if you came up with a cure for cancer. She was a glass-half-empty type. Not a lot different to Emily's own mother, really. And, as with Enid, Emily had never felt good enough in Thora's eyes.

Gerald Stratten was a dear, sweet man, though he was rarely seen in the presence of his wife. He'd made being absent an art form. He and Emily had shared a couple of great conversations along the way, but she felt she didn't know him at all. Again, in all the wrong ways he was like her own father – they were both dominated by the women in their lives.

Emily regularly wondered if Gerald had any idea of the state of their finances, and just how much had been syphoned off into the John-has-to-be-kept-happy-at-all-costs fund. Through a system of emotional blackmail, their son was slowly ruining them and they couldn't, or wouldn't, see it. Or perhaps there was a magic money tree after all. It was hard to believe that the Strattens could be so wealthy when they spent so much; weren't the rich meant to be miserly? Wasn't that how rich people stayed rich? *Could be they're still getting by through old money*, she supposed.

Anyway, soon it would no longer be her concern. What would she be entitled to through the divorce? No doubt they would have set everything up in a trust that couldn't be touched – it was what smart farming dynasties did. Part of Emily hoped she'd be adequately compensated and John adequately punished for her three years of unhappiness, but a bigger part of her said that the less there was to fight over, the less time it would take to cut all ties and get on with her life.

Except that right now she wasn't sure what she wanted out of life. She hoped it would become clear once she got out of this mess. *But the first step is to get out of this house*, Emily told herself sternly.

Patting Grace on the way past, and telling her to wait, Emily brought the car from the shed and parked it outside the glass sliding door. She packed everything carefully into the boot. It was a struggle, but she managed to fit it all in. She was glad that no one would be able to see what she was up to and that there would be no difficult conversations to be had unless she wanted to have them. She could take things one step at a time, in her own time.

Emily closed the boot lid with a bang and felt a wave ripple through her. Sadness? No. More like disappointment. She went back to the house and did a final check that she'd taken what she immediately needed. Nothing looked out of place – there weren't even any obvious signs of missing items. She wondered how long it would take John to realise she wasn't just late back to prepare his dinner but wasn't coming back at all – *ever* – and allowed herself to indulge in a brief moment of satisfaction.

Back in the kitchen, Emily sat in a chair opposite the clock above the original chimney hob that had been altered to house the modern oven. It was nine twenty-five.

Each forward movement of the second hand seemed to take ages, and its tick seemed to vibrate right through the cheap plastic cover and then roam around the otherwise silent room before being followed by the next.

Emily waited, her handbag strap over her shoulder, her left hand clutching the car keys so tightly it hurt. Grace, who had been sitting at attention, gave up and lay down at her feet. The portable phone handset became slippery in her right hand and she put it down on the table.

As the clock struck nine-thirty, Emily picked up the phone, took a couple of deep breaths, dialled, and waited.

'Barbara, hi. It's me, Emily.'

'Emily, hi! How are you?'

'Very well, thank you. And you?'

'Great. Um, is everything all right? You sound different.'

'Yes, fine thanks, but I was wondering if you fancied a visitor for coffee – only if you're free, that is. I understand if you're busy.'

'This morning? That would be great.'

'Only if you're sure I wouldn't be intruding.'

'Not at all. Would you like me to meet you in town to save you driving all the way out here?'

'Thanks for the offer, but I think the drive will do me good. I need to get out of the house – you know how it is, just one of those days.'

'Do you mean now? Are you sure everything is okay?'

'Yes, fine. And, yes, I'm actually ready to leave now. Unless it's too early for you.'

'Not at all.'

'Thanks Barbara, see you soon.'

'Drive carefully.'

'I will.'

Emily put the handset back in its charger cradle, took a final glance around the kitchen, called Grace to her, and walked out.

She stood at the closed sliding door a few moments, struck by an overwhelming feeling of apprehension.

But the feeling wasn't so much about leaving John as facing her mother, the townsfolk, and life itself.

A lump lodged tight in her throat and tears teased her eyelashes. Marriage had been horrible; John had been horrible. She'd tried to stick it out. Why shouldn't she leave? A small voice in her head – not unlike her mother's voice – told her it might be worse to be alone.

But of course there was Grace to think about now. Next time John shot at her – and there would be a next time, of that she was sure – he probably wouldn't miss. All that mattered was that they had each other; they'd muddle through somehow.

'Come on, Gracie, we're going on a little adventure,' she said, holding the passenger door open for the pup to get in, and then closing it again.

Beyond spending a couple of hours with Barbara, Emily had no plans. All the hours of thinking the night before had just resulted in her decision to leave, no matter what. She wasn't even sure if she'd tell her new friend the truth.

Chapter Twelve

For the first few kilometres, Emily's heart was leaden in her stomach, but gradually the feeling eased. By the time she was approaching Barbara's, a tiny part of her was even feeling a little excited about the prospect of going through life alone and being in control of whatever successes she had. She ignored her inner voice reminding her that the failures would be all hers as well. She would have none of that. Anyway, as her wise old gran used to say, 'Mistakes are only failures if you don't learn from them'.

'Nothing ventured, nothing gained, Gracie,' she said aloud, causing the pup to look up from the passenger's seat and flap her tail. If only she knew what she wanted to do with her life.

Emily felt like a high-powered engine sitting in neutral – all revved up but with nowhere in particular to go. She gripped the steering wheel with both hands and concentrated hard. But the more she thought about it, the less clear her thoughts. Hopefully she'd have a light bulb moment before too long – before she'd chewed through her five thousand, seven hundred and fifty-seven dollars and thirty cents of savings.

★

Barbara bounded down her verandah steps and was at the car before Emily had even turned off the engine. It took a few more moments for the old dog to ease herself from her sleeping position and waddle after her mistress. Barbara peered through Emily's open window.

'Oh. I thought you'd be all loaded up because you left John,' she said with obvious disappointment.

Without replying, Emily got out of the car. She had difficulty standing: her legs were shaking so much. Grace leapt out after her and engaged in a hearty reunion with her mother. The two friends hugged briefly before Emily broke away and silently went behind the car and opened the boot. Barbara followed her, a perplexed expression on her face.

'I have. These are my worldly possessions,' she said, sweeping her hand across the top of the tightly packed boot.

'Oh,' Barbara said, staring at the contents. Emily smiled weakly and Barbara drew her into a tight hug. 'Well done you! I'm very proud.'

As Emily clung to her friend; two tears fell. And then, as if the floodgates had opened, she began to cry. At first she tried to hide it, but with Barbara's words of, 'There, there, let it all out, it'll be good for you,' she allowed herself to openly and loudly sob.

It took a few minutes for Emily to regain control of her breathing and the tears to return to a trickle.

'Come on, I'll put the kettle on,' Barbara said, steering her towards the house.

Barbara busied herself with getting mugs of coffee and a plate of homemade ginger biscuits while Emily blew her nose and wiped away the remaining wet lines of tears streaking her face.

'So,' Barbara said, plopping down onto a kitchen chair at the end of the table. 'Did he hit you?'

'Sorry?'

'John must have done something pretty major. Yesterday you weren't happy but you certainly weren't ready to leave him. And the carefully packed boot out there suggests you're not going back – that this is not just some tiff.'

Emily stared at her steaming mug, picked it up, took a long sip, and carefully put it back down on the coaster before her. Returning Barbara's gaze, she said in a voice a lot calmer than she felt, 'He demolished the cottage across the way.'

'Oh Em, that's terrible.'

'For no other reason than to upset me,' she added.

'But I thought it was to make way for a hayshed?'

'Yes, well, apparently not; there are over five thousand other acres to choose from,' she said venomously.

'You're sure it was out of spite – lot of work just...'

Emily chose to ignore her friend's scepticism – it was understandable. 'I quote, "Maybe now you'll stop with all this bed and breakfast nonsense".'

'Oh my God! What a nasty piece of work! I had no idea.'

'It came as a bit of a shock to me as well.'

'At least he didn't hurt you or Grace. I absolutely think you did the right thing leaving.'

Emily looked away.

'What? What aren't you telling me?'

She took another breath and said quietly, 'He shot at her.'

'He what?! Why?'

'To give her a fright,' she said with a shrug.

'He shot at Grace – that's inexcusable. Bastard! So, did you have a big fight?'

'No, I didn't give him the satisfaction.'

'Good girl. So what did you do?'

'Finished dinner, did the dishes, watched some stupid reality TV show with him, went to bed. This morning I packed his lunch for the Ag Bureau day, and when he'd gone, packed my things. And now, here I am.'

'Did you leave a note?'

'No.'

'I wonder how long it will take him to realise you've gone.'

'When his next meal isn't on the table, I would think. Though he has been eating out quite a bit lately.'

'Have you told your mother?'

'I don't feel quite up to facing her just yet,' Emily said with a weak smile.

'No,' Barbara mused. 'You know you're welcome to stay here as long as you like.'

'Thanks Barbara, but I couldn't impose.'

'Actually, you'd be doing me a favour – David's taken a load of wool to Adelaide and won't be back until Saturday or Sunday. He's getting it done while the weather is too cool and damp for harvest.'

'Oh, right.'

'Anyway, where else can you go – your parents'?'

Emily, suddenly feeling very lost and teary again, concentrated on her coffee.

'Em, just because your mother's the iron maiden doesn't mean you have to be. This is a really tough time for you, and I hate to say it, but it's probably going to get a lot worse before it gets better. Don't be afraid to accept help; it's what friends are for. And I know you'd do the same for me if the situation were reversed.'

'I just don't know what to do,' Emily replied, her eyes again filling with tears.

'You've taken the biggest step – you've left the brute.'

'Yes, but now what? What am I going to do with my life? I have no job, nowhere to live, and a dog to look after. *And* I have to break the news to my mother, who thinks marriage should be endured no matter what,' she added, wincing.

'I'll tag along for moral support, if you like. Seriously. But first, you need to stop thinking big picture – whole life – and start breaking it all down into manageable pieces. Firstly, you're staying with me for the next few days – and I will not take no for an answer,' she said, holding up a hand in response to Emily opening her mouth to protest. 'During that time you can look for a job and somewhere else to live. And we'll tackle your mother together.'

Emily sighed deeply. Put like that it did seem easier. 'Thanks Barbara, you've no idea how much it means.' Her eyes filled again.

'Fiddlesticks,' Barbara said, flipping a hand. 'You'd do the same for me. Now, first things first: I need another coffee,' she said, leaping up. 'More coffee, or would you prefer tea, or something else?'

'Another coffee would be good, thanks.'

'They don't call it the "think drink" for nothing,' Barbara said from the sink.

And they don't say 'A problem shared is a problem halved' for nothing, Emily thought, staring at the tiny rose design in the floral table-cloth. She thought of Granny Mayfair, who would otherwise have been her first port of call. Even though her memory had been shot and she couldn't have given her anywhere to stay, just being in her presence would have been a great comfort. Not that she wasn't grateful to Barbara. But it just wasn't quite the same, was it? God, she missed her gran. Why hadn't she confided in her when she first realised she'd made a mistake marrying John, or any time after? A couple of tears dripped onto the table cloth, spreading upon impact and leaving small darker spots.

God, she thought with a groan, she really had to break the news to her parents soon. She'd never hear the end of it if someone in town heard first and told her mother. And it couldn't be done over the phone.

Perhaps she had her mother painted all wrong. Didn't parents always do their best to help when their children were in trouble? Didn't parents just want their children to be happy, no matter how grown-up they were?

Yes, it would be all right – she'd be offered a warm, welcoming embrace from Enid, who would then cook her a nice, comforting meal. Then together, as a family, they would devise a strategy for moving forward and putting the past behind them.

'You look a little calmer,' Barbara commented, putting Emily's mug back down in front of her.

She startled slightly. 'Sorry, I was miles away,' Emily said, recovering her composure.

'Meditating?'

'Just deep in thought.'

'Oh well, you look calmer. Care to talk about it?'

'Just talking myself into fronting my mother. I figure things are never as bad as you think they'll be. Anyway, it has to be done, and sooner would be better than later.'

'I quite agree. Would you like me to come? I'm more than happy to accompany you if you think it would help.'

'Thanks, but I really think this is something I have to do on my own. I made the decision to leave John, and now I have to start standing on my own two feet.'

'So when do you think you'll do it?'

'After I've finished my coffee, if that's okay?'

'Of course. And if there's anything I can do, promise you'll let me know.'

'Actually, there is one thing.'

'Yes?'

'Gracie. Could I leave her here with you?'

'Of course. Sasha will love having her little girl back.'

'I've got food and everything else for her in the car.' Emily gulped her coffee down nervously. 'Well, no time like the present,' she said, pushing her chair back from the table.

'Do you want to phone first and make sure someone's home?'

'No, I'll take my chances.'

Barbara followed Emily to the car. Gracie bounded up, and Sasha arrived, panting, a few moments later. Emily took Grace's bedding, bowls and food from the boot and handed them to Barbara, feeling a wave of sadness as she did.

'Do you want me to take any of your things inside?'

Emily felt a little awkward. 'Thanks for the offer, but I'm hoping if everything goes okay I'll stay with Mum and Dad – you know, being family.'

'Well, if it doesn't, there's a bed all made up and ready here. Just let me know one way or the other so I don't worry you've had an accident or something.'

'I will. And thank you so much for everything – especially taking care of Gracie; it's a real weight off my mind. Mum doesn't do dogs,' she added, forgetting Barbara had had a dose of Enid's dislike of pets just the day before.

As if realising she was about to be left behind, the pup stared up at Emily with her head to one side and whined.

'You'll be quite all right with Auntie Barbara. I'll be back soon,' Emily said, squatting down and ruffling the pup's ears before giving her a kiss on the head.

Starting to feel teary again, Emily swallowed deeply and gave Barbara, who still had her arms full of dog paraphernalia, a quick hug.

'Thanks again for everything. Speak to you soon,' she croaked, and got into the car.

★

Emily had a little over three quarters of an hour in which to pull herself together and figure out just what to say. She drove as if on autopilot, the road disappearing under the car, barely noticing the trees on the roadside. A couple of times she wondered exactly where on her journey she was, having made turns and stops at dirt intersections without remembering doing so.

By the time Emily drove into her parents' street, she couldn't quite decide if she wanted her mother to be home or not.

Chapter Thirteen

Emily parked in front of her parents' house, turned the car off and sat taking deep, calming breaths and enjoying the band of sun coming through the window. Out of the corner of her eye she noticed the pale net curtain at the front window move. Reluctantly, she exited the cool of the car into the warm, sunny day.

She was on the final step up to the verandah, ready to lift her arm, when the door opened wide before her.

'I wasn't expecting you, was I?' Enid Oliphant declared.

'No, Mum.' The words came out with a weary sigh.

'John not with you?' Enid asked, looking behind her daughter as if for a small child hiding behind adult legs.

Emily swallowed and took another fortifying breath. 'Mum, can I come in please?'

'Oh, yes, of course. Sorry,' Enid said, stepping aside.

'Is Dad here?' Emily asked, now standing in the casual lounge area and looking about her.

'Not sure where he is; bound to be back soonish. So John's not with you, then?'

Isn't it obvious? She sat down on the edge of the nearest lounge chair with another deep sigh. 'I've left him.'

'Left him where, Emily?' Enid asked, looking around again.

'Left him, Mum. As in separated, pending divorce.'

'Oh Emily, don't be silly.'

'I'm not Mum – it's true.'

'But whatever for?'

'Because he is horrible and I've been miserable for far too long.'

'Oh Emily, now you're being melodramatic. He's from such a good family – they're the wealthiest people in the district.'

'I don't care. He's a nasty piece of work.'

'So what exactly happened to cause this little tiff?'

'It isn't a little tiff, Mum. I'm not going back.'

'Of course you're going back – once you see how silly you're being. When you realise what you're about to throw away. What you need to do is go back, apologise, and cook him a lovely meal – men have very simple needs, you know.'

'I've got nothing to apologise for and I am not...'

'Well, you've left the man – he's probably quite beside himself. And what will the town think? What will people say?'

'Mum! You're not listening to me!' Emily cried, 'I am *not* apologising and I am *not* going back! It's over!'

'Now you *are* being melodramatic. I hope you haven't made a silly decision you'll live to regret. He's got very wealthy parents, you know.'

So you keep telling me. And the only thing I regret is coming here, Emily thought. Now she was angry at herself for believing things would be different. Why hadn't she just picked up the bloody phone?

'Look Mum, I only came to tell you in person. I'm going now.' She stood up on shaky legs. Thank God she'd left her suitcases in the car and hadn't turned up on the doorstep with them in hand like in the movies.

'But you haven't even told me what happened.'

'It doesn't matter, Mum,' Emily said, beginning to make her way back to the door. Enid would never understand; it wasn't worth the angst.

'Where are you going?'

'I'll stay with Barbara.'

'But we're family. You need family at a time like this.'

Emily was almost at the door when her father entered.

'Em!' he cried. 'What a lovely surprise. To what do we owe the pleasure?' He pulled her to him.

'Hi Dad,' Emily said weakly, and let herself be hugged.

'Apparently she's left her husband. Can you believe it?' Enid Oliphant said. Emily pictured her mother pursing her lips and rolling her eyes, and was glad she had her back to her and couldn't see.

'Oh, you poor thing, are you okay?' Des Oliphant asked, gently pushing her away to inspect her face.

'Of course she's not okay, Des. She's about to throw her life away over some silly little tiff. You'll have to talk some sense into her; she won't take any notice of me.'

'Dad, don't waste your breath,' Emily said wearily. 'John's horrible, I've been miserable for ages and now I've finally left him. There's really nothing to discuss.'

'Fair enough,' Des said, nodding.

'Des, at least say something *useful*. It's not *fair enough*; it's a bloody disaster!'

'You heard her – she's miserable. I don't know about you, Enid, but I don't want my daughter to be miserable.'

'Thanks Dad,' Emily said, turning and offering him a forlorn smile. He seemed somehow different.

'Oh God,' Enid Oliphant said, throwing herself theatrically into one of the plush armchairs. 'We'll be a laughing stock. A failed marriage. And the Strattens – such a good family,' she said, shaking her head. Lifting her head as if suddenly struck by a thought, she added, 'I suppose that'll mean no invitation to Thora's garden party this year.' She buried her head in her hands.

'Enid, this is not about you!'

A jolt ran through Emily; she'd never heard her father raise his voice to her mother before.

'Dad, I'm going to go. I've clearly upset Mum.'

'Well, she has no right to be upset,' he said, shooting his wife a sharp glare as he followed Emily outside. 'Don't go. Come to the pub for a drink and tell me all about it,' Des said when the door closed behind them.

Emily looked at her father, her slight frown hiding the turmoil inside her. He'd just stood up to his wife, defended his daughter to her. Emily felt a twinge of guilt. She'd spent most of her life thinking her father spineless and pathetic. Had she been blind, or just blinded by her dominant mother?

'Dad, I really appreciate you standing up for me, but I can't do this right now. I need to go.'

'But where will you go?'

'I'm going to stay with Barbara Burton for a couple of days while I sort a few things out – she's been a really good friend.'

'Well, as long as you're not going to be alone. Promise you'll call me if there's anything I can do – anything.'

'Okay, thanks Dad,' she said, gave him another quick hug, and got into the car.

Emily stopped in front of the roadhouse to phone Barbara and tell her she would be returning after all.

Barbara made soothing noises before instructing her to drive safely. As Emily put the phone back in her handbag, she was struck by just how lucky she was to have met Barbara those few short weeks ago. Wasn't it odd the way some things happened?

Again the drive passed in a blur. Emily's thoughts teetered between rage and frustration at her mother for not being more motherly, and anger at herself for expecting her to be suddenly different from what she'd always been.

If only she'd just picked up the phone instead. But then she wouldn't have seen her father. What was that about, anyway? Had he changed suddenly or had she read him wrong all these years?

She shook the thought aside. Well, it was done; it was out in the open now. The whole district would know soon enough. Though not from her mother – Enid would not utter a word about having a daughter with a failed marriage. She'd be too humiliated.

But word always managed to make its way around this small town with lightning speed – accuracy didn't stand a chance. What would the gossipmongers make of her change in circumstances?

She'd seen people's lives ruined through seemingly harmless misquotes, mistaking of names, not to mention blatant ignorance of facts. The bush telegraph seemed to only work one way: bad news – interesting news – travelled around at three times the speed of good. Corrections rarely made it through at all.

Granny Mayfair had always said that spreading gossip was the only way those with meaningless lives could get a bit of the lime-light, and that rarely did truth play a part. This advice had kept Emily going through the cruel years of high school. If only Gran were here to guide her now.

Emily thought, sardonically, that maybe she should take out an ad in the local paper announcing that, yes, she had left her husband, no, she wasn't having an affair, and no, she had not decided to become a lesbian.

She tried to stay annoyed with the world – that way at least the tears seemed to stay away.

When she pulled up out the front of the Burtons' house, Barbara and Grace raced down the steps and over to Emily's car door, with the old dog, Sasha, ambling slowly after them.

Thank goodness for Barbara, Emily thought for the umpteenth time as she took comfort in her friend's tight, lingering embrace. Grace leapt about fighting for attention until Emily finally bent down and scooped her up.

'I hope you've been good for Auntie Barbara,' she said, nuzzling the squirming, wriggling dog in her arms.

'Come on, I'll put the kettle on, and you can tell me all about it,' Barbara said, getting Emily's suitcases out of the boot.

Inside, Emily slumped heavily onto a kitchen chair, suddenly aware of just how tired she really was. She barely registered Barbara taking her cases up the hall. She thought to get up, but couldn't. She laid her head on the table, and was then vaguely aware of Barbara back in the kitchen filling the kettle and putting it on.

After what seemed only seconds, Emily was startled when a mug thudded on the table in front of her. She forced her droopy eyelids open and her posture upright. She must have dropped off; she felt decidedly groggy.

'God, you poor thing, you're exhausted. Would you prefer to have a lie down instead?'

'Actually, I wouldn't mind, if that's okay?'

'Don't be ridiculous. Of course it's okay. Just make yourself at home. Feel free to have a shower if you want – there's a clean towel in the guest bathroom for you.'

'Thanks Barbara,' Emily said, hauling herself slowly to her feet. 'For everything.'

Chapter Fourteen

Emily woke up slowly, opened her eyes and looked around. It took her a second or two to register where she was: at Barbara's house, in the guest bedroom. She sat up and rubbed her hands across her face.

Now sitting cross-legged under the quilt, she realised bright light was filtering into the room from behind the drawn curtains. She'd lain down for a nap – surely she hadn't slept right through the night? A pang shot through her stomach followed by an audible rumble.

She thought back to the day before. Had it only been twenty-four hours since she'd phoned Barbara, loaded the car, and driven away from her marriage?

She felt another sharp twinge that was too high for a hunger pang. Fear? Regret? Sadness? She wasn't sure. She'd left John. Had actually done it. But had she meant it, *really* meant it?

What if John got the jolt he needed and changed? She'd heard over and over that men didn't change; that you were stuck with what you'd got. But surely there were exceptions. *What if John was one?* Maybe he deserved another chance.

Emily climbed out of bed and began packing the few things she'd taken out back into her suitcase.

There was a gentle tap on the door, and when Emily stood upright, Barbara was standing before her.

'What are you doing?'

'Packing. I've got to go home. Thanks for everything, but I've made a mistake.'

'Okay. But I've cooked eggs and bacon, so at least have a decent meal before you go. You missed dinner last night.'

'Yes, sorry about that. I can't believe I slept right through.'

'Well, I can – you're on an emotional rollercoaster. You may as well have run a marathon. Leave that and come and have breakfast – it's almost ready.'

Emily sat down to a plate of crispy bacon, mushrooms sautéed in butter and mixed herbs, grilled tomatoes, poached eggs on lightly buttered crusty bread, orange juice, and a mug of steaming, rich, milky coffee.

'Barbara, this is amazing. Thank you,' she said, pausing after her first few mouthfuls of food. 'Just what I needed.'

'Good. In my opinion, nothing beats a big country breakfast for starting the day with a clear head.'

Emily nodded, despite her head feeling anything but clear. She was relieved Barbara hadn't said anything about her decision to leave. After the initial murmurs of appreciation, they ate in silence.

Finally Emily put her knife and fork down and, after a deep, contented sigh, said, 'Thank you, that was wonderful.'

'Pleasure. Now, I've been thinking about your predicament…' Barbara started.

'Sorry?' Emily blinked at her with surprise. She was suddenly aware that for the fifteen or so minutes they were eating she hadn't thought once of her situation and the daunting time ahead.

'Unless you really *have* decided to go back to John, which I definitely don't agree with. Obviously I'll support you if that's your wish – it's your life to live, not mine – I just want you to be happy.'

Why couldn't my mother have told me that yesterday? Emily wondered with a heavy heart.

'You've no idea how much that means to me. Did, um, John call, by any chance?' she asked tentatively. She wasn't sure what difference it would make, but couldn't help asking.

'He did, as a matter of fact. Late last night when you were asleep. Seems to think you'll be home soon. He said, and I quote, "Tell her to hurry up and get over her little hissy fit because we'll have two sheep to pack into the freezer in the next few days".'

'That's it?' Emily said, feeling both angry and disappointed.

'Well, he did say you'll probably need to get more freezer bags on the way,' Barbara said, offering Emily a crooked smile and raised eyebrows.

'The nerve! I can't believe he's that blasé.' But as the words left her mouth, Emily was forced to admit that she really hadn't expected much else – hoped, yes, but expected, no.

'So I take it you're not going back to pack the chops?' Barbara asked with an innocent lilt to her voice.

'No bloody way. He can stick his lamb chops *and* his freezer bags up his arse, for all I care!'

'Good girl, that's the spirit,' Barbara said, patting her friend's hand.

Emily scowled into her coffee.

'Now, on to other matters. I hope you don't mind, but yesterday I made a few calls on your behalf,' Barbara said.

'Oh?'

'The good news is there's a cottage available for rent a few farms away on the McFarlane place. They don't want much for it because they don't want to upset their pensions, but also don't want squatters moving in and trashing it. They've given me directions and permission to visit if you want to check it out. I didn't give your name – just said an artist friend from the city needed somewhere quiet to live for a few months.'

'Wow, that's great. And thanks for not mentioning my name.'

'Well, don't go getting too excited. There's bad news too. I phoned most major businesses around town – again, remaining discreet of course – but I'm afraid no one's hiring at the moment. The financial downturn seems to have well and truly hit.'

'Damn, I was really counting on getting a job straight away.'

'Something will turn up – it always does. You did say you had a little tucked away, so it's not too dire, is it?'

'Not totally. And Dad did offer to help.'

'Of course. I'd completely forgotten about your parents. We didn't get around to discussing your visit. So, what happened?'

'Well, not a lot really. Mum was all concerned about her reputation – having a daughter with a failed marriage and all. No great surprise there, much as I'd hoped otherwise. But Dad was a bit of a dark horse.'

'Oh?'

'He actually raised his voice to defend me – told Mum he didn't want his daughter being miserable. You know, I can hardly remember the last time he raised his voice to her.'

'Really?'

'Yeah, but now I feel guilty about thinking him weak all these years. I've been pretty disrespectful.'

'Well, maybe that's the something good that is going to come out of all of this – a renewed relationship with your father.'

'Hmm.'

'I vote today we pack a picnic, visit the house that's for rent and forget about everything else for a while.'

'Sounds like a fine plan. But I wouldn't mind getting my hair cut – like, much shorter,' Emily said, the thought just suddenly coming upon her. She ran her hands down her mouse brown hair that was pulled into a ponytail low at the back of her neck. 'I know it's a really clichéd thing to do when your relationship ends, but I don't care – I'm just suddenly sick of it. What do you think, should I do it?'

'Absolutely. I think it's a great way for you to draw a line between your old and new life.'

'Well, don't let me chicken out, then. Because I might want to if I can't get an appointment until next week.'

'No need for that; I can do it for you right now.'

'Really? You can cut hair?'

Barbara laughed. 'You don't need to sound so sceptical. I was a hairdresser for a while before I moved here. Didn't I tell you?'

'No.'

'I'm a little rusty, but not totally devoid of talent. And I certainly wouldn't offer if I didn't think I could do a decent job. So, what do you reckon?'

'Let's do it. Right now, before I chicken out. If that's okay with you, of course.'

'Great. Let me at it,' Barbara said, rubbing her hands together and looking Emily over with a critical eye.

Just under an hour later, Emily was sporting a bob that was a little longer than chin length at the front and sloped up to be very short against the back of her head, with soft feathering slightly below it.

She turned her head this way and that, trying to see in the bathroom mirror in front of her and the round one Barbara held behind her. She felt it all over with her hands and was surprised to not feel at all apprehensive about the dramatic change.

'So, what do you think?'

'Oh, I love it. Thank you. What do *you* think?'

'Perfect. You look great. It really frames your face. Come on, let's get going on our little outing now.'

Chapter Fifteen

'Now, I only roughly know where this house is so you'll have to bear with me,' Barbara said apologetically.

'Well, I don't know this area at all so I don't mind getting lost and doing some exploring.'

Emily drove and Grace stood on Barbara's lap watching where they were going. Sasha lay on the floor in the back, showing none of the younger dog's excitement at the adventure they were apparently on.

Emily tried to curb her sudden new habit of flicking her head back and forth to make her new haircut swish about, and of looking at it in the rear vision mirror every few moments. She felt a little naked at her neck without her ponytail. The style made her feel fresh and vibrant, but it would take some getting used to.

It took them fifteen minutes and a number of wrong turns before they pulled into a driveway. At the end of the driveway, approximately one hundred metres ahead, a house sat in a large barren clearing, stark white against the blue-greens and browns of its scrubby surrounds. Once, it might have been considered minimalist, modern and classy, but Emily thought the whole setting now looked lonely, depressing and uninspired. She kept her feelings to herself though – not wanting to seem ungrateful for Barbara's efforts to help her – and was relieved at her friend's next words.

'Oh! Not at all what I was expecting,' she said. 'Perhaps it's one of those places that look better up close.'

They pulled up in front of the square concrete building. The plain front door with its flaking, faded dark blue paint stood between two large, white aluminium-framed windows. If it wasn't for the windows, the house could have been an ablutions block in one of the caravan parks she'd visited as a child. It was bald faced, with minimal eaves and no verandahs.

The only vaguely homely touch was a pair of 1950s-era concrete pots sitting on either side. Strips of peeling white paint hung off them like the dog-eared pages of a book, and a couple of dry straggly wild oats waved in the slight breeze.

Grace leapt out of the car and bolted off around the side. Sasha stayed snoozing in the sun. Emily and Barbara's silence matched the eeriness of the place as they walked the perimeter of the house, which revealed nothing more of interest.

Back at the front door, Barbara squatted to tilt the pot on the left and peer underneath. She held up a single key with a smirk. Emily rolled her eyes in response.

'I'm almost too scared to open the door – this place gives me the creeps.' Barbara said.

'Not exactly the epitome of the welcoming family home, is it?' Emily said, relieved she didn't have to pretend anymore.

'Shall we, just out of curiosity?' Barbara turned the key and pushed the door ahead of her, but remained standing on the threshold. Emily joined her in peering into the hallway. They turned to look at each other with raised eyebrows before giggling.

Stretching out before them was an expanse of low pile commercial carpet in a gaudy pattern somewhere between floral and geometric that somehow managed to include more than every colour of the rainbow.

'It's like an entire paint shop threw up in there,' Barbara said with a laugh.

'Well, I guess it won't show the dirt.'

They took a few steps inside.

'Now, that's not fuchsia, not lipstick and not really musk. What would you call that pink?' Emily asked, indicating the walls.

'Now that, *darling*, can only be described as "nipple pink".'

'God, you're right – that's exactly what it is,' Emily said, putting her hand across her mouth to stop herself giggling. 'It's just awful.'

'Well, at least you'd also have a new job.'

'As renovator, painter and decorator?'

'No. As a madam. If the entrance is anything to go by, this place would make the perfect cheesy brothel.'

Emily giggled again. 'God, couldn't you just imagine it? Mum would have a fit.'

'So, shall we just close the door on this awful experience? There is no way I'm going to let any friend of mine live here. Let's go and find a nice boring green tree to sit under and have our picnic.'

'Good idea,' Emily said, relieved to be leaving the house, but disappointed she hadn't solved her accommodation problem.

They pulled the door closed behind them, put the key back under the pot, called Grace, and piled back into the car.

'You really didn't miss much, Sasha,' Emily said, looking at the old dog still sleeping on the floor. An ear lifted and fell, and the end of her tail twitched twice in acknowledgment.

After driving for a few minutes and finding a stand of gum trees in a clearing just off the road, they spread out the picnic rug and unloaded Barbara's large esky.

Again Sasha stayed in the car with the doors open. Grace, sensing the food, stayed close.

They ate in silence for a few moments before Barbara spoke.

'Now, it's really none of my business, but I think this might be a good time to ring John. Let him know you really have left him – if indeed you have.'

Emily had been thinking the same thing as she'd munched on her sandwich. 'To be honest, I was hoping to have had a bit of a plan so I'd feel more confident. If I had somewhere to live at least … This is a lot harder than I thought – maybe I *would* be better off staying with him.' A couple of tears broke through her lashes and she rushed to wipe them away.

But they didn't escape Barbara's notice. She patted Emily's hand. 'It'll all be okay – you'll see. You just have to have faith.'

'In what, though?'

'Yourself, the universe. The power of positive thinking.'

That's easy for you to say, when your life is perfect, Emily thought, instantly annoyed at herself for being spiteful when Barbara was being so good to her. 'I'll call him when we get back,' she said, taking another bite of her sandwich. She'd phone her dad as well, see if he had any bright ideas. Hopefully her mother would be out doing the groceries or something.

After they finished eating they leaned back on the tree trunk. Emily closed her eyes and found herself thinking about the old cottage and the B&B she'd hoped to have one day turned it into. She knew she had to let it go, but it was the only thing she could remember being really excited about in recent years.

Except, of course, for her wedding, she thought wistfully; the excitement of leaving her mother behind and starting a new life with a man she thought she loved. But that had been a different type of excitement – more temporary. *Indeed*, she thought, acknowledging the irony with a silent inward snort.

'You know,' Barbara said, sitting up straighter, 'I reckon you should write a list of all the things you have to do, right down to the littlest thing, and then cross them off one by one. That way it all might seem a bit more manageable. Like, first you have to phone John. I'm sure once you've done that you'll feel a weight off your mind. It's just a thought,' she added, slumping back against the tree and closing her eyes.

'Hmm, good idea,' Emily said, already beginning a mental list. She'd write it all down when she got back to Barbara's and found pen and paper.

'Ouch!' Barbara cried suddenly, slapping at her leg.

At almost the same moment Grace yelped and leapt up, and Emily felt something bite the flesh behind her knee.

'I think the ants have found us,' Barbara said.

They quickly packed everything up, being careful to shake the picnic rug and make sure they weren't taking any of the ants with them.

'I hope you took notice of where we are,' Emily said, turning the key in the ignition. 'Because I was too focussed on finding somewhere nice to eat.'

'I couldn't concentrate over the rumbling my stomach was doing,' Barbara replied, laughing. 'But if we head towards that hill over there we shouldn't be far from my place,' she said, pointing to her left.

Emily grinned. 'Well, looks like it'll be the trial and error method of navigation then,' she said as she put the car into gear.

Chapter Sixteen

Heading towards the landmark proved easier said than done. There was no direct route, and each turn seemed to take them further away.

After twenty minutes, Emily pulled off the road to let a ute past. It had been tail-gating them for a few kilometres, clearly in a hurry and knowing where it was going.

Emily hoped the driver would stop to see if they were lost – which they most definitely were. But although country folk were friendly, and would always stop to help when asked, they weren't ones to interfere without an invitation.

'Do you reckon that's a driveway – given there's a cattle grid instead of gates?' Emily asked, indicating the graded track beyond a concrete and steel apparatus breaking the fence line.

'There's no mailbox,' Barbara replied with a shrug.

'Might have a post box in town.'

'I guess it's worth a shot.'

Emily drove forward and they shook right to their bones as they crossed the steel cattle grid.

They made their way slowly along a rutted, corrugated track. Beside them, spindly wild oats waved in the breeze. On their left, a wire fence surrounded a paddock of browned-off pasture, scattered with the short, grey stubble of the previous year's cereal crop. Off to their right about two hundred metres was a large, elongated cluster of gum trees. They seemed too randomly placed to be hand-planted, and somewhat out of place in a region where the only native vegetation was relatively low-growing mallee scrub and broom bush. She was about to say something when the track took a sudden right-hand turn as the fence joined another. They were now heading towards the trees.

'There must be a soak or spring or something for those trees to be so magnificent,' Barbara said.

'Or once lovingly planted and then watered.'

'Too many for that, surely?'

'Fingers crossed there is a house just through here,' Emily said, nodding ahead at a gap in the trees. They were bathed in dappled shade as they passed through the stand of trees, which revealed itself to be a variety of large gums in rows with between-plantings of smaller, bushier natives.

When they came into a clearing, it took a few moments for their eyes to once again adjust to the bright, clear sunlight.

'My God, it's gorgeous,' Barbara said, in practically a whisper.

Before them was a magnificent, elevated whitewashed stone home with large barley-twist columns holding up an expansive corrugated iron verandah. A set of concrete steps, which began wide and tapered up to the verandah, were framed by stouter, shorter columns, complete with concrete balls on top. Emily and Barbara sat in the stationary car gaping. They could see paint was peeling from the walls and woodwork, and hear the unmistakable squeak and squawk of loose iron moving in the breeze.

'How could someone have abandoned such a lovely place?' Barbara asked.

'Maybe it just needs some TLC,' Emily said, getting out of the car. She stood a few metres away from the vehicle, shielding the sun from her eyes while she took in the details.

'No, it's definitely deserted,' Barbara said a few moments later from atop the verandah.

But Emily wasn't listening. She was too busy imagining the place in its heyday. It was as if she'd been plonked into a film, so clear were the people milling about the verandah in black-tie finery, clinking glasses, sipping champagne and chattering, while musicians played jazz off to the side.

It would have been so grand, Emily thought wistfully. *What a shame*. Her heart felt heavy for the tired old house.

Someone cared enough about it to keep it locked though, and the key hidden, so they couldn't look inside.

Instead they spent half an hour wandering around the perimeter, peering through windows thick with dust into large, empty rooms before calling Grace and joining the patient Sasha in the car.

'I'd say we're officially lost. Looks like we're going to have to call someone. David's away – any ideas?' Barbara said. 'Pretty patchy signal, too,' she added, holding her mobile phone high and turning it in various directions.

'Well, I'm certainly not calling John,' Emily said, folding her arms tightly across her chest.

'I wouldn't for a second suggest that you do!'

'Dad's bound know where we are,' Emily said, extracting her own mobile from her handbag. 'Fingers crossed Mum's elsewhere,' she said as she prodded at the keys and waited for an answer. 'Oh, hello Mum, it's Emily. Is Dad there? … No, I haven't "come to my senses".' She looked across at Barbara and arched her eyebrows. 'Is Dad there or not? I'd really like to talk to him … Oh! Well, I'm sorry he called you … Okay, I'll call him tonight … No, I am not going back … I have no idea how that will impact on the garden party guest list, and frankly…'

Emily looked at Barbara, pulled the phone away from her ear and shook her head slowly. Enid's voice kept coming from the tinny microphone. She tried again.

'Look Mum, I really do have to speak to Dad if he's around … It's not something you can help with – more up Dad's alley … I'm calling on the mobile. I need to be quick, it'll cost a fortune.'

Barbara gave her the thumbs-up sign and mouthed, 'Good girl.'

'No, I don't need a better plan, I need to make quicker calls … Mum! Is Dad there or not? … Good, thank you!'

'Dad, hi. Sorry, I need to be quick since I'm on the mobile. It's just that Barbara and I have gotten ourselves a bit lost out north-east-ish of her place. Do you happen to know a big old white-washed stone house behind a stand of hand-planted trees?'

'Yes, at least a couple of kilometres … It's a really high house, with barley-twist columns, steps sweeping down.'

'Oh no, you don't need to do that – just some directions back to a main road would be great.'

'Oh, right, well okay. Thanks Dad, see you soon.'

She turned the phone off and looked at Barbara. 'He's insisting on driving out here – says he knows it well. Apparently there's something he needs to discuss with me. Wonder what that's about.'

'Hey, why don't you ring John while we're waiting? You can use the mobile as an excuse for keeping it short, and if it all gets too hard you can use the dodgy coverage as an excuse for hanging up. I don't mean to nag, but I seriously think you'll feel better when you've got it over with.'

'But don't you think it's a bit gutless to not be prepared to talk things through?'

'It doesn't have to be the last conversation you ever have with him. But seriously, Em, it's best to let him know where he stands. And from the conversation I had with him last night, I don't think he's interested in talking anything through.'

'I know,' Emily said with a sigh. She took a deep breath and dialled. 'Probably won't be in this time of day, anyway...'

A female voice answered.

'Oh! Hello, who's this?'

'Stacy.'

'Well, *Stacy*, is John there?' Emily's face turned beetroot red.

'Who may I say is calling?'

'You can tell him it's Emily. His wife.'

'Hang on, I'll get him.'

Emily's heart pounded furiously against her ribs while she waited.

'Ah, good, Emily, thanks for calling back.'

'Jesus, John. It didn't take you long, did it? Who's Stacy?'

'Um, nobody.'

'Nobody, huh? I hope Stacy didn't hear that.'

'So you got my message? We need freezer bags.'

'John, I am not coming home – it's over.'

'I'm picking up the meat tomorrow morning; it'll need packing away.'

'You're not listening to me, John. I'm leaving you. I'm not coming back to pack meat away, or for any other reason.'

'You're not seriously throwing a hissy fit over the meat, are you? Or is this about the stupid cottage, or the dog?'

'No, this is about me seeing what a bully you are and choosing not to put up with it anymore. You're a pathetic excuse for a man and you're a bad husband – something you have just proven by bringing another woman home.'

'Well, if I'm pathetic then so are you. It takes two, you know, Emily.'

'Yes, I know, and I blame myself for making such a huge mistake. But face it, John, it's not me you want. You want a house-keeper and someone to have sex with on tap.'

'So you're just going to leave me in the lurch?'

'If that's what you want to call it.'

'Now come on, Emily, don't do something you'll regret. What will people say?'

'I really don't care what they say, John, because I know the truth. I'm going now. You'll have to get your own freezer bags and pack the meat away yourself – maybe *Stacy* will help you.'

'Don't you dare go spreading rumours about me.'

'Goodbye John.'

Emily sat staring at the phone now in her lap.

'Well done,' Barbara said, squeezing her arm. 'Now, doesn't that feel better?'

'I just feel numb,' she said, still staring at the phone.

'All part of the process, I'm sure.'

'I think maybe I was a bit harsh.'

'It obviously needed to be said.'

'Can you believe he's got someone else already?'

'I don't think you should go jumping to conclusions. There might be an innocent explanation.'

'What innocent explanation can there be? He's got another woman in *my* house, Barbara. And she's answering the phone like she thinks she belongs there.'

'Hmm. Well I guess it just goes to show you've made the right decision.'

'You know, he still thought I'd pick up freezer bags and come home to pack the meat away,' Emily said, staring at Barbara with disbelief.

'Clearly delusional.'

'Still thinks I'm having a hissy fit over the cottage and Grace and that I'll come home when I'm over it. Can he actually be that stupid?'

'As I said, delusional.'

'I can't believe I was stupid enough to marry him!'

'Be angry at him, not yourself.'

'And now Mum's worried about not getting a fucking invite to the fucking garden party!'

'*That* I cannot believe.'

'Well, I guess I've just kissed any hope of getting anything else from the house goodbye. I can't go back there now.'

'Maybe when things settle down you...'

'You know what? I don't care. I've got Grace and that's all that really matters to me right now.'

'That's the spirit,' Barbara said, giving her friend's arm another hearty squeeze.

'I can't believe he was still going on about packing meat into the freezer. Did I really mean that little to him?' she said, looking beseechingly at Barbara. Her bottom lip began to quiver and her eyes filled with tears.

'Oh, sweetie,' Barbara said, drawing her friend towards her. 'He's just hurt and lashing out – trying to hurt you in return. It'll all be okay, you'll see. You've taken the first step in changing your life. You should be proud of yourself for being so brave.'

'But look at me, I'm a mess.'

'You're grieving.'

'But I ended it. Why am I so upset?'

'Because an important chapter of your life is over. It doesn't matter how, or why, or how unhappy you were, it's still an end, and endings need to be grieved for. If you let yourself feel what you feel and not fight it, you'll be fine.'

'What would I do without you?' Emily said, returning her friend's tight hug.

'It doesn't matter, because you *do* have me,' Barbara said, patting her friend firmly on the back.

Chapter Seventeen

It seemed only a few minutes later that Emily heard the sound of car tyres on gravel, and her father's white ute pulled up beside the verandah. Emily leapt up, bounded down the steps and greeted her father with a tight hug.

'Love the new haircut,' he said when they broke away.

'Thanks,' she said shyly, feeling self-conscious. 'Dad, this is Barbara Burton. I don't know if you've met before.'

'Thanks so much for rescuing us.'

Des and Barbara shook hands. 'Hi Barbara. No worries – I wanted to see the old place, anyway. You girls would have found your way eventually,' he said absently while staring past them towards the house. 'Shame it's been let go.'

'So how do you know it?'

'Actually, my very first girlfriend lived here – a long time ago now.'

Oh, Emily thought, but before she had the opportunity to probe further, her father was up the verandah steps and making his way around the house, peering into each of the windows as she and Barbara had done earlier. The two friends looked at each other and shrugged.

Soon, Des Oliphant returned and stood leaning against the tray of his ute, staring back at the house. Emily joined him. Barbara, clearly sensing they needed time alone, got back into Emily's car.

'It's a pity we can't have a look inside,' Emily said.

'Last I heard, it was being leased by a workman, but he was put off about ten years ago,' said Des.

'What about the people who owned it – the ones you knew?'

'The parents left the district years ago. The two sons still farm the land, but they've got another property where they live. This was the original home – quite stunning in its day. The place probably held too many sad memories for them,' he added wistfully.

'What happened?'

'A fall from a horse. A tragic accident. It was a very long time ago.'

Emily waited for him to continue, but instead he picked at one of the tall strands of wild oats sticking up from the verandah concrete in front of him. It was clearly the end of the subject.

'Your mother spoke with John yesterday...' he finally said after a few moments of silence had passed.

Emily stiffened.

'He seems to think you've left him because he demolished the old cottage across the road. Did you?' He looked up at Emily.

'Not really,' Emily said. 'That was just the last straw. I knew a long time ago that I'd made a mistake marrying him. I'm just tired of being the only one making all the effort.' She wasn't sure why she didn't mention John shooting at Grace.

'Why didn't you say something before now?'

Emily swallowed. Here, now, with her father being so support-ive, she found herself wondering the same thing.

From an early age she'd turned to her grandmother for advice. It hadn't been a conscious decision, but she now saw that it was because of how negative and judgmental her mother could be. It had meant she hadn't turned to her father either.

But of course, she'd never seen this side of him – had never been allowed to see it. Her mother, his shadow, was always around, and was always the dominant force. Guilt bit at her and she pushed it back. It wasn't too late. Gran had gone, taking her wisdom with her, but maybe Des could step into the breach – if she let him. If he wanted to.

She shrugged and said quietly, 'I guess I just got used to sharing most things with Gran.' *Except this.*

Emily saw the cloud of disappointment cross her father's face before being quickly replaced by a broad smile.

'She was a wise woman; I'm glad you could talk to her.'

Unspoken words hung thick in the air between them.

'So, tell me about the cottage. I had no idea it meant anything much to you.'

'Oh, it was just a silly pipe dream, really.'

'Now Emily, I don't want to hear you say things like that – that's something your mother would say. As much as I love Enid, she does tend to be a bit "glass-half-empty".'

Isn't that the understatement of the century, Emily thought.

'So, what about this cottage?'

'Well, I wanted to do it up, turn it into a B&B or something and earn a bit extra for us. It could have worked, especially now the new ferry is up and running. I did some research.'

'But John didn't agree?'

'He said it was a waste of money and that people wouldn't want to stay so far off the main road.'

'So he tore the building down instead?'

'Yes. To spite me.'

'Surely not.'

'He admitted it.' She paused. 'It doesn't matter, it's gone now. I guess it just wasn't meant to be.'

'Maybe just not there.'

'Sorry?'

'There's nothing to say it's not a good idea and that it wouldn't work, it just wasn't meant to be *there*, in that cottage, and while you were married to John. If it's something you really want, and believe in, it'll happen – you'll make it happen.'

'Dad, that's really sweet, but I have no husband, no money to speak of, nowhere to live, and no job.'

Des Oliphant put his arm around his daughter. 'Ah, despite what some people think, you don't actually need a husband – or a man, for that matter – in order to succeed. Anyway, you have me.' He gave her shoulder a squeeze. 'And something will turn up on the job and accommodation fronts. You'll see.'

Emily looked at him through tear-soaked lashes. Who was this man beside her?

'Thanks Dad,' she said, smiling weakly.

'I'm serious. If you're really passionate about setting up a B&B, or any other business, for that matter, I'll do all I can to help. Oh, look at the time,' Des said suddenly, 'I'd better get back. And your mother asked if you could come to dinner tomorrow night.'

'Oh. Well, Dad, um…'

'She really does feel bad about what happened.'

Feels bad because she's been told to feel bad, more likely.

'Please, Em. Bring Barbara with you, if you like. At least think about it.'

'All right, I'll think about it.'

'I'd better get going,' he said, going to the driver's door and getting in.

'You'd better tell us how to get back to Barbara's before you go – since that's why you're here,' Emily said with a laugh.

'Oh, right, of course. The back way is probably the easiest. Just go back through the trees and turn right instead of left. You should only have three gates to open – they used to be easy iron ones – and you'll end up at the intersection with all the mailboxes. Then you turn left on to the road that takes you past Barbara's driveway.'

'You're sure the farmer won't mind us driving through his property?'

'Not if you leave the gates how you find them,' he said, and turned the key. The ute roared to life.

Barbara appeared next to Emily. 'Do we have sound directions?' she asked.

'I think so,' Emily said.

'You'll be fine,' Des said. 'And please, Em, think about tomorrow night – let us know what you decide.'

'Okay, I will.'

'Bye then.'

'See ya Dad. Thanks.'

'No worries. Bye Barbara. Thanks for taking care of my Emily for me.'

'My pleasure,' Barbara said, putting a protective arm around her friend.

They waved Des Oliphant off before calling the dogs and getting back into the car. Emily turned the vehicle around and headed back towards the stand of magnificent gums.

'Are you sure we're allowed to drive through here?' Barbara asked when Emily stopped at the first closed gate.

Emily shrugged. 'Dad said it should be fine as long as we leave the gates how we find them.'

Finally, they shut the last gate behind them and were facing the five-way intersection dotted with seven mailboxes of varying styles. 'Fancy being so close to our place all along,' Barbara said. 'Whose property were we on?'

'Dad didn't say.'

'Oh well, at least we know where we are now.'

Back at Barbara's, Emily couldn't shake the feeling that something significant had occurred that afternoon between her and her father.

Barbara pulled a lasagne from the freezer and heated it for their dinner.

Then, over a dessert of stewed peaches and ice-cream, Emily broached the subject of dinner with her parents the following evening. Barbara agreed to accompany her and shoulder some of the burden.

At five minutes to nine, Emily felt sufficiently fortified with sherry to make the necessary phone call to her mother. Enid didn't take calls after nine on the grounds that it was 'sheer rudeness'.

Emily held her breath while the phone connected and began ringing at the other end, and almost choked on her relief when Des answered.

'Hi Dad. Could you please tell Mum that Barbara and I will be there for dinner tomorrow night?'

'Oh, Em, that's great.'

'Is there anything we should bring?'

'No, just yourselves.'

'Okay. I'll let you go. Thanks again for rescuing us today.'

'My pleasure. It was good to see the old place again after so long.'

'Oh, is it six-thirty, as usual?'

'That's what your mother said.'

'Okay, we'll see you then.'

Emily hung up and suddenly felt exhausted. 'I think I'll go to bed, if that's okay,' she said.

'I was just thinking the same thing. These dishes can wait until tomorrow.'

'I'll do them,' Emily said, making a move for the sink.

'No you won't,' Barbara said, shooing her out of the kitchen. 'Anyway, there's hardly enough worth running the water for. We do need to conserve water, you know,' she added with mock seriousness.

It was so nice spending time with someone so sensible yet so laid-back. John would have a fit if she left dirty dishes in the sink – as would her mother.

Grace was already curled up in her basket at the foot of the bed when Emily entered the room. The dog flapped her tail a couple of times to acknowledge her mistress's arrival, but made no move to get up.

Emily crawled into bed, wallowing in the comforting cocoon of two large sherries and general exhaustion. She lay with the bedside lamp on for a moment, wondering how she was going to make her life better.

First, she needed a job and somewhere to live. And she was no closer, thanks to the house for rent being an absolute disaster. But that old house with the barley-twist columns would make a great B&B…

Her heartbeat quickened as she began to worry – she was a million miles off even thinking about making any of her dreams come true.

But there was nothing she could do about that now – there was no point wasting good sleep on something that could not be changed.

'Deal with it in the morning,' was the silent mantra her grandmother had taught her to help her get to sleep. It didn't always work, but it helped keep her calm while she waited to drift off.

Chapter Eighteen

Emily was relieved Barbara insisted on driving them to dinner with her parents, because she was a bundle of nerves. She couldn't keep her mind on anything, let alone the road and keeping them safe.

'What's the worst that can happen?' Barbara said, smiling brightly. 'You get into a shouting match with your mother and I diplomatically say we must be off.'

Emily offered a grim smile. There was no point in speculating about what could go wrong – she'd just come off sounding negative and paranoid. Barbara didn't know Enid Oliphant well enough.

'Oh well,' Barbara continued. 'Look on the bright side. By getting dinner over with now you won't have to front up again for, what, another six weeks or so?'

'Hopefully.'

Emily mentally kicked herself – something she'd been doing a lot lately. Why hadn't she just damn well said no and stopped this ridiculous happy-families-at-dinner charade?

Then she thought about the difference she'd seen in her father and how they'd begun to reconnect. Finally the real Des Oliphant

119

was starting to shine out from behind his dominant wife. When he'd asked them to dinner she'd detected a slightly hopeful, pleading, expression. No, it wasn't fair to punish him by not turning up; he deserved better.

'Well, if nothing else, do it for your father,' Barbara added with a resigned sigh. 'He seems a really nice man. Kind and gentle.'

'Hmm,' Emily said as she glanced at her friend. Had she spoken her thoughts aloud without realising? No, just great minds thinking alike – another of her grandmother's favourite sayings.

She leaned back in her seat and closed her eyes to focus on keeping her breathing slow, deep and even, and not giving in to the rising panic.

Just why had her mother summoned her to dinner, anyway? A peace offering for being so harsh the other day? An olive branch held out with the words, 'It's your life, your decision; whatever you do, you have our support – we just want you to be happy'? Emily snorted and quickly covered it up with a cough.

'Are you okay?'

'Yes, fine thanks.' *Just choking on my wishful thinking.*

Emily did a double take as they pulled up in front of her parents' garage. Just off the street, parked on the sidewalk, was a trailer loaded with household effects – some boxes, a wardrobe, a desk, a chest of drawers and a small cupboard. *Their neighbours must be moving some furniture,* she thought.

But then something near the bottom of the pile caught her attention: a hint of burgundy and gold plush brocade fabric almost identical to that on an armchair she owned. And that bentwood chair looked familiar too … Her temples began to throb. She put a hand to her chest and another to her mouth.

'Oh my God,' she gasped.

'What? What's wrong?' Barbara asked, staring in the direction Emily was looking.

'That's my stuff from the farm,' she said, pointing.

As Barbara turned the ignition off, Des Oliphant emerged from the house and rushed over to them. Emily almost fell out of the car.

'Em, I'm so sorry. I had no idea he...' Des's face was crimson beneath a mixed expression of embarrassment and rage.

From where she now stood, Emily saw the corner of John's ute, which was parked a little way away from the laden trailer.

'He's here as well?! Oh God, this just gets better and better,' she whispered.

'Stay. Please don't go. Honestly, I had no idea – this is all your mother's doing.'

Emily looked up at her father and was shocked by what she saw. He was genuinely distressed. Were there actually tears welling in his eyes?

Barbara draped an arm around Emily's shoulder and whispered, 'We are not going to give your mother the satisfaction of leaving, nor hand more power to John. You have nothing to be ashamed of. You are going in there with your head held high, and you'll put on a performance worthy of an Oscar.'

Emily nodded. Barbara was right: she had to start standing up for herself if she was going to make it alone in the big, wide, scary world. She swallowed deeply a couple of times. She was here for a pleasant dinner with her parents and her friend.

'Ready to go in, then?'

Emily set her jaw and raised her head a couple of degrees. 'Yep.'

'Right, take one, ready, *aaaand* ... Action,' Barbara said quietly as she walked forward and propelled Emily ahead of her.

Enid Oliphant was waiting on the front porch with a smug, satisfied look on her face.

'God, Emily, what on earth have you done to your hair?!' Ordinarily Enid would have offered an air kiss about six inches from her cheek. Instead she looked Emily up and down without bothering to hide her distaste.

Emily was about to answer when Barbara cut in.

'Doesn't it look great! Hello Enid, lovely to see you,' she added, grasping Enid and air-kissing.

Enid's demeanour snapped back to that of impeccably-mannered host. 'Lovely to see you both. Do come in,' she said, clearly a little startled.

John Stratten looked up from his beer. When he saw Emily he nodded, and then did a double take and frowned slightly. But he didn't say 'Hello' or comment on her new appearance, and he remained seated in the leather armchair. Emily thought it very rude of him – her father always leapt to greet anyone who entered – and wondered why she'd never noticed this failing of John's before.

'Hello John,' she said, looking down her nose at him, unable to hide the distaste she felt.

Enid broke the uncomfortable silence. 'Now, we're going to have a pre-dinner drink. Emily, you sit beside John, there's something he wants to discuss. And Barbara, you sit there beside Des. Des, get the wine, would you?'

'Why are my things in a trailer outside?' Emily asked calmly.

'Thought I'd save you the trouble of coming back out to the farm.'

'Very thoughtful of you, John. Here, have a nibble,' Enid said, offering him a bowl of assorted nuts before sitting down.

'Especially as it means I don't have to meet the slag he's shacked up with.'

'Emily! We don't use such language in this house.'

'Oh, I'm sorry, Mother. I meant the delightful young lady he's now enjoying sexual relations with. He didn't waste much time, did he?'

By the look of her mother's expression and the hand trying to hide it, Enid did not know of her soon-to-be-ex-son-in-law's new acquisition.

'Oh, I'm sorry, I thought you knew,' Emily said, reaching for a handful of nuts. 'Or perhaps I am mistaken, and it's been going on for a while.'

John, blushing furiously, was staring into his beer. Emily found she rather liked seeing him in such discomfort.

'John, I'm sure Mother would have offered an invitation if she'd known about … what's her name again?'

John spluttered slightly before mumbling, 'Stacy, her name's Stacy.'

'But she's only there helping out with the housework while Emily's away, isn't she?' Enid said.

Emily stared at her mother in disbelief, before shaking her head slowly and exchanging questioning looks with Barbara.

John cleared his throat and gave a mumbled reply no one could decipher.

'Mum, she's not the bloody hired help! He's shagging her and probably was well before the door closed behind me.'

'Emily! Language! Oh, I'd better rescue the meat before it's ruined.' Enid leapt up and fled the two metres into the kitchen.

Des turned to Barbara and asked her about the farm she'd grown up on in the south of the state.

While Des and Barbara were distracted, Emily gritted her teeth at John and said, 'Mum said there was something you wished to discuss.'

'Yeah, this,' he said, reaching into his back pocket and handing her a crumpled wad of papers. 'I need you to sign them.'

'You didn't waste any time, did you?' Emily said.

'This is for the financial settlement – thought we might as well get the complicated stuff over with. I've had the family accountant go over it. All I need is your signature,' he added, handing her a pen from his top shirt pocket.

Emily began to unfold the paper on her lap with one shaking hand while she accepted the pen with the other. She was about to sign when Barbara, turning away from her conversation with Des, put both her hands on Emily's.

Locking her gaze on John, she said, 'Emily will read this in her own time and get back to you in due course. I've got room in my handbag if you like, Em,' she added, now looking at her friend.

'Thanks.'

'Well, I need them signed and back to me by the twenty-second.'

'Why, what's the hurry?' Barbara asked.

'Just be good to get it over with,' he answered. Emily noticed he was avoiding meeting Barbara's gaze.

'Good for whom, exactly?' Barbara continued.

'Sorry?' But the bright blush making its way up his face and into his receding hairline told them he knew exactly what she was implying.

'Dad, do you have any room in the shed for my things?' Emily asked, keen to ease the tension. 'I think they're forecasting some rain.'

'Of course. I'll just have to do a bit of shuffling around.'

'You can keep the trailer for a couple of weeks, if you need to,' John offered, addressing Des.

'Very generous of you, John,' Emily said, and flashed him her most condescending smile.

John returned his attention to his beer and they lapsed into tense silence until Enid announced that dinner was served.

The meal was punctuated by clinking cutlery and stilted sentences here and there, mainly from Barbara and Des. Emily barely tasted the food, but complimented her mother anyway, and Enid thanked her daughter for the praise. They were on autopilot, as always.

Halfway through her dessert of bread and butter pudding, Emily allowed herself to relax a little. The evening was nearly over and her distress had been minimal – thanks to Barbara. But her mother's next words caused her to stiffen.

'Now, Emily, tell me it's not true that you threw away your marriage over a silly old tumbledown cottage. I really hope you won't live to regret it.'

Emily opened her mouth to speak but shut it again when no words came to her. She turned bright red under her mother's gaze. No one said a word. She glared at John, who returned a nasty crooked smile. From the corner of her eye she noticed Barbara check her watch. The room was beginning to close in on her and she could feel beads of sweat prickling under her arms.

Barbara leapt up. 'Mr and Mrs Oliphant, I'm really sorry to have to do this, but I promised I'd ring my mum – she hasn't been well. I don't like to ring her after eight-thirty in case she has an early night, and by the time we get back...'

'You're welcome to phone from here,' Enid said.

'That's very kind but...'

'I'm sure Barbara's got dogs to attend to before it gets too late as well,' Des said. 'Lovely that you could make it,' he added, pushing his chair back from the table. 'Enid, you stay there, I'll see the girls out.'

Closing the door behind him, Des looked at Emily. 'I'm so sorry about that,' he said, embracing her. 'I really had no idea Enid had invited John, or that he would bring your furniture.'

'It's okay, Dad, it's not your fault.' Emily clung to her father.

'Well, Enid has a lot to answer for. As does John.'

'Hmm.'

'And I'm sorry you've both come all this way only to be treated like that. I do appreciate you staying to eat. I wouldn't have blamed you if...'

'Let it go, Dad, it's done now,' Emily said, giving her father a kiss on the cheek before breaking away.

'It was lovely to see you again, Mr Oliphant,' Barbara said, opening her arms to give Des a hug.

'Yes, likewise. And please, it's Des,' he said, kissing Barbara on the cheek. 'Drive safely. And thanks again for looking after Em. I'm so glad she's got a friend like you.'

'We're lucky to have each other,' Barbara said, getting into the car and turning it on.

'You'd better get back inside before Mum sends out a search party,' Emily said, keen to be gone.

Chapter Nineteen

They had left the streetlights of Hope Springs far behind before either of them spoke. The trees on the edge of the road loomed large and menacing in their headlights as they passed, adding to Emily's feeling of despair.

'Are you okay?' Barbara asked, turning her head slightly and addressing her friend's reflection in the side window.

'Honestly, I don't know,' Emily replied. 'I know I should be pleased the chapter of our marriage is about to be closed so quickly...'

'But?'

'I don't know.' She shrugged and lifted her hand from her lap before dropping it again. She twisted the strap of her handbag. 'I know it sounds really pathetic and self-centred, but...'

'You wanted him to fight for you, your marriage. Or at least be a bit upset?'

'Yes. Well, at least *pretend* he cared,' Emily said with a deep sigh. 'Can you believe he brought my stuff? The bastard!'

'Maybe he's devastated and it's just his way of dealing with it. Maybe he's trying to hurt you like he feels you're hurting him,' Barbara offered with a shrug.

'I thought you were on my side.'

'I am. I didn't say he *is* upset, I was just trying to balance the books a little.'

'I wonder what sort of condition my things in the trailer are in. Not that I suppose it really matters.'

'You know, I think your mother genuinely thought he was there to discuss reconciliation. Did you see how white she went when he pulled out the papers?'

'Well, then why did she think he turned up with all my stuff in a trailer?'

'Maybe she was inside cooking and didn't see him arrive. I know you're not going to like me saying this, but I think Enid really was trying to do the right thing.'

'Sometimes I don't think she lives in the real world.'

They lapsed into silence for a few moments.

'What I'd like to know,' Emily said suddenly, 'is how the laziest man on the planet got off his arse and got settlement papers drawn up so quickly.'

'Maybe he had an inkling you were going to leave and had them drawn up already.'

Emily shook her head slowly. 'No, I don't buy that. John would never think that I'd leave him in a million years. He's such a great catch, remember?'

'Maybe they're not properly drawn up – he's just done them up himself.'

'Hmm, I didn't look that closely.

'I think the big question here is why the urgency? Three days to sign them? I hope I wasn't out of line stopping you. But I'm serious, you should have an accountant look over them. Better yet, a lawyer. You only have one shot at this and it could determine your whole future.'

'I really appreciate your concern, but to be honest, I'd rather just sign them and get on with my life. There isn't much money to be divided up; he ploughed everything back into machinery and stock.'

'All of which you own half of.'

'What would I do with half an old truck, a tractor and several thousand head of sheep?'

'Half the *value* of. It's the law, Emily; you'd only be getting what you're entitled to. Anyway, isn't his family, like, really wealthy? And what about the farm? That would have to be worth around a million dollars.'

'I think the farm, like all the big machinery, is tied up in a trust or family company or something. Anyway, I really don't want to be branded as a gold-digger – we live in a small town, remember? The last thing I want – if I ever become successful – is having everyone say it was because of John and his money.'

Barbara sighed deeply. 'I suppose you're right. But it's not fair. And for the record, I don't think you're being fair on yourself either.'

'Maybe not, but it's reality – well, out here, anyway. God, I hate this place sometimes.'

'Are you going to leave?'

'I wouldn't know where else to go. Better the devil you know, I guess.'

Emily looked at her hands in her lap. Just what was in store for her? Whatever happened, she would need money. And Barbara was right: half the assets should legally be hers.

Was she being magnanimous or just plain gutless? It was one thing to put on a brave front and try to go it alone, but she wouldn't survive long on her meagre savings. And it didn't look like there were any jobs going. A rogue tear escaped from one eye.

'You'll feel much better when you find somewhere to live,' Barbara said, as if reading her mind. 'Not that I don't love having you staying with me. But I do understand you need to start feeling independent again.'

'I think I'll try to track down the owner of the house we got lost at, see if they'll rent it,' Emily said. 'If it's been locked up it probably only needs a good clean and a fresh coat of paint.'

'Good idea. Let's hope it's better than the other place – that décor was dreadful!'

'We can only hope,' Emily said, grinning. For the first time in days, she felt good about the prospect of waking up the next morning. 'You know,' she said suddenly, 'I am actually quite relieved I won't have to go back to the farm.'

'I know. But promise me you'll at least read the settlement papers before signing them. I'm happy to read through them as well if you want, but I don't want to intrude.'

'God, Barbara. Do you think after all this I've got anything left to hide? Thanks for the offer; it is gratefully accepted.'

As they turned into Barbara's driveway, Emily saw the verandah lights blazing. She couldn't remember them being turned on when they left, but Barbara might have done it without her noticing. Anyway, it had still been daylight then.

'Oh great, David's home,' Barbara cried. 'He must have had a good run with traffic.'

Emily felt a stab of mild jealousy before she scolded herself for her pettiness. Barbara was her friend; of course she was pleased to see her happy.

David waved from the porch as Barbara pulled the car into the open garage. Emily waved back.

She was out of the car and next to David before Barbara.

'Hi David, welcome home. Hope you don't mind still having a house guest,' she said, feeling awkward. They had only met a couple of times before.

'Not at all,' he said, surprising Emily by pulling her into a brief hug before letting her go. 'I hope you don't mind, but Barb did fill me in on a few of your woes. And you're welcome to stay for as long as you like.'

'Thanks David, that's really kind of you. You've both been so good to me. But I do have to start standing on my own two feet.'

'Whatever you need to do,' he said and shrugged.

'Well, right now I'm exhausted, so I'm going to go to bed and leave you to your homecoming,' Emily said. 'See you in the morning.'

Barbara gave Emily a hug. 'Goodnight.'

She paused at the front door. 'Come on, Gracie, bedti…' she started to call, before suddenly stopping. *Shit!* David was a farmer; dogs belonged outside. She looked sheepishly at Barbara, who mouthed, 'Oops' and grimaced.

'God, you two! Don't think I didn't suspect you softies would have had the animals inside the moment my back was turned,' David said, laughing. 'Go on, I don't mind.'

'Thanks,' Emily said and stepped across the threshold. Grace darted ahead of her and bolted down the passage.

Lucky Barbara, having found such a nice man, Emily thought as she snuggled down under the plush quilt in the guest bedroom. Maybe one day she'd find someone nice too.

Chapter Twenty

As she lay in bed waiting for the fog of sleep to envelop her, Emily's mind went back to the old house where they'd found themselves after becoming lost. Even though she hadn't even stepped inside, there had been something tremendously comforting about the place. *The sort of comfort that a grandmother offered*, she thought. A familiar wave of warmth washed over Emily and she wrapped her arms around her ribs, as if to capture the feeling.

Yes, that was it: Gran's presence had settled around her like a thick quilt. She stared up at the ceiling, tired but wide awake and full of restless energy.

Tomorrow she really had to start getting her life sorted, she told herself. And she would. No more feeling sorry for herself. John was not going to change. No, that part of her life was over, and she needed to get on with the next. And the next was going to be a B&B. No matter how long it took, she would find the perfect property and turn it into a successful business. Was it the old white house surrounded by gums? She'd need a miracle, but what harm would hoping and dreaming do?

Emily climbed out of bed and fossicked in her suitcase for the scrapbook she'd kept of the cottage. Beside it lay Gran's button jar. She took it out and gave it a quick, tight hug before placing it on the bedside table.

Then she got back into bed with the folder open on her lap. Skipping quickly past the photos of 'her' cottage that was now rubble, she began leafing through the contents of the folder, trying to imagine the scraps of fabric and examples of impeccable decorating belonging to the large white house.

Soon she found herself drifting off, into that state of being neither here nor there…

She was standing with her folder in hand, making notes of measurements, the angle of the light through the windows…

…And then she was making a slight adjustment to a hung painting. She was dressed in black pants and a deep smoky blue grey formal wraparound shirt. The silk fabric crisscrossed her bodice before capturing her narrow waist in a bow at the small of her back. A strand of glossy white pearls sat just below her throat, highlighting the flawless tanned skin of her décolletage.

Emily checked her watch; in twenty minutes her guests would begin arriving. Was everything done? What had she forgotten to do? There was something. She frowned, racking her brains. She surveyed the room around her before mentally making her way through the others in the house in turn. Nothing came to mind.

'Didn't you want to put this somewhere? I seem to remember you saying so,' a male voice called from the doorway.

'Oh yes, thank you, I'd forgotten.' *Forgotten!* How could she, after everything that had happened?

'What about on this little table – swap it for the ruby vase?'

'Okay, but do you think people will think it weird, putting a jar of buttons on display?'

He shrugged. 'Sentimentality is a very personal thing. Anyway, could make for a good conversation starter. Come on, it's time. I can hear a vehicle,' he said, stretching out a hand towards her.

What was the occasion? Why were they all dressed up? And who was this man? He was a few metres from her, standing in the doorway, but she couldn't see his face. He was impeccably dressed in a well-cut charcoal pinstripe suit. She willed him to come closer so she might identify him, but her dream-filled mind wouldn't comply...

Emily woke sweating and feeling disoriented. Beams of light were peeping through the crack where the curtains hadn't quite been pulled together. She looked around and saw the button jar on the bedside table.

What had she been dreaming about? She frowned. She couldn't remember turning the lamp off. But she must have.

Grace was lying in her basket looking wide awake, not-so-patiently waiting for Emily to get up and start the day. Some-where along the line the young pup had learnt not to jump up on the bed nor whine at the door to be let out. It was as if she was an older dog in a young pup's skin. An old soul, just like Gran had often said about Emily. It had taken her until about age nineteen to understand what she meant – she'd always thought herself just boring, or 'antisocial' as her mother called her. But Gran made her see she was just a little more serious about life, and that there was nothing wrong with enjoying her own company rather than partic-ipating in frivolous activities.

'Come on, Gracie,' Emily said, getting out of bed and dragging her terry towelling robe on.

'Good morning sleepyhead,' Barbara called as Emily entered the kitchen.

'Morning.'

'Morning Emily,' David said from the sink, startling her. She'd completely forgotten he'd come home. She instinctively pulled the ties of her robe tighter around her.

'Oh, hello. Sorry, I'm still half-asleep. I had the strangest dream and feel all out of kilter.'

'I'm not surprised, though I think it was more a nightmare,' Barbara said. 'We heard you call out. You must have fallen asleep with the light on – I turned it off.'

'Sorry. Probably too much on my mind.'

It was an awful thought, but Emily wished David would go off and leave her alone with Barbara. It wasn't that she didn't like him – she did, very much – it was just that she'd got used to it being the two of them.

She marvelled at how quickly things could become the norm. This was only her third morning waking up at Barbara's – less than a week ago she'd been married with her life pretty much laid out before her.

Emily still found it hard to believe she'd actually left John. Was she mad, brave or stupid? Maybe Enid was right. Maybe it had been a hissy fit designed to provoke an ultimatum. But if so, it had backfired. John had called her bluff. She had lost.

She stared at the mug of steaming milky coffee that had appeared while her mind was elsewhere.

Suddenly she felt an overwhelming desire to cry. A giant hand clamped around her heart, squeezing, squeezing until her soul rose up to her throat. She took a tentative sip of coffee and swallowed harder than she needed to.

She was feeling sorry for herself. Barbara was right: you could choose to be a victim and blame the world for feeling the way you did, or you could decide to get on with changing things to make yourself feel better.

Gran would have simply shrugged, offered a lopsided grin and said, 'It just wasn't meant to be.' She stared down at her hands wrapped around her mug, imagining Granny Mayfair's soft, pudgy pat of reassurance – willing it.

David sat down at the table and Emily felt a slight surge of disappointment. If only she could be alone with Barbara to tell her about the dream – see if she had any idea what it could mean – before it completely faded from her memory.

It was always the same: she'd wake from a dream, the sequence of events, characters, sights and sounds still clear in her mind, but they would gradually dissipate, as if reality was the sun burning the early morning fog from the horizon.

She tried to quickly run through the scene, but found most of the detail missing. Had the button jar been dropped, scattering its bright, shiny, multi-sized, multicoloured contents across the floor?

Upheaval, chaos and panic. It was just a metaphor for what she was experiencing, nothing more. Certainly not a premonition.

'Darling,' Barbara said to David, as she put down plates of toast in front of both him and Emily, 'do you remember an old house, whitewashed, around nineteen-thirties vintage, I suppose, due north from here? Its back access road comes out near our mailbox.'

'Thanks,' Emily said, picking up her knife.

'Of course. It's the old Baker place. Such a shame to be left empty. Far as I know, it's just rotting away.'

'So why is it, do you think?'

'I don't know. Probably like lots of other farmhouses around: surplus to requirements. Sign of the times, I guess. I don't think anyone's lived there for years. Why do you ask?'

'We got lost the other day and stumbled upon it. Don't you think it would make a great B&B for Emily? That's her dream.'

Emily felt another twinge; she wasn't ready for anyone to know her plans – her dreams – yet. Why couldn't Barbara have kept it to herself? Now she'd look foolish if it never happened.

'But I'm about as far from making *that* happen as I could get,' she said, trying to sound more upbeat than she felt.

'Well, you have to have dreams,' David said sagely, before draining his cup and then spreading his toast with butter and jam.

Barbara sat down with her own plate, and they lapsed into silence while each concentrated on their toast.

'So, what are you girls up to today?' David asked, pushing his chair back and getting up.

'I need to do some baking and washing, and sort out dinner. Apart from that, not a great deal,' Barbara said.

'And I need to find somewhere to live, and hopefully a job,' Emily said.

'Why don't you give the Bakers a call?' David suggested, picking up his mug and empty plate from the table. 'They're under D.B. and T.R. in the local book. Maybe the old house is in rentable condition and they'll give it to you cheap – miracles have been known to happen.'

Emily didn't know if she could bear to live somewhere so lovely if it couldn't really be hers. If she was renting she could be kicked out any time the landlords felt like it – and she'd be back at square one again. But to say so might sound negative and ungrateful, so she stayed silent. She nodded in reply.

'Don't worry, Em. Things have a way of working out,' he said, giving her shoulder a pat. 'Well, I'd better get out and see what's been happening while I've been away. I'll be ages, so don't wait for me for lunch.'

As she watched David bend to kiss his wife goodbye, Emily felt a surge of affection for him – for them both. They really were a lovely couple, and she was lucky to have them on her side.

'Don't you two get up to any mischief while I'm gone,' he added with a grin.

They listened in silence as David's footsteps echoed down the hall. A few moments later he was back in the doorway.

'It seems your Grace wants a day out as a real dog. Do you mind if she comes along?'

Emily shrugged. 'Fine with me, if you're sure she won't be any trouble.'

'I'm just going around the sheep. I'll tie her on so she'll be safe and sound. I promise to take good care of her.' He left with a wave of his hand.

'Did you sign the papers from John?' Barbara asked.

'No. You told me not to until you'd had a look.'

'Oh, that was just so you didn't rush into it. I don't need to read them; it's really none of my business.'

'But would you? Please, Barbara, my brain's not functioning very well at the moment. And quite frankly, I'd like to get them out of the way. The sooner it's done, the sooner I can get on with my life.'

'Okay, if you're sure. But I don't think I'll have any better idea of what to look for than you. As I said last night, you really should get professional advice.'

'Well, you're less emotional and more objective than me for a start – that's reason enough. I'll go and get them.'

'How about while I take a look you ring the Bakers – use the phone in the office. Phone books are in the top left drawer and paper and pens in the drawer below.'

Chapter Twenty-one

Emily found the number easily and dialled quickly. It rang four times before a gruff male voice answered.

'Hello.'

'Hello, um, is that Mr Baker?'

'Yup, Donald, who's asking?'

'This is Emily Stra... Er, Emily Oliphant. I'm, uh, calling about the old white house on your land...'

'What about it?'

'Well, I was wondering if you'd consider renting it.'

'That old dump?!'

'It's just that I stumbled across it the other day – I hope you don't mind, but I got lost and found myself there.'

'I'd rather you took it off my hands for good.'

'Sorry? Is it for sale?'

'Well, as much as I'd like to get rid of it, I have a stubborn, sentimental older brother. I'd be happy to tear the old eyesore down but oh no, he won't have a bloody bar of it, will he? Hopefully it'll fall down soon, anyway – save me a whole lot of bother.'

'So it's not liveable?'

'The mice seem to like it. Look girly, if that's all...?'

'So you wouldn't consider renting it to me?'

'You'd be mad.'

'And if I am – mad, that is?' Emily let out a tight laugh. 'Look, I really need somewhere to live.' She almost gave in to the sob that caught in her throat.

A deep, resigned sigh came from the other end of the phone.

'Well, you'd better take a look inside before you go getting all ahead of yourself. I've got to go past in the next hour so I'll leave a key on top of the tank stand under a brick. Lock up and put it back when you've finished.'

'Thank you.'

'But don't think I'm going to do any work on the place – it's as you find it.'

'Okay.'

'Righteo then.'

There was another pause.

'Um, Mr Baker?'

'What now?'

'Would you ask your brother about selling, if it wouldn't be too much trouble?'

'Sure, why not? Not that it'll do any good; he's the stubborn one.'

'Thank you. I really appreciate it.'

'Right, if that's all...?'

'Yes, thank you very much. I'll be in touch soon. Goodbye.'

Emily hung up and sat doodling on the pad of paper in front of her, trying to decide how she felt. Surely it couldn't be as bad as Mr Baker indicated. And wow, he'd sell if it was up to him. But what was she thinking? She didn't have any money. And even if she did, the other brother – the stubborn one – wasn't interested in selling.

She tore the page from the pad, screwed it up, tossed it into the nearby bin, and put everything back where she'd found it.

Walking back down to the kitchen, her legs felt like lead.

'So how did it go?' Barbara asked, looking up from the papers.

Emily shrugged. 'He's leaving the key out for me to have a look.'

'That's great! So why the long face?'

'Apparently it's only fit for mice to live in.'

'Well, I think we can be the judge of that. Which one did you speak to – which brother?'

'Donald. Not that it matters; if he's right, I'll be back to square one.'

'Spoken like a true defeatist,' Barbara scolded.

'Sorry, but that's how I'm feeling. So, is John offering me a million dollars?' Emily asked, indicating the papers in front of Barbara.

'Um, not exactly. And you were right: it is just something he's put together. How does forty thousand sound, paid in cash?'

'Rather generous – for John Stratten.'

'That's what I was thinking – too generous. I don't mean to pry, but haven't you had a few droughts like the rest of us?'

'Of course. I'm pretty sure we've been making a loss, just like everyone else around here. Where would he get forty grand from?' Emily said, as much to herself as to Barbara.

'Bank loan?'

'Maybe, but parents more likely. So where do I sign?'

'I'm not sure you should.'

'Why? Forty grand's forty grand. I'd probably walk away with nothing to have him out of my life.'

'Something just doesn't feel right.'

'What?'

'I don't know – the timing, for a start. You'd better read through it for yourself. The land and major equipment must be tied up in a family trust or company like you said – there's no mention of it. Shouldn't you at least check?'

'I guess so, but I'd rather not bring Thora and Gerald into it. I'll have a quick look, but I am going to sign and get it over with. If he's pulling a swiftie, let him, and hope what goes around really does come around.'

'Karma won't keep you fed and clothed, Emily.'

'God, you sound like my mother.'

'Well, someone has to look out for your interests; you're clearly not.'

'What, so you think I should get a lawyer involved and go up against one of the wealthiest families in the district? I'll go through my savings in a second. And it could take years. Not to mention having my reputation trashed in the process.'

'Now who's sounding like Enid?' Barbara said, becoming visibly exasperated. 'And since when do you care what people think? You've lived here long enough to know that people are going to say what they're going to say, regardless of the truth. Come on, that's not a good enough reason not to stand up for yourself.'

'I just don't want to make my life harder than it's already going to be.'

'Good. Then help yourself and at least get some professional advice. You're selling yourself way too short, Emily.'

'It's not like I actually helped on the farm.'

'It's not about what you did or didn't do. It's about right and wrong. It's the law. From where I'm standing he's about to do more wrong by you. And you're going to just lie down and take it? Where's your bloody self-respect?!'

'Gee, thanks for the support.'

'I *am* being supportive. I'm trying to stop you doing something you'll regret.'

'Forty grand will get me on my way, and that's all I want. It was hard enough getting the courage to leave. I don't think I could fight him and his family for years in court.'

'No one is saying it has to come to that. I'm just asking you to think it through properly before signing your life away.'

'Easy for you to say, with your perfect marriage...' Emily stopped herself and put her hands to her flaming face. 'Oh, I'm so sorry, I shouldn't have said that.'

'No, you shouldn't have. Emily, I'm trying to be a good friend and help you here.'

'I know. And I appreciate it, I really do.'

'Then bloody well listen to me!'

'Please, Barbara. I don't want to fight. Can we please just drop it?'

'I don't want to fight either. And I suppose it *is* your decision to make, even if I don't agree,' Barbara said with a long, resigned sigh.

'Exactly. So, at the risk of disappointment, do you fancy coming with me to see this "dump" of a house?'

'Sure, why not? After another fortifying cup of coffee,' Barbara said, getting up, taking the remaining plates and cutlery with her. 'Meanwhile, please at least read the offer. See what you make of it.'

As Barbara made the coffee, Emily flicked through the document, the words 'if it sounds too good to be true...' ringing in her head.

Forty thousand dollars seemed like a large cash payout. Large to her, anyway. But there was likely nothing generous about it at all.

She turned the pages and checked the figures against her memory. Everything seemed included, albeit at considerably lower value than she would have thought – even taking the drought into account.

But when did they sell several thousand sheep? She wasn't sure exactly how many they ran – John shut her out when it came to farm-related business – but surely they had more than the two thousand stated here. Emily sighed; she was clearly being short-changed. The disappointing thing was that it came as no surprise.

Of course John Stratten would screw her – he was greedy, it's what greedy people did. And if she pulled him up on it, he would no doubt offer a very plausible explanation and make her look like a fool – another thing he was very good at.

Emily signed the papers and, as she pushed them aside, wondered if she would live to regret her decision. But she didn't see she had a choice if she was going to stay in the district – farmers were an endangered and protected species around here.

Chapter Twenty-two

Just as they emerged from the stand of trees, the sun came out from behind a thick bank of fluffy clouds, illuminating the white exterior of the house. It was beautiful. Emily's heart sank.

'Wow, it really is gorgeous,' Barbara cooed.

'Hmm.'

'A bit of enthusiasm, if you please. You might have found somewhere to live, to get that new start on life you've been so desperately wanting.'

'I'm sorry, but after the last place we saw, I don't want to get my hopes up.' Emily had told Barbara about her conversation with Donald Baker, but not how she really felt: that if she couldn't own it she didn't want to live there.

'We know it's not a dump – remember we looked through the windows and there wasn't anything but bare floorboards. Anyway, it's locked up. It might not have been lived in for a long time, but it's been cared for. Honestly, a bit of positive attitude wouldn't go astray, Em. Maybe if you did it up a bit, the other brother – the one you said was sentimental – might agree to part with it.'

Emily looked sharply at her friend.

145

'Don't think I can't read your mind, Ms Emily Oliphant,' Barbara said with a cheeky grin. She turned the car off, put the handbrake on and opened her door. 'Come on. I can't wait to see inside. Where's the key?'

'Tank stand, under a brick,' Emily murmured distractedly.

Her head had suddenly filled with images of a cocktail party out on the wide front verandah. Guests spilled down onto the driveway. The large sprawling gum had fairy lights strung amongst its leaves and coloured lanterns swinging from its branches. People milled about, full of happiness and laughter, gentle music playing in the still night air.

Emily closed her eyes tight to erase the vision. It was too painful. She had no means of making such a dream come true, and couldn't see how she ever would. Aching, she climbed out of the car. Being positive was one thing; losing her grip on reality was quite another.

She made her way heavily up the sweeping concrete verandah steps, and was approaching the front door when it opened.

'Found it,' Barbara said, beaming. 'Welcome!' She stood back to let Emily past.

Emily was two steps inside when she started to sneeze. 'Bloody hell, it's dusty,' she said when the bout finally subsided.

'You would be too if you hadn't been vacuumed for goodness-knows-how-many years!'

As Emily blew her nose, she stared down the wide hallway ahead of her. From the outside the house didn't look big enough to warrant such extravagance. Perhaps the rooms were small. Though she knew that was unlikely in a house of this age. Her heart sank further. She didn't have to see any more; she loved the place already.

They moved down the hall, opening each of the doors leading off it in turn, and stepping inside the spacious rooms.

Each had an open fireplace with original timber surrounds and a tiled hearth, and large double-hung windows, the tops of which held lovely leadlight panels in subdued colours and curvaceous, floral art nouveau-style designs.

The timber floors were dull, but seemed to be in reasonable condition, which Emily discovered by polishing a small section with her foot while holding a tissue over her nose.

'You know,' Barbara said authoritatively, 'only jarrah, or maybe red gum, would be in this condition after so long.'

Emily nodded and checked the ceiling. So far, each had had a different ornate moulded design – again art nouveau, but at times verging on art deco.

They opened a door two thirds of the way down the hall and stepped into a room twice the size of all the others.

'Imagine the parties you could have here,' Barbara said with wonder. 'You'd easily get eight tables of ten in here for a sit-down dinner.'

Emily nodded; she was already mentally placing them, decorating them, adding cutlery...

'Come on, I'm dying to see the kitchen – it's bound to be huge if this is anything to go by,' Barbara said.

When Emily didn't make a move, Barbara grabbed her friend's hand and tugged.

'Come on, we can come back and daydream, but I want to see everything now!'

Emily allowed herself to be swept out through the door into the second part of the hall, and then to the right where they could see the kitchen behind a set of natural timber French doors with clear but slightly wavy glass. They opened the doors and found themselves standing in an enormous kitchen.

'Lordy,' Barbara said. 'This puts even my kitchen to shame. And look at the legs on that table. Fancy them leaving it here.'

'It's so big they probably can't fit it at their other place. And I thought John's table was big.'

'This place is like Doctor Who's TARDIS,' Barbara continued. 'No way does it look this big from the outside.'

'You know, we haven't seen a bathroom or a toilet,' Emily said.

'Maybe they're through this way,' Barbara said, nodding at a second set of French doors at the other end of the kitchen that looked like they led outside. Emily followed her. *I am not living somewhere without adequate bathroom facilities*, she told herself, desperately wanting an excuse to hate the place.

'Uh-huh,' Barbara said in triumph, standing just outside on the side verandah. 'Looks like laundry one side – see, old clothes line down there – and bathroom on the other,' she said, turning this way and that.

Down a short flight of concrete steps was a long, two-stranded clothes line held up at each end by large, weathered timber posts. Barbara skipped down the steps and over to it.

'You undo this swivel, peg the clothes on the lower side, then hoist it up and secure it with this plank,' she said, demonstrating. 'My grandmother had one just like it.'

But Emily was too busy taking in the scene before her. Beyond the high verandah an empty creekbed made its way past the house. It would be stunning flowing with water. And it must occasionally do, she surmised, given the lush scrub just beyond it. No doubt that explained the magnificent stand of trees. God, everything about the place was gorgeous. She just had to find some way to own it.

Emily sighed and opened the door to her right, which, as anticipated, revealed a large bathroom.

'It's a pity they had to use part of the verandah – especially with that view,' Barbara said, appearing beside her.

'I'm just relieved it's not a long-drop out by the scrub,' Emily said, trying to make out everything in the gloom. A sheet covered the window. 'Oh, but there doesn't seem to be a toilet in here,'

'Don't worry,' Barbara said with a laugh. 'It's in the laundry.'

'Thank God for that,' Emily said, visibly relieved.

'You know, apart from being old, dated and pretty bloody filthy, I think the old girl's kept her age well,' Barbara said.

'I agree. She must have been pretty flash in her day. Were they wealthy, the Bakers?'

'I know as much about them as you – I'm an out-of-towner, remember? You'll have to ask David. Or, better yet, your dad. Come on, let's take a look at the outbuildings.'

'No, I don't want to pry. And anyway, Mr Baker said only the house.'

'All right, but at least let's see what's behind that door on the other corner. Maybe it's a cellar.'

Emily reluctantly followed Barbara out around the laundry and past the kitchen window. The house was already perfect; the last thing she wanted was for it to be too good to be true. And if the Bakers were ever to consider selling, a cellar would add significantly to the asking price.

'Bugger, it's locked – and this key doesn't open it. Wonder what they're hiding in there.'

Emily laughed. 'Dead bodies, Miss Marple? Come on, I need to sit down.' Suddenly she felt exhausted, the sensory overload catching up with her.

They made their way back inside, down the hall, and outside onto the front verandah. They sat opposite each other, leaning against the two large barley-twist pillars at the top of the steps.

'It's just so damn perfect I want to cry,' Emily said, thinking aloud.

'Well then, we'll just have to make it happen.'

'How though?'

'We could knock off the brother who doesn't want to sell,' Barbara said after a few moments of silent contemplation.

'Gee, aren't you a big help.'

'Just making sure you haven't lost your sense of humour.'

'Oh, ha ha. Well, think again, it's not a viable option.'

'You could at least speak to him, find out why. At this point we've only got his brother's word.'

'Hmm, I think you're right,' Emily said, having at that second come to the same conclusion.

'At the very least find out how much rent they want and when you can move in.'

'Honestly, Barb, I'm not sure I want to live here if I can't own it – it'd be too heartbreaking to have to leave it behind. Like the cottage all over again.'

'Since when have you been afraid of a little heartbreak? Look how far you've come, Em. It's only good things from here on,' she said.

I bloody well hope so.

'Anyway, at least if they let you move in they won't be demolishing it.'

They were in the car, about to leave, when Emily's mobile rang. She pushed the button to answer without checking the number.

'Hello, Emily speaking.'

'Emily, have you signed the papers yet?' John's voice boomed into her ear.

Emily felt like the blood in her veins had frozen solid. Her heart seemed to stop for a moment before starting up again in a series of frantic beats.

'John,' she said simply.

'So, the papers, have you signed them?'

'Yes,' she said, 'but...' she started, stopped herself, and instead let out a resigned sigh. 'I've signed them.' What was the point? *He can have this one. I'll just get on with my life.*

'Can I come out and collect them – now?'

Why now? Why the urgency? 'Hang on, I'll check with Barbara – we're out at the moment.' She put the phone against her thigh to cover the microphone. 'He wants to know if it's okay to come out to your place and pick up the papers.'

'Fine with me,' Barbara said. 'You know what I think, but it's really up to you. And why the big hurry? That's what I want to know.'

'I don't know, but I just want to get it over with.' Emily put the phone back to her ear. 'John? That's fine, but we won't be back at Barbara's for about an hour.'

She raised a questioning brow at Barbara, who nodded in return. She'd added around forty-five minutes in order to compose herself.

Chapter Twenty-three

'He's here,' Barbara called from the lounge-room window where she'd been waiting for John Stratten's arrival.

Emily was in the guest room, making notes in her 'cottage' scrapbook. She still loved the ideas she'd recorded there, but was now starting to think of them in terms of the white house. She was strangely relieved to hear Barbara's announcement. The thought of seeing John made her queasy, nervous and sad. But it would be good to get it over with.

She grabbed the envelope from the bedside table and went out into the hall. She was at the door, opening it, just as John put his hand up to lift the knocker.

Emily handed him the envelope and muttered, 'There you are,' with her hand still on the partly opened door. She liked how ill-at-ease John looked.

He opened his mouth to say something, but shut it again.

'There isn't anything else, is there?'

'No.' He looked as if he wanted to ask her something, but thought the better of it. 'Okay, I guess I'll be off then.'

What does he expect, to be asked in for a cup of tea?

As she closed the door with a clank, a wave of sadness swept over her. She ached right to her soul.

She heard John's footsteps pause before making their way heavily down the steps, and had the overwhelming desire to run out and stop him, tell him she loved him, that she'd made a terrible mistake and that they'd work things out.

But she just stood leaning against the back of the door feeling numb.

No matter how hard she tried, one person couldn't make a relationship work if the other person's heart wasn't in it. They might stay together, but it would be on the other person's terms, and that was not living truthfully.

Granny Mayfair had always said, 'You have to be true to yourself, first and foremost. That doesn't necessarily mean being selfish, but it does mean making sure the needs of your own soul are taken care of.'

Was that why she had chosen Grandpa over an Indian prince? Emily shook the thought aside. She'd never know now. But it was probably why Emily had never consulted her about John. She would have been devastated if Gran had told her she wasn't working hard enough at her marriage. She'd never quite figured out where the old lady had drawn the line between selfishness and putting the needs of one's own soul first. If only she'd taken the risk, perhaps things would have turned out differently.

She was brought back to the present as Barbara called down the hall from the kitchen doorway.

'Are you okay out there?'

Emily opened her mouth to reply that yes, she was fine, but her eyes suddenly filled with tears and her throat constricted. She nodded instead.

'Oh, sweetie, come in here and sit down,' Barbara said, appearing beside her and putting an arm around her friend. She led

Emily towards the lounge where they sat in the middle of a large, dark chocolate leather chesterfield-style couch.

'I'm sorry, I don't know what's wrong with me,' Emily said, tears now flowing freely down her cheeks. Barbara handed her a neatly pressed and folded lavender-coloured handkerchief. 'I should be happy that he's out of my life,' Emily blubbered on.

'You're grieving for the death of your marriage. Of course you're going to be upset. If you weren't, you wouldn't be normal. You need time to heal. Meanwhile, stay angry with him, it'll help. And remember, he hasn't come running after you to sort things out.'

'Maybe he doesn't know he's meant to.'

'He was the one who brought home another woman. He didn't exactly deny it.'

Emily shrugged. 'Maybe I wasn't good enough in bed.'

She knew as she said it how pathetic this sounded. It was what Enid had told her before she got married – that sex was the only sure way to keep your marriage together. Part of Emily knew there was no way this could be correct – and had known it from the beginning – but another part trusted her. Mothers were supposed to know best, weren't they?

'I'm not even going to respond to that,' Barbara said, 'other than to say that it is utter crap and you damn well know it! Have you forgotten why you left? You're just having a crisis of confidence. You need to stay strong,' Barbara said firmly.

Emily dried her eyes roughly while nodding. 'You're right. Thank you. Thank you for being such a good friend,' she said with a weak smile.

Barbara patted her friend's hand. 'You're welcome. I know you'd do the same for me. You'll get through this, you'll see. It'll just take time.'

Emily blew her nose.

'Come on, I'm in the mood for some baking,' Barbara said, getting up. 'Personally, I think the therapy of cooking is very underrated.'

A surge of warmth ran through Emily at the thought. She'd forgotten just how much she missed pottering around her kitchen with nothing else on her mind than waiting for a cake to rise, biscuits to brown, or jam to set.

'Hmm. Something smells good.'

Barbara and Emily looked up from the table where they were icing the latest batch of melting moment biscuits. David stood in the doorway, surveying the kitchen. They hadn't heard his vehicle, nor his boots being dumped on the verandah at the front door.

'Are you two starting a shop or have the shearers arrived early?'

'I suppose we did get a little carried away,' Barbara said with a sheepish grin. The table was barely visible beneath racks of shortbread, melting moments and ginger biscuits. Taking up most of the expansive bench tops that ran around the kitchen were carrot, banana and orange log cakes, a date loaf, and chocolate and plain vanilla fairy cakes brimming with whipped cream and sprinkled with icing sugar.

'Well, I'll punish you later,' David said, sidling up to his wife and putting an arm around her waist.

Emily looked away as he planted a lingering kiss on Barbara's neck, just under her ear.

'So, how are my two favourite girls doing?'

Emily felt herself blush slightly.

'We're good,' Barbara said.

He pulled a chair out from the table and sat down.

'Am I allowed to taste, or is all this for some CWA do?'

'No, have whatever you like; we were just keeping busy,' Barbara said. 'Coffee, tea?' she called behind her as she went to the kettle.

'Tea, thanks. By busy I take it you mean after John Stratten's visit? I saw him on the road into town. We both got held up by Hignett moving a mob of sheep.'

'He picked up the signed financial papers,' Barbara said.

'So that's it? He didn't muck about, did he?'

Emily shook her head, her eyes suddenly filling with tears.

'Yep, she's rid of him now,' Barbara said.

'How come it's all over with so quickly? I thought you had to be separated for twelve months before you could get a divorce,' David said.

'It's just the financial settlement we've done – you do have to wait twelve months for a divorce. Though I think that's just a form that gets rubber-stamped by the court.'

'Honestly, I think you're better off without him.'

Barbara put a steaming mug in front of David and another in front of Emily, who was sitting at the far end of the laden table.

'He's not a bad bloke – from a bloke's point of view,' David continued, 'but there's just something about him I'm not sure I trust.'

'Hmm,' Barbara and Emily sounded in unison.

'What, you think there's a problem?' he asked, looking from one to the other.

'We think he might have been a bit dishonest with the financials, but there's really no way to prove it – Emily doesn't have access to any of the records. I don't think she should have signed so quickly – not without some professional advice – but…'

'I'd really rather just put it all behind me,' Emily added, looking down into her cup.

'Fair enough, I suppose. And if he has pulled a swiftie, he'll get his comeuppance. You just hold your head high and get on with picking up the pieces. You'll be fine.' He gave her hand a friendly pat.

'Thanks,' Emily said, offering a weak smile.

'So, did you speak to him?' Barbara asked.

'Not really. I think he's giving me a wide berth, since we're clearly on Em's side.'

'Sorry if...' Emily started.

'Don't apologise; no skin off my nose. So, what else have you been up to?' David asked brightly.

'We went and looked at the Baker house,' Barbara said.

'How was it?'

'Great,' Barbara said.

'Okay,' Emily said, unable to muster Barbara's enthusiasm.

David looked from one to the other. 'Come on, it was either great or just okay, not both. So, which was it?'

'Well,' Barbara explained, 'I love the place. It would suit Em down to the ground and would make a great B&B one day. And it's empty, so she could get in right away...'

'But?'

'It wouldn't be mine,' Emily said. 'If I rent, there's always the chance I could be turfed out.'

'So, ask if they'll sell.'

'I did. One of the brothers doesn't want to. And I don't have any money – nowhere near enough, anyway.'

'So you only have to convince one person – pretty good odds, in my book.'

'But where would I find a couple of hundred thousand?'

'Well,' David said, tapping a finger on his lip thoughtfully, 'they're most likely pensioners, and wouldn't want a heap of money at once – it'd stuff up their pension. You could offer to rent to buy, or pay an annual fee that would keep their income below the threshold. They've been hit with drought like the rest of us – I'm sure they could use the money, even if it came in a trickle.'

'How many acres do they own?' Barbara asked.

'Only about twelve hundred – they're pretty small-time around here.'

'I wouldn't want twelve hundred acres,' Emily said.

'Course you wouldn't. You'd get a few – say, twenty – carved off…'

'But the house is in the middle.'

'Easy, you get an easement put in. They have the driveway fenced, so there might already be one. It's easy to find out – the Lands Department will have the details. Though I don't think they're called that anymore.'

'How do you know all this?' Barbara asked.

'Just know,' he said, shrugging.

Emily's head was spinning. It all sounded so complicated. But could it be possible, really?

'So what should I do?' she asked.

'Have you told them you want to rent the place and found out how much they want?'

'No, I wasn't sure if…' Emily felt torn: she really needed to get herself settled, but there was so much negotiation to be done. It was all too hard.

'Look, Em, there's no rush for you to leave,' Barbara said.

'But…' Emily started.

David raised his hands to silence her. 'I know you don't want to wear out your welcome or be a burden, and honestly, you're not. This is possibly the rest of your life you're sorting out – you need to take time, not rush into something you might regret.'

Wow, Emily thought. What had she done to deserve friends like this? How could she ever repay them?

'Em,' Barbara said, suddenly beside her and draping an arm around her shoulder, 'we're doing this because you've become very special to us and we know you'd do the same for us – it's what friends do.'

'I don't know what to say,' Emily said, shaking her head.

'Nothing. Just promise you'll give us jobs when your B&B becomes a huge success and farming goes completely tits up,' David said.

Emily laughed. 'You're on.' They shook on it.

'Right,' David said, pushing his chair back from the table, 'I'm going to go into the office and mull over a few figures. And you two can cook me a lovely dinner,' he added with a cheeky grin. He bolted as the tea towel Barbara threw flew towards him.

Emily stared after David with mixed feelings. It really should be her doing the sums, coming up with options for her future. Could she really find a way to make her dream come true?

Just then Grace bowled up and gave Emily's legs a nudge. She looked down into the dog's pleading brown eyes. She'd been so caught up in her own stuff that she'd hardly spent any time with the pup in the last few days.

The dog was now her only constant; the only leftover from her past. As she bent down to ruffle Grace's ears, she vowed to be more attentive. She hugged the border collie to her tightly until Grace wriggled free and wandered off, sniffing around the kitchen for crumbs.

After a few moments, Grace gave up and lay down with a humph, head on paws, on her blanket on the far side of the kitchen.

'She's amazingly well-behaved for such a young dog,' Barbara remarked.

'John wouldn't have put up with anything less.'

They fell silent, the undercurrent of truth hanging heavily in the air between them as they looked across at Grace on her rug. Emily shuddered to think what would have happened if she'd left her behind.

Chapter Twenty-four

Emily retreated to her bedroom and sat heavily on the bed. As much as Barbara told her to make herself at home, and as lovely as she and David were to her, she did feel like an intruder.

It must have been driving them batty. No, she decided, I'm going to phone Donald Baker back and get the rental settled, and then worry about everything else later. If it was meant to be it would be, when the time was right. She had to make herself believe that.

She glanced at the button jar as if seeking Gran's approval. But there was no doubt in her mind. For the first time since leaving John, she was unwavering in her decision.

Feeling a little empowered, she left the room and went to David's study and knocked on the open door. Barbara stood behind David, who was tapping on the computer keyboard. They looked up at Emily with slightly surprised expressions.

'I've decided to phone Donald Baker and see if I can move in – to rent – tomorrow.'

Barbara and David opened their mouths, but Emily ploughed on.

'I'm really grateful for everything you've done for me and Gracie, but I really need to get on with being independent. Even if it was possible for me to buy the place, it would take months to organise the subdivision and purchase, and no matter what you say, I can't put you guys out for that long.'

'But you're not.'

Emily held up a hand to silence them. 'I really value your friendship, and I don't want to put that in jeopardy. If the B&B thing is meant to be it'll work out down the track, but first things first: I need somewhere to live.'

'If you're sure,' Barbara said.

'Yes. Could I just borrow the phone, since it's a local call?'

'Sure. We'll leave you to it,' David said, passing her the handset and getting up.

'No need to leave; I won't be long.' She pulled the piece of paper that she'd written the Bakers' phone number on from her pocket. She dialled and held her breath while she waited for it to connect and then begin ringing. It was answered almost immediately, taking her by surprise.

'Um, hello. Is that Trevor or Donald?'

'Donald speaking.'

'Hi Donald, it's Emily Str... Oliphant here again. We spoke this morning about me possibly renting the old house on your property.'

'Have you been over yet?'

'Yes, and if you're happy to rent it to me I'd love to live there.'

'Really? You sure it's not too run-down?'

'No. But a lick of paint and a bit of cosmetic tidying up would make the world of difference – if you wouldn't mind me doing that.'

'Fine, as long as you don't expect us to spend anything on it – you'd be renting it as it is. I have no idea if the hot-water service is in working order or not.'

'I really don't mind that. And yes, I understand that what I see is what I get. So how much rent would you be asking?' Emily held her breath and crossed her fingers.

'How many of you are there?'

'Just myself – oh, and my dog, if that's okay. She's really no trouble.'

'As long as it doesn't get into the sheep. Make sure the house yard is secure and keep her in there. How would one hundred dollars a week sound?'

Bloody cheap! 'Great. It's a deal. One hundred dollars a week would work for me. If that's okay with your brother.'

'It'll be fine, but don't go getting the electricity changed into your name; the shearing shed is on the same meter. We'll just include the power in the rent. You won't be leaving all the lights blazing all night, will you?'

'No, and I'll happily contribute extra when you get the bill.'

'I'm sure that won't be necessary. We don't want to upset our pensions, you see.'

'Right, I see. Thank you so much for this. I really do appreciate it.'

'When do you want to move in?'

'Would tomorrow be okay?'

'Fine. The key will be where you left it. We'll drop by in a few days to see how you've settled in.'

'That would be lovely, I look forward to it. Thank you again.'

'Okay. Bye for now, then.'

'Goodbye.'

Emily put the phone back on the desk with a shaking hand and pounding heart. Her cheeks were flaming. David and Barbara stood nearby, staring at her.

'It sounds like you've found yourself somewhere to live,' Barbara said.

Emily nodded.

'What else did he say? Come on, the suspense is killing me,' Barbara said.

'One hundred dollars a week rent.'

'A hundred is a great deal,' David said.

'And that includes power, because the shearing shed at the back is on the same meter.'

'So what don't you mind about?' Barbara demanded.

Emily replayed the conversation in her mind. 'Oh, he said he didn't know if the hot-water service is working or not. But at this point I'd be prepared to boil the kettle for a sponge bath. I might be saying different come winter,' she added with a laugh.

'And they're happy for you to repaint? We've got plenty of leftover paint, brushes and rollers in the shed.'

'That'd be great. And it's fine for Grace to be there as long as I secure the house yard so she doesn't get into the sheep. No having to hide her from the landlord, how cool is that?'

'I'll take a look at the yard for you, and the hot-water service,' David said.

'And I'll help you clean and paint,' Barbara said.

'But you've both done so much for me already.'

'We won't take no for an answer. Oh, I'm so excited for you,' Barbara said, coming from behind the desk to give her friend a hug.

They leapt up and down together like children until Grace appeared beside them, barking and trying to round them up like sheep.

'Well, it's probably going to be draughty, hot as hell and full of mice, but it'll be home – at least for the time being,' Emily said.

'And we won't be far away if you need anything,' Barbara said.

Emily beamed. 'I'm just going to quickly ring Dad and see if he can bring my stuff up tomorrow, and then I am going to stop commandeering all your facilities – well, after tomorrow morning, anyway.'

'This deserves a celebration. I'll get the bubbly,' David said, getting up and leaving the room.

Chapter Twenty-five

Unable to sleep, Emily was up at five-thirty, just as the darkness of night was giving way to the first grey signs of dawn. With her few belongings packed and ready, she sat on the floor talking to Grace, telling the puppy about the new life she hoped would be theirs. The dog looked at her as though she was mad; didn't she know it was the middle of the night and they should still be asleep?

Emily was itching to get going. What the hell was she to do for the next hour or so? She held off leaving the house to pack the car as she didn't want to wake Barbara or David. She sat tapping her feet, picking at her nails and checking her watch. It was still only six o'clock. She got up from the floor and, directing a silence-warning finger towards Grace, left the room for the kitchen.

The house was quiet, except for the occasional creak of a floorboard beneath her tiptoeing feet, and the click-click of Grace's claws behind her.

She flicked on the light, filled the kettle and turned it on, willing it to be silent. Just before it began bubbling, she pulled the plug. It was amazing how much noise she was making despite every effort not to. Grace seemed to get it, though, watching silently from her position curled up on the floor.

Emily sat at the table with both hands wrapped around a mug of coffee. Ordinarily she loathed black coffee, but she'd left it black to avoid the extra noise associated with using the fridge. She checked her watch again – less than five minutes had passed since last time.

Her father was due to arrive with the trailer some time during the morning. A small part of her wished she didn't need her furniture for months, so John would have the irritation of being without his trailer. She scolded herself for her spitefulness and took a sip of her coffee, cringing at the bitterness.

Suddenly she heard loud footsteps in the side passage. A few seconds later Barbara appeared, followed closely by David. Both were fully dressed.

'Good morning – raring to go, I see,' Barbara said. 'What the hell are you doing drinking black coffee for? There's plenty of milk in the fridge,' she said on her way past Emily to the kettle.

I'm not *drinking black coffee*, Emily thought with a smirk, looking down into her still-full cup. She got up and went to the sink to tip some out and make room for milk.

Out of the corner of her eye, Emily noticed David crouching next to Grace, giving her a great deal of affectionate attention. As she looked back, Barbara caught her eye and winked. Nodding her head towards her husband she mouthed, 'Softie'. Emily smiled back.

'You know, I think I'm going to miss having little Gracie in the house,' David said, sitting at the table across from Emily.

Emily acknowledged to herself that she wouldn't be nearly as together as she was if it wasn't for the dog. Somehow she didn't feel so lonely – though she was yet to spend a night alone. Tonight was the night, she realised with a little surge of nervous apprehension. But stronger was the feeling of excitement, of budding independence. Today really was the first day of the rest of her life, as clichéd as it sounded.

'So, I've made a list of what we'll need,' Barbara said, handing her a sheet of paper. 'Take a look and see what I've missed.'

The list covered everything from the vacuum cleaner to dishwashing detergent to newspaper for polishing windows. *Thank God for Barbara*, Emily thought. She'd completely forgotten all the cleaning stuff, hadn't even thought about it when her father had asked if there was anything she needed other than the trailer. 'No, that's all, thanks,' she'd said cheerily.

But reality was suddenly dawning: she'd need absolutely everything to set up house – crockery, cutlery, sheets, towels, food...

It was unlikely there'd be anything in the trailer beyond bits of furniture and a few knick-knacks. She'd have a chair to sit on but no television to watch and – damn it – no bed to sleep in. Hopefully John had remembered the older couch – it was hers from before they were married. At least she already had everything Grace needed.

Emily's head started to swim. Had she bitten off more than she could chew? But what choice did she have? If she was going to be independent, this was the first step. She checked her watch, anxious to get going.

'Shall I start to get all this stuff together? Dad's meeting us at the house.'

'We're not going anywhere before you've eaten a decent breakfast,' Barbara warned. 'Meanwhile, make yourself useful by making some sandwiches and packing the esky – there's egg mix ready to go in the fridge. We'll also need a thermos of coffee, mugs, cups and some water – the large water bottle is just inside the laundry. And put in the big tin of fruitcake in case we get hungry later. We need to be prepared for a long day.'

'I'll just load some stuff into the ute. Be right back,' David announced, getting up.

'Breakfast will be in fifteen minutes,' Barbara called as she whisked eggs in a bowl. Bacon was already sizzling in the pan.

Emily busied herself with buttering bread for sandwiches, glad to be making herself useful.

She was filling up the kettle ready to do the thermos when Barbara put the first two laden plates on the table. At the same moment, David reappeared.

'It's pretty overcast out there,' David said.

'Hopefully any rain will hold off until we get everything safely under cover,' Barbara said.

'Forecast said afternoon showers, so let's hope they're right for a change. This looks great,' he added, sitting down and attacking his breakfast. He kept talking between mouthfuls. 'Right, I've got the fencing stuff for Gracie's yard. I've packed the swag – without spiders; I checked,' he added with a glance at Emily. 'I put in the shearing shed vacuum cleaner, lawnmower, whipper snipper and blower vac, tarps, brooms, dustpan and brush, toolbox with hammer, nails, screwdriver, et cetera. Anything you think I've missed?' he asked, looking from Barbara to Emily.

Emily shook her head. She wouldn't have thought of even half of what he'd already packed.

'Oh, and I put in some of the camping stuff: rechargeable lantern, folding chairs and table.'

'Wow, you've thought of everything,' Emily marvelled.

'What about some rope for Grace in case the fence can't easily be fixed?' Barbara suggested.

'Good idea. There should be plenty behind the seat in the ute, but I'll check before we leave. No doubt there'll be other stuff we discover we need when we get there. At least it's not far down the road.'

'It's all terribly exciting,' Barbara said, getting up with her empty plate in hand.

'And terrifying,' Emily said, also getting up. 'Thank God I've got you guys keeping me on track. I'd be a basket case otherwise.' *And not nearly as full*, she thought. *I ate too much, too quickly.* She took a deep breath in an attempt to ease her stomach.

'Well, we'd better get cracking,' Barbara said, looking at the kitchen clock. 'Lots to do.'

'I've just got to finish the thermos,' Emily said, switching on the kettle.

'I'll head off then, open up the house and start looking at the fence. Best to get Grace secure and out of trouble first off. I'll take her and Sasha for company. See you there soon,' David said, giving Barbara a peck on the cheek. 'Come on, Gracie, you're coming with me,' he called to the dog snoozing on the floor. She leapt up and trotted off after him.

'He's taken a real shine to her,' Barbara said.

'Hmm. Good of him to let her to stay in the house.'

'He probably forgets she's here half the time, she's so well-behaved. We'll miss her when she's gone. Both of you, of course. We'll miss both of you,' Barbara added, a little flustered.

'I know what you meant. Right, this is done,' Emily said, screwing the cap on the thermos.

Chapter Twenty-six

When they arrived, the front door was wide open, and David was walking around the sectioned-off house yard. Grace was following, the white tip of her tail the only part of her visible above the grass. Sasha was curled up in a small patch of sun beside the gate, as if knowing it was where they would return to. What was the point of expending all that unnecessary energy?

'I vote we start in the kitchen,' Barbara declared. 'It'll be nice to have somewhere clean to eat if those clouds eventually deliver, and you might need it as a bathroom yet. It's so big you could use it as a temporary bedroom for a while, too, if you have to.'

'Good idea,' Emily agreed. And it was. Personally, she would have started at the front of the house and worked her way back. It seemed logical, but it wasn't practical. What would be the point of having three bedrooms and an enormous lounge-dining room free of grime, when they weren't even going to be used?

How the hell was she ever going to make it on her own? Emily stood in the kitchen doorway – watching Barbara unload everything and line it up in order of presumed usage – feeling bewildered.

'We can start somewhere else if you'd rather,' Barbara said, looking up and misinterpreting her friend's hesitation.

'No, this is the right way to go. I'm just annoyed with myself because I would have wasted time doing the bedrooms first.'

'It's not a competition, Em. Everything will have to be done eventually. Don't be so hard on yourself; we each have a different order of doing things, that's all.'

'Maybe I hate cleaning ovens and scrubbing tiles, so that's why I'd leave it to last.' Emily shrugged, looking around her.

'Maybe I do too, and that's why I want to get it over with first,' Barbara said, grinning. 'So that's decided, then – we start in here.'

'Okay,' Emily said, wondering again if she'd bitten off more than she could chew. It was going to be a long day.

They worked well together, never seeming to get in each other's way, and were able to progress steadily with little discussion. First they swept the ceiling and walls free of cobwebs and surface dirt. Then they mopped everything, including the lino floor. They filled a half dozen or so holes in the plaster, sanded the repairs smooth, put down drop sheets, and then proceeded to paint the ceiling and walls, all in the same light, creamy pale yellow. Barbara did the cutting-in and the more detailed painting, having had recent room-painting practice, and Emily followed with the roller.

Both Barbara and Emily were glistening with sweat when they finished. Sitting down for a bite to eat and a rest, they marvelled at how quickly they'd got the job done considering the size of the room and how much fresher it now seemed. They laughed as they both said at once how much they liked the smell of paint.

Next they turned their attention to the ancient oven. It was electric, albeit probably one of the first. The Baker family must have been well-to-do, and no doubt Mrs Baker would have been the envy of neighbouring wives who'd still had to collect wood or nag their husbands or sons to do it.

'Reckon we should get David to check the wiring before we try turning that on,' Barbara said. 'He's pretty good with electrical stuff.'

'Good idea.' Emily stared at the old appliance, wondering what it would take to get it working. That was one of the plusses about country blokes. They were usually good with practical stuff. What were city guys good at, as a rule?

'Hey, look! This might be the key to the cellar,' Barbara said, holding up a small tarnished object she'd found down beside the oven.

'We'll have to check it out later, when we've finished.' Emily would have loved to investigate right then and there, but instead she put the key in her pocket and opened the oven door.

While Barbara went in search of David, Emily started cleaning out all the flakes of rust and peeling enamel. There was little enamel left inside, and she wondered if it made the oven unusable or just impossible to clean properly. But she was pleasantly surprised to find no sign of mouse habitation.

The first year she and John were married – before drought had set in – they had suffered a mouse plague. Emily had turned on the oven to begin the cooking for shearing, only to hear the pop and fizz of mice caught in the wiring and being fried. The subsequent stink was unbearable, sending them to the pub for dinner. Investigation revealed a mouse nest in the insulation. A new oven had to be ordered, but in the meantime the mini bench-top toaster oven, a wedding gift previously considered a bit small to be useful, was on almost around the clock, trying to pick up the slack.

Thank God for the seemingly useless wedding gift, they'd said, seeing the lighter side of their situation.

They'd been able to do that in the early days of their marriage, she and John: laugh together, pitch in together to solve problems. Not out on the actual farm, obviously, but around the house. So where had it all gone wrong?

No, she was not going to think like that today. Emily refocussed on the oven.

After the kitchen, Emily and Barbara moved on to the outdoor bathroom and laundry, respectively. The theory was that after a kitchen that could double as bedroom and living area, Emily needed a clean working bathroom and toilet.

Some time later, Emily heard a noise in the hall and a male voice calling, 'Hello, anyone here? Delivery for Ms Emily Oliphant.'

Dad. She checked her watch. It was just after two o'clock. Where had the time gone? He'd said he'd be there that morning.

Emily pulled off her rubber gloves and made her way out to the hall. Now she'd stopped, she realised just how weary she was. And the hunger pangs were starting to bite.

'Hi Dad,' she said, giving her father a hug.

'Sorry I'm late,' Des said, looking around. 'This brings back memories. She's stood up well to the test of time.'

'I hope so.'

'Where do you want me to put things?'

'I'm not sure. We've started in the kitchen, so there aren't any bedrooms cleared out as yet.'

'In that case, I suggest we unload everything onto the front verandah where it will be protected from the rain that looks as if it's about to start. Then we'll see what's there.'

'Sounds like a plan.' They went down the hall together. Emily was startled to find her mother just outside the front door, peering about with obvious distaste.

'Oh, there you are,' Enid Oliphant said.

'Hi Mum.' They hugged rigidly and briefly. *So that's why Dad was so late.* No doubt her mother had insisted on coming along for a stickybeak, but not until she'd done all her morning chores, and then, since it was near lunchtime, after they had eaten. *Oh, shit. She's going to have a fit when she sees inside.* Emily had been hoping to have sorted out the cosmetic issues before Enid saw where she was planning on living.

'Emily, you can't be serious about this!'

'I am, Mum. Isn't it great?'

'Are you mad? It's disgusting!'

'It just needs some tender loving care.' As she said it, Emily cursed her open-book personality – if only she could just keep her mouth closed. No matter how much her mother frustrated her, more annoying still was the fact that she continued to seek her approval.

'What it needs is a bulldozer – it's not fit for habitation. You can have the caravan; you only have to ask. We can set it up in the caravan park if independence is such an issue.'

'I don't want to live in a caravan; I'm going to live here – it's got character.'

'Character?! And just how much will you be paying for this so-called *character*?'

'Um...'

'It's a bargain, just one hundred dollars a week – including utilities,' David said, materialising beside them. 'Isn't it great?' he said, beaming at Enid.

Enid stood there with her mouth open.

'You must be Enid. I'm David Burton. I believe you've met my wife, Barbara? Hi Des,' he continued, not waiting for a response. He and Des shook hands. 'Do you want a hand unloading the trailer?'

'Thanks, that would be great. I thought we'd unload everything onto the verandah in case that rain comes in.'

'What's the point?' Enid said, looking up. 'It's probably full of holes.'

'Well, we'll soon find out,' Des said cheerfully.

'I've got some extra tarps in the ute, so it won't be a problem,' David said.

'And you're absolutely sure about living here, Emily? It's not too late, you know – we can easily take the trailer back home.'

'Positive, Mum. I can't wait to get myself set up, paint it, make it nice and homey.'

'You won't want to waste your energy or money on a rental – the owners get all the benefit.'

'Not if Em finds a way to own it one day,' David said.

Emily cringed. *Please don't say another word.*

'Why ever would she want to do that? It's disgusting!'

'No way, it's got loads of potential,' David enthused.

'Potential to be nothing more than a giant money pit. Desmond, speak to your daughter. Make her see what a ludicrous idea this is.'

'It looks pretty solid to me,' Des Oliphant said, looking around him.

'Des, don't encourage this ridiculousness!'

'Well, I…' Des began, sounding torn.

'The important thing is that I've found somewhere to live,' Emily cut in.

'Well, I *have* offered the caravan. It has all you need, and it's clean,' Enid said.

'I don't want the damn caravan,' Emily snapped, instantly disappointed with herself.

'Emily, language!'

'And what if you want to go off in it some time?' Emily added in an attempt to mollify her mother.

'Yes, well, I suppose that's a good point. And if this is only going to be temporary, I suppose it won't be quite so bad. I'd still put a bulldozer through it,' she added as she stepped gingerly into the hall.

Chapter Twenty-seven

Just as they were stowing the last of Emily's possessions on the verandah, the dark hovering clouds descended and opened up, delivering a heavy, prolonged downpour. There were even a few claps of thunder as the late spring storm made its way past. Emily, David and Des paused on the verandah, enjoying the change of temperature and the sound of the rain beating on the iron roof.

'Great,' David groaned. 'At this rate I'll never get harvest finished.'

'Have you got much left to do?' Des asked.

'About a third,' David replied. 'It's been so stop-start this year, thanks to the intermittent rain and cool weather; really frustrating when we've finally got a decent crop to reap. We're going to have a problem with shot grain if we get much more of this. Especially if there's a sudden burst of hot weather on top of it.'

'You farmers certainly have a lot to contend with,' Des said. 'I often used to think how lucky I was to have my regular council salary and be able to clock off properly at the end of each day.'

'In a way, I wouldn't actually mind if this turns into a hailstorm and wipes the rest of it out,' David said, nodding skywards. 'I'm insured for hail and it'll save me a hell of a lot of frustration and stuffing about.'

'Oh, really?' Des said.

'It'd make life a bit easier, that's all. But it's going to do what it's going to do. No point worrying about it. I reckon we should get into the roof space and check for leaks while it's raining,' David added, entering the hallway and grabbing his ladder.

'Good idea. Two pairs of eyes are better than one,' Des said, following him into the second bedroom on the southern side of the hall.

For about the twentieth time, Emily wondered if she was doing the right thing. She really hadn't given much thought to basics like a sound roof above her head. Fingers crossed it would all be okay. *Please don't let my mother be right*, she thought, glancing up at the creaking sounds above her head as the men now made their way inside the roof space.

Pity the drought has ended, really she thought, and instantly felt ashamed. People's livelihoods relied on rain. Except when they were meant to be harvesting, like now. The weather had become unseasonably cool and damp just when they wanted it warm and dry. Too dry, too wet, too windy, not enough breeze – there was always something for the farmers to be complaining about. And John had done more than his fair share.

Emily had been raised a townie; she'd only been a temporary farmer while married to John. And she hadn't really even been that – thanks to John's secrecy.

Townies knew the importance of good seasons to the district as a whole – both in terms of economics and emotional stability – but they didn't run out to check their rain gauge after every shower like the farmers seemed to.

She was distracted from her thoughts by her mother's raised voice coming from the kitchen, and then Barbara's normally low tone rising sharply above it.

'With all due respect, Mrs Oliphant – Enid – I think if Emily wants to do this then we, as her family and friends, should support her. The last thing she needs right now is more angst; she's suddenly alone, without a job, and with nowhere to live. She's picking herself up and sorting things out…'

'Well, she wouldn't be in this mess if she hadn't left John! And she has *family* for support, if only she'd ask for it!'

Emily cringed at her mother's words. She knew she should go in there and rescue Barbara, but couldn't make her feet move.

'And I'm of the opinion that a person's happiness and emotional wellbeing are the most important things,' Barbara continued. 'Now if you'll excuse me, there's something I need to get from outside.'

Barbara erupted from the kitchen and fled down the hall, clearly furious. Emily stepped aside to avoid being bowled over. But it was as if her friend hadn't even seen her.

Moments later, her perfectly composed mother entered the hall and strode purposefully towards the front door.

'I really wish you would reconsider. There is a perfectly good bed at home with your parents,' Enid said with a sniff.

Emily opened her mouth to reply, but closed it again. It didn't matter – she was already out the door and on her way to the ute. Anyway, what could she say? Her mother was right: she wouldn't be in this mess – setting up house in this dump – if she hadn't left John. And she *did* have family to rely on. She'd just rather not.

She was blinking and swallowing, furiously trying to stop the inevitable flood of tears, and telling herself she was just overtired and to stop feeling sorry for herself, when her father appeared at her side.

'I think you'll be all right – we couldn't find any major leaks.'

'Thanks Dad.'

'Of course, any time.' He paused. 'Are you okay? What happened?'

'Dad, you don't think I've done the wrong thing too, do you?'

'My opinion, or that of your mother, isn't what's important here, Em.'

'But what do you think?'

'Do you mean leaving John or moving here?'

'Both.'

'I think you've done the right thing. But as I said, your opinion is the only one that matters. Only you can decide what you're not prepared to live with and for whatever reason.'

Emily noticed his face cloud over slightly. But the expression was brief and he was soon back to his cheery self.

'I know it seems hard, but you'll see, everything will work itself out – it always does. It's the way the world works. Now, I'd better get your mother home – unless there's something else that needs doing immediately. I think a few days spent painting and sanding floors will bring her up quite a treat. Just let me know when you want me.'

'Thanks, I really appreciate it.'

'Better be off before your mother starts bellowing.' He gave her shoulders a quick squeeze, and was striding down the hall while Emily was still processing his words. He'd sounded so like Granny Mayfair she was suddenly a little unnerved.

Emily followed him to the front door. She felt strange, but couldn't put her finger on exactly how. Out on the verandah she waved to her parents as they turned the ute and trailer around and started down the long driveway.

Barbara and David appeared next to her.

'I'm exhausted,' Barbara said, sitting down.

'Me too,' Emily said, sinking down next to her on to the cracked, faded red-painted concrete of the verandah. It was quite dark due to the lingering storm clouds. She checked her watch – six o'clock.

'Are you sure you'll be okay here alone?' Barbara said.

'I won't be alone – I have Grace.'

'I know, but wouldn't you rather stay another night with us – have a nice soak in the bath before roughing it?'

'You're sounding like my mother,' Emily said, rolling her eyes.

'Sorry.'

'You've both been great and I really appreciate everything you've done, but I have to do this sooner or later – and I may as well start tonight.'

'Okay. But I'm going to miss you. And we're not far away – you only have to call.'

'Well, at least the power works and you have hot running water,' David added cheerfully. 'Hard to believe the old girl was so easy to start after being idle for so long. They certainly don't make things like they used to. And the roof doesn't seem to leak. We should get going so you can get well and truly settled before it gets dark.'

'Yes, you guys go,' Emily said, sounding more persuasive than she actually felt. She suddenly wasn't sure she liked the idea of being in the old house on her own after dark. 'And again, thanks for everything – I really couldn't have done this without you.'

'Well, I hope you'll still be thanking us tomorrow!' Barbara said.

Me too.

'Come on, dear.' David held his hand out to Barbara.

'Okay,' she said, accepting David's hand and easing herself onto her feet. 'Promise you'll ring or send a text first thing and let me know you're okay.'

'To let you know I didn't get eaten by giant mice or that the ghosts didn't strangle me, you mean?' Emily said with a laugh. 'Barbara, seriously, I'll be fine.' *I will be fine.*

'Just promise you'll call. Otherwise I'll be over here checking on you at nine.'

'Okay, I promise. Now go, before I set Grace on to you,' Emily said, making shooing motions with her hands.

They hugged and Emily watched as David, Barbara and Sasha made their way to the ute.

'See you,' they called as they drove away.

Emily waved and watched them until they were swallowed by the stand of gums. Then she turned and looked down the long empty hall. *Now what?* She suddenly felt the weight of the long night looming ahead of her.

Chapter Twenty-eight

Grace was whining at the gate and Emily went to let her out. Still feeling a little lost, she looked across to the west where the sun was disappearing behind the small group of hills that flanked the old shearing shed and smaller outbuildings. She hadn't yet explored beyond the immediate house.

It had all happened so fast. She and Barbara had spent the day inside focussing on making her comfortable. Only David had looked around outside. She suddenly remembered the key in her pocket. Leaving Grace in the house, Emily strode around the verandah to the locked door at the back, the one she figured was almost certainly the entrance to a cellar. She fished the key from her pocket and tried it in the lock.

It gave easily, but the door was another matter. It needed a hefty shove to budge, and when it did, the hinges gave a deep squeal that penetrated right to Emily's spine and caused her heart to quicken.

Right at that moment, the sun disappeared behind the hill, taking the last of the full light and sending long eerie shadows across the ground and house walls around her. The suddenness took Emily by surprise. She pulled the door closed, locked it, and bolted back around to the front door like a child trying to outrun her own shadow.

Back inside, with the front door shut and locked, she tried to laugh off her wildly pounding heart. Oblivious to her mistress's distress, Grace sniffed her way back and forth across the hall.

Jesus, Em, get a grip! Emily told herself with both hands on her chest. 'Right, getting a grip, getting a grip,' she muttered, squaring her shoulders. She went down to the kitchen. Despite being grimy and in need of a shower, there was no way she was going to sit out in the outhouse bathroom, vulnerable to the world. Instead she set about fossicking through the box of food Barbara and David had left.

Every few minutes she called Grace to her, hoping for some moral support. But after appearing obediently, the dog would trot off again when no further instructions were given, the click–click of her claws echoing through the empty house.

Emily rinsed her plate and cutlery at the sink, unable to see out the window because of the well-lit room behind her. Although she knew there'd be no one around to be looking in, the lack of blinds and curtains made her uneasy.

Just as she turned away there was a sharp piercing screech close by, followed by the unmistakeable flap of loose iron. Startled, her hand again flew to her chest. She turned slowly back to the window.

Something jagged flashed into view, and Emily leapt back without turning. She glanced towards the ceiling as wind whistled through the roof space above, causing the whole house to shudder and rumble. The loose iron flapped a few more times and settled back into silence. The jagged shapes came into view again at the window.

'Phew,' Emily sighed, letting her breath go. It was nothing more than a tree caught in a few gusts of wind. She stood with her hand across her heart, trying to take slow, deep, calming breaths. Grace wandered in and gave her a cursory glance, still seemingly unaware of her mistress's fear.

Emily watched the dog follow her nose, zigzagging her way across the kitchen. And then she saw it: the front half of a mouse poking out from under the cupboard.

Grace had seen it too. The dog skittered across the lino, sliding into the wall when she didn't have enough traction to stop. But the mouse was too quick. Grace whined and howled and scratched at the floor before Emily told her to stop.

Bloody hell, how many mice were hiding in shadows and crevices waiting for her to go to bed before coming out? And what if there were rats? How was she going to sleep now?

She could almost feel her skin crawl as she imagined the touch of small scratchy rodent feet, and those of the spiders and other insects that no doubt infested the old house. Why did everything have to be bloody nocturnal?

Emily let out a deep sigh. She was exhausted. It wasn't yet eight o'clock, and not even fully dark, but she didn't care. She went down to the room that she'd chosen for her bedroom, grabbed David's rolled up swag from the floor, and carried it back to the kitchen. There was no way she was sleeping on the floor – in any part of the house. But the huge kitchen table would make a perfect bed.

She paused at each light switch as she passed. Considering her fellow nocturnal inhabitants, Emily would have loved to leave the house ablaze, but she didn't want to risk a whopping power bill down the track.

She snuggled down into the swag fully dressed. Grace was lying quietly in her basket in the corner, with one eye on the cupboard where the mouse had appeared. As she lay there in the dark, Emily ran through the list of things she needed to do to be comfortable. But far from helping her sleep, she found it overwhelming.

Was her mother right – had she made a terrible mistake? Should she just swallow her pride and take up the offer of the caravan? *The holier-than-thou looks and comments would surely stop in a week, right?* Obviously it wasn't the best outcome, but it would be better than being eaten alive.

At least they hadn't wasted time, effort and money painting the whole house. *Maybe it isn't meant to be.*

But a question continued to niggle her. Which was worse? Being beholden to her mother or fending off a few rodents?

Some time later she woke with a start. It took her a moment to remember where she was. She had no idea what had woken her, but whatever it was had given both her and Grace a fright. Her heart was racing and Grace was whimpering.

Emily sat up, listening intently. Apart from a pounding pulse in her ears, her quick, shallow breaths and Grace's whimpering, the house was silent. There wasn't even any wind whistling or flapping iron to be heard. For the first time she realised just how eerie the silence was.

Then she heard a slight rustle on the floor over by the sink. *Probably the bloody mice*, Emily thought, but in the dark she had no way of knowing. She hadn't brought the torch up onto the table with her.

Or had she, and that was what had woken her? She cast her mind back. No, she'd left it on the bench by the sink. Perhaps that was what had woken her – it had fallen and then rolled a little as it settled. *Yes, that's it*, Emily reassured herself.

'It's okay, Gracie, just a little noise – go back to sleep.' But as she lay there, trying to talk herself back to sleep, Emily found herself wondering how the heavy torch could have fallen off the bench. And why not when she'd first put it there? Mice?

Bloody hell, she thought suddenly, her heart beginning to race again. *What if the house is haunted?*

She sat up again and looked around – for what, she wasn't sure. The first grey signs of morning were shining through the window over the sink and the glass-panelled doors out to the verandah.

She rubbed her eyes. They felt swollen, burning and gravel-filled. Had she slept at all? She certainly didn't feel like it. But the prospect of daylight chased the nighttime demons away. She felt ridiculously childish. There was no way she could tell Barbara how scared she'd been – it was just a silly noise.

Emily got up and opened one of the French doors, keeping the bolt on the second in place. 'Come on, Gracie, do you want to go out?'

But the dog didn't budge from her bed in the corner.

She looked back across the room to the sink. The torch was still there, exactly as she'd left it.

She frowned. Was something missing? What else had she left there? She went through the brief inventory – plate, cup, cutlery, water bottle, esky. Then she noticed something on the floor right near the end of the bench.

'Oh no!' She crossed to where jagged, broken pieces of glass stuck up like icebergs amongst a multicoloured scattering of buttons – Gran's buttons. Grace appeared beside her.

'Get away, you'll cut yourself,' she snapped, and pushed the dog away. She picked up a piece of glass and dropped it again quickly when it stung her. Blood sprung from her finger. Emily crossed her legs, put her head in her hands, and began to cry.

Chapter Twenty-nine

'What's happened? Are you okay?'

Emily looked up to find Barbara rushing through the open kitchen door. 'Yeah, I'm okay,' she said.

'There's glass everywhere. You're bleeding!'

'I'm fine. It's only a tiny cut on my finger,' she said, holding her hand up. 'I'm just sitting here feeling sorry for myself.' She tried to get up, but faltered.

'You certainly are *not* okay,' Barbara said, grabbing her friend's arm to steady her.

'No, seriously, my legs have probably just gone to sleep,' she said, accepting Barbara's help.

'How long have you been sitting here?'

Emily replied with a shrug.

'Where's Grace?' Barbara asked, looking around. The dog was in her basket, looking at them over her paws.

'Oh, Gracie, come here, I'm sorry,' Emily called.

The dog stayed where she was.

'What's wrong with her?'

'I told her off. Oh, I feel terrible. Please Gracie, come on. Mummy's sorry.'

'What did you tell her off about?' Barbara helped Emily into the nearest chair.

'I was worried she'd cut herself, but I overreacted – probably because I barely had any sleep.'

'Join the club,' Barbara said with a smirk. 'I didn't sleep a wink worrying about you here on your own – hence my arrival at sparrow fart. I haven't even had a coffee yet. Let's put the kettle on.'

Barbara busied herself at the sink and Emily tried to coax Grace over. Eventually the dog cautiously crossed the lino to her mistress's side, giving the mess on the floor a wide berth. After considerable cooing and grovelling and lots of affection from Emily, she returned to her bed, curled up and went to sleep.

'Looks like someone else had a rough night,' Barbara said, nodding at Grace as she waited for Emily to fold the swag over and dump it on the floor. She put the mugs down in front of them. 'So, tell me, what happened?'

'It's the button jar.'

'Did you drop it?'

'No, I don't know what happened. I'm pretty sure it was on the bench.'

'It was, unless you moved it last night. I put it there myself.'

'No idea how, but it must have fallen off. It scared the living crap out of us. Of course, last night we didn't know what the bang was. And when I found it broken it just set me off. I should have just left it in the suitcase.' *Why didn't I?* 'It's silly to be so upset – it's only a glass jar full of buttons, for goodness sake,' she said, sipping her coffee.

'Darling, it's not about the jar, or the buttons; it's the symbolism. Don't think I haven't noticed how special that jar is – *was* – to you. It was the first thing you took out of your suitcase when you came to stay. And when you got here.'

Emily nodded. 'It was Gran's.'

'Oh. In that case you're probably feeling like you've lost her all over again. And it doesn't help that you're stressed and really tired. You need to be a bit easier on yourself. So how do you think it fell off, anyway? I left it well back from the edge.'

'That's last night's big mystery – mice, probably. Hence the swag on the table.'

'Ooh, yuck! But hang on. It was heavy; you'd need an army of them to budge it, let alone push it off the edge.'

'Well, there are probably quite a few, but I don't think enough to qualify as an *army*.'

Barbara looked down at the buttons and the remains of the jar, then turned back to Emily. 'Shit, you don't think the place is haunted, do you?'

'I bloody well hope not. No, I think Grace would be more unsettled if there was something weird she couldn't see.'

'What else could it have been?'

'The only thing I can think of – and it makes my skin crawl to even think about it – is rats.'

'If there were rats, I'm sure your dad and David would have found droppings in the roof yesterday.'

'Maybe they just didn't say anything in case I freaked out.'

'No. David would have told me, and we would have taken steps to quietly remedy the situation,' she added with conspiratorial raised eyebrows.

'So you don't have a boot full of rat traps and baits outside, then?'

'Nope.' Barbara returned her attention to her coffee. 'I guess we'll never know.'

'Maybe it's a sign.'

'Of what?'

'That I'm not meant to be here.'

'Em, if you've changed your mind, you only have to say. Just because we helped you move in, doesn't mean you have to stay. We'd move you ten times if we needed to, because you're our friend and we want you to be happy – well, maybe not ten, but definitely five. So don't go *looking* for signs that you're not meant to be here, all right?'

Emily let out a loud sigh. 'Thanks. It means a lot; you mean a lot – both of you.'

'Having said that, could you give us a few days to recover?' Barbara said, laughing.

The both sipped at their coffees in silence.

'Right. First things first, I think we should put the buttons somewhere safe while we look for another jar. Then we're going to write a list for the day, and do what we can to make tonight better. That is, if you want to stay,' Barbara said.

'What's a few mice and cockroaches, right?' Emily shrugged, grimacing.

'Well, I could remind you of bubonic plague and a multitude of other bacterial diseases, but that really wouldn't be very helpful, now would it?'

'No, but speaking of which, I really need a shower – I was too scared to go out there last night.'

'I thought I could smell something,' Barbara said, grinning.

'Oh, ha ha.'

'Only kidding. Now, you go and have a shower. I'll tidy up the buttons and then start on the list.'

'Thanks.'

'I've found the house's redeeming feature,' Emily said, returning to the kitchen. 'That shower is to die for. I had trouble getting out.'

'I noticed,' Barbara said.

'Sorry I took so long.'

'No probs. I put the buttons in that ice-cream container up there,' she said, pointing to the top of the pantry cupboard beside the kitchen window.

'Thanks. Did you manage to get most of the glass out?'

'Yes, but I wouldn't go rummaging around in there with my bare hands. Funny the things people put in button jars,' she added musingly.

'Like, er, buttons?'

'No, other than buttons, silly.'

'Like what?'

'Marbles, belt buckles, paperclips, pebbles, shells, that sort of thing.'

'Really, in Gran's in particular?'

'Yes, didn't you know?'

'No, I never saw her take the lid off. She always bought new buttons if she needed one.'

'How bizarre.'

'I wonder when Gran took it off last. Must have been in the last ten years – since she had Alzheimer's – if there's weird stuff in there.'

'You know, there are some really old-looking military-style buttons. I wonder if they're worth anything,' Barbara said.

'Doesn't matter; I wouldn't want to sell them anyway. You didn't chuck anything out, did you?' Emily asked, suddenly feeling anxious.

'Of course not. I agree with you: it's like a complete collection.'

'You know, having a few weird things in there sort of completes it,' said Emily. 'Like it's a representation of her whole life or something. I love that.'

'I've left the lid and large pieces of glass on top so you'll know exactly what jar it was. It's got Bushells printed on the glass. It can't be too rare or old, so I'm sure you'll find another one eventually.'

'I hope so – I want it just how it was,' Emily said.

'Now, I've made a list for…'

'Hey, before we get into that, can you come and check out the cellar with me? I was too scared to go down there on my own last night as well. That key we found by the oven does fit the lock.'

'Girl, you've really gotta toughen up.'

'I know.'

They made their way outside, around the verandah to the door on the far corner of the house. When they got there, Emily turned the key in the lock and put her shoulder against the door. The hinges groaned in protest.

'Spooky,' Barbara said. 'I don't blame you for not wanting to be out here in the dark.'

Emily ran her hand up and down the doorframe, searching for a light switch before holding out her hand for the torch.

'Ah, here it is,' she said, finally locating it a few inches further across on the wall. She stood aside so they could both see. A large space stretched out below them, illuminated by a single bulb.

'Wow, it's huge,' Barbara said, making her way down the brick steps.

'Watch out for spiderwebs and creepy-crawlies,' Emily warned.

'Too late,' Barbara said, pausing to drag a dusty mess from her hair and shoulders.

They reached the bottom and looked around. Red brick walls loomed large around them. Solid timber joists ran across the room a metre or two above their heads, holding up the floor of the house. Freestanding wooden shelves stood along half of one of the long walls. Except for the absence of painted plaster and ceilings, and the lack of windows, the space was not unlike the rooms upstairs.

'It's even got a fireplace,' Emily said, gazing about in awe.

'And a paved floor,' Barbara said, moving some dirt with her foot.

'But why would you need a fireplace in a cellar?' Emily asked.

'To keep warm?'

'I know that, but wouldn't the cellar have been used for keeping vegetables and preserves cool and dark?'

'No idea.'

'It must go under half of the house.'

'No, I think this is only under the lounge-dining room, otherwise we'd be able to see the foundations. And that's about the right place to share the chimney. You know, this would absolutely make the best space for a little restaurant,' Barbara continued.

'My head's spinning.'

'With excitement, I hope.'

'Not exactly. I feel overwhelmed, a bit depressed.'

'Depressed? Are you crazy? This is a brilliant find.'

Emily took a seat halfway up the stairs. 'Because it's not mine, and at the rate things are going it never will be. I have no money and no job. And even if I did, the brothers don't want to sell, anyway.'

'Only one doesn't want to sell, remember? And you're about to get forty grand from John.'

'This place might be worth hundreds of thousands. And I'd need that much again to do it up.'

'Perhaps there's a sackful of cash stuffed up the chimney.'

'Then it would belong to the Bakers, wouldn't it?'

'Stop being a negative ninny. It doesn't hurt to dream,' Barbara said, sitting two steps below Emily. 'Just imagine: beautifully dressed tables with candles everywhere, a fire burning, the buzz of conversation…'

'I can't, it's too depressing – I want it now,' Emily said, burying her head in her hands.

'All good things come to those who wait.'

'You sound like Gran,' Emily groaned.

'I'll take that as a compliment. Anyway, it's true. Just because you can't see the dream, doesn't mean you should give up on it. If it's meant to be, it will be.'

'That's fine for you to say.'

'True passion is fulfilled eventually,' Barbara continued. 'Meanwhile you live one day at a time – by the hour, if it's a bad day. So, let's just focus on getting you comfortable and settled. If you're careful, your money will easily last eighteen months, so look at it as taking a year off. You've earned it putting up with John.'

'What would I do without you?' Emily said, leaning down and putting her arms around her friend's shoulders.

'I don't know, go mad? Seriously, please stop stressing about the future so much. This should be an exciting time – you're free to figure out what you really want from life.'

'I'll try.'

'No, you'll *do*. You realise all this means John still has a major hold over you?'

'What do you mean?'

'Well, only by being happy and successful will he stop controlling you – and before you say anything, success isn't just about money. You may have got away from him, but if you don't dare to dream and strive for those dreams, he's still in control. Same goes for your mother.'

Emily sat back. 'I hadn't thought of it like that.'

'Well, it's time you did. Anyway, enough of the psychobabble; we need to get cracking with that to do list,' Barbara said, slapping her knees and getting up. They climbed back up the steps and walked around to the kitchen door.

'Okay, so what should we do first?' Emily asked, looking around her.

'Well, if you're to get a decent night's sleep, we need to get rid of the mice and seal up the house as best we can. I vote we go into town and get some baits and steel wool for closing up the gaps.'

'Good idea. I also want to see if the op shop has any fabric or curtains that will fit these windows. And I need some groceries. I'm also going to need a small fridge, a washing machine, crockery, cutlery, vacuum cleaner … God, it's making my head spin.'

'Lucky I've got the ute! Why don't you put Gracie out in the yard and I'll meet you round the front.'

Chapter Thirty

'Hey, is that an orchard up there by the creek?' Barbara asked when Emily joined her at the ute.

'I'm not sure – I haven't been up there to check it out yet.'

'They're the wrong colour to be natives.'

'Hmm, I agree. We'll have to take a look when we get back.'

'Almost everyone had an orchard in the old days,' Barbara continued, turning the key and starting the vehicle. 'Back then it would have been a long trip to town, so they'd have made a lot of their own produce.'

'I wouldn't mind making some jam.'

For the first time Emily thought about how far she was from town. It was one thing for her and Barbara to take the backroads in the ute, but guests probably wouldn't be keen to drive that far on gravel or rubble.

Emily's mobile began to ring and she started frantically rummaging in her bag. She answered without checking the caller ID.

'Hello, Emily speaking.'

'Hi Em, it's Dad.'

'Oh, hi Dad, how are you?'

'Fine, fine. Listen, the Buckleys have sold their shack and are cleaning it out this morning. The family picked through most of the good stuff, but they're practically giving everything else away, if you're interested.'

'Like what?'

'Well, there's an old fridge, small top-loading washing machine, vacuum cleaner, double bed, a pair of singles … What do you think, can you use anything?'

'Er, everything you just mentioned,' Emily said with a laugh. 'How much are they asking?'

'Don't you worry about it, it'll be my treat.'

'Really? Are you sure?'

'Quite. I can't guarantee the height of fashion or anything, but it all looks pretty clean and functional. You can replace it later, when things improve, but I thought it would make a start.'

'Thanks Dad, it'll be a big help.'

'I'll load up the trailer and bring it out tomorrow if you'll be home – say, in the morning?'

'Perfect.'

'I hope it will all meet with your approval – but at least if it's only temporary, it won't matter so much.'

'I'm sure it will be fine,' Emily said. *I'm not my mother.* 'See you then – and Dad, thanks so much.' She hung up and turned to stare at Barbara with wide eyes. 'Wow!'

'I take it that was your father?' Barbara said.

'Yes, and we can cross fridge, washing machine, bed and vacuum cleaner off our list. Apparently the Buckleys are cleaning out their shack and practically giving their stuff away.'

'Brilliant. That'll save some money.'

'I'm taking a bit of a punt though, aren't I, trusting Dad to furnish my house?'

'At least this way you can take your time to find things you really love when you can afford them.'

'I got the impression Mum wasn't with him. Otherwise it wouldn't be happening – she can't cope with second-hand. *Fancy using a washing machine someone else has used!*' Emily added, mimicking her mother's critical tone.

'Not to mention a bed,' Barbara said.

'No worries, I'll just get a mattress protector. Honestly, Barbara, I'm just pleased I don't have to waste money buying all those boring but necessary appliances. I was all set to give the old mangle out in the washhouse a go.'

'Atta girl,' Barbara said, patting her friend's leg. 'Okay, so let's focus on groceries and dealing with the vermin today, and leave furnishing the house for another trip. And I've just thought of another thing for the list,' she added. 'You'd better organise a post box and a redirection from the one you shared with John.'

'Gosh, I hadn't even thought of that.'

'And once you've done that, you'll have to let people know your new address – starting with the bank.'

'Shit, it's suddenly so real. The whole town will know by tomorrow.'

'Sweetie, it's been almost a week; the whole town already knows.'

Emily's legs were shaking when she walked into the bank. Barbara waited just inside the door, pretending to read the sales brochures on the rotating display stand. Emily let out a sigh of relief as a teller whom she'd known since high school approached the counter to serve her.

'Hi Sam.' She handed him her keycard and, trying to sound cheerful, said, 'I'd like to change my address details, please – for both the accounts linked to that card.'

The teller looked at her and then at the card. His face clouded slightly, and then he blushed. He cleared his throat and then spoke in an unusually formal tone.

'I'm afraid I will need your, uh, husband's permission to make any changes.'

Emily's face reddened and she began to sweat. The counter beneath her palms became slippery. 'I'm sorry. What did you say?'

'Emily, John was in on Friday,' Sam said, softening slightly before recovering his bank-teller demeanour. 'He informed us of your, uh, separation, and as the main account holder he froze all joint accounts.'

'But these are *my* accounts – in my name only – and nothing to do with John.' She wanted to sound bold and forceful, but her voice came out as little more than a whine.

'Oh, well, oh, I'm terribly sorry. Let me just make those adjustments for you, then.' Sam's slight flush turned to blazing deep strawberry.

Not trusting herself to speak, Emily handed over the piece of paper she'd written her new post box number on.

'Right, all done,' Sam said brightly after a few taps on his keyboard. 'Is there anything else I can help you with today?'

'No, thank you,' Emily said through clenched teeth. She turned on her heel and was mortified to find the small bank now full of waiting customers. They all looked down at the carpet on seeing her. Emily wanted to both dissolve into tears and snap at them to mind their own bloody business. But she just fled, with Barbara close behind.

'I've never been so humiliated,' she said, leaning on the handrail outside to try to calm down.

'You might need to prepare yourself for things to get worse before they get better,' Barbara said quietly.

A few minutes later they were walking into Mitre 10.

'Hi Grant, hi Steve,' Emily called to a couple of locals, forcing a business-as-usual tone into her voice. Both men dipped their heads, grunted, and continued walking through the shop. They were agronomists from the Department of Agriculture, and normally they would both have stopped and passed comment on the rainfall or weather.

Emily looked at Barbara, who returned raised eyebrows. The sad thing about Grant and Steve snubbing her was that they had known each other since high school, well before she had married John. Where was the loyalty?

But they were being loyal, weren't they? To their jobs. John was a client, which was more important than a mere long-term friendship. She'd seen it before – the town dividing and then settling around whichever party the consensus chose to support. She just never dreamed she'd be on the wrong side of the division.

She was born and bred here too, but John was a farmer – even better, a male farmer – and they had all the power. She was just a townie, and a woman at that.

'Come on, let's just get what we need and get out of here,' Barbara said, pulling at her friend's arm.

It took a lot longer than it should have to find what they wanted because no one rushed to their side to lend assistance. And they were feeling too self-conscious to ask. Emily was glad Barbara was in charge of their list because her eyes were beginning to blur.

Finally they were ready to pay. As they joined the short queue, the hushed whispers being exchanged around them fell silent, but the stares remained. Barbara offered Emily a grim, buoying smile. Emily didn't want to think about how much harder this would be without her support.

'Hi Kate, just these, please,' she said, feigning brightness as she put three mouse traps and a big box of steel wool onto the counter.

Kate, another old school friend, turned beetroot red.

'On savings, thanks,' Emily added, handing over her keycard.

'Oh, right. Great, thanks,' Kate said, accepting the card with obvious relief.

'I'm assuming John has already been in and my name is no longer on the account because we've separated?' Emily's voice was loud enough to be heard by everyone in the immediate vicinity. She reddened for the third time that morning, but this time she was more angry than embarrassed.

She put the receipt and her card away while Barbara gathered up their bag of goodies. They turned away from the counter and glared at the next person in line, who happened to be Grant. Steve was next to him. Emily gave him a second, extra hard glare.

'You shouldn't be so quick to judge without the facts – one day this could be you,' she snapped.

And then she and Barbara hurried from the store and across the road to Barbara's ute.

'Well done you,' Barbara said, rubbing her friend's shoulder once they were safely inside the vehicle.

'Now I've humiliated myself even more,' Emily said, burying her head in her hands.

'I don't think that's possible.'

Emily frowned at her.

'Seriously, you stood up for yourself and that took a lot of guts. These towns are great at bonding together for support during a bushfire, but God, they can be cruel too.'

'I wonder how long it will take for the gossip to die down.'

'It might not seem like it, but I'm sure there's other stuff people are discussing. Like John, for instance – he's bound to be attracting his fair share.'

'As the bloody victim, no doubt. "Poor John. Did you hear? His wife walked out, leaving him to pack all that meat away on his own?"' Emily found herself grinning despite herself.

'That's the spirit,' Barbara said, playing along. '"Thank goodness that good sort Stacy turned up to help him out."'

'Lucky that,' Emily said, chuckling.

'I wonder who they've got you shacked up with,' Barbara said. 'It'll have to be someone, because you'd never leave such a good catch of your own accord.'

'Your husband, probably,' Emily said. 'They're probably all in the pub marvelling about how lucky David is to be having three-somes every night.'

'Eww!'

'Yes, eww! But seriously, I hope David won't be in the firing line for helping me.'

'David can handle himself. He's lived here his whole life too, remember – he knows how it works.'

'I can tell you it still comes as a rude shock.'

'One of the things I love most about David is that he doesn't succumb to peer pressure. He's content to be his own man. He'll be fine – we both will – so don't you worry, and don't you dare go feeling guilty on our account.'

'Thanks Barb, you're the best.' They turned towards each other and hugged for a few moments before breaking away.

'Ready to tackle the supermarket?'

'Have to sooner or later; may as well be sooner.'

Chapter Thirty-one

'Wow, that was...' Emily started, as she shut the ute door behind her.

'Interesting? Harrowing? Exhilarating?' Barbara suggested.

'All of the above. I wonder if they've got online ordering and home delivery yet. I sure as hell don't want to go through that every week.'

'It'll get better. Just remember, you've done nothing wrong. And if you really can't cope, I'll do your shopping for you.'

'Thanks, but I'm sure I'll be fine. Wasn't it you who said I had to toughen up?'

'Sorry about that,' Barbara said, looking a little sheepish.

'Don't be. You're right. I can't waste the next fifty years feeling sorry for myself and worrying about what is or isn't being said about me.'

'That's my girl. Now, let's get back and see how Grace has coped on her own.'

'You know, I think it's a first for her – hope she isn't pining too much.'

Barbara started the vehicle.

'I still can't believe old Mrs Schilling had the nerve to tell me to my face that if I'd read my Bible, my marriage wouldn't have ended,' Emily said as they left the main township.

'I thought she was going to have a stroke when you asked her which passage, exactly, she was referring to. You should have seen your face – it was priceless.'

'I guess she deserves points for being up-front.'

'For a moment she probably thought she'd found a new recruit for the church auxiliary.'

'I did feel a little mean telling her the one thing I liked about God was that he kept his opinions to himself.'

'Oh well, you weren't *really* rude, and you did give her such a lovely smile.'

'I just wish it had been a more even contest – like someone nearer my own age.'

'So, you survived your first trip into the lion's den.'

'I did, didn't I?' Emily's mobile began to ring. 'Can you believe it, it doesn't ring for days and now I've had two calls in a couple of hours.' She retrieved the device from her handbag. 'It's my cousin Elizabeth,' she told Barbara just before she answered. 'Hi Liz.'

'Hi Em. I hear you left John and moved into an absolute dump! Well done you!'

For a moment she wasn't sure how to respond. Was Liz being serious?

'Are you okay?'

'As good as can be expected, I suppose.'

'Well, congratulations! You've done the right thing. Life's too short to be miserable.'

'Thanks. I take it you've been told to try and talk me out of my silliness?'

'Yep. You do realise there's a perfectly good caravan going begging, don't you?' she replied, doing a fine impersonation of Emily's mother.

'So I've heard. Were you also charged with getting me to return to my husband?'

'That was probably part of the instructions from your mum to mine, but mine wouldn't have had the nerve to pass it on, what with her own daughter's, quote, "embarrassing refusal to settle down".'

'Well, consider your duty done. So, how is life in the big city?'

'Hectic as usual – way too much fine dining, attending art exhibition openings, and definitely way too much champagne. I haven't had a night in for at least a month.'

'You're sounding like an A-lister.'

'I wish,' Liz groaned. 'I'm only about C, I'm afraid. But seriously, Em, what's the story with the old house? Is it really as bad as Mum says?'

'Your mum hasn't even seen it. But probably. Still, at one hundred dollars a week it's all I can afford at the moment.'

'God, you don't even get a car space for that over here! So is it a huge old farmhouse?'

'Pretty big. Not *huge*; it's a typical double-fronted house. Around nineteen-thirties vintage. Three bedrooms, lounge-dining room, kitchen...'

'Brilliant, there'll be somewhere for me to stay when I visit!'

'Liz, you never visit!'

'Well, I might.'

'Yeah, right.'

'Actually, I might. I met up with an old friend the other week. He's...'

'He, huh?'

'Yes, *he*, but nothing romantic – we're just friends. Anyway, he mentioned wanting to get out bush to take some photos – he's a keen photographer. So could he, or we, stay some time?'

'Sure, if you don't mind roughing it. The motel in town might be a safer bet.'

'I don't know about that – I stayed there before, remember? Anyway, by the time we get around to visiting you'll probably have a thriving B&B. We might be your first paying customers!'

'Liz, I'm only renting. And anyway, I don't have enough money to set myself up, let alone open a B&B.'

'What do you mean? I thought John was well-off. Isn't he from, like, the richest family in the district?'

'Apparently not,' Emily said with a sigh.

'What, no cheque for half a mil?'

'Try forty thousand.'

'What, that's all he's offering?! No, surely not.'

'Afraid so. And I've accepted. It's a done deal.'

'A lawyer let you agree to that? You need a better one – I can give you a couple of names…'

'Liz, it's done. I know I've probably been shafted, but I just want to get on with my life.'

'But how are you going to live? There can't be that many jobs out there, what with the GFC and all.'

'It's nowhere near as expensive as living in Melbourne. I'll be fine.'

'Well, if you need any money – don't tell Mum, but I've got a bit stashed away – I'm happy to lend it to you. After all, you're family. And I know where you live.'

'Actually, you don't,' Emily said with a laugh.

Liz laughed also. 'You're right. But I know where your *parents* live. Which, remember, is the reason for my call. Now, just so I don't have to lie to my mother, or yours, please, please, *please*, Emily, would you reconsider the offer of the caravan and give up this ridiculous notion of independence?'

'No. And thanks for the offer, it means a lot. But I'll be fine.'

'Right. Okay then, I'll go.'

'Thanks for the call, Liz. It's good to hear from you.'

'Same from me. And remember, I'm here if you need anything at all. You just have to ask. I'm not really into plastering walls and painting, but I have an address book full of people who are!'

'I'll just charter a private plane to fly them in then, shall I?' Emily said, chuckling again.

'Better yet, I'll get Jeeves to fuel mine up – just give me the word. And if you need me to sort out a kneecapping, you have my number. See ya! Speak to you again soon.'

'Thanks Liz. See ya.' Emily hung up, laughing. She loved the way they could still banter back and forth, even though they rarely caught up these days.

'That sounded like a good call,' Barbara said.

'Yeah, guess who's asked her to talk me out of my, quote, "ridiculous notion of independence"?'

'She didn't try very hard.'

'No. She rolls her eyes at them as much as I do.'

'She must be fun. She's got you laughing properly for the first time in days.'

'Yeah, she can be hilarious.'

'I didn't mean to eavesdrop, but was she offering you money?'

'Yeah, but I told her I'm fine.'

'That's the spirit, Em. With an attitude like that, you really will be. You just have to keep telling yourself.'

'I know,' Emily said thoughtfully. They remained silent as they drove the last section of the long driveway, turned the corner, and passed beneath the canopy of trees.

'Hey, where's Grace?' Emily said as they pulled up in front of the house. 'It doesn't look like she's in the yard. God, I hope she hasn't got into the Bakers' sheep,' she added, starting to feel concern creep in. They sat for a moment, scanning what they could see of the large fenced-off yard.

'Perhaps she's asleep under a tree, or on the back verandah in the sun,' Barbara said, getting out of the vehicle. Emily followed.

'Hang on, here she is,' Emily said, relief surging through her as the dog appeared at the gate and gave a yawn and a stretch before beginning to wag her tail. She rushed over, let Grace out, and ruffled her silky ears affectionately. 'Did you miss us, sleepyhead?'

They proceeded to unload everything from the ute into the house.

'Let's get the cold stuff into the esky,' Barbara called, carrying the two bags of ice they'd collected along the way. Emily followed her with the groceries. She hoped her father was indeed bringing a fridge tomorrow. In the meantime there was a spare esky for the non-cold items – it was probably the only thing mice couldn't get into.

'I need a cuppa before I can do anything else,' Barbara said, sitting down at the table once the groceries had been stored.

'I can't wait to sleep in a real bed again,' Emily said, glancing at the swag in the corner while she waited for the kettle to boil. 'Not that I don't appreciate the swag,' she added. She wondered how many mice had been in it since it had been on the floor.

'I know what you meant,' Barbara said, waving the comment away with a flap of her hand.

'I can't believe how weary I am – and I haven't done anything today yet,' Emily said, putting the mugs down on the table and slumping into the nearest chair.

'All the anguish over facing the townsfolk for the first time. That's why we're having a sit down and a cuppa – to gather our energy for some real work.'

'Slave driver.'

'You bet. If I know you're safe from the mice and other critters then maybe I'll sleep tonight,' Barbara said with a laugh.

'I'm so tired I probably won't even notice them.'

They ate a few Tim Tams from the packet on the table. Emily never usually indulged in chocolate biscuits, but Barbara had bought them as a treat to give them extra energy. They certainly went down well, Emily thought, crunching her way through her second.

'We can have the last of the zucchini slice for lunch – unless you want to keep it for your dinner.'

'No, that's fine. I'll just heat a tin of soup on the stove. Which reminds me, I should have told Dad I need a microwave as well. I can't believe I forgot to put it on the list.'

'It'll take you ages to stop thinking of things you need. Everything you do and every recipe you make will remind you of something you don't have. Just keep a list handy. Anyway, we can heat up the slice in the oven – it's what they did before microwaves, you know. And David did check it was in working order.'

'You know, that man of yours is an absolute gem.'

'I do, which is why I have to be back home by five-thirty. He's going to an Ag Bureau meeting and needs to take a plate.'

'I wonder if I'll ever find Mr Right,' Emily said wistfully.

'Of course you will. When the time is right, he'll just pop up. Chances are it'll be when you least expect him to.'

'Is that how it happened with you and David?'

'Pretty much. You just have to be in the right place – emotionally, I mean. It's weird the way it seems to work. When it's the last thing on your mind, it just happens.'

'Well it *is* the last thing on my mind because right now it's the last thing I want.'

'Don't worry, the universe knows that.'

'Well, I wish the damn universe knew how much I hate filthy rodents!'

'Come on, let's at least see what we're dealing with. I vote we start in here and see if we can mouse-proof the cupboards.'

'It's like a bloody open highway in here,' Barbara said a few minutes later from inside the cupboard under the sink. 'There's a gap all the way round the pipes. This is probably their major access point. Pass the steel wool and scissors. And while I do this, why don't you check the other cupboards?'

It took Emily two minutes. The other cupboards were free of gaps and, thankfully, free of droppings. She felt a little guilty at having Barbara do all the work.

'Right,' Barbara said, emerging from under the sink. 'Hopefully that'll do the trick.'

'As much as I hate setting and emptying traps, I think I'd rather that than the smell of corpses I can't find. And I don't want Grace getting poisoned.'

'Fair enough. That can be plan B. Let's just do a quick check of the rest of the house for gaps. It doesn't look like it's ever had wall-to-wall carpet, so hopefully the skirting boards go right to the floor. That's where the gaps usually are.'

They enjoyed a late lunch of leftover zucchini slice and wilted salad.

'Well, I think we've done enough for today,' Barbara said, putting their plates in the sink. 'But before I go, I want to take a walk up the gully and see if that is an orchard.'

The gully was steeper than it looked from the house, and Emily and Barbara were a little breathless and red-faced when they got to the top. They stopped in a gravelly clearing that was obviously a creekbed and discovered a couple of dozen different fruit trees. The trees had definitely been hand-planted, likely decades before. Their branches were sprawling and gnarly, and tall weeds grew against their thick trunks.

Despite the obvious signs of neglect, there was an abundance of ripe and ripening fruit: apricots, peaches, nectarines. Others had finished or were yet to fruit.

Emily recognised a plum tree with just a few remnants of fruit pulp hanging from seeds still attached; clearly a favourite with the local birdlife. There was a large fig tree off to the side and what looked like a few different varieties of citrus – though without seeing the fruit, it was impossible to tell. It seemed like the typical old-fashioned home-gardener's orchard, designed to have fresh fruit available for most of the year.

'Fine looking crop of apricots, considering they probably don't get hand-watered,' Barbara said.

'I wonder if they'd mind me using the fruit.'

'I wouldn't have thought so. These trees don't look like they've had any attention for years. It's probably the first time they've fruited in a few years too, because of the drought,' Barbara said, plucking an apricot and taking a bite.

Emily followed her lead.

'Oh, yum,' they said in unison, and then laughed.

They munched their way through a couple of apricots each, oohing and ahhing and groaning with delight at each bite.

Chapter Thirty-two

Emily waved Barbara off from the front verandah before going back inside. She made a cup of tea and sat down at the kitchen table, feeling unsure of how to occupy herself.

She was keen to make some jam – damn those were good apricots – but it was too late in the day to start picking fruit. She couldn't leave them in buckets in case there were mice still lurking about. Not that she had any buckets to put them in, anyway.

She'd had such a busy, emotion-filled day with Barbara that it seemed odd and a little unsettling to once again be alone. Though when she thought about it, why was this evening any different to the many John had spent at the pub, leaving her at home alone while he got up to goodness knows what with goodness knows who?

The difference now was that she didn't have to go to bed with the slight edge of apprehension as to what state and mood he would be in when he climbed in beside her. And what he'd want from her.

Here she was free. Broke and lonely, and with few of the home comforts she'd learnt to take for granted, but free nonetheless.

Would he come looking for her? Again threaten her not to tell tales out of school? Of course he'd know where she was living – nothing in this district stayed a secret very long. Not that it was a secret.

Given her experience that morning, it was clear to whom the town had declared its allegiance. But would it support him if everyone knew John had shacked up with someone else so soon? Surely that would go against the fine moral standards they liked to pride themselves on.

Silly even giving it thought. Attitudes hadn't changed in the last hundred years – John Stratten's wife had abandoned him and he had needs to be met. And he was a farmer. End of story.

Emily found herself wondering about her replacement, Stacy. She realised she knew nothing about her. Who was this girl? Did she realise what she was getting into by involving herself with John?

Emily shook her head to try to get rid of the anger threatening to overwhelm her. She forced herself instead to think about turning the fruit from the orchard into jam, and was instantly calmer. She loved to cook when she had time to relax into it. And she had plenty of time on her hands.

Then she remembered all the jars she'd collected over the years. Not to mention her large pans. They had all ended up staying with John. They hadn't been boxed up and in the bottom of the trailer like she'd hoped. At the time she'd been disappointed, but now she was downright annoyed. But there was no way in hell she'd give him the satisfaction of asking for them back.

Emily wondered if Stacy would be using her things to make her own jam. The trees at home – correction, John's place – would be overflowing.

'Come on, Gracie, let's lock up and have something to eat,' she said. Her voice reverberated through the almost-empty house.

It would be good to have some curtains and more furniture to soak up the sound.

Emily went through the house to check all the doors were locked. It made the place a little stuffy, but she wasn't game to leave them open. She wasn't sure what exactly she was keeping out – there was no one around for miles and she'd hear and see a car well before it turned up. But it made her feel safer.

Later that night as she lay in the swag, again rolled out on the table, Emily pondered the problem of acquiring jars for jam. The only place to come to mind was the op shop. But it was a long shot and it meant going into town again. She sighed.

Barbara was probably right when she said that people don't think about you nearly as much as you think they do. Yes, she'd brave the town again soon, but only because it was a means to an end – the peace of spending a few pleasant days holed up in the kitchen.

That was the trouble with fruit trees: all the fruit was ready at once and you had to beaver away before it went to waste. If only someone could breed species that would stagger their produce over a couple of months. That was the last thought Emily had as she drifted into sleep.

Emily sat up quickly, startled from a deep sleep. Her mobile phone was vibrating and ringing over on the bench. It was still grey out the kitchen window, but morning was obviously on its way in.

Her heart was racing as she leapt out of the swag and off the table. In her experience, unexpected calls at unusual times of the day and night only brought bad news.

'Hello, Emily speaking,' she rasped.

'Em, it's Barbara. Sorry to call so early.'

'What time is it?'

'Six-thirty-ish.'

Wow, she'd actually managed to sleep right through. Emily peered out the window again. The sky was filled with thick cloud. She was brought back to the phone by the tension in her friend's voice.

'Look Em, my mum's not well. I have to go to Millicent and take care of her...'

'What's happened? How bad is it?'

'She's okay, recovering from the flu. She's fine, just a bit weak. My sister Jill has been keeping an eye on her, but she's booked to go away. She just needs someone to fetch groceries, clean the house, and generally keep an eye on her.'

'I'm really sorry – I didn't know she was even sick.'

'Join the club. She told me it was just a sniffle when we spoke on Sunday. Jill rang last night – she's concerned Mum's not up to cooking a decent meal for herself.'

Emily found herself wondering why Barbara would call her so early in the morning when there was something like a nine-hour car trip ahead during which she could make the call by mobile.

'Anyway, the reason I'm calling is – just while I think of it – I won't be back in time to do anything with the apricots this year. So I wanted to offer you my pots and pans, and of course the fruit on our trees – if you can cope with doing two lots.'

'How long are you going for?'

'At least a week. If she has a relapse or gets pneumonia – it's happened before – I could be gone for longer.'

'I hope not, for her sake. Are you going to be okay?'

'I'm fine. Listen, I picked eight buckets of apricots when I got back last night and they won't keep for more than a few days. It's up to you whether to use the fruit or not, but I just wanted to let you know, and also tell you that you're welcome to use all my stuff while I'm gone.'

'The thing is, though, I left all my jars at John's place.'

'Don't worry about it. I've probably got enough for both of us anyway – Jill brought me a heap when she visited at Easter.'

'Oh, that would be great. I'd really appreciate it. I was beginning to psych myself up to face the town again and see if the op shop had any.'

God, here she was rambling on about her own problems when her dear friend was probably quite beside herself with worry.

'So, can I do anything for you while you're away?'

'Thanks, but I don't think so. Perhaps just check on David occasionally to make sure he hasn't pinned himself under a tractor or something.'

'When are you leaving?'

'In the next half hour. I'm flying. David's taking me down to Port Lincoln. There's no point me driving all the way when I can use Mum's car once I get there.'

'Well, let me know if you think of anything – anything at all. And thanks so much for the offer of your fruit and equipment – I'll call David and arrange to pick it all up this evening when he gets back. I hope everything is okay when you get there. Good luck.'

'Good luck yourself! And thanks, I'll need it, living with my mother again,' she laughed. 'Okay, see you.'

'Safe travelling.'

Emily hung up. *Poor Barbara*, she thought. But her friend didn't seem all that worried. She could only assume Barbara's mother would be easier to deal with than her own. She'd never cope if Enid was housebound or bedridden and ordering her around – she'd put a frying pan through her head for sure before a week was out.

Now that she was up, Emily remembered that her dad would be arriving later. She couldn't wait to see what he'd found. The place would look much better with more furnishings.

He wasn't due for a few more hours, so she had time to have breakfast, tidy up and pick some apricots. They'd be okay to store in the eskies for a few days while she dealt with Barbara's. She'd keep them separate and present Barbara with her own batch when she returned. It was the least she could do after all her friend had done for her.

But how would she get the apricots down from the gully? Full eskies would be too cumbersome to lug back on her own. And anyway, she couldn't empty them until her dad arrived with the fridge. She really needed a stack of buckets. Emily picked up her mobile again and called home.

'Hi Dad, just the man I wanted to speak to. You're still coming out this morning, aren't you?'

'I certainly am.'

'Well, do you have any spare buckets I could borrow?'

'I could probably manage about three or four. What are you up to?'

'I've found some apricot trees that I want to pick for jam – the Bakers wouldn't mind, would they?'

'I shouldn't think so. Is there anything else you need, other than the load of stuff I got for you yesterday?'

'No, I don't think so. Thanks heaps, Dad. I'll see you a bit later.'

'It's my pleasure. See you in a few hours.'

Emily hung up and then went into the laundry to look for something useful for storing the apricots in the meantime. She was itching to get started now. There was an old copper in the corner. She dragged it to the bathroom for a rinse, then sat it on the kitchen floor. It was perfect, and would hold heaps. She'd take her chances with any mice still lurking about – hopefully they couldn't get over the sharp lip.

But there was still the problem of getting the apricots from the trees to the copper. Then she spied the pile of green eco grocery bags in the doorway. *Perfect!* She grabbed them and headed outside, Grace trotting happily beside her.

Chapter Thirty-three

Emily had filled three of the green grocery bags and was well on her way with the fourth. She was engrossed in the meditative process of selecting the ripe apricots and removing them from the tree, enjoying not having to give too much thought to what she was doing.

Grace had given up investigating the multitude of nearby scents to lay quietly in the sunshine. Suddenly she gave a bark.

Emily, startled from her near trance, looked up to see her father trudging slowly up the gully towards her.

Grace bounded the few metres to meet him, the tip of her tail bobbing up and down through the long grass and heads of wild oats.

'Ah, there you are,' Des Oliphant said, leaning on a nearby tree trunk for support. He was a little red-faced and out of breath. 'That walk is deceptively hard work,' he said, tossing the words over his shoulder.

'Sit down, Dad,' she said. 'You look like you're going to have a heart attack.'

'I'm fine,' he said. 'Just need a second to catch my breath. Hello girl,' he added, bending to pat Grace, who was waiting patiently by his side, flapping her tail. Emily went over and gave her father a hug.

Looking a little brighter, he surveyed their immediate surroundings. 'I remember when that fig was a mere sapling...' he said wistfully.

'So how did you know the Bakers, again?' Emily asked, hoping this time he'd be more forthcoming.

'Their sister – the child who was killed – was the first girl I ever loved,' he said, sounding even more wistful. 'And I think it's true when they say it's something you never really recover from...'

Emily stared at her father, waiting for him to continue. A series of questions filled her mind, but she stayed silent. He was standing there near her looking ... what? Mournful? Morose? Regretful? It was hard to tell.

'Dad, are you okay?'

'Sorry? Oh, yes, just thinking of days past.'

'Happy memories, I hope.'

'Some good, some not so good. You know how life is, Em. You look back over things and despite knowing you couldn't have done anything to change the outcome, you still wish things had been different. They say hindsight is wonderful, but it can also be a curse.' He let out a big sigh.

What was Des talking about? She felt decidedly uneasy with where this conversation was heading. Should she shut it down, shove the cork back in the bottle before the genie was let out? Of course she should, but she was also desperate to know.

When the silence had stretched beyond reasonable, Emily ended it.

'I'll just finish filling this bag, and then you can help me carry them back, if that's okay,' she said. 'It'll save me a trip. You sit there in the shade and relax – I won't be long.'

'Righteo.' Des settled himself on the ground against a trunk. Emily had always marvelled at how he'd never lost the flexibility to sit cross-legged. Grace curled up in front of him with her head resting on the cross of his ankles.

Emily began picking apricots again. But the more she picked, the heavier the silence grew between them. A couple of times she looked across to check on her father. And then it became so excruciating that she could stand it no longer.

She swallowed. Forcing her tone to be casual, she said, 'So, who was she, this girl you loved?' She thought to add, 'before Mum', but as she was about to utter the words it suddenly struck her. Maybe he'd never actually stopped loving this person. Apprehension and fear bit her again.

'It was a long time ago...'

And you're remembering it like it was yesterday, Emily wanted to say.

Des Oliphant sighed again as if resigned to speaking. 'Her name was Katherine. Katherine Rosalind Baker...'

She looked sharply at Des. *My middle name is Katherine!* It couldn't be a coincidence.

'Yes, you have her name,' her father said, looking up at her.

Emily stared back slightly wide-eyed. Should she say something? What was there to say? Katherine was a lovely middle name; she'd always liked it.

'We met the first day of kindergarten, and when we finished school we started courting – going together, you'd say these days. She had the most brilliant sapphire blue eyes that sparkled when she laughed. And this one dimple would appear right here,' he said, pointing to just below the right side of his mouth. 'I remember it like it was yesterday.' He smiled, but it was a sad smile that made Emily's heart ache.

She was dying to yell, 'So what happened?!', but she knew there was a lot more going on here than her father telling her a story. She bit her bottom lip and continued to pick apricots and put them in the bag, being deliberately slow.

'We were only eighteen, but we knew. We'd been best friends – companions – our entire lives. I asked her father if I could marry her...' Des Oliphant gave a tight little laugh. 'He said, "Of course, but what's taken you so long? You've been part of this family for years, Des." We decided to wait until we were twenty-one. It seemed the right thing to do. If we hadn't waited perhaps the story would have been different.' He lapsed into silence.

'Dad, what happened?' Emily asked gently.

'She died.'

Emily paused with an apricot in each hand, a multitude of questions running through her head. She stood there, staring at this cross-legged man sitting nearby. He was her father, but he looked more like a forlorn little boy as he plucked at the grass beside him. She forced herself to stay silent.

After a few moments Des Oliphant gave a sigh. He seemed to be fighting some internal battle over what to say next. He opened his mouth a couple of times but only a moan or part of a word came out.

'A terrible, terrible accident.' The words were uttered more like a long, drawn-out weary sigh.

How long had he kept this to himself? Had he ever spoken of it? With her mother? She went and sat down beside him, resisting the urge to put her arm around him. She wasn't sure why, just that it didn't seem right. He didn't need her sympathy, he just needed her to listen.

'Oh, Em,' he said, patting her leg and offering her a tight, bleak smile. 'It was just a sad, sad accident – nobody's fault.'

'Tell me,' she whispered, not sure if her words were even loud enough for him to hear.

There was a shrug of his shoulders and another deep, resigned sigh. 'She was out riding. Trigger was his name; a lovely creature.

A big, dark chestnut. The most handsome thing, and with the kindest nature. They were inseparable. He'd never been broken, in the true sense of the word. Katherine thought it was cruel. Said she wanted a horse who did as it was asked, not told. Respect through love, not fear. Of course the old Pony Club stalwarts thought she was bonkers.' He paused and smiled at Emily. 'Katherine always did things her own way – whether it was the right way or not. You know, you're a lot like her, in some respects.'

He paused, but Emily again chose not to interrupt. She was thinking about how, when she was twelve, Des had refused to let her join Pony Club with her friends. They'd fought for nearly a month until Emily gave up. Enid, normally the one to disagree with Emily, had been on her side for once.

'Well, Katherine was the only one to ever ride Trigger. And she was right, he would have done anything for her. But that day there was nothing he could do. In some ways I'm glad he died too – I'm sure it would have broken his heart to know he'd killed her.'

The tears began to gather behind Emily's eyes and then well in the corners. She tried to stop them by blinking them back and swallowing hard.

'I know it sounds silly, but he was almost human.' Des Oliphant wiped roughly at his nose as a few tears dripped from it.

'What happened, Dad?'

'No one really knows for sure. When Katherine didn't come back from her ride, her father and I went looking. When we found them, Trigger was still on top of her. It was in the gully just around that bend. She had a short course of fallen logs she used to jump. It must have been an embolism or aneurysm, or something. He looked like he'd died mid-stride and just collapsed. Or perhaps he fell and broke his neck – though if he had, I'm sure

Katherine would have been thrown clear. There was no blood, no outward sign of trauma. It was eerily peaceful. I had to bury him. They were too upset, too angry. I was too, but it's what Katherine would have wanted. I planted a native pine tree to mark the spot. I could never bring myself to check if it ever grew.'

Emily looked to where he indicated, but there was no sign of the tree from here.

'Katherine's parents moved to Adelaide a few years later and we lost touch. Donald and Trevor moved into a house on another farm they'd bought. I see them occasionally, but since the funeral we've never spoken of it. I suppose you'd put it down to men just being men.' He offered a wan smile.

'Oh, Dad, I'm so sorry,' Emily croaked.

'It was a long time ago. Look at me getting all weepy and silly.' He wiped his face with his sleeve and got up. 'Come on, let's get those apricots in before they turn themselves into jam.' He held out a hand to help Emily up. She was both relieved and a little disappointed that the discussion was closed.

They walked back down to the house in a thick, thoughtful silence. As she pondered his words, Emily realised that maybe this was the real reason for her father's vehement refusal to get her a horse all those years ago. At the time she'd been surprised at his stubbornness – he'd objected to the cost, time and effort that looking after a horse would take – and his unwillingness to discuss things rationally. Enid was normally the one who refused to see reason, but on this occasion she had actually been quite encouraging. Now she wondered what her mother had been thinking. Did Enid not know – had she never known – about Katherine?

Impossible. Enid had spent her life here in this district. She was probably the same age as Katherine, could have been in the same class at school, and might even have been friends with her.

Anyway, the accidental death of an eighteen-year-old girl

would have been on the tip of every tongue for months, years, probably decades. Her mother must have known about Katherine's relationship with Des, no question.

Something else stirred in Emily's mind. She'd always been hopeless with figures, but now she found calculations running through her head. Her parents must have married only a few years after Katherine's death.

Rebound? It would explain the seemingly strange match. Emily watched her father's back, half a stride in front of her. His shoulders were hunched like he was carrying the weight of the world. No, just the weight of the past four decades.

Did he regret his decision to marry her mother? She didn't think he seemed unhappy. He'd always been a quiet man, perhaps, but then, Enid was so dominant there wasn't a lot of leeway for him.

And she could only remember him seriously standing up to Enid twice. The first was around the subject of her getting a horse and the second, only very recently, was over her choice to leave John.

'Right, where do you want these?' Des asked as they entered the kitchen from the side verandah.

'Just in the corner, thanks. I'll deal with them later. I need a cuppa, and then I can't wait to see what you've got in the trailer for me.'

'Don't get too excited – it's only the contents of a shack, remember.'

'Yes, but a bed, a real bed.'

'Well, there is one of those, and I did check to see it wasn't too dirty or lumpy.'

'Thanks Dad, you're the best,' Emily said, suddenly feeling the need to give her father a hug – which she did.

'My pleasure, dear heart,' he said, patting her back in return. 'But I do need a fortifying cup of tea,' he said, breaking away and sitting down at the table. 'Is Barbara coming over today?'

'No. She had to rush off to Millicent to help her mother out

– she's recovering from the flu. I was actually hoping we could have got a couple of rooms painted.'

'Well, why don't I help you do it? I'm not in any rush to get back. Your mother's gone shopping in Port Lincoln with Wilma. I've got the whole day to myself, and actually I wouldn't mind feeling a little useful – if you'd like my help.'

'I'd love it. But only if you're sure – or you can just keep me company, if you'd like.'

'Hey, don't write me off as too old just yet, my girl!'

'In that case, I'd love your help – thanks.'

Chapter Thirty-four

Emily waited until her father's ute was out of sight before going back inside. She was physically exhausted, but at the same time energised by thoughts of how much they'd got done. They'd filled the holes in the plaster walls of all the remaining rooms, prepared and painted the lounge-dining room, and finally unloaded the trailer and put the whitegoods and few pieces of furniture in place.

She flopped into one of the two chairs – poo-brown vinyl with wooden arms – that now occupied her lounge area. Des had brought her an old television, but she couldn't even muster the energy to get up and turn it on. Just having a TV gave her an odd sense of comfort. It was a bit like knowing there was someone to call if you needed help, but never actually needing to.

God, she couldn't believe what a machine her dad was. He'd sweated and worked all afternoon, and here she was, so many years younger, barely able to lift her arm.

It was like he was making up for something. *Ah, Katherine.* At some point he mentioned that the house was to have eventually become their home. She had felt a little twitch of something at the comment, but let it go. How could you be jealous of someone you'd never met, someone who had been dead for forty years?

Again she found herself wondering how much her mother knew about Katherine. Had she felt second best – second choice – her whole married life? Was that why she was so unhappy?

If that was the case, why would Enid stay in a marriage that made her miserable? Though of course, this was all pure speculation. If her mother *was* miserable, she had no evidence that her marriage was the cause.

A thought suddenly struck her as she stared at the blank TV screen a few metres away: was her mother's reaction to Emily's changed circumstances born out of jealousy?

Was it what psychologists called 'projection' – that she was angry at Emily because she didn't have the courage to do what Emily had done? She sighed deeply. All the analysis in the world wouldn't change the fact that there was a gulf between her and her mother.

Emily looked around the room. It was amazing that a house that had been unoccupied for decades could scrub up so well, and so easily. They'd just had to patch up a few sections of missing plaster and some minor cracks and paint. All the woodwork had needed was a good rub with a damp cloth. It had saved them a mountain of work.

It would have been nice to decorate each room in a different colour, but that would have cost her a fortune. *And it is only a rental,* she reminded herself. We only need to be clean and comfortable.

Speaking of which, she thought, *this chair is amazingly comfortable.* What a find Des had made. Bless him. Tomorrow they would tackle the hall and then her bedroom. *It'll be so nice to be back in a real bed again – only one more night in the swag...*

Emily woke to the sound of banging somewhere nearby and someone calling, 'Anybody home?' She rubbed her eyes as her brain tried to reconcile where she was and what was going on. She must have fallen asleep. The view from the undressed window ahead of her told her it wasn't yet dusk. She could only have been out for a few minutes.

The banging started again. Someone was at the front door. She leapt up, pulse quickening. *Who could it be?* Hardly anyone knew she was there.

She could hear male voices. Making her way down the hall, she offered silent prayers for it not to be John standing on her verandah. She wasn't sure she was strong enough to deal with him on her own just yet. She opened the door slowly and peered out.

'Hello?'

Two men of around her father's age stood in front of her looking awkward. Then she remembered – Donald Baker had promised to drop in. She opened the door. 'Donald and Trevor, isn't it?'

'Yes, I'm Donald Baker. We spoke on the phone.'

'I'm Emily, Emily Oliphant,' she said, holding out her hand. Donald appeared the slightly younger of the pair, but not by much. He took her hand and appeared to relax.

'Trevor Baker,' the other man said, offering his hand. 'You must be Des's daughter,' he said as more as a question.

Whether being Des's daughter was a good thing or not wasn't immediately clear. 'Yes, yes I am. Hello, nice to meet you,' she said, smiling warmly as they shook.

'Sorry to drop by unannounced, but we were checking some troughs and thought we'd stop by and see how you're settling in,' Donald said.

Emily had the odd thought that they could have hardly announced themselves when there was no phone on and she hadn't given them her mobile number; Donald hadn't asked and she'd forgotten to offer. She had no idea why – must have been her slightly groggy state – but she suddenly found this quite funny. She closed her eyes and blinked a couple of times in an effort to ward off the chuckle rising within her.

'Saw your father on his way out. Sounds like you've been hard at it,' Donald said, regaining Emily's attention.

'Nice looking dog,' Trevor said.

Emily cast a quick glance in the direction of the gate, and there was the little dog sitting silently at attention. *Phew*, she thought. Thank goodness they'd thought to shut Grace in the yard while they worked.

'Thanks, she is lovely. I've only had her a few weeks.'

They lapsed into an awkward silence. Suddenly Emily wondered if they were there to collect rent. 'I put a cheque in the post for the rent – you should get it in the next day or so.'

'Oh, we're not here looking for money. Just wanted to make sure everything was okay. Really didn't mean to intrude.'

'Oh, right. Well, everything's just fine. Brilliant – thank you so much. Sorry, where are my manners? Would you like to come in, for a cup of tea, perhaps?' Emily asked, finally recovering her composure. She stepped aside.

'That would be nice. What do you think, Trev?'

'Excellent idea,' Trevor said, beaming as he moved past Emily into the hall.

The two men walked slowly up the hall looking about like real estate agents taking everything in.

'Scrubs up okay, doesn't she?' Donald said, pausing to peer into the lounge room on his way past the door.

'Sure does,' Trevor said.

'Hard to believe it was left empty for so long,' Emily said.

'Nothing like a lick of paint to freshen things up,' Trevor replied.

Emily had the sudden fear that now they were seeing the house clean they'd turf her out and move in themselves. She shook it aside. There was nothing she could do about it if they did; it was their house.

'You don't have much furniture,' Donald said, peering past his brother to where the two armchairs and television were dwarfed by the huge space of the combined lounge-dining room.

'No,' Emily said. She was about to say, 'You should have seen it before Dad turned up this morning', but didn't.

'Good to see you have more financial sense than that husband of yours,' Trevor muttered.

A blush crept across Emily's face. 'We'll sit in the kitchen,' she said, trying to hurry them along while at the same time work out what Trevor meant by his comment. 'Please, have a seat while I put the kettle on,' she said, waving at the chairs before going straight to the sink.

'I see you've found the orchard,' Donald said, nodding at the bags lined up against the far wall.

Emily flushed again. 'Yes, I hope you don't mind.'

'Not at all. It's good to see them not go to waste for a change. And that the trees have fruited. They haven't the past few years, thanks to the drought.'

Donald and Trevor stayed long enough for one cup of tea, but they didn't linger. They didn't seem to have a lot to talk about, and the men didn't seem totally comfortable being in the old house. Half an hour later they made their excuses and got up to leave.

Emily thanked them again for renting the house to her and assured them she would take good care of it. They said they were pleased she was so clearly taken with the place.

'I am, very,' Emily replied, and had to literally bite the inside of her cheek to stop herself asking them about selling. She stood on the verandah and waved them off, waiting until their battered old blue ute had been swallowed by the trees before heading back inside.

Chapter Thirty-five

'Yoo-hoo, Em, it's me.'

Emily stood back from the sink and pushed her hair away from her damp face. 'I'm in the kitchen,' she called.

After collecting the jam-making things from David the evening before, she'd got up early to start the mammoth task of doing two large batches.

The first lot had gone very well – Emily had used her fruit for the trial run so as to not risk botching up Barbara's – and the top of the bench was covered in clear jars of bright orange jam. The consistency, the thing she usually had the most trouble with, was perfect, and the flavour was a delicate balance of sweetness and tang. She was now washing everything and getting ready for the next batch.

Des entered the kitchen and kissed Emily on the cheek. 'Ah, looking good,' he said, scrutinising the line of plates on the bench with small test dollops on them. 'Can I have a taste?'

'Please, I've had so many samples my tastebuds are ruined. I'd love a second opinion.'

'Mind if I have it on some bread? I'm not so keen on it by itself.'

'Sure – in the freezer. You'll just have to zap it for a few seconds.'

Thank goodness for the fridge and microwave, Emily thought as Des got to work. The microwave was an oldie with just two dials, but it did the trick. The night before, while waiting for her dinner to heat up, she'd wondered at all the functions microwaves now came with. She'd only ever used 'high' and 'defrost'. The only time she'd tried another program it had ended in disaster. The whiting fillets were ruined, causing John to berate her for her incompetence. He'd had a point, but there was no need to be nasty about it; everyone made mistakes.

Like letting your dick fall into the barmaid at the pub, she'd thought snidely as she'd watched her dinner spin slowly around.

She was pleased that the thought hadn't lingered, or particularly upset her – she was finally beginning to feel detached.

'A fine jam,' Des Oliphant declared, nodding thoughtfully. 'As close to your gran's as I think I've ever tasted. She'd be proud.'

'Thanks Dad. Cuppa?'

'Yes thanks.'

'Not too thick, not too thin – and just the right balance of sweetness and tartness,' Des continued. 'Yum,' he said, licking each of his fingers in turn.

Emily beamed. 'Let's hope Barbara's turns out just as well, though her apricots are a little riper and squishier.'

'Have you heard from her? How's her mum doing?'

'Yes, she rang while I was over seeing David. Everything is okay, though she did say she's feeling about as useful as a hip pocket on a sock. Apparently her mother won't even let her cook dinner.'

'Sounds like she's not the only one around here with a strong mother.' He winked at her.

They sipped at their tea.

'Trevor and Donald Baker dropped by just after you left yesterday – said they saw you on the way out.'

'Yes. We didn't speak for long. Came to have a nosy about, did they?'

'Yep. They seemed quite impressed with what we've done. I hope they don't suddenly decide they want to live here now it's starting to look loved again.'

'Don't worry, they're true to their word, those two. Straight down the line. They'd be genuinely pleased to see it looking nice again.'

They lapsed into silence. And then Trevor's mention of John and money came back to Emily. 'Dad, have you heard anything about John?'

'Like what, the barmaid? Sorry, Em, but the whole district knows – about everything, I'd say: the truth and what they've made up.'

Emily blushed slightly. 'Yes, but not that, Dad. About him splashing money around – not that I guess it's any of my business now we've done the settlement.'

'Why, what have you heard?'

'Oh, nothing really,' she said, removing a hand from her mug and waving it. 'Just something Trevor said in passing.'

'Like what?'

Emily spent a few moments racking her memory for the exact words. 'Something like, "Good to see you've got more financial sense than that husband of yours".' She looked at her father, who was concentrating intently on the blue stripe running around his mug. 'Dad?'

He was silent a few more moments, obviously arranging his thoughts and words carefully. The longer he took, the more concerned Emily became.

Des Oliphant let out a deep sigh. 'You'll find out sooner or later. May as well be sooner, I suppose.'

Emily held her breath.

'Apparently he signed up for one of the tractors at White's on Monday – around two hundred grand's worth.'

'Shit! Where'd he get that sort of money?' Emily had the sick, sinking feeling that she'd not just been diddled a few thousand; she'd been well and truly screwed. No wonder John had pushed her to sign so quickly.

'Apparently they dissolved the family company.'

Emily's face began burning and gradually turned crimson. She hadn't even considered his stake in the company when she'd looked at the figures. 'I had no idea he was part of Gerald and Thora's operation. Jesus, he got off lightly with me, didn't he?'

'Em, remember, what goes around comes around. You're better off without him if he's this deceitful. No matter what it cost you, I'd say it's probably worth it to be rid of him.'

'But how could he do this to me? It's not fair!' The rational part of Emily's brain told her that money wasn't everything. But her heart burned with the clear realisation that the man she'd loved – the man she once vowed to be with forever – no longer had any feeling for her. Perhaps he never had.

'Thank your lucky stars you don't have kids to tie you to him. I'm just so sorry I didn't see him for what he was.'

But how could he have? John had been so romantic in the beginning. He'd proposed so beautifully, and for a short while he'd been everything she needed – emotionally, financially and physically. Emily sighed. She'd held up her end of the marriage bargain. Not always willingly, no, but she had done her wifely duties – all of them. And what had he given her in return? Forty thousand dollars.

'You're right, probably a lucky escape,' she said, trying to sound upbeat while fighting the big lump forming in her throat. *Why did I sign that damn paperwork?*

'You know you'll be all right, don't you, Em? You're young – you'll meet someone down the track who will treat you right.' He got up with his mug in one hand. With his other he gave her shoulder a tight squeeze as he crossed to the sink. 'Come on, you make the next batch of jam while I paint your bedroom.'

'The next lot can wait until tomorrow. I'll just wash all this and give you a hand. Give me ten minutes,' Emily said, also getting up.

Emily stacked the jars in the eskies, placing breadboards between the layers for support. The eskies were the only place she could think of where mice couldn't get in and chew their way through the cellophane seals, and she didn't need them for her food now that she had a fridge.

Not that she'd seen any mice since she and Barbara had stopped up the gaps they'd found. And Grace hadn't been sniffing around after anything in particular. *Still, you can't be too careful*, she told herself as she put the lid on the second esky. She wondered how long David would be content to be without his eskies. Sooner or later she'd have to learn to trust the house and the cupboards in it. But not today.

'Right, what can I do?' she asked from the doorway, staring up at her father, who was on the ladder painting the ceiling.

He paused and looked down at her. 'I brought a dustless sander. You could start giving the floor in one of the other rooms a light going over if you want. And I've got some tung oil for them after that.'

'Hey Dad? You don't think we're going overboard here, do you?'

'Not at all. It wouldn't seem right to leave the floors untouched with the floors and ceilings freshly painted. I honestly do think it'll be worth the effort.'

'Right, where is it?'

'In the blue box in the hall – there's an extension cord in there too. Just remember to empty the dust catcher fairly often – it's not very big. Start wherever you like; it'll all have to be done eventually.'

Emily went into the first empty room and plugged in the sander. It was so nice to look around and see no mess, no clutter – a bare, blank canvas stretched out before her.

She started in the far right-hand corner, as it would be the least visible if she stuffed up a bit before getting the machine figured out.

But she needn't have worried. Soon she had a good rhythm going, kneeling on a folded towel with the sander out in front, working the length of her reach before shuffling across to her left. She enjoyed having her mind fully occupied with the vibrating machine, leaving a smooth, even finish behind her, and keeping an eye on the level of dust in the catcher. It would take ages to do the entire house, but at least the machine was easy to handle.

One bit at a time, she told herself every time thoughts of the size of the room and then the whole house threatened to overwhelm her. One bit at a time.

Chapter Thirty-six

'Hello, anyone here?' Barbara's voice sang from the front door.

Emily leapt up and bolted down the hall to greet her friend. They embraced in the hallway. 'I'd swear you've been gone months,' Emily said, not caring how she sounded.

'Tell me about it. It's only been a week, but boy is that a long time when you're sharing a house with someone who drives you mad.'

'So how is your mum? All better?'

'Fit as a fiddle. I don't know why I went! She had a constant stream of bowls ladies and little old men from the senior citizens' club dropping in and taking care of her every want. Honestly, there was no need for me at all, except of course to be seen doing one's daughterly duty.' She tapped her nose knowingly. 'But wow, haven't you been busy? These floorboards look amazing,' Barbara added, squatting to stroke the gleaming timber that had come up a deep earthy red colour.

'Yeah, but being so dark, the amount of dirt they show is ridiculous. I'm running the vacuum over the hall every day. Thank goodness the kitchen has lino.'

'Well, I think they look great. 'And it smells beautiful in here. What is that?'

'Tung oil. You can thank my dad for that. Cuppa?' Emily asked.

'Great, thanks, but only after a stickybeak through the house. Lead the way!'

Emily showed Barbara through each of the rooms, pointing out where she and Des had patched the walls and sanded and polished the floors. After five minutes of Barbara oohing and ahhing, they finally arrived in the kitchen.

'I can't believe the transformation in just a few days.'

'Well, it's still pretty sparse, but it's clean and fresh and comfortable. And heaps better than it was.'

'God, I wonder what the Baker brothers will think now it's looking so good. Have they seen it yet?'

'Not since Dad and I totally finished. They came over the other day though, and they did seem genuinely happy it's being given some TLC. Oh, Barbara, I've become so attached to the place,' Emily said with a sigh. 'I have to keep reminding myself it's just a rental.'

'Well, we never know what the future holds. Who knows? One day this could all be yours,' Barbara replied, extending her arms with a lavish flourish. 'It could be a thriving B&B with a world-renowned restaurant, with homemade jams and preserves for sale. Speaking of which, thanks so much for the jam. You really could have kept it all for yourself since you did the work.'

'Then I'd have to eat it for every meal for the next twelve months, and as nice as it is...'

'You should sell it. It's some of the best apricot jam I've ever tasted – beats mine hands down. Even David says so, and he fancies himself as something of a connoisseur!'

'You're way too kind, both of you.'

'Seriously, at least put some in the op shop for sale.'

'Someone's already got a stack in there. I noticed the other day on my way past.'

'Ah, so you've ventured back into the lion's den, then?'

'Had to, didn't I? I ran out of bread to put under my jam,' Emily said with a laugh.

'How was it?'

'Er … *awkward* is probably the best word for it. But I didn't hang around – got my groceries and left. Dad's been doing all the trips into Mitre 10, thank goodness. I suppose David's told you the latest about John?'

'I've hardly seen him – he had another Bureau meeting last night and left early for a ram sale this morning. What's the latest?'

'Apparently he's just about to put a deposit on a two-hundred-grand tractor.'

'Jesus, where'd he get that sort of money?'

'Rumour is, he's being bought out of the family company.'

'I'm sure David didn't know he was part of a company; he would have mentioned it when we were discussing your settlement.'

'Yeah, well, looks like I was royally screwed, not just diddled.'

'Maybe you can sue him for non-disclosure or something.'

'No. It was my mistake. I should have listened when you told me to get advice. I should have, but there's nothing I can do about it now. It doesn't mean I'm not bloody pissed off about it, though. Just think, for a hundred grand I could have nearly bought a house in town outright.'

'Oh, sweetheart. I'm so sorry I turned out to be right.'

'Me too,' Emily said ruefully. 'Live and learn.'

'Well, maybe you're meant to be out here closer to me,' Barbara said. 'Now, I can't stay long,' she continued. 'I've got mountains of washing to do and a house that looks like a bachelor pad to sort out. But I just wanted to know if you'd like to come over for dinner tomorrow night. Nothing fancy – I'm just going to throw a roast in the oven.'

'I'd love to, but I want to have you guys over here now it's looking half-decent. Can you come here instead and be my first guests?'

'Are sure you want the hassle?'

'God, Barbara. After all you guys have done for me, it's the least I can do. It would be my pleasure.'

'Well, I'm certainly not going to argue!' Barbara said, getting up. They made their way back down the hall to the open front door.

'It's so good to have you back,' Emily said as she hugged her friend goodbye.

'It's good to be back. See you tomorrow night. See you Gracie,' Barbara added, bending to ruffle the ears of the dog sitting beside her mistress on the verandah.

Emily went back to the kitchen feeling buoyed with the prospect of plans to work towards. Since she and her father had finished working on the house, she'd been feeling a bit lost and bored.

With another cup of tea in front of her, she idly flicked through her cookbooks for inspiration. She wanted to do something a little more special than the average lamb roast. She'd missed the excitement of planning a meal and cooking for guests, and she vowed to do more entertaining now she was settled. Maybe she could even do Christmas.

But who could she invite? All her and John's friends had clearly sided with him – she hadn't heard from a single one since the separation. And she'd been too scared to make contact lest she experience further rejection.

Oh well, she'd start by having David and Barbara around, and then her parents – to thank her dad for all his help. And to prove to Enid that the house was indeed fit for habitation. Definitely.

Emily sighed. Why did she keep seeking her mother's approval when she knew none would be forthcoming? She smiled wryly and shook her head. Freud was sure to have an answer to that.

Chapter Thirty-seven

Emily stood spooning coffee into three mugs. She was beaming. The night had gone perfectly. She silently congratulated herself for keeping things simple.

She'd chosen slow-cooked Greek lamb; if you kept the oven low it really couldn't be overcooked. Having it fall from the bone was much better than trying to keep it restaurant-pink. And it had turned out perfectly – melt-in-the-mouth meat with strong but not overwhelming flavours of garlic, lemon and oregano.

The trifle had been a hit for dessert and they'd demolished almost half of the huge bowlful, despite making great inroads with the shoulder of lamb before it.

After delivering the mugs, she sat back down at the table with a sense of satisfaction and calm, the likes of which she hadn't felt for months. Maybe everything really would be okay after all.

'Well, that was absolutely the *best* meal!' Barbara declared.

'Yep,' David said heartily. 'I hope John knows what he's given up.'

'Thanks guys,' Emily said, grinning and blushing slightly.

'Sorry to hear about the settlement – for what it's worth, I didn't know he had anything to do with Gerald and Thora's operations. That must be one of the only secrets this town has ever kept.'

'Oh well, money isn't everything,' Emily said, trying to sound upbeat, but failing.

'No, but integrity is,' Barbara said. 'Don't worry. Somehow, some time, somewhere, he'll get his comeuppance.'

'It wouldn't worry me so much if I could find a bloody job. A hundred grand would have been very handy right about now.'

'You should sell some of your jam,' David said. 'It's incredible.'

'Thanks, and no offence, but who'd buy it? Everyone around here makes jam.'

'Have you thought about speaking to a financial counsellor? They might have some suggestions. Not about the jam, obviously,' Barbara added with a laugh.

'I know what you meant,' Emily said, rolling her eyes at her friend. 'But how would investment advice help when *not* having any money is the problem?'

'No, you're thinking of a financial *planner*,' David said. 'Financial counsellors are supposed to help people suffering financial difficulty. They're government-funded, so it wouldn't cost you a cent. Seriously, it might be worth seeing if they can help.'

'Ah, you're talking about that Cameron guy who used to be in the State Bank. No way. I wouldn't trust him as far as I could throw him,' Emily said.

'No, he's been sent down to Lincoln – there's a new one. Another bloke, Ben somebody-or-other, started a few weeks ago. Word is, he's nice enough and seems to know a thing or two,' David said. 'Apparently he was raised on a farm over in the east. He took over when he was eighteen, after his father died. Then apparently he headed off to the big smoke and got a couple of degrees or diplomas or something.'

'I wonder why he's not still running his own farm, then,' Emily said.

'Saw the light, probably,' David said. 'Realised he could make more from the sidelines than being a mug farmer?'

'Listen to Mr Cynical over here. Must be time to get him home before he depresses us all and ruins such a lovely evening,' Barbara said lightly.

'Sorry, I'm a bit tired. *And* I was at Jones's ram sale yesterday – the average price was well over two grand. Couldn't afford to buy any and I wanted three. How the bloody hell can ram prices be going up when lamb and wool prices are still dropping?'

'Dunno, but come on, let's get you home. Are you sure you don't want a hand with the dishes, Em?'

'Absolutely. I'm not tired enough to go to bed yet so it'll give me something to do.'

Emily was still waving at their tail-lights when she heard the distinctive tone of her mobile phone echoing through the almost silent house. She saw her cousin Liz's name on the display as she pressed the button to accept the call.

'Hi Liz.'

'How's things? All settled into your *ghastly* house?'

Emily smiled, picturing Liz using two fingers to indicate quotation marks. 'Yep. As a matter of fact, I've just seen my first dinner guests off.'

'Sounds like the B&B is open! So, do you have somewhere for me and my friend Jake to sleep yet?'

'Depends if you mean together or separate.'

'Separate, definitely separate. He's lovely but really not my type – way too nice!'

'Well, I've got a spare room with twin single beds and another empty room that I could put a swag in – if one of you could cope with that.'

'That would be fine – he's terribly easygoing. As I said, too nice.'

Emily wondered how being easygoing made someone too nice.

'So when can I expect you?' She didn't think for a second that her cousin would ever actually turn up. Elizabeth was strictly a funerals, weddings, christenings visitor, and usually only then because it was easier than dealing with her mother's silent treatment.

'We thought we'd try for a quick visit before Christmas. Saturday week – is that too soon?'

Emily's attention snapped back to her phone conversation. 'Seriously?!'

'Yep, is that okay?'

'Absolutely. It'll be great to see you. Are you driving or do I need to pick you up from Lincoln?' As she said it, Emily hoped they'd make their own way. Now that she was settled, she was watching her pennies like a hawk. Forty thousand dollars wouldn't last long if she was filling up on petrol every week.

'Jake wants to do the whole road trip catastrophe. And don't worry, we're not coming to eat you out of house and home either. We'll stock up in town on the way.'

Emily didn't realise she was holding her breath until she heard it escape as a sigh. She put her hand over the mike of the phone.

'We'll aim to get to Wattle Creek in time to catch the shops then we'll call for directions. You know what I'm like with maps.'

'Sounds perfect. Can't wait.'

'Okay, I'd better get going – heading out to dinner.'

Emily checked her watch. It was just after nine o'clock – nine-thirty Melbourne time. The thought of waiting that late to go out – let alone eat – made her stomach grumble in sympathy. She hoped Liz and this Jake fellow would be happy to eat at six-ish while they stayed with her.

'Okay, see you soon.' As she hung up, Emily suddenly realised Liz hadn't said how long they would be staying. 'Stocking up' sounded like they were planning for more than a couple of days.

Standing at the sink, she found she was genuinely excited at the prospect of visitors. It was another thing to look forward to and to plan for.

Thinking of which, she'd better have her parents around to dinner. She decided on Sunday night – while Liz and Jake were there to run interference. Liz was more than capable of holding her own with Enid, and her mother was sure to be on her best behaviour in Jake's unfamiliar company.

Chapter Thirty-eight

Emily leapt up from the kitchen table at hearing a vehicle approaching. She'd been deep in her book.

Even with the rest of the house done, she'd been spending most of her idle time in the kitchen instead of the lounge. The room was lighter and more airy, and it also had a better energy or something – it just felt more welcoming.

Heading to the door, she suddenly felt a little nervous about greeting her first guests – even if they were her cousin Elizabeth and her friend Jake. She looked about her for signs the house wasn't ready. Ridiculous, really – she'd spent days manically clearing, positioning and repositioning furniture and knick-knacks, being short of anything better to do.

She'd sent out résumés and pestered a number of local businesses for a job by phone, but lingering caution from the global financial crisis and fears of a looming recession seemed to have a firm hold on the town. Emily had finally given up phoning when an old family friend jokingly suggested that if she didn't stop he might have to take out a restraining order. Thank God the conversation had occurred on the phone because she'd turned tomato red with embarrassment.

She was frantically rubbing her palms down her jeans as a four-door silver hatchback, covered in a layer of caramel-coloured dust, came to a stop just beyond the verandah.

Liz opened the passenger's door, and a man emerged from the driver's side. He wore denim jeans that hugged his long legs, dark brown leather dress boots, and a plain navy rugby top with the R.M. Williams logo on it. His hair was dark with a sparse peppering of grey.

Emily bounded down the steps to meet them while Grace whined at the gate, upset at being confined. She felt dreadful about it, but until she knew how this friend of Liz's felt about dogs, it had to be done.

'Brilliant to see you,' Liz said, embracing her cousin in a tight, quick hug. 'Love the new haircut,' she added, giving Emily's hair a flick with her finger.

'Thanks,' Emily said.

'Hi, I'm Jake Lonigan.'

'Emily Oliphant. Welcome,' Emily said, accepting his smooth hand and allowing him to pump hers firmly but gently.

'What a gorgeous dog,' Jake said, wandering over to Grace. 'What's his name?'

'He's a she – Grace. She's normally a house dog, but I locked her up in case you had a phobia or allergy, or something.'

'I love dogs. Come on, girl, out you come,' he said, opening the gate. 'Aren't you just lovely?'

Having been freed, Grace now lay on her back in the hopes of having her belly scratched. After a few moments obliging, Jake stood up.

'Come on, we'd better be sociable.' He went to help unload the car and Grace followed at his heel.

'Looks like you've found a new best friend.'

Seeing everything on the verandah – suitcases, bags of groceries, a large esky and boxes of wine and beer – Emily found it hard to believe they'd managed to fit everything into the small car. *How long are they staying?* Christmas was only two weeks away.

'Just leave everything here while I show you around,' she said, standing aside at the threshold to let them in.

'Em, it's just perfect,' Liz said as Emily led them into the house. 'I don't know what your mother is on about. Sure, it's rustic and a bit old-fashioned, but it's lovely: the setting, the house, everything.'

'Well, don't get too excited; there's no air-conditioning, so you'd better hope this cool weather lasts,' Emily warned.

There had been a few really hot days in the last week, but the position of the house seemed to attract the cooling gully breezes at night. And just in case, she'd set up three old pedestal fans in the bedrooms.

'Bags the room with the French doors,' Liz suddenly yelled, pushing Jake aside to run down the hall to claim her room.

'You'd swear she thinks she's back at Brownie camp,' Jake said, grinning.

Emily smiled back. She noticed for the first time just how attractive he was. Not drop-dead gorgeous, but handsome in a warm, friendly sense. He had lovely, dark hazelnut-coloured eyes with very long lashes. *What was his story?* In her experience, nice guys over thirty were usually married, gay, or both. She couldn't see a wedding ring, anyway.

'Bathroom is out this way. Feel free to shower if you're feeling grotty from your trip,' Emily said as they continued down to the kitchen.

'We've only driven from Whyalla – we stayed there last night – so it wasn't too arduous a journey. I'd love a coffee, though. I'm happy to get it; just point me in the right direction,' he said, looking around him.

'You plonk yourself down. I'll do it. I was about to put the kettle on, anyway.'

Emily filled the kettle and turned around to find Liz in the doorway.

'We're having coffee. Do you want one?'

'Yes please,' she replied. 'Hey, are these Gran's buttons? What happened to the jar?'

Emily moved to the far end of the bench where Elizabeth stood staring at the mass of buttons spread out on a tea towel. She'd got them out the day before to clean them, having run out of things to do.

'Yes. The jar broke a couple of weeks ago and I'm trying to make sure there are no more bits of glass. Figured I may as well give them a bit of a rinse while I was at it.'

'What happened? I've never seen them out of the jar.'

'Somehow it fell off the bench the first night I was here. It scared the living daylights out of me!' Emily said with a laugh.

'I can imagine,' Jake said.

'I still don't know what happened. I doubt mice could have done it, not that I've seen any on the bench. I wondered for a moment if perhaps there was a ghost, but I haven't seen any other signs,' she added, shrugging.

'So it belonged to your gran?'

'Yes. She gave it to me the day before she died, so it's pretty special to me. I've only had it a little while and I'm really annoyed that I let it get broken.'

'Well, it's not like you did it on purpose. I'm sure she would understand,' Jake said, offering her a sympathetic smile.

'Wow,' Liz said. 'There are all sorts of things in there: leather, fabric, bone. I had no idea.'

'I need to find a replacement – it was an old Bushells Coffee jar from the thirties and I want another one the same.'

'Fair enough,' Elizabeth said, running her hands through the buttons. 'Are you going to take out the paperclips and other non-buttony bits and pieces?'

'No. Call me sentimental, but I want to keep it all exactly how it was.'

'What are these little pebbles? There are a few of them.'

'What pebbles?' Emily asked, appearing at Liz's shoulder.

'These.' Liz held up a small, smoky blue-grey stone with an odd lustre to its surface.

Emily took it from her and examined it. It was cold and smooth – definitely a stone. Most likely quartz, though the colour and texture seemed a little unusual. She frowned. Something stirred at the back of her mind.

'No idea,' she said, handing it back. 'Probably something Gran collected near the end – she became quite the bowerbird. You remember her place. The drawers were full of all sorts of odd, irrelevant things.' She turned to Jake to explain. 'You know those little square plastic bread ties? There would have been dozens of them.'

'Wow, look at the colour,' Elizabeth said, holding it up to a beam of sun catching the edge of the kitchen window.

'Hmm,' Emily said, taking another look. There was that odd feeling of a memory, or something struggling to be known. But still she couldn't grasp it.

'I loved how sure of everything she was,' Liz said absently, placing the stone back on the pile. 'Well, you know, before...'

'Yep, me too,' Emily said, smiling. 'It wasn't that she was stubborn, was it? Just that she took the time to form an opinion, and once she had, it was final – end of story. I loved that about her; you always knew where you stood. God, I miss her'

'Well, I didn't spend as much time with her, but I think it's great you're going to keep all these together and in the same sort of jar,' Elizabeth said wistfully, giving the pile one last caress.

'You never used to be so sentimental,' Emily said, looking at her cousin.

'Must be a sign of age. Now I really do need that coffee,' she said, moving to the kettle at the other end of the bench.

'Okay, but I'll do it – you sit,' Emily instructed.

'If you insist,' Liz said, settling into a chair. 'So, how are you, Em? *Really?*'

'Pretty good.' She wasn't sure she wanted to be having this discussion with Jake in the room. While Emily and Elizabeth were discussing Granny Mayfair, he'd gone across to pat Grace, who was sitting on her bed in the corner. He was still over there now, but definitely within earshot.

'I haven't found a job yet, but Dad and I only finished here a couple of days before you rang.'

'You could always come to Melbourne. The offer's open.'

'Thanks, but I don't think I could leave here now I've got settled.'

'Well, the house certainly has a good energy about it.'

'It does indeed,' Jake said, returning to the table.

Chapter Thirty-nine

'Are you guys hungry at all?' Emily asked as she put some bread into the toaster. 'I was going to have some toast and apricot jam. I didn't get around to having any lunch.'

'We had lunch, but I'd love some if it's your famous apricot jam,' Elizabeth said.

'Well, I don't know about famous, but I did make it. It's Gran's recipe.'

'Yum, my favourite,' Jake said, licking his lips.

'When did you ever have our gran's apricot jam?' Liz asked, looking puzzled.

'I haven't, silly. I mean *apricot* jam is my favourite. Honestly, Em, sometimes you'd swear this girl was blonde.'

'Yes, well, we're all allowed our ditsy moments, Mr Where-are-my-sunglasses-oh-they're-on-my-head.'

'Touché,' Jake said. 'Okay, *thank you*, Elizabeth. Truce?'

They all started chuckling. *It really was going to be fun having them here*, Emily thought, spreading the first two slices. 'Now, before you get too settled, you need to know I've invited Mum and Dad for dinner tomorrow night. So now's your last chance to escape, otherwise I'll assume you're committed to helping me entertain them.'

'She really means playing buffer – Auntie Enid can be a little scary,' Elizabeth explained to Jake.

'Oh, right.'

Emily caught Liz's eye. 'She's just a little, um, *intense* – that's probably the best way to put it.'

'Just the usual mother-daughter dramas, then,' Jake said with a dismissive wave of his hand. 'I do have a sister, remember,' he said to Elizabeth. 'I will be more than happy to serve as a distraction. I promise to be on my best behaviour and to be utterly charming,' he added, batting his eyelashes at Emily.

'Don't do that. She'll have you two married off before the week's out,' Elizabeth said with a laugh.

'Hmm, could be fun,' he said, flashing Emily a cheeky, boyish smile.

Emily blushed and looked away.

'I'll give you a full briefing later,' Elizabeth said to Jake.

Emily felt a small stab of annoyance at her cousin speaking disrespectfully about her mother. It was fine for her to be annoyed with Enid, but Elizabeth was different. She returned her attention to the toaster, where the second lot of toast had just popped out.

'God, this jam is amazing!' Jake said, swallowing his first bite.

'Yeah, Em. This is even better than what Gran used to make – even in her heyday.'

'Thanks,' Emily said, smiling coyly.

'This would go down a treat at the South Melbourne markets,' Jake said.

'I'm glad you like it,' she said.

'Seriously, we should take some back and see if it sells,' Jake said.

Was he just flattering her?

'So, Liz tells me you want to do some photography while you're here...' she said.

'That's right.'

'What of? Maybe I can help you find the right spots if I know what you're looking for.'

Jake shrugged. 'Old buildings, farmland, anything really. I'm just dabbling. Still trying to figure out where my talent lies, and if I have any, for that matter.'

'Oh, right, fair enough,' Emily said, not quite sure what to say. She thought Liz had brought a professional photographer to stay, not some guy in the midst of a midlife crisis.

'I think you should carry on with the series of Melbourne landmarks, since they're selling so well,' Liz said.

So he really is a photographer, Emily thought, feeling relieved, before wondering why it really mattered, anyway. *Who am I to judge?* It wasn't like she was anywhere near sorting out her own life. She pushed her empty plate aside and leaned back from the table.

'I probably will,' Jake said, 'but I just want to see what else I'm good at.'

'You know, I think I left my phone in the car. I'll go take a look,' Liz said, suddenly getting up. 'Won't be long.'

'Okay. I'll get the slow cooker organised. I hope lamb shanks are okay for dinner. Simple fare around here, I'm afraid.'

'Sounds perfect,' Liz said from the door.

'I'll give you a hand,' Jake said, gathering up the plates and mugs and taking them over to the sink.

'There's really no need,' Emily said. 'Feel free to put your feet up in the lounge or take a nap or something.'

'Can I at least stay and watch? Unless of course your recipe is secret. I'd hate for you to have to kill me,' he added with a chuckle.

Emily let out a nervous giggle. 'Of course not. I'm just not used to having an audience – I get a bit flustered. I'm used to having a husband watching the footy on TV while I slave away over a hot stove…' *Shit, did I actually say that out loud?* Emily reddened, wishing she could take back the words. God, she sounded like such a bloody victim. She was grateful for the cool rush of air as she gathered all the vegetables from the fridge's crisper.

She returned to the bench to find Jake with rubber gloves on, searching the cupboard underneath the sink for the bottle of bright green detergent.

'Thanks,' she said, smiling at him.

'Least I can do. We're not here to have you wait on us hand and foot.'

So how long are you here? The words were on Emily's lips but she couldn't quite seem to push them any further.

Chapter Forty

The following morning, Elizabeth wandered into the kitchen wearing a pale pink plush dressing gown over white and multi-pink, striped light-cotton shortie pyjamas. She plonked herself heavily onto the nearest chair. 'God, I slept like an absolute log,' she said.

'I thought you were going to sleep all day,' Emily replied.

'You sound like our mothers. What's the time, anyway?'

'Eight-thirty-five,' Emily said. Liz was right; it *was* something their mothers would say. So what if they slept all day – they were on holidays.

'Thanks,' Elizabeth said, as Emily placed a mug of steaming coffee in front of her. 'So, no sign of Jake yet?'

'No.'

'Wow, he's normally up with the sparrows, no matter how late he goes to bed.'

A couple of minutes later, Jake came in looking barely awake. He was dressed in the same clothes he'd been in the day before, and his hair was sticking out in all directions except for a flat patch on one side. Emily suppressed an urge to giggle.

'Good morning,' Emily and Elizabeth said in unison.

'Good morning,' Jake said with more cheer than his appearance suggested he felt.

'I hope Grace didn't disturb you,' Emily said, noticing the dog trot in after Jake and take her spot in the far corner.

Emily had let her out early for her customary morning wee, but hadn't seen her for ages.

'Yes and no. She demanded I open my door at around seven, and then proceeded to commandeer half my bed. I guess we fell asleep. I hope you don't mind – she was quite insistent.'

'I'd believe it. And no, she's generally allowed to do as she pleases – I'm a bit of a sucker like that.'

'I'm not surprised – she really is a lovely dog.'

'Thanks. I don't know what I'd have done without her this last month. As clichéd as it is, she really has been my saving grace.'

'Liz told me you've been through some tough times. She wasn't gossiping or anything,' he hastened to add, 'was just explaining how you came to be living here.'

'Really, I wasn't,' Liz said.

Emily waved a dismissive arm. 'When you've lived in a small country town all your life, you get quite used to people talking about you.'

'Not that it makes it easier – it still hurts when people talk behind your back, right?' Jake said.

Emily sensed a flicker of camaraderie.

'I think what really hurts is the division – people you thought were friends no longer giving you the time of day,' she said. 'And the lies that are peddled about so freely – without anyone actually asking the people involved to confirm or deny them. That's what really pisses me off.' Emily shut her mouth abruptly to stop herself from ranting. 'Sorry, it's all still a bit raw. Coffee?' she asked, getting up.

'Don't be sorry. And yes, thanks, coffee would be great.' Jake said.

'So, you must have grown up in a small town as well to be so aware of how things work?'

'Not really,' Jake said. 'I wasn't born into one, but I spent a few years in one doing an apprenticeship. Of course it had its good points, but I found it quite toxic at times.'

'If you two are going to have a deep and meaningful about small-town living, I'm going to take a shower and get organised,' Elizabeth said. 'We're going out this morning, right?' She drained her coffee and got up.

'Yes. I told my friend Barbara we'd be there at ten. But we've got plenty of time,' Emily replied on autopilot. She was focussed on what Jake had last said. 'Toxic'. That's exactly the right word for it,' she said, keen to continue their conversation. 'Though I have to be fair. I'm just a bit jaded at the moment – ordinarily I love country life.'

'Me too, but it's like anything – there's good and bad aspects, and you have to just make the most of what you get.'

'So where did you do your apprenticeship?' Emily asked, placing his coffee in front of him.

'Small town down near the bottom of Victoria. I did a building apprenticeship. I wasn't so keen on it.'

'The building or the small town?'

'Both, really,' he laughed. 'I don't want to sound like a total snob, but I realised I don't relate well to rednecks and bogans. I'm not into sitting around in a dirty flannelette shirt and steel caps getting hammered in the pub every night after work.'

Emily found herself giving him a mental tick of approval. 'So you left?' she prompted.

'Well, I did get my ticket – I've got this stubborn streak where I have to see things through,' he said, smiling at her.

'Ah, a qualified builder in the house – good to know,' Emily said, grinning back at him. 'Lucky for you this is only rented. Otherwise I'd find all sorts of jobs for you to do to pay your way,' she teased good-naturedly, surprised at hearing herself. She couldn't believe she was actually engaging in such banter. She'd known him less than twenty-four hours.

'And I would certainly oblige,' he said, doffing an invisible hat. 'But seriously, it's got heaps of potential. And not just as a house.'

'Like what?'

'Well, with the plumbing already along the outer verandah, turning it into a B&B wouldn't be too difficult, or a small restaurant. And with such nice big rooms it would make a great art gallery. The possibilities are endless, really.'

Emily felt a little overwhelmed just thinking about it. 'Hmm, lots to think about. So you're a builder in Melbourne now?'

'No. I actually run my own business – as an architect.'

'Oh, wow.'

'I realised I needed to create something of my own, not just follow someone else's awful design. Although I do think training as a builder first made me a much better architect. It's helpful when I'm on site and can talk the talk *and* walk the walk. You've no idea how much easier it makes dealing with tradesmen.'

'Do you do commercial or residential?'

'Bit of both, actually. To quote my website, I specialise in designing modern, sympathetic versions of older buildings where clients want old-world charm with modern conveniences. And I'm also a bit of a greenie, which fits in well because it means I can use wide eaves much of the time. The pioneers had the right idea with their expansive verandahs and breezeways. Sorry, now you've got me on my soapbox.'

'No, it's fascinating. I hate those boxy, bald-faced houses with square porches that seem to be popping up everywhere these days.

Hopefully that trend will be over before it makes it out bush,' she said. 'That's another good thing about country living,' she added with a laugh. 'We're slow to adopt new trends.'

'Well, there's nothing wrong with that. Give me rickety and rustic over sleek and sophisticated any day.'

They chuckled and then lapsed into silence.

'Ah,' Emily said suddenly, 'so that explains your photographic interest in old buildings.'

'Yes, I like to show the techniques they used to use. Some of the pictures are just corners of buildings on interesting angles; blown up they can look quite arty. When they started to sell at the market my ego got a fine stroking and I began fancying myself as a photographer...'

Emily couldn't imagine him being egotistical – he seemed far too down to earth.

'So now I'm seeing what else I'm good at photographing. Another habit of mine is trying different things – pushing my boundaries.'

'Which brings you out to little old Wattle Creek.'

'Exactly.'

At that moment, Elizabeth wandered back in with a towel wrapped around her head. 'That really is a fabulous shower.'

'I can't believe how quick you were. I thought you city types spent ages under hot running water,' Emily said with a tight laugh.

Liz shrugged. 'There's been a drought on, hasn't there? We're under water restrictions in Melbourne too, you know.'

'And our Liz is a bit of a greenie at heart too. Aren't you, sweetie?'

Emily flinched at hearing the term of endearment. 'Really?'

'I try to do my bit,' Elizabeth said, looking a little uncomfortable.

'Ah, she's being far too modest. Your cousin here had me convert a small warehouse rather than buy one of those boxes we were talking about, even though it cost her nearly twice as much.'

Chapter Forty-one

Emily dumped her keys in the bowl on the old wooden chair in the hall and rushed down to the kitchen. They were an hour late and she really had to get the roast on or else suffer Enid's silent – or not so silent – disapproval, which would depend on just how late dinner was and how much she liked – or didn't like – the people in the room.

She'd cut all the vegetables up and prepared the lamb that morning, but was now regretting her choice of meal. A roast was a cheap, easy and delicious way of feeding a group without having to spend all day in the kitchen, and had always been a family favourite with the Oliphants, but it would heat up the inside of the house – and that was something she wasn't keen on. It was nearly thirty-five degrees outside.

It was still definitely cooler inside, but not nearly as comfortable as it had been that morning. Hopefully the gully breeze would cool it down again overnight. Emily much preferred the cooler months – having to rug up rather than trying to stay cool.

As she fired up the oven and took the lamb out of the fridge to bring it to room temperature, Emily wondered how cold the house would get in the middle of winter. She'd really have to get some kind of heating organised. Were the fireplaces in working order?

They weren't the most efficient form of heating, but she loved an open fire – sitting watching the flames flicker, listening to the gentle crackle, perhaps a glass of red wine in hand ... It was so romantic. Well, it would be if you had someone to share it with.

'Can I give you a hand?' Jake asked, sauntering in. 'I'm next in line for the bathroom, unless you want it first,' he said, absently running a hand through the buttons, which were still on the tea towel at the end of the bench.

'Oh shit, I've got to hide those. Can you grab the ice-cream container and bundle them in? Shove the whole lot into the cupboard under you, towel and all,' Emily said, a little breathlessly.

'Sure, but why?'

'Just in case they're not totally dry yet. I don't want the leather bits going mouldy.'

'No, I mean why are we hiding them?'

'Mum doesn't know I've got them, and I'd rather not tell her.'

'Okay,' Jake said, sounding sceptical.

'She thinks I'm a sentimental fool, and the last thing I need tonight is her criticism,' Emily said wearily as she strained the water that had been keeping the cut vegetables fresh all day.

'Right.' He still didn't sound convinced.

'You'll see what I mean when you get to know her – probably not tonight though, because she'll be on her best behaviour.'

'You make it sound like I'm to become a permanent fixture around here,' Jake teased.

Emily blushed and turned so he couldn't see. 'You and Liz haven't said how long you're staying. For all I know, you *are* to be a permanent fixture,' she shot back, still avoiding his eyes.

At that moment Emily realised, with a bit of a shock, she couldn't imagine living alone in the house again. They'd only been here a little over twenty-four hours, but their company made the house feel more homely.

Well, if she was being honest with herself, it was Jake's presence that she enjoyed the most. Not in a romantic sense – of course not – but not really in a brotherly sense either. He was just great company. Emily especially liked that they could have different opinions and hear each other out and then agree to disagree.

Unlike with Liz. There had already been a couple of stark reminders of why they didn't spend a lot of time together. At Barbara and David's house that day, Liz had openly flirted with David and seemed quite hostile towards Barbara – as if she was jealous of her, for some reason.

Within minutes Emily had regretted bringing them over. But Barbara had taken her aside while the others were talking and told her not to worry about it – it wasn't up to Emily to account for her cousin's behaviour. Emily was grateful, but continued to bristle for the rest of the afternoon.

It had almost been worth it to see Jake so excited at the sites David took them to by four-wheel drive. And the photos he got were great – or so he said. Jake wouldn't show them to anyone; he insisted he had to check them out on his laptop first.

'Just call me a temperamental artist,' he'd added, laughing, deflecting their pleas to see them right then and there.

Emily found Elizabeth hard-going, but beyond a minor person-ality clash, she couldn't put her finger on why. They weren't what you'd consider great friends – they were family; that was it, really. But Liz was also a guest, and Emily was a good host, so she'd let her furniture be moved around at her cousin's whim, and just cringed inwardly at the wildly exaggerated stories she told about Emily growing up.

Emily took a deep breath. They'd had a long day, and she was just on edge because she had her mother to deal with. And she was tired. As good as it had been, their day had been jam-packed.

'What's going on?' Liz asked, suddenly materialising in the kitchen.

'Just putting these away. Apparently Enid Oliphant wouldn't approve,' Jake said, sliding the container into the open cupboard and closing the door. 'Do you want to shower, Em, or should I go?' Jake asked.

'No, you go; I've got a few things to do here,' Emily said. She was liking the way he said the shortened form of her name.

'What can I do?' Liz asked.

'Actually, if you could set the table, that would be great – everything should be there on the bench. And would you mind doing a quick check that the rest of the house is presentable?'

A few minutes later, the lamb was in, the table was set, and the vegetables were ready to put in in half an hour. The bread rolls would follow when the meat came out. Even the lemon pudding dessert was organised.

It was really too warm for a hot dessert, but Emily figured she may as well cook one since she had the oven on anyway and the kitchen heated up as a result. She'd open the verandah doors later, when the cool of evening had settled in. With the front door also open, a nice gully breeze would flow through – and she'd keep the can of bug spray handy for any creepy-crawlies that came in with it.

All she had left to do was have a shower and get dressed. And then relax with a fortifying drink before her parents arrived. Hopefully there would be enough time, and enough water – she had no idea what the ancient hot-water service's capacity was.

'Right, your turn.'

Emily turned to find Jake standing at the kitchen door open to the verandah.

'Wow, you were even quicker than Liz,' she said, trying to drag her eyes away from his pale, bare torso, which had a nice patch of fine dark hair and was surprisingly muscular. She forced her imagination away from what was beneath the forest green towel around his waist.

'Don't want you being told off by your mother for being late.'

'Thanks.' Emily untied her apron and threw it onto the bench, and then bolted to her bedroom to get her robe.

It's like art, she told herself. Nice to look at, even if you had no intention of buying. The last thing she needed in her life was romance. As Emily dragged her robe from the doorknob, she wondered if she'd ever trust herself to have a relationship with a man again.

Maybe. But not for a very, very long time.

Chapter Forty-two

Emily was back in the kitchen when the sound of crunching gravel signalled her parents' arrival. Taking off her apron, she heard Elizabeth welcoming them in and introducing Jake. She listened at the kitchen door for a few moments, out of sight.

'Nice to meet you, Jake. I hope you're enjoying your visit,' Des Oliphant said.

'Yes thanks, Des. Emily has been a very gracious host.'

'Ooh,' Emily heard her mother coo. 'Where has she been hiding you? Your mother must be pleased you've done so well, Elizabeth. She never mentioned you had such a lovely man.'

Emily rolled her eyes at the absurd and blatant fawning, and chanced a look down the hall. The shock of what she saw made her retreat, frowning with confusion. Elizabeth was positively draped around Jake, every bit the doting girlfriend. Why? For whose benefit?

'Emily, your parents are here,' Elizabeth called.

Emily forced a smile on her face, ran a quick, smoothing hand down her hair, and strode out into the hall.

'Ah, here she is,' her father said, meeting Emily halfway. 'Something smells delicious,' he said as he hugged her tightly.

'Thanks Dad. Nothing too special, I'm afraid. Just a lamb roast.'

'How can you say that when you know it's my favourite?' he said, giving her a final squeeze before letting her go.

Enid Oliphant gripped both of Emily's shoulders and air-kissed her from a distance of about six inches. As she let go, Enid gave her daughter a cursory inspection from top to bottom and back up again, ending with a slight frown as she let her go.

It was always the same, and while Emily had come to expect it – even accept it – it still never failed to unsettle her. As much as she tried to force herself not to, Emily's response was to always give herself the same critical appraisal, as she did now. Every time, she mentally kicked herself for taking the bait, but it didn't help – next time she'd do the same thing. Without fail. And find herself lacking, again, without fail.

'You didn't tell me you had such a gorgeous visitor, Emily,' Enid accused.

'Shame on you, Emily,' Elizabeth said quietly beside her, with a grin and a wink.

Emily relaxed slightly. *Ah, so Liz is playing games with my mother. That explains it.*

'Jake, darling,' Elizabeth continued. 'Why don't you settle Auntie Enid and Uncle Des in the lounge and get them a drink – there's a dear.'

'Actually,' Emily said, 'the kitchen would be better. There's a nice breeze and dinner isn't too far away.'

'Okay, the kitchen it is,' Des Oliphant said jovially, and led the way.

Emily noticed her mother's nose wrinkle with distaste, and felt the slightest shimmer of satisfaction.

Everyone settled around the table, except Emily, who retrieved her apron from the bench. She carefully manoeuvred Jake around to sit him next to Enid. Her father sat himself opposite with Elizabeth, and the end was left for her.

She'd really wanted her father to be the head of the table, but she hadn't got in quickly enough, and now it was too late. What sort of a fool would she look now if she shuffled everyone around like chess pieces for no apparent reason?

Anyway, it doesn't matter, she told herself, turning to put the finishing touches on her simple cheese platter. It was too hot for her usual starter of pumpkin soup, but one of those fancy cold soups would have been just the shot. She must see if Barbara had any good recipes for starters; she needed a larger repertoire.

'Em, would you like to open the red wine now, or wait for dinner?' her father asked.

'Actually, I wouldn't mind a white – I put a bottle in the fridge earlier,' Elizabeth said. 'Could you get me one, Jake sweetie,' she cooed.

Emily bristled. *God, Liz. You're laying it on a bit thick.*

'Uh, sure. Des, Enid, what can I get you? I brought some beer, if you prefer.'

'Actually, that'd be great,' Des said. 'But only if you have a light – designated driver and all that.'

'I certainly do, it's my preference.'

'Great.'

'Enid?'

'I think I'll join Elizabeth in a white – as long as it's not chardonnay; too bitter for me.'

'No, I think it's a sauvignon blanc,' Jake said.

'Yes, from the Marlborough region in New Zealand.'

Emily was pleased to hear no endearments. Jake clearly wasn't going along with Elizabeth's charade. Or *was* it a charade? And why did it matter, anyway? She started slightly when he appeared beside her and leant against the bench.

'Are you okay?' he asked in a whisper. 'Sorry Liz's being a bit full-on – nothing to do with me.'

'I'm fine, thanks,' she said, her answer giving away nothing of the appreciation she felt at his acknowledgment of the situation.

'What can I get you to drink?' he asked.

'Actually, I'd love a beer, if that's okay.'

'Your wish is my command,' he said, giving a little bow, which Emily thought must have been a deliberate attempt to lighten her mood.

She smiled in response, and added the crackers to the platter.

A few moments later there was a nudge at her leg and she looked down to find Grace gazing up at her with a cocked head and a pleading expression.

'Ah, dinner time, is it, darling girl?' *You could almost set the clock by the dog*, she thought with amusement as she put the completed platter onto the table.

'Tuck in, everyone,' she said. 'Dinner won't be long.'

She then gave the dog a quick pat before going to the fridge for the raw lamb bone she'd bought to keep her amused for the evening. She was just pouring Grace's dry food into the bowl behind the table when Enid cried out.

'You're not having that filthy creature eat where we are, surely?! It's disgusting! And what's it doing inside, anyway?'

So it had started. Not fifteen minutes had passed and her mother was already picking on her. Even the presence of a stranger hadn't been enough to prevent an outburst.

'She's an inside dog, Mum. It's her home as much as mine.' *And she's more welcome here than you are at this point in time.*

'Enid, it's Emily's house, and if she chooses to keep a dog inside then I think that's her choice.'

'Thanks Dad,' Emily muttered as she patted Grace, who was tucking heartily into her bone, clearly oblivious to the tension around her.

'Well, it's not hygienic,' Enid huffed, and sat back with her arms folded.

'Mum, she gets bathed every week, and the floor gets mopped regularly, and...' Emily stopped herself, wondering why she should have to defend herself in her own home. If Jake wasn't here, she'd have given Enid a piece of her mind.

But who was she kidding? She'd spent her whole life kowtowing to her mother and then internally seething for days, weeks.

'I can attest to Grace's cleanliness,' Jake piped up in the tense lull that ensued. 'We shared a cuddle in my bed this morning.'

'You didn't tell me you'd been unfaithful, darling,' Elizabeth whined.

Just what the hell is she playing at? Emily silently cursed, as she opened the oven to check the meat. At least Jake had the decency to look confused.

'He must have snuck her in when I went to the bathroom, naughty boy.'

Emily glanced, frowning, at the table and noticed a look of annoyance cross Jake's face before disappearing just as quickly.

'So, Jake. What brings you so far from home?' Des asked, much to Emily's relief.

'Change of scenery. For a bit of photography, actually, Des.'

'Uncle D, he's the most *talented* photographer – you should see his shots.'

'I'd love to.'

'Maybe another time,' Jake said quietly, fiddling with his glass of beer.

'Ooh, so do you exhibit?' Enid asked.

Emily helped herself to some cheese while closing her eyes briefly and rolling them at the euphemism. She may as well have just said, 'Are you famous? Are you worth being associated with?'

'No, that's not why I do it. I prefer...'

'He's too modest, Auntie E. He's sold heaps…'

'Only at the South Melbourne Market.'

'Well, it's only the *best* market in the whole of Melbourne,' Elizabeth said.

'Oh, you must be *very* good,' Enid cooed.

Emily quietly seethed as she concentrated on her cheese and cracker. Just what was this Uncle D and Auntie E business? It was ridiculous, almost funny. She was thirty-four, for goodness sake!

'It's just a hobby, really – and part of my work as an…'

'It doesn't sound like a hobby if they're selling so well,' Enid cooed.

'He's really *very* talented. It's only a matter of time before one of the big galleries picks him up.'

'Well, I hope to get an invite to the opening when the time comes,' Enid said.

Out of the corner of her eye Emily noticed her mother give Jake's hand a brief stroke. *Oh, for God's sake, get me a bucket*, she thought, closing her eyes and shaking her head ever so slightly.

'So what is it you do – other than the photography?' her father asked.

'I'm an architect. I run my own small firm.'

Emily could almost hear the cogs turning in her mother's brain as she tried to calculate his net worth.

'Dad, Jake's also a qualified builder,' Emily said.

'Really? That must put you in a better position than most architects.'

'Yes, especially when the trades like to pretend you don't know anything about getting your hands dirty. I've had a couple of fun times trotting out *that* revelation.'

'I'll bet. Did Em tell you we've just done a bit of work here? She's a dab hand with the tools – sanded all the floors herself, you know.'

Now it was Emily's turn to blush slightly as she got up to take the meat out of the oven and put the bread rolls in.

'No, she didn't tell me any of that,' Jake said, giving Emily a lingering look – of what, Emily wasn't sure.

She felt her face getting warmer as she placed foil over the meat and set it to rest. *All that slaving over a hot stove*, she told herself.

'This really is lovely cheese, Emily,' Jake said, smiling at her.

'Mmm, lovely,' Des agreed. There were a couple of other non-committal murmurs.

'Thanks.'

'So how long are we to have your lovely company, Jake?' Enid asked, putting her half-eaten cheese and cracker down on her bread plate and looking expectantly at him.

'We're heading back Tuesday morning,' Elizabeth said, driving the knife into the block of cheese.

Hang on. Tuesday is only the day after next. Why so soon? Emily stared at her cousin's roughly cut lump of cheese and thought she knew how it felt.

'I have to get back,' Elizabeth shrugged, as if it was all the explanation needed.

Why hadn't Jake mentioned it when the two of them had been chatting yesterday? The prospect of suddenly being alone in the house again filled Emily with dread.

She forced herself to calm down and concentrate on pulling off a good meal. She'd been doing fine prior to their arrival, and she'd be fine after their departure. Yes, it would be good for things to get back to normal. The distraction of guests had been fun, but she really did have to knuckle down and find a job, or at least work out some other plan for her future.

'I'd offer more cheese, but we have roast, and then lemon pudding and ice-cream for dessert,' she said, getting up and collecting the decimated cheese platter from the table.

★

Emily tried to suggest they leave the dishes for the morning, but Jake's insistence had been stronger. Elizabeth didn't exactly heartily agree, but stayed to lend a hand nonetheless. The cynic in Emily wondered if it was more to do with not leaving Jake unattended than pulling her weight on the domestic front.

Lying in bed later, Emily scrutinised the evening with her exhausted mind. Just what was the story with Jake and Elizabeth? Maybe they *were* an item, despite Elizabeth saying otherwise. They could be what people called 'friends with benefits'. But really, why did she care, anyway? It had nothing to do with her. She'd had enough of men and their games.

Speaking of which, the latest talk around town was that Stacy had left John. Barbara had shared the news during their visit that afternoon. Emily let herself bask in the slight satisfaction that at least it wasn't just her – another woman had left the almighty John Stratten. And with a slight smile upon her lips, she rolled over to get some sleep.

It was only ten o'clock, and she could still hear the hum of the television, but she was exhausted from all the cooking and, more so, the emotional tension of being in the same room as her mother. She shouldn't have bitten back over Grace, but it was too late now. Oh well, the food had been pretty good.

She sat up slightly, struck by a sudden thought. Her mother had not passed one comment about how much better the house looked. Not even when the new golden-haired boy – Jake – had raved about its features. Enid had given a quiet harrumph, which only Emily had noticed because she'd been looking and waiting for some sort of response.

That was probably the most annoying thing about her mother – the way she had of refusing to pass comment when proven wrong on something. She was so damn opinionated about nearly everything and everyone, but when proven wrong she'd remain silent, or pretend she hadn't said anything at all. The woman really was wasted on domestic duties and community service – she should have been a criminal, a lawyer or an actress. Better yet, a politician!

Emily was annoyed, but mostly with herself, for getting into a state that meant she'd now find it hard to get to sleep despite her tiredness. She turned over a couple of times before forcing herself to concentrate on the gentle rustling of trees outside, and remembering Granny Mayfair's bedtime mantra: 'Deal with it in the morning'.

Chapter Forty-three

Next morning, Emily was flicking through some old interior design and garden magazines at the kitchen table when Jake came in, followed by Grace. The dog really had taken a shine to him. Emily had stopped letting Grace on her bed at night because she kept disturbing her with bouts of snoring and startled barks in her sleep. *But if Jake's was willing to put up with it, good luck to him*, she thought, smiling.

'Have you had coffee?' he asked. 'And if not, would you like one?'

'No. And yes, that would be lovely, thanks. I only got as far as boiling the kettle.'

A few minutes later Jake put two mugs on the table and sat on the end, around the corner from Emily. 'The house cooled down nicely overnight,' he said.

'Yes, I'm probably going to freeze here come winter.'

'Is there insulation in the roof?'

'No, I don't think so. Dad and David went up there and I'm sure they would have mentioned if there was.'

'It might be worth putting some in, even though it's a rental. It can make quite a difference and it's not all that expensive.'

'How "not all that expensive"?'

'I'd say less than a grand, if you do it yourself – even for a place this big. And it's not hard; you just have to make sure you don't fall through the ceiling. It's a pity we're going tomorrow. I could have done it for you.'

'Thanks, but I'm sure Dad will help if I decide to do it. It's just that my finances are all over the place at the moment, and I need to see where I am when things settle down a bit.'

Emily felt embarrassed being so open with a mere acquaintance. She'd been raised to believe that discussing finances with strangers was terribly crass.

'I know what you mean. Some things need to sort themselves out. Things will get easier, Em, you'll see.'

Emily looked at him. *Just how much had Elizabeth told him about her circumstances?* Her cousin chose that moment to enter.

'What time do you call this?' Jake teased.

'Far too bloody early,' Elizabeth said, frowning. 'God knows how, but I think I've got a hangover.'

Emily had mixed feelings about them leaving in twenty-four hours. Gran had had an old saying that guests were like fish – they should be off after three days. Before the Alzheimer's, she'd had a perpetual line of visitors and never seemed to tire of the intrusion, though they were usually people just staying overnight on their way to somewhere else. Emily wondered how the hell she'd done it week after week, year after year.

It struck her now that running a guesthouse wouldn't be too dissimilar. How could she do that if she couldn't cope with having her cousin stay? She couldn't use the excuse that Elizabeth, in particular, rubbed her up the wrong way, because her guests would come in all personalities, with all sorts of peculiar demands and – no doubt – complaints.

No, Emily decided, she really would be rethinking the idea of a B&B – if she ever had the means to go down that path. But it didn't hurt to dream, now did it? *Certainly not*, she thought, returning to the magazine in front of her.

She let out a small gasp when she turned the page – the sight before her was spectacular: a modern lounge room decorated in the rich red and gold of a past era of opulence. Two coffee bean-coloured studded leather chesterfields faced each other. A magnificent trunk – in leather or painted timber, she couldn't tell which – sat between them, a Persian prayer rug laid on top as a table cloth. Her mouth was practically watering as she tore the double-page spread out.

'What is it?' Jake asked.

'Oh, I'm just collecting ideas in case I ever get to own this place and do it up. You know, when money's no object,' she said wistfully. 'I love this look,' she added, turning the pages towards him. 'Just feeding my delusions, really,' she added with a laugh.

'Hey, it's important to have dreams to strive for – it's what keeps us going.'

Elizabeth sat down across from Emily with a mug of steaming milky coffee. 'I love those ottomans,' she said, pointing at the picture laid out in front of Jake. 'I saw some in a shop selling Moroccan imports the other week. They were hundreds of dollars. Couldn't believe it.'

'Wow, why so expensive?'

'Well, the ones I saw were leather. But they were only stuffed with rags. For that price I'd want gold or silver coins, or something.'

'I suppose you prefer a more modern look, Jake?' Emily said. 'Given you're an architect.' She was mesmerised by his long fingers tapping against the side of his mug.

'Actually, I love the imperial look. There's not a large, white, shiny Italianate tile to be seen at my place – not that it's anything as grand as this. Remember, I'm an architect who specialises in old-world charm.' He grinned. 'I'm minimalist only in that I'm not a fan of clutter. Also, I have a slow and steady approach to decorating, so...'

'That's code for "haven't got around to it yet",' Elizabeth cut in.

'No, it's not,' Jake said, looking sharply at her. 'It means I like to slowly gather things that mean something to me. I prefer to wait until I find something that insists I buy it, rather than just filling the space as quickly as I can,' he explained to Emily.

'Unlike me, you mean?' Elizabeth shot back.

'I didn't say that.'

'But it's what you meant.'

'We're all allowed our differences, Liz. Don't be so damn prickly. You like to shop and buy, I like to spend ages browsing,' he said, shrugging. 'I tend to suffer buyer's remorse if I jump in too quickly,' he added by way of explanation to Emily.

'I'm starving; what's for breakfast?' Elizabeth said, obviously keen to change the subject.

Emily moved to get up. 'I was thinking of doing bacon and eggs.'

'Great! That's exactly what my stomach's craving,' Elizabeth said.

'Yum,' Jake said. 'But I'm doing the cooking – if that's all right with you, Em. You've been waiting on us hand and foot since we got here.'

Again Emily enjoyed the way her abbreviated name rolled off his tongue. 'I really don't mind,' she said, smiling warmly at him.

'Good, just point me in the direction of the frypan, then.'

'I mean, I don't mind doing the cooking,' Emily protested. 'You're guests.'

'I know what you meant,' Jake said, grinning, 'and I *insist*. Now you sit there with your magazines of dreams and just tell me where things are when I ask.'

'Okay, if you insist.' Emily found she rather liked him gently ordering her about.

'Indeed I do, m'lady. Would you like another coffee?'

'Thanks, that would be great. White…'

'White with one. Yes, I know, I've been taking notes. One for you too, Liz?' Jake asked.

'No thanks. I think I'll have a shower if you've got breakfast under control. Won't be long.'

She left the room and Jake stared after her for a few moments, frowning. Emily tried to re-focus on her magazine, but found her attention constantly returning to his back.

'That was fantastic,' Emily said, three quarters of an hour later, pushing her plate away from her. 'Thanks Jake.'

'Mmm, thanks,' Elizabeth agreed, absently flicking through one of Emily's magazines.

'Glad you enjoyed it, missy, because it's your turn to do the dishes,' Jake said.

'Fair enough,' Elizabeth said, getting up to clear the table. 'Then what are we going to do?'

Maybe that's what's up with Liz – she's bored. Fair enough, she supposed. They had only left the house to drive around the local district. No doubt her cousin was suffering shopping or café withdrawal.

'Why don't we take a drive over to Charity Flat for a late lunch?' Emily suggested. 'The pub's been done up recently and by all accounts now does half-decent food. It's only forty minutes' drive away. Jake, there's a couple of old buildings you might find worth photographing too.'

'Sounds perfect,' Jake said.

'There are a few antique shops and a place with lovely gifts.

Probably a little too rural for you, Liz, but it'll be a change of scenery.'

'Great. Should we invite David and Barbara along? They were such good company yesterday,' Elizabeth said.

'I think they've got something on already,' Emily said. But it was a white lie; she wasn't actually sure what they were up to that day and wasn't about to ask. She really wasn't up for a repeat of Liz's sparring with Barbara and flirting with David.

Chapter Forty-four

'Hello, anybody home?'

Jake, Emily and Elizabeth exchanged questioning expressions. Emily got up, leaving Jake at the table and Elizabeth drying the last of the dishes. 'Coming!' she called, hurrying down the hall.

The voice wasn't familiar, and it was weird that Grace hadn't announced the visitor's arrival by barking. The dog was curled up in her basket with a bright, satisfied grin after being given a few pieces of bacon rind by Jake.

When Emily got to the door, a woman dressed neatly in jeans and an emerald green polo shirt was standing at the threshold. The woman's car, a nondescript white sedan, was parked just beyond the verandah steps.

'Can I help you?' Emily said, cursing the house for not having a basic wooden screen door.

'I hope so,' the woman said, pushing a pair of sunglasses up onto her head. 'I think I've got myself lost,' she added, slapping what looked like a folded map against her thigh. She had friendly pale brown eyes, and her dark reddish hair was tied in a bun at the back of her head. She appeared to be quite a few years older than Emily, but perhaps that was just because of her freckled complexion. She'd always found it hard to tell people's ages.

'I'm Emily Oliphant,' Emily said, smiling warmly and holding out her hand.

'Tara Wickham,' the woman said, shaking hands. 'Sorry, I'm a little flustered,' she said, pushing imaginary strands of hair from her face. 'I've been driving around for ages…'

'Um, well, would you like to come in? I could get you a glass of water, or a coffee.'

'That would be great. As long as I'm not intruding.' It was clearly a throwaway line; Tara Wickham looked to Emily like she very much wanted to come in. She was peering inquisitively into the darkened hall.

Emily should probably have said something about them actually heading out, but instead she led the way back down the hall. Hopefully this Tara woman wouldn't want to hang around too long.

'Jake, Elizabeth, this is Tara Wickham – Jake and Elizabeth are visiting from Melbourne.' Emily thought Tara was right behind her, but as she turned to introduce her, she saw that the other woman was still at the open door to the lounge-dining room, looking in. Emily was a little annoyed. Even if it wasn't technically her house, it was her *home*, and she didn't like this stranger scrutinising it. She cleared her throat.

Tara recovered herself and hurried into the kitchen. 'Hello,' she said, thrusting out her right hand.

They exchanged handshakes as Emily repeated the introductions.

'Are you sure I'm not intruding? I didn't realise you had guests,' Tara said, taking a seat at the table. 'I seem to have got myself lost,' she explained hastily to Jake and Elizabeth.

'Well, we are off to Charity Flat soon,' Emily said, 'but we do have a few minutes. Tea, coffee or Milo?'

'Ah, Charity Flat, haven't been there in years. A Milo would be great, thanks.'

'Do you guys want another drink?' Emily asked.

'No thanks,' Liz and Jake said in unison.

'Are you from around here originally, then?' Emily asked, filling the kettle at the sink.

'No, but I have family in the area. I used to visit when I was a child, but not in the past twenty years or so. I was planning a surprise visit,' she said with a tight laugh, slapping the map on the table, 'but I can't seem to find them.'

'So who's your family?' Liz asked. 'Everyone knows everyone around here; Emily here's bound to know them. She's probably even related to them,' she added with a hearty chuckle.

'Oh. Just a couple of old bachelor cousins. They're brothers. I think they keep pretty much to themselves.'

At hearing this, the hair on Emily's arms stood up and her back tightened. *How many old bachelor brothers could there be around here?* She had the distinct feeling Tara was being evasive. She wasn't sure why, but she was suddenly uneasy. Hoping Tara would say more, Emily took her time to plug the appliance in and get the things back out of the cupboards. But Tara didn't elaborate.

'You don't mean the Baker brothers, do you? Donald and Trevor?' Emily finally offered.

'Actually, yes. Do you know them?'

'This is their house. I'm renting it from them.'

'Ah, so this is the original Baker home, then?'

'I think so,' Emily said reluctantly. She remembered how nosy Tara had been on her way down the hall. Her back stiffened again as she wondered if Tara Wickham was really lost and there by accident.

And so what if she isn't? she thought. She's not going to just bowl up and say, 'Hey, my great-aunt and uncle used to live here, do you mind if I come in and take a look around?' Emily could imagine her mother doing just that, though she was country born and raised. This Tara woman seemed to have more of a city air about her.

'Isn't it a small world?' Liz said.

'It is indeed,' Tara agreed.

Emily frowned as she made the one mug of Milo, unable to judge Tara's tone, and with her back to her, unable to read her expression.

'I haven't actually been to their other house,' she said, putting the mug in front of Tara.

'Thanks. I think they must be more to the north-east.' Tara said.

'I don't know. Sorry, I'm no help at all.'

'Oh well, I'll just have to drive to the next place and ask,' she said, taking a sip.

'I'm afraid I don't know where the nearest house is,' Emily said apologetically. 'I'm not really from around here either. I've only just moved in.'

'So, Tara, what do you do when you're not out driving around the countryside looking for old relatives?' Jake asked.

Emily was a little taken aback at his forthrightness. Perhaps it was normal in Melbourne to ask relative strangers straight up what they did for a job. Not around here. Around here most men were on the land and most women were stay-at-home wives and mothers, or they held dull jobs on check-outs or in offices. There was no need to ask, and certainly not as a conversation starter.

'Oh. I'm a financial planner. I advise people on the best strategy for their financial future. Freedom now and in retirement, making sure they're getting whatever Centrelink assistance they're entitled to. It can be quite a juggling act.'

'I'm sure. Tell me, what are your thoughts on subdividing?'

'Can be a way to make a lot of money, depending on where the land is. I've actually done quite well out of a couple of city blocks.'

'What about farmland?'

'As in rural living blocks?'

'Yes, farmers selling off small parcels of land to free up some extra cash.'

'I could put you in touch with some developers if it's something you're interested in.'

'Thanks, but I'm more interested from a financial planning perspective. Is it something you'd recommend farmers do?'

'Carve off portions of a much larger holding to access the value?'

'Yes.'

'Well, obviously every situation is different, and I would need to know your full financial history, goals, et cetera, before giving any sort of advice.'

'It's not for me. I'm speaking hypothetically. Say a farmer was near or past retirement age and they wanted a bit of cash to make themselves a little more comfortable. Is it something you would recommend?'

'Oh, well, *hypothetically* speaking, no, it's not something I would generally recommend to someone near to or past retirement age. I'd be more inclined to suggest selling everything up, investing in superannuation or managed funds, and seeing if they qualify for the aged pension.'

'You mean, you'd have them leave the land completely?'

'That's usually the better outcome. For those in difficulty, freeing up the equity in their land can often give them more financial freedom and peace of mind.'

'And if they didn't want to sell up? *Hypothetically.*'

Emily wondered about Jake's line of questioning. He was becoming slightly combative, and she asked herself why. Had someone in his family received poor financial advice? Had he?

'Well then, *hypothetically*, I probably wouldn't be of much help. I sell investment and superannuation products. So my clients are usually those with money to invest, seeking advice and options.'

'Are there options other than selling up?' Jake continued.

'Well, you asked about subdivision. If you're now talking financial planning options, generally, then yes, there is usually more than one option. But as I said before, it would all depend on the individual's circumstances.'

Emily wondered now if Tara was visiting the Baker brothers to talk them into selling up. Perhaps they had asked her to come out and give them some advice. No, hadn't she said her visit was a surprise?

'My dad knew Donald and Trevor's parents before they left the district,' she said, desperate to change the topic of conversation. 'Were your parents from around here as well?'

'Yes, but they left before I was born. I actually grew up on a farm over in Western Australia – cereal and wool country, like around here.'

'So you'd have to understand a farmer's connection to the land. Where's your compassion and understanding?' Jake asked, looking incredulous.

'Compassion and understanding don't pay the bills. And it was a hypothetical discussion we were having, remember?' Tara offered a tight smile and shifted in her seat.

Jake changed tack, but clearly wasn't giving in. Emily was intrigued to see a different side of him, but was also concerned that he was being less than hospitable. 'So, what are the old farmers meant to do all day, once they've sold up?'

'Travel, potter around in the garden, take up bowls, do what most other retired people do: enjoy their retirement!'

Emily hated the way Tara waved her arm dismissively. It must be so bloody easy when they were just clients and there weren't any consequences to directly affect her.

'What are your thoughts on investing in shares? Any hot tips?' Elizabeth suddenly asked.

'Shares are fine if you're talking long-term. Though you have to be careful – the market is still pretty volatile thanks to the GFC. No sure bets, I'm afraid.'

'The trouble with what you do,' Jake interrupted, 'is that it's still only another opinion. And you can be wrong, can't you?'

'Well, I have had extensive training.'

'But it's just sales, really, isn't it? It's not really about helping people, it's more about filling your company's coffers.'

'Jake, I'm sure Tara has better things to do with her time on a Sunday than defend her profession,' Emily cut in quickly. 'Tara, would you like me to phone your cousins and get directions?' she asked.

'Thanks, but I have their number in my mobile. I'd better get going and let you head off,' Tara said, pushing her cup away and getting up.

So why didn't you call them when you got lost? Unease wound its way through her again.

'Thank you, Emily, for the cuppa, and you, Jake, for the stimulating conversation. Elizabeth, lovely to meet you. Emily, here's my card if you ever need any advice of a financial nature. I'm based in Adelaide. No point giving you one, Elizabeth or Jake, is there?' she said brightly – a little provocatively, Emily thought.

'No thanks,' Jake mumbled.

'I've got some friends in finance in Melbourne, but thanks anyway,' Elizabeth muttered.

The three of them followed Tara down the hall and out onto the front verandah. As she walked, Emily marvelled at Tara's ability to remain cool despite Jake's criticism and refrain from getting into a full-blown row. She frowned at his behaviour. It was rude. Sure, he might have issues with financial planners, but it was her house, and Tara was her guest. Well, not exactly. But she'd invited her in. And she still had the unsettling feeling that Tara hadn't been totally honest with her.

'Jeez, Jake, what was that all about?' Elizabeth demanded when the car was out of sight.

'What was what all about?'

'The interrogation.'

'Interrogation? I was only satisfying my curiosity.'

'Yeah, Hitler-style.'

'I wasn't that bad, was I, Em?'

'Well, actually you were a bit aggressive,' she said, carefully choosing her words.

'Oh well, she seemed able to take it.'

'I hope she doesn't talk her cousins into selling everything up,' Liz said.

'Hmm. That's what I was thinking.'

'It's interesting, isn't it, how she wouldn't support selling off bits of land to free up some cash,' Liz said. 'It sounds like a good idea to me.'

'Me too.' A thought suddenly struck Emily. *Hang on, was Jake's hypothetical questioning about* this *place,* me? He'd said 'not for me'. Had he cast his eyes briefly in her direction when he'd said it? The more she thought about it, the more she was convinced he had been asking on her behalf. She felt herself blush ever so slightly before returning her attention to Liz, who had carried on talking.

'But I guess they're all about super and allocated pensions and getting the most out of Centrelink.'

'And I hear you're only allowed to earn a miniscule amount each week before it affects your pension,' Emily said.

'So, seriously, Jake, what's your beef with Tara?' Liz asked.

'I don't have a beef – I just don't trust financial planners, advisors, whatever you want to call them. I went to see one once and I'd be broke if I'd taken his advice. What people don't seem to realise is that their advice really is subjective. At least accountants have concrete facts to work with – this is how much you've got, this is how much tax you're going to pay, this is what you can do legally to minimise it. And don't forget, most of the advice financial planners give is about investing in products that they receive a commission on. So you tell me whose interests they have in mind.'

'I hear the government has changed the regulations so they won't get commissions anymore – they'll just charge hourly for each service they perform,' Liz said.

'Yeah, and about time too,' Jake said. 'Shall we go and see what Charity Flat has to offer?'

Jake offered to drive since the road was sealed. Emily was content to sit in the back and enjoy the scenery. But her head was still whirring with the thought of buying the house and a few acres. It crept into her mind whenever she let it.

First David had mentioned it and now Jake. They were both intelligent, sensible men, which told Emily there must be some merit to the idea. Though of course, even if she could get Donald and Trevor to agree – which was unlikely, especially if they asked their cousin for advice – there was a major hurdle. Money.

Why the hell hadn't she got professional advice on the settlement? If only she'd spoken to a lawyer. Though, like Barbara had said, it really wouldn't have mattered much; the figures were cleverly fudged.

Emily looked at Grace sprawled across the back seat beside her and thought how good it was of Jake to let the dog in his car with its lovely leather upholstery. He really was a very nice man.

Chapter Forty-five

'Is that a giant kangaroo up ahead?' Jake asked after they'd rounded the last bend and were slowing on their approach into Charity Flat.

'Big,' Emily corrected, leaning forward into the gap between the two front seats. 'And it's not a kangaroo, it's a wallaby. It was originally a kangaroo, but a big wind took off the top section a few years back and it got shortened during repairs. That's why it's a little out of proportion. You'll see when we get alongside it,' she explained. 'I think it's made of fibreglass.'

'Oh, right,' Jake said.

'You're kidding,' Liz said.

'Nope,' Emily replied, smirking.

Jake followed her directions and before long they were parked where they had a full side-on view of the enormous sculpture that stood about two stories high.

'Welcome to the Big Wallaby-Once-Kangaroo!' Emily declared, putting her hands on Liz and Jake's shoulders. 'Isn't it something?'

'Yep, it's that all right,' Liz said.

'The question is, why?' Jake said, shaking his head.

'The big ram was already taken, as was the big farmer, and pretty much everything else that relates to this area. There is actually another kangaroo somewhere. I wouldn't have minded an emu – there are plenty of live ones around here. But anyway, it's a bit late now.'

'I've just got to get a photo of this,' Jake said, undoing his seatbelt and getting out.

'Don't say I don't present you with the best photo opportunities,' Emily said, laughing. 'Come on, Gracie.'

Liz and Emily got out. Grace trotted over to where Jake already had his camera out and was lining up the object for a photo.

'The sign says Giftware. I wonder if there's anything suitable for Mum for Christmas,' Liz said, looking in the direction of the nearby shop.

'I wouldn't bet on it, unless you want to get her a set of placemats, coasters or stubby holders adorned in pictures of a kitsch, stumpy wallaby-slash-kangaroo sculpture.'

'Come on, you all have to pose for me,' Jake called. 'It's a pity the pouch is so high up – how cool would a photo of Grace peeping out of it have been? Oh well. Gather around, gather around.'

Emily and Liz put their arms around each other and pulled silly faces while Jake snapped away. They allowed him one serious one with them smiling like well-behaved, mature adults.

'One more serious one with Grace, though I can only fit up to the pouch. It looks like you're standing in front of a big pile of poo from here,' he said with a chuckle, his eye on the viewfinder. 'What fun,' he said, when he'd finished and was putting the lens cap back on the camera. 'Now let's see what the shop has to offer.'

'I'll wait outside with Grace,' Emily said.

'Are you sure?' Jake said.

'Trust me, you won't be long,' she said knowingly.

Ten minutes later, significantly longer than Emily had anticipated, Liz and Jake emerged carrying a couple of small, thin paper
bags, and three bulging ones. They crossed to where Emily was
perched on the wallaby's long back feet, in the shade of its front
paws. Grace was snoozing at her feet.

'For you,' Jake said, handing Emily one of the small bulging
paper bags.

'Er, thank you. What is it?' she asked, taking it from him,
instantly detecting warmth.

'A kangaroo hotdog. The sign above the counter says they're
famous for them.'

Emily was doubtful.

'If you don't like it, I'm sure Grace will happily take it off your
hands.'

At hearing her name, Grace sat to attention, her gaze shifting
between Jake and Emily. She was concentrating so hard her tail
was completely still.

Liz and Jake settled on the base of the town's mascot and they
all unwrapped the tops from their hotdog packaging. Emily hadn't
thought she'd want lunch yet after the big breakfast they'd had a
mere few hours earlier. But as the warm bread, onion and meat
smells wafted out of the bag, her mouth began to water.

'Mmm,' Jake murmured through his first mouthful.

'It's actually quite good,' Liz said.

'Mmm, it is. Thanks very much. Sorry Gracie,' Emily said. But
she gave in to the dog's pleading look and ripped a bit of bread off
and fed it to her.

'Surely there's something wrong in celebrating an animal with
a giant monument and then selling its meat stuffed into a bread
roll,' Jake said, looking down at his food and shaking his head
slowly with wonder.

'Oh well, it tastes great to me,' Liz said, taking another large bite.

Emily was surprised Liz was tucking in with such gusto. She'd been a little concerned at the prospect of taking her to the pub for lunch.

'So, what else did you buy?' Emily asked, nodding at the other white paper bags lying beside Jake and Liz.

'Fridge magnet and a postcard,' Jake said.

'I got a fridge magnet too,' Liz said. 'It says "I hopped through Charity Flat". I've never seen anything so tacky – I just had to have it for a laugh. And to provide proof of actually being at the Big Wallaby. No one in Melbourne will believe me otherwise.'

'Oh, come on, surely the Big Wallaby has made Charity Flat famous right across the country,' Emily said, in mock consternation.

'Afraid not. I hope there'll be somewhere else here that might have something for Mum for Christmas,' Liz said.

'Oh God. Christmas, what a pain!' Emily declared. 'We stopped exchanging presents and doing all the Christmas palaver years ago. We don't even put up a tree anymore.'

'Where's your Christmas spirit?' Liz asked, aghast.

'Gone. As far as I'm concerned, it's just far too commercial. It's all about presents. And these days everyone has everything they need and you just end up exchanging useless crap or vouchers. I don't see the point.'

'And spending the day with people who drive you mad – that's also what Christmas seems to be about,' Liz added thoughtfully.

'Listen to you two,' Jake chided. 'You should start an anti-Christmas club.'

'I'm already in one, remember,' Emily said with a chuckle.

'Unfortunately, I don't think my parents would let me get away with it,' Liz said soberly. 'No idea why Enid has subscribed; I would have thought she'd be clambering to have a houseful to impress.'

'I know, who would have thought?'

'Right, where to next?' Jake asked, giving Grace the end of his bun before scrunching up his paper bag.

'There's not a whole lot to see – just a couple of streets. But there are a few nice old stone buildings you might like to take some photos of. The pub's worth seeing, and the Institute. And the War Memorial Garden is quite pretty.'

'Sounds good to me. Ready to go, then?' Jake asked.

'Yep, let's do it,' Liz said.

They got up and made their way back to the car, putting their rubbish in the bin on their way past.

They drove up and down the few streets, which were laid out in a north-south, east-west grid, the same as Wattle Creek and many other South Australian towns.

In addition to Emily's suggested stops, Jake pulled up alongside the huge white grain silos and old railway siding. Emily didn't see what was interesting about the huge white concrete structures – she saw silos most days of her life – but she kept her opinion to herself. The girls waited in the car with Grace.

Jake was particularly taken with the hotel, as Emily knew he would be. Its stonework was lovely, and the unbecoming nineteen-sixties features had been removed during its full restoration. She'd left it until last so they could have a late afternoon tea or early dinner before setting off home.

They parked the car in front of the hotel and walked the almost empty main street, each taking turns to hold Grace and wait outside while the others went into the shops. Across the road was a newsagent, a bank and a clothing store with a giftware section out the back. The side with the hotel also held the post office, a pharmacy, another bank, and a farm supplies and fodder store.

Emily hadn't thought Jake and Liz would be remotely interested in the fodder store, and followed them in bewilderedly. She was becoming bored of feeling like a tour guide; there was nothing worse than shopping when you had no money to spend. Thankfully she hadn't seen much she would have bought, anyway.

The last stop before the hotel was another gift shop. Emily expected more kitsch giftware, as had been in the shop across the road, but gasped when they walked in. As did Liz. Surrounding them was a fine selection of good quality merchandise: photo frames, homewares, accessories like scarves and wraps, gloves and hats. It was a case of sensory overload, but in a good way – except for the depressing fact that she had no money to spend. She ambled around picking up bits and pieces and showing an interest. She would have loved some of the gorgeous red-and-white and black-and-white-spotted mugs. She sighed to herself and put them back down; the mugs her dad had picked up from the shack sale were perfectly fine. She went outside to relieve Jake of Grace and let him have a look around the shop.

Emily got a shock when she checked her watch and found it was almost five o'clock. The lady would want to shut up the shop soon. A few minutes later Liz appeared beside her, laden with parcels, and announced she was done. Jake followed soon after, also carrying a parcel.

'I think I'm in need of a beer,' he declared as they left the shop.

'I'm starving,' Liz announced.

They put their shopping in the car, and after Jake had taken some photos of the exterior of the hotel, they went inside. They agreed Grace was probably tired enough to stay in the car for a little while.

'Oh, isn't this lovely?' Liz said as they entered a small area set up with café tables and chairs and a glass display full of pies and cakes. 'Ooh look, a coffee machine. I'd kill for a decent latte!'

'You girls get settled, I'm just going to have a quick look around,' Jake said.

Emily chose a seat with a clear view of Jake's car through

the window. She was pleased to see no sign of Grace looking distressed; the dog was no doubt fast asleep after walking the street on her little legs.

As Emily sat, she marvelled at Jake's confidence. Walking through a country pub was disconcerting when you were an outsider; people tended to stare. She couldn't imagine taking photos while being openly stared at.

'Coffee, Em? My buy,' Liz called from the counter.

'Thanks Liz, but I'd prefer a hot chocolate if they have it.'

'No worries.' A few moments later Liz returned with three laminated menu cards. 'I wouldn't mind a piece of the chocolate torte, but it's too close to dinnertime. The menu looks good,' she said, handing Emily one.

Soon after, Jake put a large glass of beer on the table and his camera on an empty chair and sat down.

'Nice place,' he said. 'And the people seem friendly enough.'

Moments later a waitress appeared beside them.

'Latte?' she asked.

'Yes, that's me. Thanks very much,' Liz said.

'There you are,' the woman said, putting the two mugs down.

'Cheers,' Jake said, raising his glass to their mugs. 'Here's to another great day and Emily's wonderful hospitality.'

They clinked glasses and then took their time over their drinks, perusing the menus while waiting for the clock over the counter to reach six – the time stated on the menu when evening meals could be ordered.

Emily had a battle between her tastebuds and her conscience before deciding that one T-bone out wouldn't break the bank. She hadn't bought steak since leaving John – it was so much dearer than lamb. But now she had an intense craving for some.

When the clock showed six, Jake got up and took their

orders – three steaks cooked medium and with mushroom sauce. Emily moved to get her wallet from her handbag, but Jake put a hand on her arm and told her he was paying. She could still feel the warmth of his hand on her sleeve long after he left the table. She had to forcibly stop herself from staring at his jeans-clad backside as he stood with his back to them.

The food was divine and they all raved over their first few mouthfuls before settling down to eat. Emily felt a sense of pride and satisfaction at hearing the city slickers enjoying their country pub meal so much.

Chapter Forty-six

They got back just on dark and Emily was pleased they'd taken Grace with them. Otherwise she'd have been left alone outside the house, most likely terrified.

'I'm just going to pack all my stuff so we can get an early start,' Elizabeth announced as Emily closed the front door behind them.

'I think I'll do the same,' Jake said.

'I'll put the kettle on,' Emily said, feeling her heart sink at the reminder her guests – particularly Jake – were leaving so soon.

'That was quick,' Emily said when Jake appeared in the kitchen less than ten minutes later. He went to the table and sat down.

'Now, Em, about the jam,' he said. 'I was serious the other day when we were talking about the markets.'

'But wouldn't heaps of people be selling homemade jam already?' Emily asked.

'I haven't seen any,' he said. 'I could buy some from you and then if it don't sell I could keep it – that would be fair, wouldn't it?'

Emily nodded. 'I guess.'

'So, how would you feel about me taking, say, twenty jars with me?'

If he'd said two, she would have willingly given them to him. But twenty?! 'Hmm, okay.'

'Would one hundred dollars cover it?'

'That's five dollars a jar! Jake, that's way too much.'

'No, it's not; five dollars is about right.'

'The op shop and CWA trading table here wouldn't sell it for more than two dollars.'

'That's because they probably have heaps to sell. It's all about demand and supply, and about what people will pay. Em, seriously, I think I could get more than five dollars a jar for it at South Melbourne.'

'How about you pay me two dollars fifty a jar, and whatever else you make on top of that you keep. How's that? Fair?'

'Okay, if you insist,' Jake said with a shrug, and put one of the fifties back in his pocket. 'Write down your postal address, so I can send you a cheque when I prove you wrong,' he said, grinning, and pushing the pad of paper and pen that lived on the end of the table towards her.

'Okay,' Emily said, smiling back. She almost wrote the number for the post box she and John had shared, and only caught herself just in time. She automatically added her mobile number to the bottom and then had second thoughts. But it was too late; it would look weird to scrub it out or screw up the page and start again.

As she folded it in half and handed it over, Emily wondered if she should have added her email address. She wasn't really much into emailing; all she seemed to receive was junk. She'd checked her email at Barbara's a couple of times, but since moving in here hadn't given it another thought. Until now.

'Thanks. I'll let you know how we go.'

'No, thank *you*,' she said, pocketing the fifty-dollar note. 'I'll find you a box and some packaging so they don't rattle and drive you mad all the way back to Melbourne.'

'No rush,' he said, putting a hand on her shoulder. 'Let's have a cuppa and then deal with it. You sit, I'll get it – Milo, I presume at this hour?'

'Yes thanks,' Emily beamed back at him, and went to sit in what had now become her regular seat at the end of the table. While she watched Jake, she marvelled at how thoughtful he was, and decided she'd like to keep in touch and stay friends. Oh well, it was up to him – he had her number. She was pleased about that now.

For a fleeting moment Emily imagined herself visiting him in Melbourne. But she couldn't do that without spending most of her time with her cousin, and after the last few days, she was beginning to realise she didn't even like Elizabeth all that much.

Emily had always thought it was some weird tall-poppy, competitive thing she felt towards her older cousin. Now she wasn't so sure.

Chapter Forty-seven

'I'll let you know how your jam goes,' Jake called from the passenger window as he and Elizabeth drove away.

'I look forward to it. And thanks so much again for the mugs – I love them.'

A big smile was plastered on Emily's face and she waved until they disappeared into the trees. She couldn't believe they'd bought her two black-and-white and two red-and-white mugs as a thankyou gift – the very ones she'd been admiring. Perhaps the woman in the shop had told them.

She bent down and patted Grace, who was sitting beside her.

'It's just us again now, Gracie.'

Back inside, she flicked the switch on the kettle and slumped into her chair at the end of the table. She felt strangely heavy of heart. Grace looked just as forlorn.

'It's ridiculous, us being all mopey. The world hasn't stopped because they've left.' Maybe it was hormones. She'd stopped taking the pill when she'd split from John and no longer knew where in her cycle she was. Perhaps these unexplained waterworks meant her period was near.

She got up and changed chairs to where she'd sat prior to Jake and Elizabeth's arrival, facing the bench and the window above it.

Jake's last words, 'I'll let you know how the jam goes,' ran through her head as she sat tapping her fingers on the table. She looked over at Grace and tried to calculate just when that would be.

'If they get back to Melbourne on Friday or Saturday, will Jake have time to put the jam in Sunday's market? If he does, he might call Monday, or even Sunday night. If we're lucky.'

Grace cocked an eyebrow, as if unused to hearing her mistress talking to herself.

'Stop staring at me like that. It's about the jam; I'm keen to hear about how the jam sells. That's all.' Emily let out a deep sigh and knelt down to scratch Grace under the chin. And then it hit her. 'Oh God, I've got a crush on him, haven't I? Bloody hell, that's the last thing I need. I guess it's for the best that he lives in another state.'

She looked at Grace for answers, but the dog wandered over to her bed and lay down with a loud groan.

'Thanks, you're a big help. Come on, Gracie, let's go for a walk to cheer us up.'

As soon as she said the words, Grace bounded up and over to her again. Emily liked that about having a pet – that you could confess your innermost thoughts and you wouldn't be mocked. And you'd always have good company for a walk. She pulled on her comfortable walking shoes and Akubra hat.

Emily returned to the house an hour later, feeling a little hot and sweaty, but on the whole, much better. She was startled to find Barbara sitting at her kitchen table. Grace trotted in to meet their guest.

'You really ought to lock up when you go out – I could have been anyone!' Barbara said with a grin, looking up from the magazine on the table in front of her. 'Hope you don't mind, but I helped myself to a coffee – didn't know how long you'd be. I could do with another – can I get you one?' she said, rising.

'Oh, Barbara, you have no idea how good it is to see you,' Emily said, a sudden rush of emotion causing her eyes to fill. The friends hugged.

'Are you feeling a bit sad and lost now the house is empty again?' Barbara asked kindly.

'I am a bit. It's weird, though, Liz drove me nuts, but here I am being all depressed now she's gone.'

'Well, I'm not surprised you're pining for Jake – bit of a dish, that one.'

Emily blushed slightly. 'Knowing my luck he's probably gay. Either that or there's something going on between him and Liz. You should have seen her the other night when Mum and Dad were here.'

'I know she's your cousin, but I reckon she could be trouble if she wanted to be.'

'Hmm, funny you should say that. Mum always called Liz "Trouble with a capital T". Never thought she and I would agree on anything. And I'm sorry she was so rude the other day – I have no idea what that was all about.'

'Bit of insecurity, I suppose. For some reason she saw me as a threat,' Barbara said with a shrug. 'Doesn't matter, and you shouldn't have to apologise for her – she's an adult and you're not her bloody mother! Speaking of which, what did she do when your parents were over?'

'Oh, I don't know. She was all over Jake – literally draped over him – calling him "sweetie" this and "sweetie" that. The poor bloke didn't know where to look half the time. He seemed genuinely embarrassed, even a little annoyed.'

'Well, there you are, then. He's a free agent.'

'But if they're not an item, why would she pretend they were?'

'Two reasons spring to mind. One, she's just messing with your head. Two, wishful thinking on her part – he's a pretty good catch, remember. There's probably a mix of both, but having spent a day with her – and no offence – I'd put my money on option one. She's just messing with you, probably because she has some insecurity where you're concerned.'

'What?! How the hell could I make Elizabeth feel insecure? She's a successful, I don't know, corporate-somebody-or-other, has a brilliant life, tonnes of friends, eats out *all* the time, shops whenever she wants ... And here I am, unemployed, barely able to pay my miniscule rent, and with little hope of the situation improving any time soon.'

Barbara shrugged. 'Just a thought. And anyway, Em, really, you need to lighten up on yourself. If you live on the smell of an oily rag – which we all do out here – your money will last for ages. Be thankful you don't have all the shops and restaurants to tempt you. Enjoy the freedom while you have it – that would be my advice. Get a hobby, fill your time with things you enjoy – like making jam and baking.'

'I guess.' Emily was doubtful.

'Seriously, don't compare your life to your cousin's. Usually we only ever know what people want us to know about them. For all you know her credit cards are maxed out and she's barely affording her mortgage. I'm not saying it's the case, but things aren't always what they seem.'

'Hmm. Hey, speaking of jam, you won't believe this, but Jake took twenty jars, he loved it so much. He's going to try and sell it at a Melbourne market.'

'Wow, that's great. Maybe you won't need a job after all.'

'Well, let's not get ahead of ourselves,' Emily said with a laugh. 'One box of jam does not a millionairess make. They might not even sell.'

'Don't they say just turning up is half the battle won? So, anyway, when will they be back in Melbourne?' Barbara asked.

'Friday or Saturday night, I think. Why?'

'Well, that's when Jake will ring you – you gave him your number, didn't you?'

'Yes. He's going to let me know how the jam goes – but that won't be until Sunday at the earliest. More likely the following weekend.'

'Oh, trust me, he'll ring you the night he gets home,' Barbara said.

'Why do you say that?'

'He'll no doubt use the excuse that he's just got home and had a piece of toast with your jam on it, or something, and wanted to say how much he liked it again. Though, I could be wrong – he might ring you in a day or so to thank you again for having him stay.'

'You're making it sound like he's going to ask me out or some-thing.' She laughed. 'Anyway, I'm pretty sure he's gay, Barbara.'

'Oh, come on, Emily. Have you even *looked* at him? If Jake's gay then I'm the Queen of Sheba. You're just trying to stop yourself from developing romantic feelings for him – which is only to be expected, given what you've been through.'

'Maybe you're right.'

'There's no maybe about it. Your subconscious knows it's far too soon for you to consider getting involved with another man, and it's protecting you. But at the same time, it's letting you get distracted to take your mind off John and all the other crap that's not so good in your life right now.'

'So, if I follow your logic, the universe has sent me Jake so I can be distracted but can't get involved with him and get hurt?' *I suppose it makes sense.*

'Yep.'

'Barbara, you are *so* wasted out here as a farmer's wife. You should be a psychologist or something.'

'Ah, yes, but then I'd have to bite my tongue instead of telling clients to just get over it. I did seriously consider psychology once, but the short stint I did as a hairdresser was bad enough. So are we putting, say, five dollars on Jake calling Friday or Saturday night when he gets home, or not?' Barbara asked.

'Well, I think he'll wait until after the market this Sunday or the following one – but I'll happily take your five dollars,' Emily said, full of conviction.

'Right, you're on.' They shook. 'Honestly, Em, regardless of what happens, I think Jake could be a really good friend to you. David liked him too, thought he was a really nice bloke.'

'I hope so.'

'You know, I wish we'd been able to have the townsfolk see you and Jake hanging out – now that would have set tongues wagging,' Barbara added with a chuckle.

'Well, we did go to Charity Flat yesterday. Word is bound to filter back. But Liz was with us, so I guess they'll assume they're together.'

'Oh well, maybe next time.'

'If there *is* a next time.'

'Oh, there'll be a next time,' Barbara said.

Emily raised her eyebrows. 'Are you psychic as well?'

'Maybe. You'll have to wait and see.'

They laughed, and Emily thought again how lucky she was to have Barbara as a friend.

'So, what's been happening in your life?'

'Well, David's dad isn't well. He's probably going to drop off the perch any day now...'

'Oh, I'm sorry. You only just got back from your mum, and now this. Is David okay?'

'You know men and hiding their feelings. He's a little sad, but I think he'll be relieved when it finally happens. The old darling's been miserable up in the old folks' home since David's mum, Beth, died last year. It's not much of a life when you're ninety-six, deaf, half-blind and lonely. I don't know if it's worse for him or us, seeing him like that.'

Emily couldn't help but think of Granny Mayfair.

'It's like a switch was flicked. Almost overnight he became frail and sickly. Even lost interest in coming out to the farm. It's like he just gave up when Beth died.'

'And they say a broken heart can't kill you,' Emily said wistfully.

'Well, whoever said it didn't have the elderly in mind. I reckon I'd be the same. I wouldn't want to live without David – it would seem pointless. We really are just so lucky to completely adore each other.'

'Yes, you're so lucky,' Emily said quietly.

'I'm sorry, I didn't mean to rub it in.'

'You didn't. And why should you apologise for being happy? Yes, I'm sad that my own marriage didn't work, but at least seeing you guys gives me hope. Maybe it could even happen to me one day.'

'It will happen, Em. You just need to believe that. Meanwhile, do your best to pick up the pieces and regain your strength.'

'Thanks for being such a good friend.'

'Thank *you*. Just because my life isn't in the turmoil yours is at the moment doesn't mean I don't need and treasure your friendship. And now, please change the subject before *I* get all sad and weepy!' Barbara said with a laugh. 'Did you find anything interesting at Charity Flat? I haven't been up for ages. Is it worth us doing a trip of our own?'

'Yes, but I'd rather pop across to Hope Springs first – I haven't been there for ages either. Well, except for visiting my parents, but that doesn't really count.'

'No, I quite agree. What about tomorrow? Leave early – say, just after lunch – and do some groceries and collect the mail on the way back through Wattle Creek?'

'Sounds brilliant. I just hope Mum is safely tucked away in someone's house.'

'Best we take my car, then, so no one spots yours and tells her you were in town.'

'Thanks, I really appreciate it.'

They made their arrangements and then Barbara set off. Emily spent the rest of the day rearranging the furniture and knick-knacks Elizabeth had moved, conceding that she was more doing it out of stubborn principle than anything else. Liz had good taste when it came to interior decorating, but it was Emily's house so she'd damn well have her things where she wanted them! It would be different if her cousin had made suggestions or asked before making changes. But she hadn't, and that irked Emily.

Chapter Forty-eight

Emily felt a sense of calm as they turned the corner of the long driveway and drove towards the stand of gums. It really was starting to feel like home. She and Barbara had had a great few hours in Hope Springs, browsing the combined gift shop-café-art gallery and enjoying an inexpensive lunch of chicken salad and crusty bread.

Barbara had bought a lovely soft upholstered pyramid-shaped doorstop with a tassel. There was another one that would have been perfect for Emily's front door, but she hadn't been able to justify the fifty-dollar price. Maybe one day. Meanwhile, she'd continue using the brick she'd wrapped in fabric to protect the floor and door from being scratched.

On the way back they'd stopped in at Wattle Creek for their groceries, because it was easier than having to figure out the layout of a different supermarket.

That day many of the usual people were in the street, but those she'd once chatted excitedly with about the rain and promise of a good season, or commiserated with on the drought and falling grain prices, didn't even acknowledge her presence beyond a curt nod.

Until recently, she'd thought of them as friends. But friends were people you could rely upon in times of need, who supported but didn't judge. It was with a bit of a shock that Emily realised that the only friends she really had were Barbara and David. These other people had only ever been acquaintances. And when they'd had the opportunity to step into the role of true friend, they'd failed. Every last one of them. Most of them couldn't even look her in the eye. Why? Was it that they didn't want to be seen taking sides? Or was it simply that they didn't know what to say to her?

'Not sure what I prefer,' she said to Barbara, 'the whispering and pointing, or being totally ignored.' She let out a tight laugh.

'Hmm.'

'I can see why people become reclusive. If I could order online and have everything delivered, I wouldn't ever need to go to town.'

'Then they would have won. You're not doing anything wrong, Em. You left a husband who didn't treat you right. You didn't bloody shoot him!'

'Only because he's not worth going to prison for.'

'Well, if you become a recluse, he's effectively put you in prison, anyway. You realise that, don't you?'

'I suppose. Isn't it funny how small country towns are portrayed as the epitome of mateship, the Aussie spirit, banding together in times of catastrophe – blah, blah, blah. If only people knew how cruel and oppressive the postcard-picture-perfect little town can be.'

'Thinking of leaving?'

'Nah. Where else could I rent a house for a hundred bucks a week, including electricity? Anyway, I wouldn't want to give them the satisfaction.'

'Good to hear,' Barbara said, giving her friend's leg a pat.

'But I might still consider becoming a recluse.'

'Ah, yes,' Barbara said, playing along, 'but for that you will need a computer, internet connection and a supermarket that delivers out in the sticks. And I doubt old Mr Barnes at the IGA is about to embrace the world wide web any time soon – he's coming up on ninety, according to the notice in the paper last week.'

'Well, one can dream. Anyway, didn't you once offer to do my groceries for me?' Emily asked.

'Yes, but only as a temporary measure. I will not be responsible for you becoming the scary old axe-wielding hermit who boils up small children in her cauldron in the woods.'

'I'll have to think of something else, won't I?'

'Yes, you will!'

'Though it would give them something interesting to say about me. It might be fun to become a proper urban myth.'

'And have teenage boys wandering around all the time as part of initiation pranks and dares?'

'Yeah, you're right. Scrap that,' Emily said.

'You know,' Barbara said thoughtfully, stopping the car in front of the house and turning to look at Emily with a serious expression. 'If you became successful, *really* successful, outside the district, say, interstate – like Melbourne – that would be the best way to get back at everyone.'

'You mean by becoming the Jam Queen?'

'Why not? Maggie Beer started small, and look at her.'

Emily rolled her eyes at her friend. 'A friend of a relative bought twenty jars of jam – that's hardly worth noting. It's even worse than a friend of a friend.'

'Regardless of who it was, it technically makes you a professional – because money changed hands.'

'Probably only out of pity.'

'Well, you can think what you like,' Barbara said, 'but Jake didn't strike me as the sort of fellow who says things he doesn't mean.'

'Are you coming in for a cuppa or do you have to get going?' Emily asked with her hand on the door handle of the car.

'Thanks, but I'd better get going. I need to water the roses.'

'Okay, I'll see you later.' As she gave her friend a quick hug, Emily hoped she hadn't annoyed her by being so negative. She was just being realistic, wasn't she? No point setting your expectations too high and being disappointed, right?

Nonetheless, as she waved Barbara off, Emily vowed to try to be more positive.

She propped open the front door and left the two bags of groceries in the cool of the hall while she went to let Grace out of the yard. She was relieved to find her lying in the shade looking resigned to being contained, but not unhappy.

She hated leaving her alone, but decided she'd have to start doing so unless she was going to end up with a totally neurotic dog who would work herself into a frenzy at the very thought of being left. It had been David's suggestion, delivered via Barbara. Apparently you had to be a little cruel now to be kind later.

'Sorry girl, Uncle David insisted,' Emily told the dog as she opened the gate. It sure made it a lot easier having someone else to blame!

As she stood watching Grace racing about enjoying her renewed freedom, Emily's thoughts went back to Barbara. She had been absolutely right when she'd said John had eroded her self-confidence. She was only now realising to what extent. At their wedding, Aunt Peggy had described Emily as a self-assured, confident young woman who knew what she wanted and set about making it happen. What had happened to that Emily? She had to find her again.

Chapter Forty-nine

On Friday night, Emily was surprised to hear her mobile vibrate on the chair beside her and indicate she had received a text message. It was just before nine o'clock at night. She'd gone to bed extra early and had lost two hours to the book she'd settled in with, which was almost finished.

Her heart leapt as she remembered the bet she'd made with Barbara over when Jake would call. Did a text count? *Would* he text instead? She hoped not; it was so impersonal.

Emily thought to ignore the phone and get back to her novel, but curiosity got the better of her. The number on the screen was unfamiliar. She opened her inbox to find a striking image of her jars of bright orange jam lined up in rows on a pale stone bench top. Beneath was the simple message: *All arrived safe and sound. Jake.*

Emily frowned slightly, wondering why he'd felt the need to reassure her – it was only jam, for goodness sake!

It felt weird to know he was somewhere, almost on the other side of the country, looking at his phone just like she was. Was he out to dinner with a group of friends? Out with someone special? Just passing time at home? Alone?

What should she say in return? *That's great?* She sat back to try to think of something better. She'd rather just speak to him, but that might look desperate, and anyway, she really couldn't afford to be making unnecessary calls.

She settled for *Thank you*, and started looking for the letters and putting them in one by one.

What she really wanted to say was that she was glad he had got back safely, that she missed him and that the house was feeling strangely empty without him. But she certainly wasn't about to get into anything personal – she had no idea where he was or who he was with. Anyway, she hardly knew him. He was probably just making contact out of politeness, not because he was interested in her.

Emily halted her thoughts and reminded herself that she wasn't either. *You've just left your husband, for goodness sake! It's the last thing you need.*

She was halfway through typing the two-word message, cursing all the time she was spending deleting the wrong letters and replacing them, when the phone began vibrating and then ringing in her hand. She got such a fright she almost dropped it.

With a slightly shaking finger she pressed the accept button and answered tentatively, wondering as she did if she'd lost her half-done message.

'Hello?'

'Em, hi, it's Jake. Did you get the picture I sent?'

'Yes, it's great. Sorry, I was just trying to reply. I so rarely text, I'm a bit slow.'

'Hey, I'm not calling to tell you off for not replying. I'd just rather pick up the phone than send messages back and forth. Call me old-fashioned. But I did want you to see how pretty they looked all lined up on the bench – how the gorgeous colour lights up against the pale background. They're like an art installation in their own right. Far too beautiful to eat.'

'I can always make some more,' Emily reminded him with a laugh.

'You might have to when I sell all these for a fortune at the market.'

'So you had a good trip back?'

'Well, Elizabeth nearly drove me mad, but yes, we did arrive back safe and sound,' he said with a laugh. 'I would have liked to have taken it a bit easier, but she insisted we rush back for some reason, which she wasn't prepared to tell me. Thanks again so much for having me stay.'

'You're welcome. Thank you again for the lovely mugs. I'm sorry the accommodation was a bit basic.'

'You have nothing to apologise for. I had a great time, and got some fantastic shots, which was why I was really there. I'll send you some when I've gone through them all. Are you on email?'

'Not here, but I do check it occasionally at Barbara's or the library.' She rattled off her email address and added, 'I look forward to seeing them some time. So when did you get back?'

'Yesterday. We stayed in Adelaide Tuesday and Wednesday nights – Liz had some friends she wanted to catch up with – and then drove right through yesterday.'

'Sounds exhausting,' Emily said as her mind started going through the reasons why he hadn't called her sooner. He was tired. He ran a successful business and probably had a stack of work to do after his time away. Or perhaps he had a girlfriend he had to catch up with.

She was surprised at how much this thought stung, and instantly told herself to stop being so ridiculous – it wasn't like there'd been anything between them.

She gasped as Grace launched herself onto the bed and then into her lap. She let out a laugh as the dog tried to bury herself in

the covers, obviously trying to gain some of her mistress's attention. Emily giggled, for a second forgetting she was on the phone.

'You still there, Em?'

'Yeah, sorry, Grace is being naughty. Apparently I've been
talking to you quite long enough.'

'Does she want to talk to me?'

'No, silly,' Emily giggled. 'She just wants all my attention.'

'Well, I'll let you go…'

'No, don't be ridiculous – it'll do her good to be ignored for a
few minutes, won't it, Gracie – naughty girl?' Emily said.

'I'm happy to wait if you need to sort her out.'

'No, that's okay, but I don't want to keep you if you have other
things to do.'

'Nothing pressing. But there is something I did want to discuss
with you.'

'Oh, what is that?'

'Would you mind if my sister swapped your labels for something a little more eye-catching? It's just that she was over here
and is terribly keen to do it – she loves the chance to be creative
and she thinks it might help with sales. But only if you don't mind
– it's your jam.'

'No, it's not – you bought it, remember?' Emily said with a
laugh. 'But seriously, go ahead, if she can be bothered.'

'She's very talented. And she's really keen to give them the best
chance of selling.'

'Jake, I don't want you getting your hopes up – it's only a bit
of homemade jam.'

'Try telling that to my sister,' he said, laughing. 'Well, I'd better
get going. I'll let you know how it goes.'

'Okay, thanks.'

There was a moment's silence on the line before Jake spoke
again. 'Hey Em, I know you've been through some stuff, but you

shouldn't let your past adversely affect your future. Take a risk, believe in yourself, do something new – you never know where it might take you.'

'Um, okay,' she said. *Are we still talking about jam?*

'Bye Em.'

'Bye Jake. Thanks for calling.'

Emily put the phone back down, feeling a little unsettled. Had he phoned out of friendship, or just about the jam and his sister's involvement? It seemed so businesslike. And had ended quite abruptly. Had she said something wrong, inadvertently given some signal that she didn't want things to be friendly between them?

Perhaps she should have shown more interest in his sister. But he'd caught her on the hop – it was the last thing she'd expected. Not that she wasn't pleased and grateful. She was incredibly chuffed he'd thought enough of her and her jam to even mention it to his sister.

Emily picked up the phone again and dialled Barbara's number, telling herself it was just one quick phone call, and it was necessary.

'Hi Em, what's happening?'

'About that bet we had…'

'He's just called, has he?'

'You are psychic!'

'No, but you don't normally sound this flustered at nine o'clock at night. So, what did he have to say?'

'Not much. And I do not sound flustered, do I? No, don't answer that. He sent a picture of my jam lined up on his kitchen bench – they look quite pretty really, the orange against the pale stone…'

'And…?'

'And what?'

'When I asked if he'd just called, you said he had – so, what did he want?'

'To check if I minded if his sister did some different labels for them. Apparently she's very talented and really wants to do it.'

'Wow, that's great. It'll help them sell.'

'That's what he said.'

'So why aren't you sounding more excited?'

'Barbara, it's just homemade jam, for goodness sake. Why is everyone behaving like I'm the next Maggie Beer?'

'Who's to say you won't be? And anyway, it's not just homemade jam – it's *excellent* homemade jam.'

'Thanks, but honestly…'

'Seriously, Em, you need to stop being so negative. That's your mother's gig, not yours. Don't let her way of thinking jeopardise your future. You've been given this opportunity for a reason. You just need to trust it and accept that if it's meant to be, it will be. Dare to be brave and think outside the square.'

'That's sort of what Jake said. Except for the bit about my mother.'

'That's because he's too polite. But he is a smart man. Seriously, Em, don't stress so much. You're a strong and independent woman – the world is your oyster.'

'Thanks Barbara.'

'What for, confusing the hell out of you?'

'No, silly. For being my friend, and keeping me on the straight and narrow.'

'You're welcome.'

'Well, I'd better go – this thing costs a bloody fortune.'

'Pop over tomorrow for a cuppa if you want – David's off to Adelaide with another load of wool so I'll be all on my lonesome. I'm doing some cooking for the CWA trading table so I could do with the company, if you're interested.'

'Sounds like fun. Is nine too early?'

'No, I'll be up to see David off at five – so any time after that will be fine.'

'Okay, see you in the morning.'

'Okay, bye.'

Chapter Fifty

Grace patiently waited on the passenger seat of the car while Emily got out and walked around to open the door for her. Sasha appeared beside Emily, her tail wagging furiously but her sagging, overweight body struggling to join in.

'Hello girl,' Emily said, giving the robust dog a hearty pat. 'I've brought you a visitor.' She never ceased to enjoy the way Grace would greet her mother. No matter how recently they'd seen each other, Grace would clamber about like they'd been separated for years, trying to lick her mother all over her face while Sasha twisted her head this way and that to avoid her daughter's tongue.

The ritual was always the same. After ten minutes of frantic licking and clambering on Grace's part, Sasha would take her out of sight, probably to proudly show off her stash of old bones or to dig one up. Or to explore any rabbit or rodent scents they could find.

Barbara gave Emily a prolonged hug at the door. As they separated and Barbara stepped aside to welcome her friend, Emily saw that her eyes were red-rimmed. She silently followed Barbara down the hall, wondering whether it was just tiredness from getting up so early to see David off, or if something had happened.

Barbara flicked on the kettle before sitting down heavily on one of the wooden kitchen chairs.

'Barbara, are you okay?'

'I'm so glad you're here, Em,' she replied, patting her friend's hand. 'Doug passed away last night,' she said with a sigh.

'Oh, I'm so sorry.'

'We got the call at three this morning, and then David had to leave at five with the wool.'

'He went? He's still going to make the trip?'

'He had to. It's booked in for a sale on Tuesday. Anyway, Doug wouldn't want everything to stop on his account,' she smiled wanly.

'So are you stuck with all the funeral arrangements, then? What can I do to help?'

'Not quite – David's going to call in and see the funeral people on his way through Whyalla. His brother William is going to meet him there. Works out quite well, really. We're aiming for Thursday for the funeral. It's going to be tight, but we wanted to get it over with before Christmas.'

'Of course.'

'So anyway, today we get to cook for both the CWA Christmas trading table Tuesday *and* the funeral afternoon tea. We're going to need our strength.' Barbara started to get up. 'Tea, coffee or Milo?'

Emily put a hand on her friend's. 'I'll get it. You stay there.'

'Okay, thanks, but bring the green tin of biscuits from the pantry too.'

'What would you like? Tea or coffee, or something a bit stronger?' Emily asked.

'Coffee would be good, thanks. I'll leave it a while longer before I hop into the brandy.'

'Are you sure it's wise, David driving all that way on his own – you know, when he's upset?'

'He'll be fine. He knows to stop if it all gets too much. He assured me he will. Part of me thinks it will be good for him to be alone with his thoughts and memories. It'll give him plenty of time to start on the eulogy in peace too.'

Barbara lapsed into her own memories of her father-in-law, a kind and generous man whom she'd never heard raise his voice.

Emily had met Doug Burton a few times over the years at various town functions and at her grandparents' place. She couldn't remember ever sitting down and having a decent conversation with him, though, and now regretted not making more of an effort.

'Oh hell, look at the time,' Barbara said suddenly, looking up at the clock on the wall above the oven. 'I can't be sitting around here all day feeling sorry for myself. We've got a stack of cooking to get through.'

'Can't you get someone else to do the CWA's stuff?'

'They're relying on me. I'm one of the youngest members they've got, so I have to do more than my share. Anyway,' she added, smiling weakly, 'I have you, don't I?'

'Yes, you do. Okay, come on then, what first?'

They started by making a list of everything they could do that was suitable to freeze. That way they could double or quadruple recipes and get one variety out of the way before moving on. It was hardly *MasterChef*-appropriate, they laughed, but good enough for the country. Before long they had a fine, well-oiled production line working.

'We should go into business,' Barbara said, standing back at one point to stretch.

'We are,' Emily reminded her. 'This is CWA business.'

'I meant...'

'I know what you meant. Anyway, haven't you already suggested I become a world-renowned jam queen?'

'Have you heard again from Jake?'

'Barbara, he only called last night!'

Barbara looked at her knowingly.

'He won't call until he has some news on the jam.'

'You never know. He might just call to say hi, see how you are.'

'Well, if you're right, I hope only as a friend. I really don't need a relationship just yet. My life's a mess.'

'No, it's not – it's a ball of wool just waiting to be unravelled. You've already found one end and have started unravelling.'

'How do you figure that?'

'Well, leaving John, taking a stand for the future, renting your own place, and exploring possibilities, like the jam.'

'But nothing might come of that.'

'So what? If that's the case you'll find something else to explore. But at least you're considering different avenues. That's the problem with this town, Em, far too many people are content to just go along with the way things have been forever. Nothing can change without you first having an idea or a dream.'

'Speaking of which, remember I was telling you about the visitor we had while Jake and Elizabeth were at the house – the Bakers' cousin? I can't help feeling I'm even further away from one day owning the house now Tara Wickham is in the picture.'

'Put her out of your mind. I doubt Donald and Trevor could be talked into something they didn't agree with. If it's meant to happen, it will. Meanwhile, just keep on dreaming. It's a good distraction.'

'Hmm, you know, I really didn't like how nosy she was about the house,' Emily said, beating the sugar, butter and eggs in her bowl more furiously than was necessary. 'I might be just being paranoid, but she seemed to be really looking it up and down as she passed through.'

'Well, it *is* looking great now you've painted and done the floors.'

'She didn't offer any compliments, but that must be it,' Emily said, frowning.

As she continued cooking, Emily's mind kept wandering back to thoughts of owning the house and the bit of land around it. It had become a common theme in her head of late, and in her dreams. Just the romantic in her – wanting to fulfil the great Australian dream of home ownership, she supposed.

Forcing the subject from her mind, she tried to concentrate on ensuring each spoonful of biscuit mixture on the tray was the same size.

Chapter Fifty-one

The late afternoon sun was streaming through the window when Barbara finally declared that their work for the day was done.

They'd created dozens of chocolate and strawberry lamingtons, and plain and chocolate-cream cupcakes, slabs of fruit cake, loaves of jubilee and date cake, and several small mountains of scones and biscuits.

Everything for the funeral had been put in the freezer, and the produce for the CWA stall had been sealed in plastic bags, priced, and stored in large Tupperware containers.

'I'm exhausted,' Barbara said, putting the last of the dishes on the rack for Emily to dry. She pulled the plug and then peeled each rubber glove off, slapping them onto the side of the empty sink in a deliberate gesture of finality. 'You must be too. Thanks for all your help.'

'My pleasure. It's been fun, though I'd rather not see another baking tray, cake tin or cooling rack for a few days.'

'I second that. But boy does it feel good to have it all done. So, now we have to find something for dinner.'

'Oh, don't worry about me. I can have something when I get home. I'd better get going soon, anyway – Madam Grace will be wanting her dinner too.'

'It's really no trouble. There's leftover lasagne in the fridge. Otherwise there's a chicken casserole in the freezer that won't take long to defrost.'

'In that case, lasagne would be lovely.'

'That's that solved, then. Oh, I've just remembered, David asked me to check out a couple of things online – I'd better do that before he calls. Did you want to check your email?'

'That'd be great, if you don't mind.'

'Of course – let's do it while the food heats up.'

'Good idea. My head's still in sweet mode. I'm not quite ready to face real food just yet.'

They settled in front of the computer in the small office in the back room of the house. It only took them a few minutes to finish what they needed to do – Barbara to print out the latest Bureau of Meteorology weather maps and grain and wool prices, and Emily to sort through her emails that, disappointingly, consisted mainly of advertisements for male sexual performance enhancers and very generous offers of money from associates of the (non-existent) Pakistani royal family.

Emily let out a sigh, unaware she'd done so until Barbara shot her a glance.

'Were you expecting something else?' Barbara asked.

Emily flushed slightly. 'No, not really, just wishful thinking,' she said with a wan smile. 'Jake said he'd send some photos through. I clearly do not have enough occupying my mind – I'm getting obsessed,' she said, forcing a laugh.

'Nothing wrong with being distracted by a nice man. Hey, why don't we check out his company's website.'

'I don't know what it's called.'

'His business card should be right here,' Barbara said, starting to rifle through an almost overflowing document tray beside them. 'Here it is,' she said, extracting a matt laminated card in black, burgundy and white, with a logo that looked like initials entwined. 'JKL and Associates dot com dot au,' she said aloud as she typed.

After a few moments they were greeted by a large version of the logo and a welcome message. According to the site, the company specialised in blending old and new architecture, using the best features of each era to create something truly special with modern-day comfort. A series of changing interior and exterior photographs occupied the right-hand side of the page.

'Wow, isn't that lovely,' Emily said, pointing to an exterior image.

'Hmm,' Barbara said and clicked on it. 'Do we want to watch the video?'

'Yeah, why not?'

They were taken on a 360-degree tour of the outside and then inside of the building while the narrator – whose voice was instantly recognisable as Jake's – discussed the project's brief and pointed out particular features.

When the camera was back on the view of where they had started, it zoomed in on a brass plaque with the name SOMERSET MEWS engraved in large capital letters.

'I thought it looked familiar – that's one of the most famous new developments in Melbourne,' Barbara said in awe. 'It was on the news a few weeks ago. I think it's up for an international award.'

'Wow,' said Emily. 'I got the impression Jake was doing okay, but bloody hell! That he's so humble makes me like him even more,' she added, sounding almost wistful. But what she was really feeling was overawed and disappointed. How could someone that talented, that successful, ever be interested in her? A meek, plain, country girl with a failed marriage and no immediate prospects.

It was easier to think of Jake as just some nice guy who lived in Melbourne and was friends with her cousin. Of course he was rich and successful – Elizabeth didn't bother with people who weren't. How could she not have seen past the plain R.M. Williams dress boots, jeans and well-worn polo tops?

'Let's check out his associates,' Barbara said, clicking the mouse again. Three head-and-shoulder shots appeared – one woman and two men – all of whom looked to be in their mid-thirties to early-forties.

At seeing the name Simone Lonigan underneath the woman, Emily's heart sank right down to the wooden chair beneath her. *So he has a wife.*

Perhaps he'd come away with Elizabeth because he was going through some personal stuff, needed the space. She wanted to despise the face smiling back at her, but the woman looked nice and warm and friendly. Her generous smile included her eyes.

'She looks nice,' Barbara said absently, as if reading Emily's mind. 'This must be his sister.'

'Wife, more like.'

'No, he's not married. Definitely his sister – he adores her apparently; was telling David all about her. She runs the office.' Barbara clicked on the photo and a small bio appeared beside it. 'See, it says Office Manager.'

'Are you sure she's not his wife?'

'Positive. Why are you so worried, anyway? I thought you were convinced he's gay,' Barbara said with arched eyebrows.

'Well, you keep telling me he's not.'

'Anyway, no romantic thoughts, remember. Not until you get yourself back on an even keel.'

'Totally. And I'm not worried, just curious.'

'I suggest we stop now before we look up to find we've lost three hours,' Barbara said.

'Good idea. I can't begin to imagine how much time I wasted surfing the net while John was at the pub,' Emily added absently.

'You know, that's the first time you've mentioned his name all day.'

'I know you must be totally sick of me moaning about how crap my life is.'

'Emily, I meant it as a compliment – a sign of progress. Don't be so defensive. It's going to take time and I'm here for however long it takes,' Barbara said, closing all the open windows on the computer and then turning it off.

'Thanks.'

'You're welcome,' Barbara said, giving Emily's leg a firm pat. 'Well, I'm hungry now, let's eat,' she said, getting up.

'Gosh, it's already six-thirty – see what happens when you go online.'

As Emily's headlights flashed across the windows of the house, she felt a mix of emotions swamp her. She turned the car off and sat thinking for a few moments until Grace, sitting beside her on the passenger seat, started whining with impatience to be let out.

It was odd. On the one hand it was nice to be coming back to her own home and not have to cook or make polite conversation with anyone.

Nonetheless, it would be nice knowing there was someone else to come home to. After such a busy day with Barbara, she'd love to be welcomed by a husband who poured her a glass of wine, ran the bath and then sat by her side while she soaked, discussing their respective days.

Better yet, she thought, *to have a man to share the deep bath with, the room flickering with candlelight, floating languidly in the warm water, then going to bed all relaxed together...*

Emily let out a deep sigh as she climbed the verandah steps. She hadn't left a light on – wary of ending up with an unexpected power bill – so the place was in complete darkness.

'Hello house,' she said, less than enthusiastically, pushing the front door open and flicking the hall light switch.

Having been shut up all day, the house was stuffy. The warm air hit her in the face as it escaped outside, adding to her low disposition. The heat would make it difficult to sleep.

Emily went through the routine of opening up the house and feeding Grace, and then stood watching the dog tuck in heartily while thinking that if she didn't have Grace relying on her she might have just crumpled into a heap she couldn't get up from. The thought was depressing.

She decided to make herself a cup of Milo, but as she stood waiting for the kettle to boil she found herself wondering about her life with John.

Had it really been that bad? Had she really meant to leave him or just to teach him a lesson? Had she expected – wanted – him to come after her, beg her to come back, to prove he really did love her and that she was important? Could her mother be right? She shuddered at the frightening prospect.

Emily recalled Enid's stern words the one time she'd made the mistake of confiding in her, about a year into her marriage: 'Emily, you've made your bed. You can't just go throwing childish tantrums at the first sign of trouble. Men hate that sort of thing. To make a marriage work you need to cook and clean for them and give them, well, you know, *it*, when they want it. It's really quite simple.'

At the time Emily had been too shocked to react – mortified at her mother's unusual frankness, and devastated by the very real prospect that life was indeed just a cruel joke. She'd hoped for a sympathetic ear when she'd voiced her disappointment and frustration at not being considered a partner in running the farm, and at John spending more and more time in the pub rather than at home with her.

As long as she could remember, she'd dreamt about meeting a lovely man, falling in love, getting married and spending the rest of her life being devoted to her husband, and being adored and cherished in return. How could her own mother shatter the dream so spectacularly?

But if it was as Enid had said – that all men needed was food, clean clothes, sex and a respectable place to live – then what did that say about Des? No, Des was nothing like John.

The kettle gave a loud click to signal it had boiled, and something shifted in Emily's brain. As she stood there staring at the steam rising from the spout, she realised she was actually no more lonely than she had been while married.

Many nights John had been at the pub until closing, and most days he'd been out in the paddock or off chinwagging with neighbours. When he was at home, he barely gave her the time of day except to enquire when lunch or dinner was to be served. She'd been little more than a servant, she realised with a jolt.

I might be alone now, but at least I'm free.

She spooned Milo into one of her new red-and-white mugs, and poured in half water and half milk. She took the mug to the table and sat down. Taking a long sip, she closed her eyes to concentrate on the warm chocolate-malt taste as it moved over her tongue. She felt herself relaxing.

Half an hour later, after saying goodnight to Grace, Emily closed the kitchen doors, turned out the light and made her way down the hall to her bedroom. She turned on the fan beside her bed. With its high ceiling and large size, the room wasn't nearly as hot and stuffy as she thought it would be.

Chapter Fifty-two

Emily spent most of the next day making more jam and trying not to think about how the market in Melbourne was going and when – or if – Jake would call.

She had just settled in for an early night with her book when her mobile began vibrating and then ringing on the chair beside her. She picked it up, excited at the prospect of it being Jake, but almost put it down again when she saw her parents' names and home number on the display. Hoping it was Des, she took a deep breath and pressed the green button to answer the call.

'Hello?' she said, a little gingerly.

'Oh, there you are!' Enid cried. Emily's back immediately stiffened.

'Hi Mum. How are you?' she asked, the words sounding more like a long, drawn-out groan.

'Very well, thank you. You sound terrible. Don't tell me that dreadful house is making you sick already.'

'No, I'm fine. I'm just lying down. I was reading,' she said, sitting up and forcing a lighter, cheerier tone into her voice. 'There, is that better?'

'Yes. Now I can't talk for long. Calling mobiles costs a fortune, you know. I wish you'd get a landline.'

'Maybe when I'm more settled,' Emily said, while thinking that right there was a very good reason not to. 'So, to what do I owe the pleasure of the call?' she asked.

'I'd like you to come for dinner tomorrow night. We've got the Lucases coming down. You remember them; he used to be in the bank here years ago.'

'Yes, I remember.' On the tip of her tongue was, 'But why me?'

'So are you able to make it?'

Emily briefly toyed with making up some prior engagement – Barbara would back her up – but in the end she couldn't be bothered. Enid would insist on all the minute details and Emily really just didn't have the energy to lie. When it came to her mother, grinning and bearing it was generally the easiest option.

'Sure. Okay. What can I bring?'

'Emily, "Sure. Okay" is hardly a gracious response. "Yes, thank you" would be more appropriate. And there's nothing you need to bring, thank you very much. Six for six-thirty. We look forward to seeing you then.'

'Right, okay. Thank you. I'll see you tomorrow night, then.' Emily hung up feeling annoyed with her mother, but more annoyed with herself.

I should have just said no.

Emily leaned back into the pillows and wondered about the dinner invitation that had come out of the blue.

Not so long ago her mother had paraded her around as someone who'd done well for herself. 'You remember our daughter, Emily? Well, she's now married to John Stratten. Yes, *the* Strattens – largest landholders, biggest wool producers in the district. Oh, yes, she's very lucky to have found such a fine catch.'

Not anymore. One thing was for certain: Emily was not going to be held up as a shining example of anything tomorrow night. She was surprised her mother didn't prefer to pretend she didn't exist at all.

Perhaps it was some kind of intervention – she was going to be bundled up, returned to her husband, and both of them told that divorce was absolutely out of the question. Thus, Enid Oliphant could again be considered a good mother. Emily felt a small, slightly hysterical chuckle bubble in her throat. She swallowed it down, shook her head, and picked up the book lying face down on the bed beside her.

She'd just got settled into the first paragraph when her phone signalled another call. 'What now?' she muttered. 'Hello, Emily speaking.'

'Hi Em, it's Jake.' Emily's heart instantly started to flap and her face blushed.

'Oh. Hi Jake, how are you?'

'I'm really well, thank you. Great news! Your jam was an absolute hit at the markets! We could have sold ten times what we had.'

'Wow, really?'

'Yes. I'm sending you a cheque.'

'Oh, that's really not necessary,' she said, her mother's years of refusing to discuss money instantly coming to the fore. 'Didn't we agree that you would keep the profit?'

'Let's call it business.'

'But you're the one who went to all the trouble of selling it.'

'And you're the one who went to all the trouble of making it. So let's agree to disagree. Anyway, my sister Simone did gorgeous labels, and she did all the work at the market. Once she tasted it, she insisted on making scones and serving samples of scones, jam and cream.'

'Wow, that was very good of her.' *So Simone is your sister.*

'She's always been a sweet thing. And always looking for a new cause to support – lucky for you your jam was it! And it really is the best apricot jam this side of the black stump.'

'Well, what can I say? Thank you,' Emily said, blushing even deeper.

'You're very welcome. So when can I have some more?'

'How much do you want?'

'As much as you can spare.'

'I'll have to figure out how to get it there safely. There's a transport guy in town. I'll speak to him about it tomorrow. When do you want it?'

'If you could get it here this week, that'd be good – keep the momentum with the punters going.'

'I'll see what I can do.'

'So how's everything else going? You sounded a little down when you answered. Or were you actually lying down already?'

Emily laughed. 'Bit of both actually. I'd just hung up from my mother.'

'And how is the lovely Enid this evening?'

'As annoying and as frustrating as ever!'

'Care to talk about it?'

'I don't know. Not really. Maybe.'

'Hmm, not very decisive, Em,' he said with a laugh. 'Come on,' he added, more seriously. 'I'm all ears.'

Emily took a slightly deeper breath. 'Nothing much to tell, really. I've just been summoned to a dinner party. God only knows why. It used to be so she could hold me up as the trophy to her excellent motherhood because I'd married so well, but of course, that particular trophy is now tarnished well beyond what Silvo could deal with.'

'Maybe it's a set-up ... with another guy or something.'

'God, I bloody well hope not! Sorry, excuse the language.'

'No need to apologise – sometimes no other word will do. Who else is going to be there?'

'Just some long-lost friends – the term "friends" being used rather loosely. I'm sure Mum and Dad haven't seen them for years, even though they still live around here.'

'Do they happen to have a son around your age?'

'Hmm, yes, but last I heard he was married or engaged or something.'

'Well, there you go. It's a set-up. Maybe he's in a similar situation to yourself and they're intent on saving you both from lives of desperate loneliness.'

'Oh, God,' Emily groaned.

'Chin up. He might be fabulously rich and great in bed.'

Emily tried to answer, but all that came out was a gasp. The heat of her blush flowed red-hot down her neck and onto her chest.

'On the other hand,' Jake continued, 'your mother might just be making sure you eat a decent meal once in a while.'

'Well, in that case I wish she'd just send a care package,' Emily said with a laugh.

'It's good to hear you laugh, Em. My work here is now done.'

'I guess I haven't laughed much lately. So thank you.'

'My pleasure. And I really must go. I've a few work things to get done before tomorrow.'

'Barbara and I checked out your website – it's very impressive.'

'Thank you. We've had some luck along the way.'

'Maybe if I ever get to own this place you can help me turn it into something truly special.'

'You're on. Let me know how you get on with sending the jam.'

'I will. Thanks so much for that, and please thank your sister for me.'

'I certainly will. See ya, then. And good luck with dinner tomorrow night. I wish I could be there to take the heat for you.'

Me too.

'Thanks. Bye.'

Emily ended the call and put the phone back on the chair. When she thought about Jake's last words, warm comfort surged through her. She was truly lucky to have his friendship.

She lay back against the pillows and replayed their conversation. She really hoped her mother wasn't up to something too sneaky or embarrassing. Oh well, in a matter of hours she would know. Meanwhile, she had to get some sleep.

Chapter Fifty-three

Emily woke early and, knowing she wouldn't get back to sleep, got dressed and took Grace for a brisk walk before the day started heating up. She was excited about the jam – it was a sign things were finally turning around – and she ignored the nagging voice telling her that she'd have to sell more than a few dozen jars for it to make any difference to her dire financial situation.

Instead she told herself that it wasn't just about the money. She was starting to find her feet, coming out from the shadow of her marriage.

Maybe she could do a lot of little things and it would all add up to some financial stability. As she walked the last few hundred metres back down the hill to the house, Emily made a to do list.

Inside she quickly committed it to paper while waiting for the kettle to boil. She had to pack up the jam so it would travel safely, find the most reliable and cost-effective method of transport, and buy a bottle of wine for dinner with her parents. When Enid had said there was no need to bring anything, what she really meant was nothing other than the customary bottle of wine or box of chocolates that well-brought-up guests appeared with. Emily wouldn't dare turn up empty-handed, even to her parents' home.

She added a list of groceries to the right-hand side of her note and doodled while she waited to see if anything else would come to her. Suddenly the phone in the light jacket beside her began to ring and she fumbled in the wrong pocket before dragging it out while pressing the accept button.

'Hello?'

'Hi Em. It's me, Barbara. Have I got you in the middle of something?'

'No, just back from a walk with Grace. I was thinking about calling you, actually. Are you up for a trip to town today?'

Barbara laughed. 'I was ringing to ask you the same thing. I need to do a few things for the funeral. It's all booked for Thursday at two o'clock. Anglican Church, then graveside, then back to the bowls club for afternoon tea.'

'How's David holding up?'

'Okay. He's pretty worn out from all the driving. It's going to be a tough few days, but we'll get through it. Any special reason for you heading to town?'

'Yes, actually. I've got to sort out sending a couple of boxes of jam to Melbourne. Jake rang and...'

'Wow! That's brilliant news. Woohoo! You go girl!'

'Barbara, are we still talking about jam?'

'If you like.'

'Well, apparently it sold like hotcakes because Jake's sister served samples on scones with cream. Wasn't that nice of her?'

'Very. So how is Jake?'

Emily censored her first response, and instead said, 'Good. I told him we were impressed with his website.'

'Now there's a come-on if ever I've heard one. "Hey Jake, love your website. All that stone and glass. Be still my beating heart!"'

'Barbara!'

'Oh, come on, Emily, lighten up. It's just a bit of fun. Anyway, you're smitten, just admit it.'

'I could be, but I hardly know the bloke. And for all I know, he's shagging my cousin.'

'That isn't exactly a denial, now is it?!'

Emily was glad Barbara wasn't there to see the red racing its way up her neck and into her cheeks. 'He is rather lovely,' she said with a sigh.

'But?'

'But he lives in Melbourne...'

'Geography, smeography. He'd be up for living in the country with the right woman. I'd put money on it.'

'And he's sophisticated, wealthy and successful.'

'What's wrong with that?'

'Well, I'm not – sophisticated, wealthy or successful, that is.'

'So?!'

'What do I have to offer a man of that calibre?'

'Bloody hell, Emily. How about charm, wit, personality? And for all I know, you might be dynamite in bed.'

'Barbara! Anyway, I'm not.'

'Only because you haven't met the right bloke.'

'Why are we even having this conversation – the last thing I need is...'

'Yeah, yeah, I know: another relationship. But you *do* need a distraction, and I think Jake Lonigan is just the man for the job!'

'Fine, whatever. Can we just get back to sorting out today?'

'If you insist. How about I pick you up at ten at the mailboxes?'

'Perfect. See you then.'

'Righteo. See you.'

As she hung up, Emily thought how right Barbara was. Jake was a good distraction. And there was nothing wrong with some harmless wishful thinking. He lived in Melbourne. She'd probably never see him again, anyway. Meanwhile she was free to dream with the safety of distance.

Visiting town no longer inspired the same level of anxiety in Emily. Everywhere they went, Barbara received condolences and offers of a 'plate' for the wake. Emily found it a nice change to be ignored as she stood beside her friend. Occasionally someone would ask, 'And how are you bearing up, dear?', to which she always answered, 'Fine. Thank you.'

Emily felt a strange mix of emotions as she paid for the freight and then pushed the two boxes of jam across the transport company's counter. On the one hand she was excited, but on the other she was a little nervous. What if it didn't sell?

'Then Jake and Simone will be eating their way through dozens of jars of lovely apricot jam,' Barbara said when Emily voiced her concern.

'You're right – I'm worrying over nothing.'

'Now when has that ever stopped you?' Barbara said, grinning at her friend.

Emily slipped her arm through Barbara's and tugged playfully. 'Right, come on. We're eating at the pub. I've been far too good for far too long.'

'Finally, the girl doth make some sense!'

After pressing and hanging her best black pants, Emily positioned her favourite charcoal shirt on the ironing board. She'd have much preferred to just throw on some comfy jeans and a t-shirt, but Enid had phoned two hours earlier specifically to tell her to dress up; jeans were a no-no.

The charcoal shirt always garnered comments about how well she looked because of the way the colour reflected in her eyes. As she started to iron, Emily noticed that one of the small faux-pearl buttons was missing. *Damn it, when did that happen?* She checked her watch. There would almost be enough time to sew another one on – if she had one.

There might be one in Granny's lot – it looked common enough. But the thought was fleeting. No matter how much Emily wanted to wear her favourite shirt, there was no way she could bring herself to take a button from Granny's collection.

No, she thought with a sigh, *I'll have to wear the pink one instead.* She crumpled the black shirt into a ball on the end of the table, made a mental note to take it with her next time she went to town, and went back to her bedroom.

As she did, her thoughts returned to Gran's buttons. *Why couldn't I just use one of them?* She smiled at the ridiculousness of the tradition that she just couldn't bring herself to break.

It was somehow nice that she stuck to it, even though she found herself thinking of the old lady less often. It wasn't that she had forgotten her, more that the memories were settling, shifting like sand over time.

God, I miss her, Emily thought, pulling the pink shirt from its hanger and willing herself to stay focussed on getting to her parents' on time and getting the evening off to a good start.

She had no idea what the night would hold, or why she was being asked to dinner with the Lucases. But at least there was no confusion over what to wear.

Chapter Fifty-four

Emily was right on time when she pulled up outside her parents' house, and was relieved to see no other cars. Her father greeted her at the door with a firm hug.

'Chaos in the kitchen, foul temper, beware,' he warned. He continued in a whisper, 'You have to say the pumpkin soup is *brilliant*. I'm in trouble because I only said it was nice. Apparently "nice" is not nearly good enough.'

'Thanks for the heads-up,' Emily said, breaking away and pecking him on the cheek. Walking into the kitchen, she steeled herself for the tornado.

'Hi Mum.'

'Thank God you're finally here,' Enid said and thrust a spoonful of pumpkin soup at her. 'Quick! Try this!'

Noticing the steam rising, Emily pulled her head back, took hold of the spoon, and made a big show of taking in the aroma.

'Smells *absolutely divine*, Mum.'

'Hurry up, taste it. They'll be here any second,' Enid said, flapping her hands. Emily hadn't seen her mother this uptight since Gran's wake.

Emily took a sip. It was indeed very nice, which is what she would have said if she hadn't already been warned by her father.

'Mmm, lovely. Just perfect.'

'Does it need anything – more pepper, salt?'

Emily shook her head while putting on a show of looking deeply thoughtful. 'No, I think it's absolutely perfect just the way it is.'

'You're not just saying that?'

'No, there's a nice subtle kick to it. What is that, ginger?'

'Yes. But there's not too much, is there?'

'No.'

'You can taste it, right? But it's not overpowering?'

'Yes, I can taste it, and no, there's not too much. There's just the right amount.'

'You're sure?'

'Mum, it's perfect,' Emily said, trying not to snap. What she wanted to say was, 'For Christ's sake, it's only bloody soup!' But it was never *only* anything with her mother.

As Enid turned back to the pot of soup, Emily watched and wondered how she had got herself in such a state. Just who were the Lucases in the scheme of things, anyway? Then it came to her – this wasn't about food, it was about Enid's standing in some unspoken, unseen hierarchy of womanhood. Emily found herself actually looking forward to what so far was pointing to an interesting evening.

There was a knock on the door.

'Oh shit! They're here!' Enid cried.

Emily almost said, 'Mother, language!', but one look at Enid and she swallowed it quickly. 'Anything I can do?' she asked with fingers crossed. It was another perfunctory part of the ritual; whatever she did would be wrong.

'Stir that soup – gently. Just keep it moving,' Enid said, thrusting the wooden spoon towards her. There was a flurry of voices at the door – exclamations and compliments becoming louder as the group moved inside.

Emily turned from the stove to see a couple of her parents' vintage, and a younger man standing next to her father but a good head taller. He was trendily dressed in a bright striped shirt, designer jeans with fancy panels and long, square-toed cream shoes – obviously he'd missed the 'no jeans' memo.

'Emily, come and meet the Lucases,' her mother crowed with an outstretched hand.

'But...' she replied, shooting the soup a stricken look.

'Come on,' Enid beckoned. 'So rude, children these days,' she whispered to Mrs Lucas, but so loudly that the cat next door would have heard.

Trying not to feel like a scolded fifteen year old, Emily lifted the pot off the hotplate and placed it onto a cold one, then turned off the stove and walked across the room.

'Hello Mr and Mrs Lucas,' Emily said, holding out her hand first to Mrs and then to Mr Lucas. 'It's lovely to see you again.'

'Oh, please, I think you're a little old for that, dear. It's Bill and Nancy,' Mr Lucas said jovially, giving Emily's arm a solid pumping before letting it go. She couldn't bring herself to repeat their names. Enid would have had a fit.

'And I'm sure you remember Nathan,' Enid said, practically shoving him into her chest.

'Hi Nathan,' Emily said, grasping his outstretched hand.

Nathan Lucas's broad smile but dull eyes told her he was as thrilled to be there as she was, and a slight connection passed between them.

She had a flashback of him as the overweight kid at her tenth birthday party who'd pulled her hair and then tried to kiss her cousin Elizabeth. It had ended in tears – his – when Liz had simultaneously punched him in the face with one hand and in the stomach with the other.

The 'adults' moved away and left Nathan and Emily standing there alone. *Definitely a set-up*, she thought. Otherwise they too would have been shepherded to the table.

Emily was trying to think of a way to break the ice when Des called out, 'What can I get you to drink, Nathan? How about you, Em?' Her father's shout was cut off by another hiss from Enid.

'Let them have a few moments to get reacquainted, Des. Just give them both a glass of bubbly.'

'Get the feeling we're being set up?' Nathan asked, grinning.

'Wherever did you get that idea?' Emily said, putting on her best sugary voice and smile. 'I really should tell my mother that the point of whispering is that it *isn't* heard right across the room.'

'Your mum's not real subtle, is she?'

'About as subtle as a sledgehammer.'

'So I take it you're divorced? Or are you still on the shelf?'

'Speaking of subtle. Is that how you talk to all the girls?'

'Sorry,' he said, colouring a little.

'That's okay. Newly separated. Mum probably thinks if she gets me paired up again quickly enough no one will notice. Shall we play along?'

Before he could answer, Emily's father appeared and handed them both a glass of bubbles.

'I hope this lolly water stuff is okay with you,' he said with an apologetic grimace to Nathan. He raised his eyebrows and rolled his eyes at Emily, and mouthed a silent, 'Sorry'.

'Cheers,' Emily said loudly, raising her glass towards Nathan. 'Nice to meet you – again.'

'Likewise,' Nathan said, clinking his glass against hers. This time his smile included his eyes, which were a nice hazel colour. He was actually quite good-looking.

'So, you were going to tell me your story,' she said, after taking a sip of champagne. 'Divorced, widowed, or sad sack?'

Nathan coughed, putting his hand over his mouth.

'Sorry, I *so* didn't mean to say that.' Emily blushed slightly, which Nathan had the good grace to ignore. He dabbed at his lips with a handkerchief.

'Divorced. What about you – kids?'

'No, thank God. Not that I didn't want them, just not with him. And thank goodness for realising that early on. Much easier to start afresh without that level of complication, don't you think?' Emily suddenly realised she was rambling and abruptly shut her mouth.

'Yes, I quite agree. Well put. Come on, we'd better join the others before they start making wedding plans.'

'Or set us up on a kids' table in another room,' Emily said with a chuckle.

'I thought that only happened in our family.'

'Don't flatter yourself,' Emily said, grinning.

'After you,' Nathan said, stepping aside.

Emily and Nathan sat in front of steaming bowls of soup and exchanged subtle smirks across the table. Enid had placed them opposite each other but next to their respective mothers.

'Please start, before it gets cold,' Enid said, picking up her soup spoon.

Emily coughed quietly to try to quell the giggle rising up in her throat as she watched Nathan. While his mother paused in her eating and turned away to wipe her mouth with her napkin before answering a question from Enid, Nathan made a childish show of slumping down into his chair, folding his arms across his chest and pouting. Because his legs extended so close to her chair, Emily couldn't resist putting on a scowl of her own and giving him a gentle kick.

'Ow!' he exclaimed.

Both their mothers turned and glared at them, and this time Emily had to actually bite the inside of her mouth so she didn't laugh.

'Stop it, you two!' both women said at once.

'He started it!'

'No, she did!'

The mothers frowned at them and looked a little puzzled before returning to their conversation, which was punctuated with the careful consumption of soup. As she tore her bread roll apart, Emily poked her tongue out at Nathan, and he did the same in return.

Des cleared his throat quietly before speaking. 'So, Nathan, your dad tells me you've followed in his footsteps and gone into banking.'

Emily took the opportunity to start her soup. Thankfully Enid had only served up a small amount – the weather really was far too warm for it. She cast a glance around the table. Clearly she'd been deemed too plump that evening, because hers was the smallest serve.

'Yes,' replied Nathan.

Emily swallowed her mouthful and let her mouth drop open slightly in surprise. She'd picked him for a graphic designer, advertising executive or something else in the creative arts. Definitely not a banker.

'I've actually put in for a posting at Wattle Creek – Assistant Manager. I should hear in the next few weeks.'

'You'd come back out here after the city? God, you're either mad or desperate.' *Oops, I didn't mean to say that out loud.*

'Emily! Manners!' Her mother shot her a fierce scowl.

'Sorry,' she muttered, taking a less than ladylike gulp of champagne, which took a few moments and considerable concentration to swallow lest it come back up and out her nose.

'Neither, actually. A country stint is usually a good career move,' he said without hint of being unsettled.

'Hmm. So, tell me, Nathan,' Emily said after composing herself, 'are you in favour of helping struggling farmers stay on the land, or would you prefer they walked off completely? I met a financial planner the other day who'd have them all sold up and moved away.'

'Emily,' Enid warned.

'It's all right, Mrs Oliphant,' Nathan said.

'Enid,' Enid corrected, patting her hair.

'Enid,' Nathan said to her with a smile and a nod before looking straight at Emily across the table. 'Wow, usually I get asked if I can get someone a good discount on their home loan,' he said with a laugh. 'I can't, by the way.'

'So what about it?' Emily persisted.

'No idea. I don't think I've ever even met a farmer. I've been based in the city, remember? Ask me again when I've got the job out here.' He chuckled again.

Emily took the opportunity to tuck back into her soup.

'But seriously, without knowing a person's individual circumstances, I couldn't give any specific advice. Sorry,' he added, shrugging.

'What, not even an opinion?'

'Nope. Afraid not.'

Out of the corner of her eye, Emily noticed Mr Lucas nodding with approval.

'Do all bankers have splinters in their butts from sitting on the fence? Ouch!' Emily cried as her mother pinched her leg.

'Emily, to answer your question would be like trying to answer "how long's a piece of string?". If there's someone who needs some *specific* advice, maybe if I get the job you can send them in...'

'Not really, I was just being curious.'

'You know what they say about curiosity?' he said, grinning at her.

'Indeed I do.'

Touché, she thought, as she silently took the final spoonful of soup, then put her spoon down into her bowl as if driving the point home. Emily folded her arms and sat back to wait for everyone else to finish their soup. A few minutes later, Enid was up and collecting the empty bowls.

One course down, just two more to go.

Mrs Lucas got up to help and Mr Lucas lapsed into conversation with Emily's father at the end of the table. She was having trouble even *thinking* of them as Bill and Nancy.

'So are you living back here with your parents now you're separated?' Nathan asked as the silence between he and Emily stretched into awkward territory.

'God, no! No, I'm renting an old farmhouse outside Wattle Creek.'

'Are you wanting to buy then, hence the earlier badgering?'

'I wasn't badgering. It was a simple question. And yes and no; as much as I love the place and would like to own it, I don't have the money, and the owners don't want to sell, anyway.'

'Ah.'

They lapsed into silence again. A few moments later, Enid and Mrs Lucas brought out plates piled high with meat, three roasted veg, and peas.

'This looks lovely, Enid,' Nathan said, starting a rumble of agreement that went right around the table.

Suck! Emily thought as she picked up her knife and fork. The evening was slowly turning into the stock standard Enid affair she had dreaded. Things had briefly looked up when she'd met Nathan and noticed the cheeky glint in his eye. Now they were all serious again.

Why couldn't she have just stuck to the so-where-in-Adelaide-do-you-live, what-sort-of-car-do-you-drive sort of questions, instead of ambushing him about work stuff? And why was she so bloody fixated on the subdivision, anyway?

Emily speared a piece of crispy baked potato. *Because I want that house and a few acres around it.* Her shoulders slumped a little. Nothing but a pathetic pipedream. She dragged her knife through the tender pink roast lamb, and was then pleased to be distracted by her father waving a bottle of red wine.

'Yes thanks, Dad,' she said, putting down her knife and fork and handing over her empty wine glass.

Chapter Fifty-five

Emily kept checking her watch, barely able to believe it was just past eight o'clock. If only her mother would hurry up and serve dessert. She could eat it and then, after a short but respectable interval, get in her car and go home. *Ah, home.*

Despite its run-down state and how cold it would be in winter, and her sparse, daggy collection of pre-probably-not-even-loved furniture, it really did feel like home. Even the farmhouse she'd shared with John hadn't given her the same feeling of emotional security. *Weird*, she thought, forcing her attention back to the chatter around her.

'Oh no! I'm a complete idiot!' Enid Oliphant screeched from the open fridge. She turned towards the table with her mouth frozen in an 'O', one hand covering it and another on her chest. Before anyone could ask the obvious question, she continued. 'I've forgotten to get cream for the apple turnovers!'

What's she playing at? Emily wondered. *Enid Oliphant never forgets anything.*

'I'll go,' Des said, pushing his chair back. 'The shop on the corner will still be open.'

'No, Des. Emily will be quicker. You wouldn't mind, would you, Emily?' Enid really was just too much. So good were the theatrics – or bad, depending on how you saw it – they were almost laughable.

'No,' Emily groaned, pushing her chair back and rolling her eyes at Nathan.

'Nathan, why don't you keep Emily company – it's almost dark out,' Mrs Lucas said, prodding her thirty-something son like a stage mother.

'I'll be okay,' Emily said, thinking she'd be quite happy for a few minutes of peace.

'Oh no, I doth insist on accompanying the lady,' Nathan said, almost equalling Enid's previous theatrics.

'I'm driving. It's only two minutes up the street.'

'Oh, but your car is blocked in,' Enid said, with a tone that sounded gleeful rather than apologetic. 'And so is ours.'

'So I'll walk. It'll take me twenty minutes, tops, and the fresh air will do me good.'

'In that case, I'm definitely not letting you go alone. Can't have you walking unescorted in the almost-dark,' Nathan declared.

'That's enough from all of you. Come on, then. Just cream, Mum, or is there something else you need?'

'No, that's all, thank you. Get the thickest one you can find.'

It had got quite chilly outside since she'd arrived, and Emily set out on a long stride in order to both warm up and get the mission over with.

'Hey, slow down,' Nathan said, breaking into a skip to catch up. 'We're on a romantic stroll, remember.'

'Oh God, don't you start! Can you believe the blatancy?! "Nathan, you'd better keep her company",' Emily said, doing a fine impersonation of his mother.

'I don't mind. It's been a while since I was alone with an attractive, intelligent woman.'

'Please don't tell me that line has ever worked before,' Emily said, returning her attention to the dark street underfoot.

'No, actually.' He laughed. 'But I keep using it in the hope that some day it will. Call me optimistic. Anyway, you are.'

'Sorry?'

'You – you *are* attractive. And intelligent.'

Emily sneered at him. 'Flattery, flattery. Should we just stop for a quick romp in the park now the foreplay's been covered?'

'Hey, now, since when did you get so cynical that a bloke can't even give you a compliment without you getting all prickly?'

'When he's only doing it because his mother told him to. For all I know, you're involved with this ridiculous farce our mothers have cooked up.'

'I certainly am not and I resent the suggestion,' he said, folding his arms hard across his chest.

They continued on in silence.

'Sorry,' Emily finally said. 'I'm just so sick of everyone thinking they know what I need – like a replacement husband. It's only been just over a month, for Christ's sake! And anyway, the way I feel right now, I'm not sure I'll ever want to get that involved with a man again.'

'You obviously got badly hurt.'

'Your powers of observation are incredible.'

'I'm sorry, I mean it. But you shouldn't let your past determine your future. Don't let it stop you getting close to someone else down the track.'

'Oh, like you, you mean?'

'No, not necessarily me.'

Emily breathed out. 'So what's your real story, anyway?'

'Walking cliché, I'm afraid. Wife of seven years ran off with my best mate.'

'How long ago did she leave?'

'Just over twelve months – divorce papers signed last week.'

'Kids?'

'Nope. She told me she didn't want them. But apparently only didn't want them with *me*, because they now have one – a boy.'

'Well, I'd be counting my lucky stars if I were you. At least this way you won't have to hand over money for a kid you only see half the time, or exchange pleasantries at family functions with two people who put you through misery. Especially when you're single and they're the epitome of the happy family. Be cheered by the fact you don't *ever* have to have *anything* to do with them *ever again*.'

'God, you're really bitter, aren't you?' he replied, frowning.

'Anyway, you're still young enough to find the woman of your dreams and have a small tribe. With a nice stable career as a bank manager I imagine you'd be considered quite a catch.'

'I suppose so,' he said with a shrug. 'So, you said you realised you didn't want kids with your husband.'

'Yes. He turned out to be a nasty piece of work. I don't know what I'd do if I had to look at someone who reminded me of him every day.'

'So what did this guy do that was so horrible? He can't have been *that* bad if you married him in the first place.'

'Look, I'd really rather not talk about it – him.'

'Okay. Sorry.'

'That's okay, no need to apologise.'

They walked the last few hundred metres in silence until Emily said, 'Here we are.'

'The Corner Shop,' Nathan said, reading the faded sandwich board out front. 'Original.'

Emily pushed the door open and the bell above it jangled. She grabbed a large plastic tub of cream from the fridge and put it on the counter while Nathan stood taking in the quaint surroundings of the old-fashioned shop.

'See anything else you'd like?' Emily prompted him while the lady behind the counter silently waited.

'No thanks, I'm good.'

Emily handed over her money, thanked the lady, and headed back across the scuffed dark floorboards to the door. Nathan rushed to open it for her.

'Here, let me carry that for you,' he said when they were outside, tugging at the pot of cream Emily had tucked under her arm while she was trying to shove the change back in her purse.

'Thanks,' Emily said, releasing it. 'I should have asked for a bag.'

They trudged back down the street in silence. It was dark now.

'Hey, sorry about being so prickly before. I'm sure you're probably a really nice guy. I'm just not interested.'

'I *am* a really nice guy,' he said, grinning at her. 'No "probably" about it. But I get it – wrong time, wrong place. For the record, I do think you're attractive and intelligent...'

'Thanks.'

'But I doubt we'd be compatible.'

'Oh. Why's that?' Emily asked, feeling the tiniest stab of hurt.

'What star sign are you?'

'You can't be serious!'

'Come on, humour me. What are you?'

'Capricorn. Why?'

'As I suspected. I'm a Cancer. We wouldn't work at all.'

'Are you seriously into all that?'

'I never used to be. There's more to it than you think. Probably just too much time on my hands and looking for answers.'

'And did you find any?'

'Yes, actually. Kate and I would never have worked out in the end.'

'That's called hindsight, and it's got nothing to do with star signs.'

'Touché.'

'Sorry, maybe that was a bit harsh. But you said you were married for seven years, so you can't have been *that* incompatible.'

'I think it probably only lasted that long because neither of us were willing to acknowledge that it wasn't working. We kept things going for longer than we should have out of stubbornness – didn't want to have to fess up to our parents and all that.'

'Oh, I know what you mean.'

'It's a hard thing to admit when you've made a mistake. Especially when it's a mistake as big as marrying the wrong person – or for the wrong reason.'

'Sometimes I think I only got married to stop the withering looks of my mother and half the town. "Poor Emily, still unmarried at twenty-eight. Tut tut."'

'That isn't old.'

'What are you talking about? Unmarried and over twenty-three is considered left-on-the-shelf around here!' she said, shaking her head.

'Well, I spent my high school years at boarding school and then stayed on in the city. But I'm hoping to reacquaint myself with the country way of life. The good bits, anyway.'

'I really hope you get the job. But if you do, just remember that what is quaint and cosy one week can be stifling and oppressive the next.'

'Are you telling me it's not all brandy snaps and cream cakes?' he said, bringing a hand to his throat.

'No, it's not!' Emily said, giving him a half-hearted slap on the arm.

'Well, luckily I'll have you to keep an eye on me,' he said, putting an arm around her waist and pulling her to him.

Emily liked the closeness and his touch, but wasn't sure what it meant. 'It might not be wise to associate yourself with me too much,' she said.

'What have you done? Did you let out the secret CWA scone recipe or something?'

'No.' Emily giggled. 'I'm being serious. Farmers are a protected species around here, and I left one. A divorce means I'll get a settlement, which, no matter how small it is, means I am a gold-digger, and, therefore, the enemy.'

'Well, the law is pretty clear when it comes to dividing up marital assets. I hope you get a decent payout, especially if he was horrible. It might teach him a lesson.'

Emily considered telling him about her mistake – settling for a fraction of what she rightly deserved – but habit stopped her from talking about money matters with a stranger. Instead she said, 'Unfortunately, John Stratten would never connect those two particular dots. I'm just the cow who left him and does not deserve a cent.'

'Stratten. Why does that name ring a bell?'

'They're the biggest landholders in the district.'

'Oh! Clever girl to choose so well.'

'I wish. Look, I really don't want to talk about it. I'd rather just move on.'

'Fair enough. But if you ever need any help with banking or financial advice, let me know.'

'And if you ever need help deciphering the weird ways of the country, let me know.'

'Deal,' Nathan said, pausing and holding out his hand. They shook on it before walking the last few steps to the front door of Emily's parents' house.

'We should have dishevelled ourselves and given the mothers some hope,' Nathan whispered as he held open the door for Emily to pass.

With the door now closed behind them they were just in view of the dining table. Emily winked at Nathan before grabbing him and planting a firm kiss right on his lips.

'Right, one large tub of thickened cream,' Emily said, depositing it on the table and throwing herself into her chair.

'Not on the table, Emily!' Enid said, gathering the tub as if it was a ball of smelly socks. 'Now let me get those turnovers.'

The evening wrapped up quickly after dessert. The guests declined tea and coffee, and just a few minutes later, made their goodbyes.

Emily stood at the door beside her parents as the Lucases left. She was slightly shocked, but not totally surprised, to be pulled into a loose embrace by Nathan.

'This will get them talking,' he whispered in her ear, before pulling her slightly closer and kissing her. He turned and followed his parents out. Emily noticed Enid exchange a satisfied expression with Mrs Lucas on the step outside.

'Can I help with the dishes before I head off?' Emily asked, hoping her offer would be declined, as usual. It was only nine o'clock but she was longing for the sanctuary of her new home and Grace's comforting presence.

'No, thank you. I'm going to leave them for the morning.'

Enid Oliphant was the queen of the guilt trip. Emily knew all too well she wouldn't leave dirty dishes in the sink until the morning, no matter what she said. But it was habit to shun an offer – even from her husband – and then stay up late rattling around so the kitchen would be spick and span in the morning. And then she'd invariably pass carefully worded comments the next day about how late she'd been up.

Enid's emotional blackmail had once really bothered Emily, but she was beginning to accept it as her mother's martyr gene. Well, she was trying, anyway.

'Okay then, I'll get going,' she said, retrieving her handbag from beside the front door.

Des gave his daughter a big hug and said, 'Thanks for coming, Em.'

'Are you going to see that nice Nathan again?' Enid asked.

Out of sight of her mother, Emily gave a silent groan. 'Maybe if he asks me, Mum,' she said, turning back to Enid for an air kiss.

Chapter Fifty-six

Emily had been so busy helping Barbara organise the food for her father-in-law's wake that she forgot that Gran's funeral had been the last she'd attended, less than two months ago.

But when she sat down on the hard, shiny wooden pew and gazed around the whitewashed interior of the small stone church, it all came flooding back.

Last time she'd had Liz on one side and John on the other. Now she was surrounded by people she knew reasonably well, but who were not her friends. Barbara and David sat two pews ahead in the space set aside for immediate family. Emily focussed on the backs of their heads, thinking she couldn't remember a time she'd felt so alone.

As the organist began to play *The Lord is my Shepherd*, Emily began to quietly sob. All the dabbing she did with her fistful of tissues did nothing to stem the flow.

Oh Gran, I miss you so much. My life's a mess – where are you now when I need you?

Emily watched through swimming eyes as David delivered his eulogy, but didn't take in any of his words. She was trying to

362

remember Granny Mayfair – the details, the words of wisdom she'd had for every occasion. What would she say to Emily now?

Would she have approved of her leaving John, or would she have encouraged her to stay and work it out? It was impossible to know. On the one hand, Gran had advocated that life was too short to be miserable, but on the other she said things should be seen through to the end, no matter how difficult.

Well, it really was too late now. She'd made her decision, she had to live with it. No regrets. It wasn't like John had shown any sign of distress, except over not having her there to pack meat away in the freezer.

The tears subsided and Emily settled back against the high, hard back of the pew, and dabbed her eyes with the dry wad of tissues in her other hand.

The organist continued now with *Amazing Grace*, and Emily swallowed back another wave of tears.

As supportive as Granny Mayfair had been, she'd never tolerated self-pity for long. If she was here she'd be sternly telling Emily to pull herself together: 'Leaving John was your decision – no one else's. Right or wrong, you now have to live with it and get on with your life'.

Just suck it up, princess, Emily thought, allowing herself a slight smile. Gran would have so loved the new expressions generation Y used.

No matter how many weddings, funerals, morning and after-noon teas, and luncheons Emily attended, she always marvelled at the quality and quantity of the offerings. Trestle tables occupied the centre of the bowls clubroom, along which all the sweet and savoury delights were set out. There were piles of plates and paper serviettes at each end.

At Gran's funeral she'd been too busy to eat – hugging long-lost cousins, catching up with old family friends, and avoiding dribbling smooches from great-uncles. So this time – despite the circumstances – it was nice to get the chance to sample the wonderful array of food. Most local women had brought their signature dish, and Emily had attended enough functions that she could identify what had been made by whom.

Mavis Bertram was known for her small, round jelly cakes and brandy snaps, Diana Timms her cream puffs, Mary Rickets for chocolate éclairs, Tiffany Rogers for melting moment biscuits...

With plate in hand, Emily surveyed the table. Right across from her – and too far to reach and still appear ladylike – was a plate piled high with Beryl Egbert's homemade sausage rolls, identifiable by the triangular cuts in the puff pastry rather than the traditional fork marks. It was this telltale sign Emily looked for.

Beside them was a plate of Carole Turner's egg sandwiches, distinguished by her trademark of using three slices of bread and cutting them into chunky fingers.

Emily moved around the table and was hovering over the sandwiches, deciding whether to take one or two, when she heard a male voice beside her. 'So, what do you recommend?' Taking only one, she turned to the voice. Nathan Lucas stood beside her with an empty plate.

'Oh, hello, I didn't know you knew the Burtons.'

'I don't. Mum and Dad dragged me along to start meeting some of the locals – for when I get the job. They're convinced.'

'Nice to have supportive parents. Well, this is certainly the best place to meet everyone.'

'God, the food looks good – I'm starving.'

'It is – well, from past experience anyway.'

'So sausage rolls and egg sandwiches are obviously a good bet,' he said, nodding at Emily's plate.

'Ah, but not all of them. See those egg sandwiches over there?' Emily indicated surreptitiously with her plate. 'The bright orange ones? Don't touch them. Old Mrs Bates lost her tastebuds years ago. They've got so much curry powder in them they'll make your eyes water.'

'Thanks for the tip. Which sausage rolls are edible?'

'Those and those,' Emily said, pointing. 'The ones with the random fork marks are okay, but not as generous with the meat and herbs. Beryl's are the best.'

'What about these? They look great.'

'Best avoided. Maggie Semmens is a lovely lady, but not blessed in the culinary arts. She uses tinned Spam as filling.'

'Surely not,' he said, reaching for one.

'Don't say I didn't warn you.'

Nathan bit into the roll and Emily stood beside him with an angelic I-told-you-so expression on her face, enjoying his discomfort as he struggled to swallow.

'Yum, that's better,' he said after clearing his throat and tasting the second of the two samples he had on his plate. 'So, did you make anything?'

'Yep. I helped my friend Barbara make a stack of stuff, including those scones and pin wheels,' she said, indicating two plates piled high in front of them.

'I notice you're not having any.'

'Only because I overdosed the other day. Honestly. Ask Barbara over there, if you don't believe me.' Right at that moment Barbara caught Emily's eye across the room and raised her cup of tea in acknowledgement. Emily raised her plate and smiled back.

'So do you know everyone by their culinary abilities, or lack of?' Nathan asked.

'Pretty much,' Emily said, grinning and tucking into a mini quiche, which she knew by the carefully arranged slices of cherry tomato on top to be Dorothy Price's.

Nathan followed Emily as she sought out her favourites, quietly steering him clear of this and that and providing encouragement here and there.

As they moved around the table, she noticed the signs that people were discussing her: the odd blush, averted eyes, hushed voices when she got too close.

They'd never be able to recruit spies from around here, she thought, glaring icily at a couple of people.

'Do you reckon they're talking about us?' Nathan asked in a whisper from behind her. 'Just, you know, you can sometimes tell.'

'You wait, this time next week we'll be engaged. Sometimes the lack of anonymity around here drives me nuts,' Emily added, pursing her lips.

'Oh well, the good with the bad, I suppose. They do do a damn good spread for funerals,' Nathan said, grinning and biting into a ham-and-mustard sandwich.

'Indeed they do. Come on, I'll give you a heads-up on dessert. My ultimate favourites are Mavis Bertram's brandy snaps,' she said, picking one up and putting it on her plate. 'Identifiable by their golden colour and the cream running the entire length,' she continued, holding the plate up for Nathan to see.

'Those darker ones,' she said, pointing across the table, 'are most likely Jill Dupont's. Hers, in my opinion, are too bitter and a little burnt tasting. And she never puts in enough cream.'

'You should be a food critic.'

'Maybe one day I will be,' Emily said, tossing her head jauntily. 'So what do you like the look of?' she asked, adding a mini chocolate cream cake dusted in icing sugar to her plate.

'Think I'll be a copycat,' Nathan said, putting both a brandy snap and a cream cake on his plate.

Emily finished with a miniature meringue topped with cream and small chunks of strawberries and said, 'Come on, let's get out of the way.'

She turned and made her way through the throng converging on the heavily laden trestles. She nodded and mumbled greetings to people she passed, all too aware that their gazes were set beyond her to Nathan, whom she could sense was right on her heels.

'Either they know I'm a banker or I've got too much food on my plate,' he said when they were settled, standing against the far wall of the large room. 'Or maybe they can smell I'm an interloper and didn't know the deceased,' he added.

'No, it's because you're with me. I haven't mourned my marriage for the requisite period,' Emily said, through a mouthful of brandy snap.

'How long's that?'

'No idea – probably no one else does either,' Emily said with a shrug.

'So two people of the opposite sex can't be seen together without conclusions being drawn?' Nathan asked, sounding aghast.

'That's right. Oh, unless they're about a generation apart in age. Even then it can be touch and go.'

'But we might be doing business – talking banking.'

'We might be.'

'If they knew I was in banking.'

'Oh, they know. Anyway, us talking business might be even worse, because if I've got enough money to be discussing it with a banker then I've obviously ripped off one of their precious bloody farmers.'

'The protected species.'

'You're catching on,' Emily said with a wink. 'You might just fit in here yet,' she added, before popping the last half of her brandy snap into her mouth.

'You're far too young and attractive to be so bitter, Emily,' Nathan said, taking a bite of miniature meringue.

'Can't help it,' Emily said after she'd swallowed her mouthful.

'Well, I will make it my mission to change that when – if – I get the job.'

Emily shrugged her shoulders and bit into her cream cake. She was beginning to feel a little full, but the food was just too good to pass up.

'So, is he here?' Nathan asked, looking around him.

'Who?' Emily said with a hand over her mouth.

'Your ex?'

'Probably,' she said and finished swallowing. 'Most likely at the bar or outside having a smoke.'

'Sorry, I shouldn't have asked. It's none of my business.'

Emily tried to analyse how she'd feel about seeing John, and was surprised to realise she hadn't thought about it until now. *Of course he's here. The whole bloody district is here.* She was a little nervous, apprehensive, but not like she might have felt a few weeks ago. She just didn't want to see him, and hopefully, with so many other people there, she wouldn't have to.

But if she did, she'd be okay.

Emily and Nathan were finishing their plates when Barbara appeared beside them.

'How are you holding up?' Emily asked, hugging her friend.

'Glad it's almost over. How about you?'

'Oh, I'm fine. Barbara, this is Nathan Lucas. Remember I told you he was at dinner at my parents' the other night? He's hoping to become the new assistant manager at the State Bank.'

'Lovely to meet you,' Barbara said, exchanging handshakes with Nathan and covert raised eyebrows with Emily.

'It's Barbara's father-in-law's wake we're eating our way through,' Emily explained.

'I'm so sorry. Please accept my condolences. I hope you don't mind my being here.'

'Not at all,' Barbara said, indicating the long table with a sweep of her arm.

'Can I get you ladies a cup of tea or coffee?' Nathan asked.

'Oh, would you? That would be great. Tea, thanks. White with one,' Barbara said.

'Same for me thanks, Nathan,' Emily said.

'He seems nice,' Barbara said, staring after Nathan as he wove his way through the crowd. 'Better looking than you had me believe too.'

'Oh God, don't you start!' Emily said and rolled her eyes at her friend.

'Just passing comment. I'm not starting anything.'

A few minutes later Nathan reappeared and swapped their empty dessert plates for cups and saucers.

'You're a life saver. Thanks Nathan,' Barbara said, sipping on her tea.

'My pleasure.'

'Yes, thanks very much,' Emily said. They lapsed into silence and watched as the crowded room gradually thinned.

Suddenly Emily yawned. It felt like evening, but when she checked her watch it was only four o'clock.

'You don't have to stay on my account,' Barbara said. 'Seriously, I've got all David's lot already insisting on hanging around to clean up. You did all the setting up this morning, not to mention all the cooking. You've done more than your fair share.'

'I am pretty weary, actually. It's suddenly hit me,' Emily said sheepishly.

'Well, get on home then, silly. Off you go,' Barbara said, taking Emily's empty cup from her.

'If you're sure you don't need me.'

'Yes, positive.'

'Nathan, do you need a ride anywhere?' Emily asked.

'No thanks, my parents are over there,' Nathan said, pointing. 'Anyway, it would probably be best *not* to be seen leaving together,' he said with a cheeky grin.

'Ah, so Emily's filled you in on the rumour mill then, has she?' Barbara said. 'Nothing you do around here passes unnoticed. Unless you happen to want it to be noticed. It can be very frustrating.'

'Right, I'm off,' Emily said. 'I'll see you soon, Barbara. Call if you need anything,' she said, giving her friend a hug.

'Lovely to see you again, Nathan,' she added, pecking him on the cheek.

Chapter Fifty-seven

Emily checked her mailbox on her way out of town and was surprised to find a card indicating she had a parcel awaiting collection inside the post office. She hadn't ordered anything.

As Emily returned to her car, she turned the package over in her hands. It was about the size of a shoebox, and the printed sender details showed a post office box number in Melbourne, but no name. And, damn it, it was so securely taped she'd need scissors to open it.

She looked at the object on the passenger seat beside her as she pulled away from the kerb, feeling excited at receiving an anonymous parcel. It might have been from her cousin – another thankyou gift for her hospitality the other week. Not really Elizabeth's style, but people did always have the capacity to surprise.

Despite her interest in the parcel, Emily felt a strange heaviness settle upon her as she drove out of town that day, the likes of which she hadn't felt since … since when? Since she'd first left John? Yes. But also before that. At Gran's funeral. That was it. Now the hoopla of the wake was gone, the sense of loss had seeped back in.

★

When she let Grace out of the yard, the border collie stayed by her side rather than tearing off to check out who and what had left new scents on her patch.

'It's okay, Gracie, I'm just a bit sad. I'll be okay,' she said, ruffling the dog's ears.

Emily put the parcel on the kitchen bench, her curiosity over-shadowed by more thoughts of Gran and how much she missed her. Deciding to walk it off, she got changed into her old jeans and faded windcheater, put her walking shoes on, and took a stroll up the small hill behind the house.

Back inside the kitchen she still couldn't settle. She put the kettle on and then fossicked in the drawer for scissors and sliced through the tape binding the parcel. Peeling back one of the flaps, she found a large nugget-shaped object wrapped in brown paper. It was slightly squishy and quite heavy when she removed it from the box. She tore away the outer layer to reveal a generous amount of bubble wrap. Still no hint of what it was or who had sent it.

Emily paused for a moment. It wouldn't be John sending something nasty, would it? *Or perhaps he was doing something to try to win her back*, she thought, feeling slightly hopeful. But why now? He hadn't made any effort to seek her out at the funeral. Her heart sank again. She was being ridiculous. She carefully undid the tape and began to unwind the bubble wrap.

When she was finished, Emily stared at the object in her hands: a large Bushells Coffee jar with a faded, slightly rusty, red tin lid. Granny's button jar, minus the buttons. She didn't need to check the writing on the large broken pieces still in the cupboard under the sink to know it was exactly the right jar – she'd run her fingers over the letters too many times over the years to need to do that.

She also didn't need to take out the note she could see inside to know it was from Jake. She couldn't believe he'd remembered. He'd only seen it in pieces, and only the once.

It was one of the nicest things anyone had ever done for her. And she hardly even knew him. Her throat tightened and it took her a few moments to swallow back the tension, regather her composure, and unscrew the lid.

In the jar was a loose roll of cash encircled by a slip of thick cream-coloured notepaper. She tugged the contents free and separated the money from the note. She counted it twice. One hundred and fifty dollars! With the fifty Jake had already paid her it meant she'd earned two hundred dollars just from selling her jam. That was two weeks' rent. She stared at the money in disbelief.

Hang on. Was this for the total of forty-four jars or just the original twenty? Could the second batch of jam have been sold so soon? She'd only sent it Monday and today was Thursday – the market wasn't until Sunday.

So that meant her jam had sold for ten dollars a jar. That was insane! But the numbers didn't lie.

Her mind started whirring with possibilities. If she could produce jam right through the year, could she, maybe, make enough to not have to find a job?

No, it was really too much to expect Jake and his sister to practically run a business on her behalf – especially without taking a commission. But it was a start.

She set the money aside on the table and focussed her attention on the letter, which she now flattened out to make reading easier.

Dear Em,

I hope this finds you well.

Please find enclosed the proceeds of your first batch of jam, as promised. I hope it signifies the start of a very lucrative venture for you.

Emily felt her heart ache a little. He was practically a stranger, and his sister certainly was. And here they were helping her for no other reason than just because.

> *I took the liberty of purchasing this jar for you. I hope it is the same as the one that contained your gran's buttons. If not, let me know and I will keep searching.*

Bless him. How could he have possibly deciphered the pieces of broken glass so accurately, let alone remembered? Emily shook her head in wonder.

> *I will let you know how the next jam sales go and forward the proceeds again in due course. Until then, stay well.*
> *Yours truly,*
> *Jake*

Emily reread the note, marvelling at its contents but feeling a little off-put at its formality.

How should she respond? By letter? By phone? Did she need to respond at all? He was merely sending the proceeds as promised. And of course, the jar. No, that was a gift. It had to be acknowledged.

She picked it up and turned it around again in her hand. It did indeed feel the same size as that which she'd held so many times over the years.

She ran her fingers over the raised letters, remembering the day, when she was four, that Gran had first shown her her treasured button jar.

Emily was shaking as she picked up her mobile and found Jake's number in her list of contacts. Her heart rate increased with every ring. By the fifth she was feeling perspiration breaking out. She waited for the voicemail to activate, feeling slightly relieved when it did.

She silently cleared her throat as she listened to Jake's message. She was surprised at how calm her voice was when it came to leaving her own.

'Hi Jake, it's Emily. I've just received your parcel. Thank you so much. I can't believe how much you got for the jam. Please thank your sister for everything she did. And you. And thank you so much for the jar. I can't believe you found one. Thank you. It's perfect. Anyway, I'll stop now. Thanks again, Jake. Bye.'

She hung up and went back over what she'd said, looking for any peculiarities, idiocy or rambling, until she told herself to stop it. The message was fine, and it was too bad if it wasn't; it was done.

As she put the kettle on, Emily was nagged with wondering if she should have added her surname. She hoped Jake didn't know too many women named Emily. Though, she reminded herself, there wouldn't be too many Emilys he'd sent a glass jar to.

'Idiot,' she muttered and shook her head while tapping a teaspoon on the bench and waiting for the kettle to boil.

Chapter Fifty-eight

Emily was startled when Grace sat up to attention and gave a single bark. A moment later she heard a voice.

'Hello, anyone home?'

Emily stiffened slightly as she tried to place the voice coming from her front door. Male, old, raspy. Ah, one of the landlords.

'Wait Grace. You stay here,' she told the dog, who had crossed the kitchen and was at the doorway into the hall. 'Coming!' she called as she bundled the cash and note up, stuffed them back into the jar, and quickly screwed the lid on. She shoved it into the cupboard below the sink behind the fly spray, bottle of cream cleanser and dishwashing detergent. 'Hello,' she said from halfway down the hallway.

'I hope we're not interrupting you at dinnertime.'

'Not at all. Come in. I've actually just put the kettle on if you'd like a cuppa,' she said to the two men standing outside the wide open door.

'Lovely, thank you,' Donald said.

'That would be very nice, thank you,' Trevor said.

They looked a little awkward, but that might have been because they were unaccustomed to wearing suits and ties. She hadn't seen them there earlier, but they looked like they were on their way home from the funeral.

'You should keep the door closed,' Donald said, entering the hall.

'Yes, it's not safe for a girl living on her own,' Trevor added.

'You're probably right,' Emily said, knowing they were. 'But I like the fresh air in the house while it's cool.' She'd always thought she'd hear any vehicles crunching on the gravel as the pulled up, but she hadn't heard their ute today, nor Tara's car the other day.

Emily wondered how much a second-hand screen door would cost – maybe that would be a good use for the wad of cash under the sink. She'd look into it, she decided, following the two men as they clomped heavily on the wooden floorboards.

'Hello there,' Donald said to Grace, who was curled up in the corner of the kitchen. The small dog flapped her tail in response. 'Very well-behaved.'

For a moment Emily couldn't remember if she was allowed to have a dog in the house or not. *Oh well, too late now.*

'Tea?' Emily asked.

'Yes thanks, white with one,' both men said at once.

The two men sat on chairs pushed back from the table and fiddled with their stiff Akubras before placing them on the floor beside them. As Emily made the tea, they exchanged small talk about the weather and long-range forecast, a wrap-up of the recent harvest, and speculation over the next season's outcome.

There was a pause in the conversation as Emily put the mugs on the table.

'You seem more settled since we were here last,' Donald suddenly said, looking around him.

'Yes, I love it here. I'm really so grateful to you both,' she added, suddenly feeling the need to defend her position. *God, please don't be here to turf me out now I'm finally finding my feet.* The brothers exchanged a glance and her stomach knotted.

'We, er, have a *proposition* to put to you,' Donald said, breaking the silence that had become awkward.

Emily swallowed back the dryness in her throat. 'Yes?'

'We're thinking of selling,' Donald said.

Oh God. Tara has spoken to them, then. Just when I'm settled, I'm being kicked out. Her worst fear was coming true.

'And wanted to give you the first right of refusal,' Trevor said.

'Oh!' A wave of relief washed over her, but it was short-lived. 'Well, that's very good of you, but I'm not really in a position to buy a farm.'

'Not the whole farm. We mean the house and a few acres with it,' Donald said.

A lump formed in her throat. *A few acres? The house?* It was everything she wanted. It was so close, but she'd never afford it. She shook her head as she spoke, her voice a croak.

'I'm sorry. I really do love the place, but I...'

'Please, hear us out,' Donald said, holding up a silencing hand.

She stayed silent with her hands wrapped around her mug, shifting her gaze back and forth between the men as they took turns speaking.

'You'd probably be aware we're on the pension,' Trevor said. 'And with it comes certain ... rules ... one must adhere to.'

'Well, the pension isn't exactly – how shall I put it? – *generous*, and with the recent droughts we're in need of a bit of *supplementary income*,' Donald added. The fact the term was new to Donald was obvious given how carefully he uttered the words.

'We want to take a trip to Ireland before we're too old. You know, see the family heartland while we're young enough to make the trip,' Trevor said, sounding quite excited. 'There's a family reunion planned for this time next year.'

'Right. That sounds exciting,' Emily said, wishing they would get to the point. She took a sip.

'So we've come up with an idea that might help all of us out.'

'We heard that husband of yours took you for a ride,' Donald said.

Emily snorted with surprise, her mouth still full of tea.

'Donald, the poor lass isn't interested in your gossip,' Trevor chided.

Oh, yes I am. Emily dabbed at her nose and looked down at her mug. Was she hearing right, that a pair of farmers was sympathetic towards the estranged wife of one of their fellows, another of this 'protected species'?

'Right, yes. Well, anyway, we were thinking that we could strike some kind of rent-to-own type deal...'

'With a small down payment...'

'To get us to Ireland and back.'

'Oh, right.'

'So this is what we've come up with,' Trevor said, pulling a small folded wad of paper from his inside pocket and pushing it across the table to Emily.

'We'll leave you to read it at your leisure,' Donald said.

'But we'd appreciate an answer by the end of next week, if that's possible,' Trevor added.

'All right. Okay. Thanks very much.' Emily thought she was lucky to get that many coherent words out. She was completely gobsmacked.

'Well, we'd better keep going,' Donald said. 'A couple of troughs to check and clean while we're out this way.'

They pushed their chairs back, put their hats on their heads – each shook Emily's hand – and clomped back down the hall.

Out on the verandah, Emily thanked them for dropping by and for thinking of her regarding the house. They thanked her for the tea, and suddenly their leaving was awkward and formal. Not that she knew them very well, but they'd been a lot more relaxed last time. They got in their battered old blue ute, with its rusty, creaking doors, and waved from the open windows as they departed.

Emily turned and walked back down the hall with her heart thudding against her ribs. Part of her was dying to see what the terms were, but part of her didn't want to know. They'd have to be even better than too-good-to-be-true for it to be at all possible. She was broke. Well, she had John's forty grand, but that might have to last her a while if nothing came up on the job front.

Where there's life, there's hope, she found herself thinking – another of Gran's favourite sayings. And it was sort of true. While she didn't know the specifics, and that they were absolutely beyond her reach, there was still a chance.

She turned the small wad of paper over and over in her hands for a few minutes before putting it back down unread. Then she headed outside for another walk in the cooling evening air.

Chapter Fifty-nine

An hour later she walked back inside to find Barbara sitting at the kitchen table, fiddling with the still-folded wad of paper. Grace ran up to Barbara with her tail wagging furiously.

'Jesus! You scared the shit out of me!' Emily cried.

'Sorry. I had to escape for a bit. I'm a bit peopled out.'

'I'm not surprised, you poor thing. I was going to phone later and check on you.'

'David and co. are still finishing up tea at the pub. It's a bit naughty, but I pretended to have a slight migraine coming on. Now how many times have I told you to keep the house locked,' Barbara said, grinning up at her friend.

'You're the second – actually, third – person to say that just today.'

'Oh?'

'I had Trevor and Donald Baker visit earlier.'

'I hope they haven't changed their minds about your peppercorn rent now you've done the place up.'

'No. They're thinking of selling...'

'Oh, Em, I'm sorry. And just when you've got settled.'

'…the house and a few acres. To me.'

'Wow, that's brilliant! It's just what you want.'

'Well, it would be if I had any money. I'm almost broke, remember?'

'Ah details, schmetails,' Barbara said, flapping a hand about. 'So how much are they asking?'

'I'm not sure. It's all in those pieces of paper you're fiddling with.'

'What, you haven't read them yet?!' Barbara cried, dropping the wad of paper like it was red hot.

'No, I wanted to savour the dream for a bit before having to let it go.'

'You never know, it might be doable.'

'Doubtful. They'd have to be practically giving it away.'

'Maybe they are. Aren't they on the pension? Large lump sums would wreak havoc with that.'

'Hmm.'

'Well, I can't stand not knowing!' Barbara said.

'Open it, then,' Emily said.

'Oh, I couldn't. Anyway, stop being a wimp. Whatever terms are in there, I'm sure they can be negotiated on. And you know David and I will help if you need it.'

Emily shook her head at her friend. 'Thanks Barbara, but you know I could never borrow money from you.'

'Well, you mightn't need to. Just open the damn thing.'

Taking a deep breath, Emily unfolded the wad to reveal three pieces of lined A4 paper that had been torn from a pad and stapled together in the top left-hand corner. The handwriting was a scrawl of straight lines that she found difficult to decipher. Gradually her expression went from close attention to astonishment and disbelief.

'Wow!'

'What?'

'They only want ten thousand up front. Five to each of them.'

'That's pretty good.'

'Yes, but it's a quarter of my entire life savings. It's a big risk.'

'Life's a big risk, Em. These opportunities don't come up very often, if ever. When did the last person offer you a house and land for a ten-thousand-dollar down payment? Think about that. What are the other conditions?'

'After that, five thousand to each of them per year for twenty years – that's, what, two hundred and ten thousand all up?'

'Yep. So what exactly are you buying?'

'Hang on, it's hard to read this handwriting,' Emily said, frowning. 'Okay, it's around twenty acres, including the house, the stand of gums and the creek with the fruit trees. Oh, and the shearing shed and the small plant shed next to it. What would I do with a smelly, run-down old shearing shed?'

'It doesn't matter. It sounds like a bloody good deal to me. Are there any catches?'

'Um. Yep,' Emily said after a few moments' silent reading.

'Well?!'

'I have to pay for all the costs associated with subdividing. How much do you reckon that would be?'

'No idea, but I'm sure the council will. And if they're sticking to the current fence lines, you won't be up for anything there. It's a great deal, Em.'

'It would be if I could afford it.'

'But you *can*. You only need to come up with ten thousand now and you've got twelve months before the next payment.'

'And however much it's going to cost to subdivide.'

'And that. It's good to be cautious, Em, but not if it means knocking back a damn good offer. I say bite the bullet. You'll have your own home.'

'As run-down as it is.'

'What? Last week you would have done anything for an offer like this. You're just looking for the negatives because you're scared. Which is fine, as long as you don't let it paralyse you. Forget the state of the place. You wouldn't have moved in if you didn't think it was safe and sound for the foreseeable future.'

'I suppose you're right. Ooh, and Mum would have kittens if I bought it,' Emily added, grinning naughtily at Barbara.

'Emily Oliphant, that is not a good enough reason to buy a house!' Barbara said in a warning tone while struggling to hide her grin.

'No, but the look on her face would be priceless.'

'Yes, that it would be. Hey, speaking of priceless, thanks again for all your help with the food. I couldn't have done it without you.'

'Any time. So have you got an absolute houseful?'

'Yes. And I'm exhausted.'

'If this place was in better nick, I could have helped share the burden of guests,' Emily said.

'I know. I'd say, "hopefully next time", but I hope there won't be another funeral for a very long time.'

'I did really enjoy our cooking day, though. See how pathetic my life has become? I *so* need a job!'

'Still nothing?'

'Nope.'

'You just have to trust everything will work out. Feeling hard done by and getting depressed won't help. Apply for the dole; you've always paid your taxes, and you're genuinely looking for a job.'

'The thought makes me physically queasy. Anyway, I did actually make enquiries,' Emily said, colouring slightly. 'Apparently I have too much money in the bank. Anything over five thousand and they make you wait. You have to use up *all* your savings before they'll help.'

'What a bummer.'

'Yeah. It's fair enough, but bloody frustrating. I had psyched myself up, got over the stigma, and was all set to apply.'

'Well, I'm glad to hear you're not letting pride get in the way of common sense. Apply and then just wait it out – then it's done. That's what I'd do.'

'Yeah, you're probably right. I'll call them back.'

'Wouldn't it be good if you didn't need it by the time you became eligible for payment,' Barbara said wistfully. 'I wonder how else you can make money around here?'

'Oh, that reminds me. Jake sent the proceeds of the jam – the first lot. Can you believe they sold it for ten dollars a jar?'

'Yes, I can – it's some of the best apricot jam I've ever had.'

'You're way too kind.'

'No, I'm not; it's the truth. What you need to do is make jam all year round.'

'Well, I suppose that's what the cellar was originally for, but I used all the fruit in one hit – there wasn't any left to put in storage.'

'No, silly, I mean following the seasons. What's up there in the creek other than apricots? Figs, quinces, citrus?'

'There are a few nectarines, but not many, and I've never made nectarine jam before. Other than that, I'm not sure. I can't tell what trees are what until they have fruit on them.'

'I wouldn't mind betting it's like the orchard David's parents had. Old Beth made jam and preserves all year round.'

'You'll have to show me what's what. Pity it's too late now.'

'And I'm not exactly dressed for traipsing.' Barbara sighed heavily. 'Actually, I'd better get going,' she said, getting up slowly. 'It'll be embarrassing if everyone beats me back home!'

'Is there anything at all I can do to help?' Emily asked, following her friend down the hall.

'No, just being here to whinge to is enough. I feel so much better. Anyway, everyone is leaving tomorrow. Thank God they haven't decided to stay on for Christmas.'

'Well, you would have just told them they can't; you have other plans. With me!'

'I know. Thanks so much for that. I think we would have been quite lost with the house suddenly empty. Thanks for rescuing us for Christmas day.'

'My pleasure, but I am warning you that it will be very low-key.'

'Oh, no you don't; you're not getting out of it that easy. There's far too much to be joyous about this year.'

'Okay, but no presents.'

'No presents. But I'm bringing tinsel, crackers with appalling jokes, champagne, and plenty of good cheer. Maybe I'll pop in a cheesy Christmas CD or two as well, just to irk the Oliphants who don't *do* Christmas,' Barbara said, laughing and giving Emily a nudge.

Emily was about to reply, but Barbara held a hand up to silence her.

'Seriously, Em, this year we are going to celebrate. No arguments. You're halfway to being a professional jam maker, you've finally left that awful husband behind, you've got a beautiful, *beautiful* puppy, and you've just received the best Christmas present ever – this offer,' Barbara said, giving her a hug at the front door.

'Yeah, I suppose it's not bad for someone who doesn't do Christmas *or* presents,' Emily said, grinning.

'And you never know. Maybe there's a new man somewhere in your future too. Seriously, though, you can do the house thing – you just have to believe in yourself. It'll all work out for the best, you'll see.' The two best friends hugged again.

'Hmm,' Emily said thoughtfully. And right then even she believed it was possible.

Turn over for a sneak peek of
Book 2 in *The Button Jar* series by

Fiona McCallum

TIME WILL TELL

OUT APRIL

Chapter One

Emily Oliphant and her best friend Barbara stood on the verandah, staring out into the still country evening. Birds rustled in the trees, settling themselves for the night, and a multitude of insects chattered and sang in the summer air.

'What a gorgeous evening. And what a really lovely spot, Em,' Barbara said with a sigh.

'It is, isn't it?' Emily reached down to pat her border collie pup, Grace, who was at attention by her feet. 'I could stay here forever.'

They were out the front of Emily's house — the house that would be hers if she accepted the Baker brothers' proposal. She thought of all she'd been through in the last two months — leaving her husband, meeting Barbara, saving Grace. And now, finally, settling into a home of her own. Could she find the courage to do this too?

'Seriously Em, you can do this — the house, everything. Don't let fear stop you. And don't worry about your mother.'

Emily nodded. Her friend was right; being offered the house was one hell of a Christmas present. And not too shabby as a thirty-second birthday gift either. Forget what Enid had to say about it. *This is my life.*

'Well, I'd really better go before they send out a search party,' Barbara said, kissing Emily on the cheek.

'I'm so glad you stopped in.' The two friends hugged, neither wanting to be the first to let go. As always, Barbara had turned up at just the right time.

Finally they broke apart, and Barbara made her way down the steps and over to her car. 'See you Saturday,' she called.

'Don't forget the tinsel,' Emily called back sardonically.

'No fear there. And the champagne; we're going to celebrate.' She got in the car with a wave of her hand.

Emily watched until Barbara's taillights were out of sight. She smiled wryly. Her mother would indeed have a fit when she found out she was buying the run-down old place.

Thankfully it didn't matter what Enid thought. It was to be Emily's home and no one else's.

As she stared out into the last fading light of the warm summer day, her head began swimming with possibilities, risks, and calculations. The chance to buy the house really was a huge opportunity, if a little daunting — well, very daunting. But it was meant to be, wasn't it? A home of her own.

A home that was as much Grace's as hers, she thought, looking down at the small black and white dog beside her. Grace was a typical border collie except for the missing white ring around her neck. Emily still found it hard to believe it was only six weeks since the day she had picked her up as a tiny puppy — it felt like Grace had always been a part of her life. And Barbara; they'd become firm best friends almost instantly. She was so blessed to have met her. Along with Grace, Barbara had been her saviour; her rock, her voice of reason.

She bent down and ruffled Grace's ears. The puppy looked up

at her with love and adoration. Emily smiled. That look would melt anyone's heart. Well, except her estranged husband's.

At the thought of John Stratten, her face clouded. Thankfully the bully was now out of her life. He'd completely ripped her off in the financial settlement, but at least he was gone.

'Come on Gracie, let's go inside.'

They made their way down the hall, Grace's claws clicking on the bare floorboards punctuating Emily's thoughts.

Why didn't I leave him sooner?

Her mother had told her that once she had made her bed she had to lie in it. If only she had ignored her. It was the twenty-first century for Christ's sake, not the nineteen-fifties! *How could I have been so damned gullible?*

But of course Emily knew. It had nothing to do with gullibility and everything to do with that old chestnut that shaped your life growing up in a small country town: what will people say? What could possibly make a woman like her give up a marriage to one of the wealthiest farmers in the district?

She cast her mind back to the afternoon she had finally decided to leave him. John's threat to shoot Grace had been the last straw. A shiver ran the length of Emily's spine. At least she had saved her from the brute.

Forty thousand dollars?! It wasn't fair. Perhaps if she'd known she was going to be offered the old house to buy she might have fought for more in the settlement.

Emily sighed. At the time she'd just wanted to get it over with, to get on with her life and never have anything to do with him again. She had hoped that feeling would last; that when twelve months had elapsed it would just be a matter of the divorce papers being signed and rubber-stamped.

She paused in the hallway and looked around her. The old place had so much potential. She'd love to turn it into something worthy of *Home Beautiful*. But her meagre funds would barely cover updating the kitchen — even the most basic design.

The Baker brothers were only asking for ten thousand up front and then ten thousand per year for twenty years — and the costs associated with subdividing, however much that would be. It was a bloody good deal in anyone's book, but still felt precarious to Emily in her current situation.

She had approximately forty seven thousand dollars in savings, but no job, and nothing on the horizon thanks to the Global Financial Crisis and a couple of years of drought since.

But she was going to stay positive. 'Fake it till you make it', Barbara had said not so long ago. She had to have faith that it would all work out. Really, what else did she have?

She could see now that Barbara had really been gently telling her to stop feeling sorry for herself and get her act together. It was something Emily's gran might have said if she'd been born fifty years later than she had. As it was, Granny Rose would have been more likely to say something gentler, like: 'Put on a happy face, dear. No one likes a sourpuss'.

With that thought Emily hoicked her shoulders up and carried on into the kitchen.

She filled the kettle and waited for it to boil. She really had to start believing that good things could happen. Like her cousin Elizabeth turning up with a friend who just happened to be an architect and a qualified builder; what were the odds of that?

Jake would be able to give her a good idea of how much the house would cost to fully renovate. He'd certainly indicated it was worth looking into. And he wasn't just humouring her or being polite. He was genuine — the gift and proceeds from the jam he had sent were proof of that. It was such a pity that he lived so far away in Melbourne.

She looked across at the old Bushells coffee jar on the kitchen table. It was an almost identical match for the original jar from the nineteen-thirties. Even the tone of the faded red tin screw-top lid was the same.

The night before she died, Granny Rose had given Emily her button jar. The thought of how serious Gran had been — her insistence that she take good care of it — still brought a sad smile to Emily two months on. The Alzheimer's had made her wise old gran say the strangest things.

The jar was precious to Emily too. It had been since she'd first seen it as a four year old. She'd always loved the bright colours and the rattle it made when gently shaken. She'd especially loved the weird tradition that buttons were constantly put in on top, but none ever removed, nor the contents ever tipped out and rifled though. Since Gran's death, she had felt a sense of comfort whenever she held it.

And she felt dreadful that in just a few months it had got broken. She still had no idea how the jar had fallen from the bench to the floor in the middle of the night. It would remain one of life's mysteries.

Emily forced thoughts of Gran aside — she was getting too melancholy thinking about her — and wondered if she should phone Jake again. She'd rung him earlier to thank him, but had got his voicemail. She could try again later.

No, that would be weird and stalkerish. You've already left one message, she told herself. *But I'm really grateful to him.* The replacement jar was such a thoughtful gift.

The roaring kettle distracted her and she set about preparing a mug of Milo.

At the kitchen table sipping her drink, she looked around the large space and wondered who else she could ask for advice about the purchase. Her dad would be her first port of call — he'd already helped her repaint the inside of the house and sand the floorboards — but he wasn't in the actual building game, so he wouldn't know about how much things would cost.

Suddenly Emily yawned. It was only eight o'clock, but it had been a big day; with the funeral for Barbara's father-in-law and the Bakers' visit afterwards. She was weary, but her brain was still spinning a little too fast and her thoughts were too disconnected. She needed some down time to let it all seep in.

She would have loved to soak in the tub for a while, but still didn't like the idea of lying naked and vulnerable in the bathroom outside on the back verandah.

As she brushed her teeth and waited for Grace to have her last pee for the night, Emily found herself daydreaming of a plush ensuite, right off her bedroom, with plenty of heating for the cold winter months. When the time came, and funds permitted. That would be a long way off, she thought pessimistically as she followed Grace inside and closed the kitchen door behind them.

She said goodnight to Grace, who was settled on her bed in the corner of the kitchen, and made her way slowly and heavily down the hall to her bedroom, turning off the lights as she went.

She changed into her summer pyjamas and climbed into bed. She ignored the small wad of paper from the Bakers that contained the conditions of the purchase — she was way too tired to study it again — and picked up her book. But she couldn't focus on that either.

Was she about to open a can of worms by trying to buy the old place? It sure would be easier just to stay renting and trying to find a job. But wouldn't she then be letting herself down; not fulfilling her full potential?

Perhaps she didn't have any unfulfilled potential. Her mother had certainly never seen her as more than wife material. And John had never let her help out on the farm. That had been her dream; for them to stand shoulder to shoulder and run the place together, as a true partnership. But he hadn't even let her do the books.

Oh for God's sake, stop feeling sorry for yourself, Emily! When haven't you been prepared to work hard for something?

Barbara was right; she could do this. She had been brave enough to finally leave John, and she'd be brave enough to do this too. Somehow she'd make it happen. On her own.

One of Gran's sayings came to her now: 'Nothing come by quickly is ever as satisfying as that which has been waited for or toiled over'.

She was right. Yes, bit by bit, slow and steady wins the race, and all that.

Emily banished the quotes from her head and picked up Donald and Trevor Baker's handwritten offer. Her whole body began to tingle with excitement. She reread it carefully and was making notes and listing questions to ask — of whom she wasn't yet sure — when her mobile chirped into action beside her. Her heart rate doubled as she saw Jake's name lit up on the screen. *Oh!* She took a deep breath and pressed the button to answer.

'Hi Jake,' she said cheerily.

'Hi Em.'

'I got your parcel this afternoon. Thanks so much. It does seem rather a lot of money for just some jars of homemade jam.'

'Well, it's very good jam.'

'Thanks. And thank you so much for the jar — I can't believe you found one the same.'

'I hope it's the right one. The antique dealer seemed to think there weren't many variations.'

'It's perfect. Thank you again.'

'My absolute pleasure. Now I would love to chat, but I don't have long. I actually called to ask you a favour.'

'Oh. Okay.'

'I'm in Whyalla — working on a project with a friend of a friend. Bit of a long story. I was wondering if I could come and stay for the weekend. You did say you don't do anything special for Christmas, right? I'm sorry about the short notice.'

'Of course you can stay — I'd love to have you!' As soon as the words left her mouth, Emily blushed. She was glad he couldn't see her embarrassment at her poor choice of words.

'It's just I have to be here again next week — we're working right through while most businesses are shut — but I'd rather not spend the Christmas weekend here on my own. I hate to impose, but this project has come together in a bit of a rush,' he added, sounding a little breathless.

'Jake, really, you wouldn't be imposing. I'm just having Mum and Dad and Barbara and David here for lunch Christmas day, and you're very welcome to join us. It's just casual. And absolutely no presents are being exchanged,' she added.

Emily had always hated the awkwardness of being given a gift and not having one to offer in return. It had almost become a phobia. When she had invited Barbara, she had put the 'no gifts' rule on the table and had been relieved when Barbara had agreed, albeit reluctantly.

'Okay. Well, perhaps I can have a bit more of a look at that house of yours if you like — to earn my keep,' Jake offered.

'Your timing would be perfect actually; there's been a bit of a development on that front.'

'Oh?'

'Yes, the old brothers who own it have offered to sell it to me.'

'Wow, that's great.'

'It's a bit of a long story, but I really would appreciate your opinion on the structural aspects of the house, and any other advice you can offer.'

'It would be my pleasure.'

'So when should I expect you — and do you have someone with you or are you on your own?' She hoped it was the latter.

'No, it's just me. And Saturday — Christmas day — if that's okay? Say mid-morning?'

'No problem at all.'

'And I'm really sorry to have to cut this short, but I'm being collected for dinner and my hosts have just arrived.'

'Okay. See you Saturday then. Drive safely.'

'Thanks very much, Em, I look forward to it. See ya.'

'Me too,' Emily said quietly, but she suspected the call had already been disconnected.

Her heart rate subsided to a thud of nervous excitement. Wow, Jake wanted to visit — alone; without Elizabeth! And for Christmas, no less! She couldn't wait to see him. This would make the day a bit special.

Emily was no longer tired, and in fact couldn't imagine how she'd get to sleep at all now. She mentally ran through her list for Christmas; what she still had to do, what ingredients she had on hand and what she had left to buy.

When the reminder of the expense seeped in, she picked up her book. She'd found reading fiction the best antidote to the pressures that regularly threatened to overwhelm her.

Especially the thought that she wouldn't be in this mess if she'd listened to her mother and continued to lie in the bed she'd made — her marriage to John Stratten.

For a moment she wondered what her husband was doing for Christmas. Had John arranged to see his parents, or would he be spending the Christmas weekend alone on the farm? She cut off the thought before letting herself feel any sympathy for him — he deserved everything he got.

More heart-warming stories by bestselling Australian author

Fiona McCallum

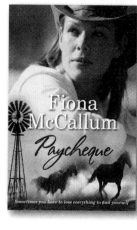

HARLEQUIN®
™

Find out more about our
latest releases, authors
and competitions.

 Like us on facebook.com/harlequinaustralia

 Follow us on twitter.com/harlequinaus

 Find us at harlequinbooks.com.au